The Four Queens of the Buttonbush Museum

"Written with a playful hand and impeccable wit, Beth Brookhart's uplifting debut novel will have you rooting for her endearingly flawed characters and eagerly awaiting her next release."

—Sandra Kring, bestselling author of *The Book of Bright Ideas.*

"You are going to love this delightful trip through the realm of *The Four Queens of the Buttonbush Museum*! Beth Brookhart has created a playful and rich world full of fabulous, feisty characters and oodles of charm and humor, all while staying true to the realities of a complex time period when it was difficult for women to thrive. You will be rooting for the strong women at the center of this story—each one fighting serious odds as they reach for their dreams."

—Shana Kelly, book editor, writer, publishing consultant

"A fun romp with the serious theme of fighting gender oppression, *The Four Queens of the Buttonbush Museum* will keep you reading—and laughing and groaning until, finally, you're cheering. Beth Brookhart's lively prose and captivating characters rule!"

—Jennifer Wortman, author of *This. This. This. Is. Love. Love. Love.*

"Beth Brookhart is a wonderful writer—smart, funny, and insightful about the tangles of small towns. *The Four Queens of the Buttonbush Museum* is a rich and engaging read."

William Haywood Henderson, author of *Augusta Locke*

"In *The Four Queens of the Buttonbush Museum*, Beth Brookhart crafts a spellbinding tale of ambition, resilience, and the intertwining legacies of remarkable women in mid-century California. Equal parts heartfelt and hilarious, this novel blends sharp social commentary with rich historical detail, inviting readers into a town bursting with grit, gossip, and unyielding charm. As the museum becomes both battleground and sanctuary, we witness how determination and identity collide, proving that history is written by those brave enough to claim it. A must-read for anyone who cherishes stories of redemption, rivalry, and finding one's place in the world."

—Mike Young, author of *The Farmer's Code*

"When Buttonbush Museum is under threat, four wildly different women band together to save it, only to discover they are up against a greater force within their own town. Through creativity and determination, The Queens first fail and then discover a strength they didn't know they possessed, a path forward for the museum, and how the power of friendship can transform us. A beautiful novel about the complexity of female friendships and the powerful things it can do."

—Carrie Talick, author of *Beware the Mermaids*

"This book will make you laugh and cry. If you're old enough, then it will remind you of the way you used to feel when you read a Fannie Flagg novel, or watched *Steel Magnolias*. If you're not that old then you're in for a real surprise treat—women who fight hard, love hard, and support each other. *The Four Queens of the Buttonbush Museum* is a delightful book about what really matters in life, and how to protect it."

—Jonatha Kottler, University of New Mexico Honors College, author of *Fat in Every Language*

"With rich humor and unforgettable characters, this captivating story is a love letter to friendship and the unstoppable force of determined women."

—Jacquelin Cangro, Developmental Editor and Book Coach

To Cindy —

My good, good friend and fellow Queen!

love you —

[signature]

The Four Queens of the Buttonbush Museum

A Novel

BETH BROOKHART

Sibylline
DIGITAL FIRST

Sibylline Press

Copyright © 2025 by Beth Brookhart
All Rights Reserved.

Published in the United States by Sibylline Press,
an imprint of All Things Book LLC, California.

Sibylline Press is dedicated to publishing the
brilliant work of women authors ages 50 and older.
www.sibyllinepress.com

Sibylline Digital First Edition
eBook ISBN: 9781960573636
Print ISBN: 9781960573841
Library of Congress Control Number: 2025931633

Cover Design: Alicia Feltman
Book Production: Aaron Laughlin

This is a work of fiction. Names, characters, places, brands, media, and incidents are either the product of the author's imagination or are used fictitiously. Any resemblance to similarly named places or to persons living or deceased is unintentional.

Sibylline Press

For Grandma Pauline, a true queen

1953

DIDDLY-SQUAT

Irene

There she was, in all her dang glory. Odilia Delgado pranced up to the stage, surprised and demure, oozing humility. She might as well have popped up fairy wings on her skinny back and a halo on her head. The crowd clapped and cheered as if she was the savior of us all, the heroine. I knew better. She hadn't saved us. We'd survived her.

Odilia liked to think she was the only person who'd worked her tail off for the Buttonbush Museum, the only one with a brain in her head. Preening in her fancy dress with little sparkles on the sleeves and her big, ole, fat diamond necklace jingling around her neck, Odilia planted herself at the microphone like a spring daisy, smiling at the banquet room full of people. It was pure horse hockey.

But there she was at the podium of the Buttonbush County Commissioner's Dinner, soaking in the adoration while knowing I'd put in exactly the same amount of blood and tears as her for three years. And there I was, invisible as a clump of dirt. Sitting in the back row where my chicken dinner smelled like disappointment. I clapped for her, too, because I was nothing if not polite, along with Betty and Maye Marie.

Well, I'd had it. She was about to be handed a shiny trophy while the three of us got diddly-squat. I stood up, hands on my hips.

"Yoo-hoo! Odilia!" I shouted across the room. She didn't see me because I was too far back. But she wasn't going to get away with it this time. Maye Marie tugged on my dress to try to sit me down, but I shrugged her off. For once, Odilia was not going to win. No, she wasn't.

1949

BEEF NOODLE CASSEROLE OR A FEDERAL WATER PROJECT

Irene

A.J. McCorkle, Editor-in-Chief of the *Buttonbush Daily*, smiled at me. He never smiled. Crud.

I ducked into his office, a fortress of paper and ash trays framing him. I rubbed my cheeks. I'd put on a new rouge that morning and it occurred to me he might be smiling because I looked like a circus clown.

"You wanted to see me?" I paced the room. I was certain this was going to be my big break. I'd written a story about the lights going out at a meeting of the Buttonbush County Power and Light Company, a situation almost too ironic to be true. In my five years as a news assistant, it was the first story he'd given me.

"Nice little story there, Irene."

"Thanks. I've got some other ideas and ... So I was thinking that next ..."

He interrupted me.

"Hang on. I need to talk to you about something." He adjusted his considerable backside in a well-worn chair and took off his spectacles. "Some things are going to be changing around here. You know there are lots of men coming back from war, still ... men who got hurt or who stayed on for rebuilding."

He was still smiling. I slumped into a chair, the pencil hanging from my ear feeling heavy all of a sudden.

"Irene, you've been a great assistant in the newsroom. We couldn't have gotten through the war without your help. And I know you wanted to get a job as a reporter one day ... But I've got two young Navy men just out of college who were in the Pacific Theater. One was injured and now he's recovered. They need work. You understand, of course," he said, and I nodded because to do anything but agree to that would have been unthinkable. The men were heroes.

"Sure, I was just holding down the fort. But isn't there somewhere you could use me?"

"There really isn't. Sorry, Irene. You'll find something to do with yourself," he said. "And you're married, so it's not like you need the work."

"But I think I'm good at this. I think I could be a good news woman."

"No doubt about that. Doesn't change the fact that these men need work."

"How come you need two of them to replace me?" I asked, and he narrowed his eyes.

"You'll find plenty to do at home. My wife is always complaining about how she can't get things done around the house. And you've got two kids, right?" He flipped open a file and started reading.

This was the way things always seemed to go with me: with no intention or planning on my part. I'd only stumbled on the job by running into old McCorkle at the gas station one day in 1944. He needed help, so I jumped in, despite having two kids, Pauline and Willy, and a husband, Jimmy. God seemed to enjoy tossing me like a rock into the air where I sometimes plunked into a river, sometimes landed in a dirt pile, and sometimes crashed through a window. Where was I going to land now except in a haze of housewifery? I blubbered the whole way home.

* * *

Two days after getting booted from the newspaper, I grabbed my second sugar cookie from a tray and took a bite that crumbled all over my navy-blue blouse. I wiped it away, crumbs scattering on the floor as all the muckety-mucks wandered around at the grand opening celebration of the new Buttonbush Agricultural Commissioner's office. It wasn't the most exciting thing to do on a Wednesday morning, but it beat cleaning my oven, which was what I'd be doing if I wasn't there.

"Irene Pickett, how are you doing?" a familiar voice rang out from behind me.

"Senator Delgado! How are you? Nice building you've got here," I said.

"Where's that husband of yours? Is Jimmy here?"

"No, I'm his substitute. He's planting seed," I said. Senator Ignatius "Iggy" Delgado was an air force pilot in the war and now a state senator. Jimmy met with him several times in the past to discuss farming issues and I'd talked to him for the newspaper once or twice. Smart and politically sly, his smile was disturbingly dashing, and his knifelike, dark eyes bored into mine.

"Sorry I missed him. What have you been up to, Mrs. Pickett? Still at the newspaper?"

"No. They hired some men back from the war. So I haven't been up to much at all. Cooking better dinners for Jimmy, I guess."

He laughed as a startlingly attractive woman with short, pin-curled, raven hair, intense brown eyes, olive skin, and a tiny and sharply thin build sauntered up to us. She was wearing a cream-colored dress with blue brocade on the sleeves and a sparkling pin on the neckline in the shape of a bow. I could smell her fancy perfume.

"This is my wife, Odilia. Odilia, this is Irene Pickett." The Senator's wife stared at me with wide eyes, like she knew me, but I knew I'd never met her before. "Odilia and I just moved back here from Sacramento, although we still have a home there. I'm retiring at the end of my term in three years, you know."

"Did you say 'Pickett'? That's interesting," she said. "And what do you do?"

"What do I do? Well, I wash my kids' dirty socks, make mashed potatoes, feed fifteen sheep and can peaches. I figure I've got the most exciting life in Buttonbush," I said, chuckling, but she didn't smile back at me.

"Irene, I've just had a thought." The Senator glanced at his wife out the sides of his eyes. "The Buttonbush Museum needs a new board member. Would you like to serve on that board? No pay, but it might be interesting."

Odilia snapped her head around to glare at him and a chill crept over the conversation. I wasn't sure why she was unhappy about this idea, but a gush of excitement washed over me.

"That sounds like something I might like to do. I've always loved the museum," I said. "Would they even consider me? I've never served on a board before."

"Dear, she's never served on a board before," Odilia said, her hand gripping her husband's arm. Her painted fingernails dug into his suit coat. "I'm sure she's got other things to do."

"Not to worry. You leave it to me," he said, shaking off her grip. "Good seeing you, Irene."

Odilia stared at me with a look so vicious it made me want to sink into the floor. Later, I saw her talking vigorously with the Senator in a corner, which didn't look too fun at all, at least for him.

I was tickled pink Senator Delgado would even think of me, but figured he'd forget about it.

★ ★ ★

I decided to make a go of being a first-rate housewife. I swept under all the beds and found three missing socks, cleaned out the junk drawer in the mud room, took all the books out of the bookcase and wiped them all down but got distracted when I found my copy of *The Good Earth* so I re-read the first six chapters. I even made dessert every night for a week. At least I was busy.

My household duties were one thing, but finding something to keep my mind occupied was another. I knew there were plenty of things to do in Buttonbush, but I wasn't sure what I was cut out for and what was open to me now that the war was over. One thing I knew for sure: In Buttonbush, a farm and oil town in the Central Valley of California, it was how hard you worked and who you knew that got you places.

I knew people always said their hometown was different, but it was really true about Buttonbush. Buttonbush was full of simple, hard-working people, but they weren't stupid. They were smart as bumble bees: working, planning, building, making things happen, all in a dry, dusty place that got hotter than a hey-who in the summer. The Dust Bowl brought many of them to California, but lots of them came from other places because there was so much opportunity. They didn't come for the scenery; they came because there was money to be made, but it was mostly men doing the making. This included my husband, Jimmy, who had been doing well farming cotton, potatoes, wheat, and alfalfa. But that was his little kingdom, and I didn't have much part in it other than to keep him fed. And happy, which wasn't too hard because he was good-hearted by nature.

Buttonbush, like most places, was the kind of place where you had to know somebody. I don't mean, know somebody like, "Oh you really *must* know Serena Vanderpoof Clausbinker." But more like you had to know the right person to get something done or get connected to the right thing.

My Ma used to tell me that when she and Daddy moved us here in 1919 from Texas, right away there were five neighbors who dropped by with biscuits and cookies and cakes. And when Ma mentioned she needed to find someone to fix a broken window, one neighbor said, "Hey Al, didn't your brother get his window fixed last May?" And Al chimed in, "Yeah, let me see who did that." And the very next day Ma had the name of a window repair man. Things like that happened all the time.

Buttonbush buzzed with crusty oilfield workers, jolly farmers, hustling equipment salespeople, and lots and lots of good-hearted folks who, for the most part, gave you the straight story when you asked them something and who did what they said they were going to do, once you actually got them to say they were going to do something. They didn't apologize for making money. I didn't think they were at all like the people in San Francisco or Los Angeles where the men had office jobs in cooled buildings and wives wore dresses and practical pumps to clean house. Their kids played in city parks on swing sets and slides instead of climbing on old tractors or surfing on a piece of plywood in an irrigation canal while holding a rope being pulled by a pickup truck. In Buttonbush County, the more dust you had on your shoes, the more likely you were to have some money piled up in the bank and the dirtier your kids were.

Buttonbush sat quietly smack dab in the middle of California, never claiming to be northern or southern. It was just Buttonbush. You might have characterized San Francisco and Sacramento as the head of the state, the brains where all the important thinking gets done. And Los Angeles, with its fast freeways and glamorous lifestyle, could have been the legs of the state. So you might think that Buttonbush was the heart of the state. But it wasn't, because the heart would make it too sentimental, too romantic. No, Buttonbush was the guts of California. The place that pushed and ground, dug and churned. Buttonbush did all the dirty work.

My newspaper job had put me in the catbird seat to find out what was going on around town, but that was all out the window. Other than making sure Jimmy, Pauline, and Willy were doing fine, I just didn't know where I fit into all of this and I had a big hankering to fit in somewhere.

Resigning myself to my fate, I continued my quest to be the best housewife I could be. I organized my spice cabinet so all the jars were in alphabetical order, flipped all the mattresses, then disinfected everyone's toothbrushes in boiling water. I put Pauline's hair barrettes in order of color and size and hung her hair ribbons up in descending lengths.

Over the next weeks, I cleaned all the wallpaper with ammonia and baking soda, which gave me a terrible headache. I polished the bit of silver I had, made squash bread and vegetable soup. I put Willy's baseball card collection in little envelopes, labeled with the name of the teams, and hung everyone's clothes in color categories. Borax soap became my best friend, and I washed down all the Venetian blinds, cleaned the upholstery in my car, unclogged the drain in the bathtub, and washed out the inside of the icebox. I drove tractor for Jimmy and organized his little farm shop office until he told me to stop when I put a vase of daisies in the window.

For a change, Ma was pleased with my activities.

"Lookie there, your china cabinet is sparkling," she said one day, and I knew I should have beamed with pride, but I didn't. I was always hard-pressed to impress Ma with much of anything I did. My sister could get Ma's attention just by crocheting a potholder or gluing buttons on a cigar box to make an ugly jewelry holder. Ma had a mysterious ranking method.

I glanced in the mirror one morning and realized I hadn't put on makeup in three weeks. So I went to Dempsey's Department Store and bought something called a "Perk Up Stick" which was advertised as a whole makeup kit in one little stick.

"It was made by a woman who flew bomber planes over the Atlantic during the war," the salesclerk told me. I figured I couldn't go wrong with a woman who could fly a bomber and do her makeup right.

"What did you do today, honey?" Jimmy said that night.

"I cleaned out all the drawers in the laundry room. Then I read a news story about a belly dancer who joined the Egyptian army. There's a plumbers strike in Montana and a lady from Beverly Hills is coming to Buttonbush to talk about a 'fountain of fabrics' for home decorating. It's a free lecture. Can you believe that?" I asked, rolling my eyes. "And the county code commissioner captured a monkey-faced owl outside his office yesterday. He named it 'Buster.'"

"Been reading the newspaper cover to cover, have you?" Jimmy said.

"Clothesline posts are on sale at Burt's Hardware for ten dollars."

It was a dismal representation of my day.

Three Thursdays later, I opened up the newspaper to see a small headline about my sister.

Mrs. Raymond Hankins wins contest for baked beef and noodle recipe. Page 12.

And there on page twelve was my sister, Agnes, gazing into the camera like Miss America. Her skinny face scrunched in a smile as she held her casserole that must have weighed fifteen pounds. She even got twenty-five dollars for the dang casserole.

I was washing out the breakfast dishes, thinking about how I was going to avoid hearing my sister gush over herself, when Ma called, chirping like a red robin.

"Did you see your sister in the paper? Wasn't that something? They gave her a big 'ole plaque along with the money. You should put your chicken divine recipe in there next year. You could get your picture in the paper and a plaque, too."

"Ma, you realize I used to ... oh, never mind."

I glanced at my little certificate on the wall, the one I got at the Valley Press Club awards two years ago for my contributions to a story on the new federal water project. Apparently, a federal water project was no match for a beef noodle casserole.

"I should try to be more like Agnes, right Ma?"

"I didn't say that, but ... she seems much more agreeable with life than you are. You're always trying to be something big."

Maybe Ma was right. I hung up the phone and took a gulp of coffee. Maybe I needed to take myself down a notch. Simmer instead of boil. There was a lot to admire in doing other things that were more normal. Housewife things.

So I joined some ladies' committees. There was a bunch of coffee drinking and a good dose of gossip: ladies who were gaining weight, ladies who were losing weight, husbands known for enjoying a few too many cocktails, kids with harelips and cowlicks, kids with bad tempers and bad behavior, but never anyone's own kid, always some other kid. I didn't mind listening to it. It was a tad bit like being at the newspaper and far more salacious.

The ladies were friendly enough and willing to foist responsibility on me.

"How about you bake the treats for the teenage social?" they asked me at the Lutheran Ladies Lunch Bunch meeting. By treats, they meant eight batches of marshmallow marvels. I had no idea a person could make such a mess with Knox gelatin. I took punch to the book fair at Willy's school and helped sort books. I decorated the cafeteria for Halloween and made pumpkin centerpieces for the carnival. I learned how to draw little cats out of black construction paper, hung potato sacks to lower the ceiling and make it spooky, and built a scarecrow that slightly resembled Bess Truman. I also learned the room mother for the sixth-grade class used to be a Rockette in New York; Miss Nancy, the third-grade teacher, decorated her house in a Dalmatian spotted theme; and the principal liked to ride motorcycles on weekends with a group called "Riders of the San Joaquin Wind."

Those ladies at both church and school were so organized and dedicated. They appeared to me to be the pinnacle of motherhood and marriage, delicate yet strong workhorses who carried their families along in life in so many ways, with enthusiasm for the everyday details. Seemed to me like they spent all day thinking about what their children and husband were doing and what they could do for them to better their lives and not one second thinking about themselves. It occurred to me I might be selfish.

★ ★ ★

Odilia

Odilia Terésa Soliz Delgado does not let anyone impede her goals, even a husband, I told myself as I marched up the steps of the Buttonbush County Administration Offices, my arms swinging side to side, high heel shoes staccato-clicking on the marble steps. I was ready for battle; I was most always ready for battle.

I pushed open the wide glass door to the Buttonbush County Clerk's office. Standing at the front counter was a petite woman holding an enormous cake on a red plate and talking to the woman behind the counter, Noreen Winton, secretary for the county administrative office. Noreen's head popped to the side when she saw me.

"Mrs. Delgado, I'll be right with you."

I crossed my arms and nodded.

Greying hair bun perilously perched on top her head and black cat glasses sitting high on her hooked nose, Noreen picked up a phone and punched a button.

"Ethel, Maye Marie Shadwick is here for Henry."

In a moment, Ethel waddled up to the front desk.

"Maye Marie. Look here. Another cake. How nice." Ethel picked up the phone. "Henry, guess who's here again, with another cake?"

A chair scraped in a back office and heavy footsteps shuffled towards the front counter.

"Hello, Maye Marie. Good to see you. Another cake. Wow. We've barely finished the last one." Chief Tax Collector Henry Downs raised his eyebrows and frowned.

"Oh. If you don't want it, I can take it back." The woman holding the cake took a step backward and her lower lip quivered.

"No, of course we want it, don't we, Ethel?" Henry smiled and took the cake from Maye Marie. "This looks delicious."

"It's a caramel cake. It's all the rage in San Francisco right now," Maye Marie said.

"I'm waiting." I tapped my foot. What was all this cake nonsense?

Henry ignored me, pursed his lips, then cocked his head to the side like something had clicked in his brain.

"You know, Maye Marie, I heard the Buttonbush Museum is going to be losing some board members in a few months and they could sure use someone like you. They've had some trouble over there, according to the newspaper. I could nominate you. As a county boss, I think I could get you on that board. Would you like to do that? Something different for you to spend time on."

I let out a yelp.

"There's no opening on the board." I curled my fingers into the palms of my hands.

"There is one opening that will be filled this month, and I hear rumors that there will be others soon enough," Henry said, ignoring my scowl.

"You can't just nominate someone like that." I stepped up to the front counter, staring at Henry.

"I think I can. They always ask county administrators to find candidates. I think Maye Marie would be outstanding."

"Me? On the museum board. I don't know, I ..." Maye Marie stammered.

"I think you'd be great. Your family are old California pioneers and you're a whiz bookkeeper. I bet they could use someone with a head for numbers. They're usually in the red over there," he said.

"But ... this just isn't ... You can't do this!" I spit out the words. This was not how it was supposed to go. This was supposed to be me, not Irene Pickett and not this cake-carrying simp.

Henry came around the counter, snatched the cake out of Maye Marie's hands, and handed it to Ethel. Then he grabbed Maye Marie by the arm to escort her out.

"Gosh, I don't know about that. Well, maybe ..." Maye Marie said, and Henry opened the door.

"I'll let you know, Maye Marie. Bye now," he said and quickly shut the door. He strolled back to his office without glancing at me, even though I was certain my face was on fire.

"Mrs. Delgado. What can I do for you?" Noreen said, knocking a cup of pencils across the counter.

I ran my hands through the crown of my hair and yanked at it.

"I'm here for my husband, Noreen. He submitted a recommendation for the Buttonbush Museum board. For one opening. A letter that he sent Tuesday. I've come to retrieve it. He changed his mind." I tapped my fingernails on the counter. And now this Maye Marie person was in line for the spot. I was going to fix Iggy's stupid mistake of nominating Irene Pickett, a no-name ninny, to the museum board. That pompous stuffed potato did it just to spite me, I just knew it. I'd been telling him for months I needed to join important boards and commissions now that we were back in Buttonbush. The museum was the perfect spot for me. Lots of public attention, lots of ways to make myself known. He'd done this on purpose just to hurt me, a task he seemed inclined to do at every turn. And he was so very good at it.

"We received it yesterday. But it's not here."

"What do you mean, it's not here?"

Noreen bit her lip.

"I mean we copied it and sent it off to all the commissioners. It's already on the agenda for the meeting next week."

"Well, take it off. He doesn't want to nominate her, Noreen."

I crossed my arms and leaned on the counter. Noreen took a step backwards and stumbled on her chair leg, knocking her little glasses onto the floor. She left them there.

"I'm so sorry. I can't. The meeting has already been advertised with the agenda made public and to the press. We can't take it off at this point." Noreen's lips trembled.

"Are you certain? Can't you just call all the commissioners and withdraw it?" My voice rose, and I arched my neck forward as if ready to hurl myself over the counter at her. Noreen squared her shoulders as a visible shiver ran down her body.

"I can't. I'm so sorry. But you can go to the meeting next week and publicly oppose the nomination. That would work." Noreen sat back down, cowering in her chair.

"I can't believe there's nothing you can do. Ugh. Never mind." I turned and stomped out the door, my high heels clicking even louder than before.

I was going to make a name for myself in Buttonbush, a big name, a name no one would forget. My mind flashed back to my Mama in her thin dresses, tied-back hair, always puttering behind my Papa who never gave her a compliment for any of the thousand things she did for him each day, always seeking some meager form of approval. That would never be my life and even Iggy would not stop me. That rat, Iggy. That no good, dirty rat.

THE FIRST QUEEN

Irene

Right before Thanksgiving I got a call notifying me that my nomination had gone through and my board term on the Buttonbush Museum would begin in January 1950. I'm not certain but I think I hollered "whoo hoo" when I got off the phone. The Western Union of Buttonbush, otherwise known as my Ma, dropped in right away to stick her nose into my new venture.

She carried six heaping sacks of red beets into my kitchen and dumped them on the table. I hadn't seen her in over two days, which meant she was overdue on her commentary about my life.

"What do you want to go and do that museum silliness for?" she said, her cotton dress clinging to her in all the wrong places from perspiration.

"Senator Delgado asked me to be on the board. My job is gone. So why not?" I said.

"Don't see how you're going to have time for that mess, Irene. There's Jimmy and the kids to take care of. I don't know what you're thinking ... Here, Jorge brought these to your pa. They're just right for pickling. I'll bring you some more tomorrow," she said.

"Ma, I don't have time for pickled beets. Do you know Gwen Hatch, the museum manager?"

"They say she's hard to deal with. Can't see why you want to get involved with her," Ma said, then lowered her voice. "I hear she walks around all day with a teacup filled with liquor." Ma snorted her nose in that church-lady way of glorious judgment.

"I've had some practice dealing with a difficult woman." I watched Ma swipe a cobweb from my dining room ceiling with one of Jimmy's farm magazines.

I didn't know when I got to thinking there was something more for me than just being a wife and mother. I'd never shared that thought with anyone because no decent wife would ever say that, and I loved my husband and kids to pieces. It might have been because my Ma shot down every idea I ever had for doing something different, like the time in fifth grade when I wanted to enter the turkey calling contest at Thanksgiving, or the time I wanted to make some money by delivering dead flowers on Valentine's Day to people who wanted to break up with their sweeties. In my junior year, I told Ma I wanted to become a poet, and she told me that was only something weird people did in the 1800s. And when I told her I might like to have a career covering news in London because it might lead to me getting to meet Princess Margaret, she told me I didn't have the wardrobe for it and besides, Princess Margaret was a fast woman.

In high school, I gave it a shot. I knew I couldn't be like the class brain, Lauri Fienberg, who used words like "exegesis" and "inextricable." So I became the pep club secretary and ended up running the dang thing because Fern and Jane, the girls who were president and vice president, were too busy learning to dance the Mambo at Miss Poteet's Dance Studio and chasing down two basketball players who ran in terror every time they saw those girls coming. I put on the sock hops after the basketball games and made all the posters to cheer on the teams. But at the end of high school, Fern and Jane got service awards. I didn't. I wasn't too upset. It was enough for me to know that I did something. At least that's what I told myself, and Ma confirmed it.

"Virtue is its own reward, Irene," she said to me about a million times.

Just about every girl I knew from high school had made it her prime goal to find a decent husband and get married, have kids, and then spend every day doing an exceptional job at it, to the point of exhaustion. It seemed to reward them in ways I couldn't quite see. I kept waiting to feel accomplished for unrolling my Willy's dirty socks or ironing Pauline's white blouses or cleaning out the crumbs from the toaster. I didn't mind doing all that. But I had a need for something else, if only I could figure out what that was.

"They say women who don't pay attention to their husbands end up with a husband who finds happiness elsewhere," Ma said, arching her eyebrow. Ma was queen of the "they say," an invisible group of people with opinions about everything.

"For Pete's sake! Jimmy would never ... honestly!"

"Who's going to pickle the beets? I know Jimmy loves them. So do your brothers. You've got enough jars, don't you?" She opened my pantry door. "They must be in the shed. I'll go get them."

"I have to go to the museum for something called an 'orientation.' That means they're going to show me how to be a board member."

"That's just foolishness. You make better pickled beets than anyone in town. You should enter them in the fair ... What do you want to go get involved in the museum for? You're going to have to drive into town all the time."

"Ma, I drive into town all the time anyway and we live right on the edge. It's not far. And our history is important. I want to do something to preserve it ... let people know about it," I said. "I want to be, I guess ... relevant."

"'Relevant!' That's a weird word. Relevant! Ain't being a wife and mother enough? It was good enough for me ... Don't Jimmy need your help?"

"Jimmy's got his hired man and I'll still help him plenty. Jimmy thinks it's just fine that I'm on the museum board."

"What about the kids? Pauline and Willy don't like seeing you flitting off like this. Not even getting paid."

"It's not flitting. I'm doing community volunteer work. I think the kids will be proud of me."

"Don't see how. If you got to do something, Pastor Foster needs help cleaning his house. Why don't you do something like that instead of something so uppity, like a museum?"

"It's not uppity!" I looked at those beets like they were going to bite me.

"I'll be back Friday. I hope you get these beets pickled by then." Ma went out the back door and started up her Chevy. She rolled down the window and shouted at me as I stood at the kitchen door.

"You'll do what you want, Irene. You always do."

★ ★ ★

It sort of surprised me I needed training for the board and hoped it would not be so hard that I couldn't figure it out. So I took it upon myself to learn more about the museum and spent a lot of time wandering around the place in the days before the training. The first thing I noticed was that hardly anyone was there, and it was pretty run down.

But the dang place fascinated me from the start. To me, the Buttonbush Museum—which was more of a village with lots of little historic houses and old buildings set along walking paths and surrounded by grass and landscape—was a treasure. Sitting on twenty-one acres near downtown Buttonbush, fenced in and secured, it was surrounded by city offices, old two-story houses, baseball fields, open grass areas, and a grammar school to the north. It looked like a little piece of history, frozen in time, preserved for the citizens of a city that was now growing and changing into something different while still recognizing that its past had a lot to do with its future. Those buildings were like big suitcases, packed full of the stories of countless Buttonbush people—people who lived ordinary and extraordinary lives, people who had given over their lives for the dry, desert climate that they'd forced into a shape that meant something and yielded so much. Gold mines, heavy crude oil, farms that could grow just about anything. I was genuinely excited to see what I could do there.

Gwen Hatch, the museum manager, greeted me with a clipped "hello" and whiskey on her breath for the training session in early January. Ma was right. She appeared to me to be a cantankerous, sturdy woman with strong opinions. Gwen wore velvet collars and Red Cross shoes. She smirked rather than smiled and told me herself that she often backed her car into light posts. But she was brimming with oodles of historical knowledge, and she liked to talk about it. Talk a lot. And when she did, it was like going on a magic carpet ride because she'd take you from a piece of Buttonbush history to some distantly related gun battle in Oklahoma to a Buddhist temple in Indonesia to a giant river in the Congo to a disgraced earl in Great Britain to a shanty in Virginia. I wrote down twenty-seven pages of notes that day.

We wandered around from building to building, with Gwen giving me a history of each of the twenty-four buildings at the museum and commentary on how expensive it was to keep them up.

"Paint, electricity, heating, sometimes cooling, roofs. They get rats and bugs in them. We have to look for donations everywhere and it's hard to pry money out of these rich folks in town," Gwen said. "You'll soon see that as a board member, part of your job is to sweet talk these high and mighty folks into giving money. Good luck with that."

"Eeeeeks," I said, wondering if maybe Ma was right. "I'm not sure I'll be good at that."

"You'll learn." Gwen smirked and walked me out the door.

★ ★ ★

Agnes chased me down outside church that following Sunday as I walked out with Jimmy and the kids. I'd seen her up front, her enormous maroon hat taking up two seats, covering up her husband. She was always in the front row, singing every hymn at the top of her lungs, sometimes singing the harmony which I found annoying as all get out.

"Too bad you're joining that museum thing. It's going to take up too much time." She pulled up her skirt which was riding a bit low on her non-existent waist.

"Gee, thanks, Agnes. Glad you're so proud of me." Ma must have gotten to her.

"You're always trying to be more than your station in life, like you're better than everyone. Can't you just be content? I'm having my quilting ladies over Tuesday. Why don't you go start a new quilt with us? That's something you could use."

Oh Lord, my sister, and her quilting ladies. I did not want to sit through an entire evening hearing about which wanton woman forgot to bring the Saltines to the chili feed at the Elks Club.

"Pretty sure I'm busy on Tuesday. I think I need a bunion removed."

"Ma said you wouldn't come. You never want to do the things all the other ladies want to do. Why can't you be normal? Like me? She grinned and slung her giant purse over her shoulder.

"I'm normal as anyone, Agnes. Why can't you just let me be what I want to be?"

"Whatever that is."

Agnes stood preening like a flamingo: little strands of hair wisping around her face and her skinny ankles wobbling in her shoes. I grabbed the kids and headed for the car before she could launch another verbal bellyache at me.

"What's wrong with Aunt Agnes?" Willy said, yanking the tie from his neck. "Can I go shoot squirrels today?"

"Shoot squirrels all day, sweetheart," I said, as I slid into the car. "Ma! She must have told Agnes about the museum. Those two never want me to do anything."

"Don't worry about what your ma says, honey," Jimmy said, waving his arm out the window to make a left turn. "Your ma don't recognize you can't put a whirlwind in a cage."

We turned down Hastings Avenue, and I shook my head and gazed at the rows of old houses, grand Victorians, which lined the avenue. Ma never missed an opportunity to tell me I thought too highly of myself.

"Your career should be your home. Anything else will make you unhappy," Ma said to me back when I graduated high school and asked to go to university in Los Angeles. I settled for some courses at the local junior college and even that was a bit much for Ma.

Jimmy turned the car down the highway that led back to our farm and I noticed a tiny stubble of whiskers on his chin that he'd missed shaving that morning. He was my finest achievement, according to Ma.

"Why, he's got four hundred and thirty acres of land and river water rights," Ma told me when Jimmy and I were dating. "You need a good Christian man like that. Handsome, too. Just as easy to love a handsome man as a toad face."

I was glad Jimmy wasn't a toad face. But he had the farm business handled.

"I just want to be a little part of something, something important. A town's history is important, right?" I said as we pulled into the gravel road in front of our house. The second story windows were eyes staring at me, twinkling yellow in the sunlight as if teasing me.

"Honey, you do what you want. I like it when you get excited about things," Jimmy said, tugging at his tie as we pulled into the carport and got out of the car. "I'm going to go shoot squirrels, too."

★ ★ ★

Right on time for my first board meeting on January 10, 1950, I opened the carved wooden doors of the main museum building. I turned around and looked back at all the little buildings: the small houses that stood silently, the warm afternoon setting in, the sunshine sparkling on my face. I took a big breath and went through the door.

Gwen greeted me with a skeptical look. I seated myself at the oak board table while six old men, either white-haired or balding, nodded in welcome.

"Our first woman on the board," the chairman said. "Aren't we lucky? That Senator Delgado has a sense of humor."

There were a few grunts in the room, and I could not tell if he was serious or not.

I confess, I was powerfully ignorant. So I stayed quiet, making sure I knew *Robert's Rules of Order* just so I didn't make some egregious mistake yelling "yay" when I should yell "nay." I determined it was going to be a fine learning experience with me and six old men: bankers and real estate men, even a judge, sitting on that board. A couple of them were old as dirt and I think one fell asleep during the reading of the minutes. I was certain they'd talk about the financial situation which, if I read the documents correctly, was not great. The only bright side seemed to be a healthy savings reserve, given to the museum years before by an oil company tycoon.

In a dark corner of the room sat a slim woman with twig brown hair, a thick neck, and an irritated face. It was Carlotta Eustice, the curator, who informed the board that the museum had received a donation of an incredible relic, a feat that didn't seem at all interesting to anyone but me. One man coughed, and another dropped his glasses on the floor and leaned over in his chair trying to pick them up.

"It's a mud wagon made by Henderson & Sons in Stockton from about 1850. A real beauty," she said. "It was used here in Buttonbush for mail delivery for many years. It needs a bit of work."

"Where will you exhibit it?" I asked.

"Exhibit it? We can't exhibit that. Children will climb all over it, light will fade the paint. There'll be no exhibiting it. I plan to put it in the back warehouse," Carlotta said. Gwen nodded her head in agreement.

"You mean we're getting this wonderful relic, and no one is going to see it?" I blurted it out without thinking. All the men stared at me.

Carlotta, dark eyes burning, turned to me.

"I realize you're new here, Mrs. Pickett. Our relics must be protected at all costs. They cannot be exposed to air and light," Carlotta said.

"Do you store them in an airtight room?" I asked in all sincerity, but Carlotta tossed her head.

"We store them in the basement or the warehouse," she said, and all the men settled in their seats like nothing had happened and moved on to a different topic. I'm pretty certain my mouth dropped open. Carlotta grinned like a cat with a mouse in its belly.

Kosta, the caretaker, sat quietly in a corner and winked at me.

"Is the caretaker cutting the grass the precise length?" one man asked. "Winter grass should only be cut to two inches."

The grass discussion went on for seven more minutes. I timed it by watching the big black clock on the wall. Kosta put his head in his hands and sighed. This was what these learned men did at meetings? I expected lofty thoughts out of them. Being new, I didn't want to point out that the museum was not in good financial shape, and we were getting a spectacular relic that no one would see and maybe the grass height shouldn't be top of the list of things to discuss. I was pretty sure I'd had more serious discussions at the beauty shop. I wrote all this down in my notebook for future reference, but I couldn't imagine what I'd need to refer to out of all that nonsense.

I told Jimmy all about it that night.

"Those men don't seem to pay much attention to the museum. I can't see how this place has stayed open since 1874 because there is hardly any money in the bank except for a reserve which we are not supposed to touch unless it's an emergency. The county wants to cut our budget next year by five percent, too. It's going to be a challenge," I told him in what would become the biggest understatement of my life.

* * *

Odilia

Iggy went back to Sacramento, missing my birthday on January 12 and the cocktail party at the Wakefield home, a stunning estate on the outskirts of Buttonbush. Phillip Wakefield, president of Pinnacle Road Oil, and a titan in the community, could have been useful to me. I'd wanted to impress him since he was vice president of the Gold Seal Club, a prestigious men-only club, but as usual, Iggy upended my plans.

"I have to get to Sacramento to oversee a bill on a new power plant regulation. Just go to the party. You don't need me."

"But it's my birthday. Who am I going to celebrate with?" I sounded pathetic, even to my own ears. My birthday was always a sore spot. Iggy didn't care about birthdays anymore and I didn't really care except that it indicated his level of interest in me. As a child, no one ever acknowledged my birthday. In the early days of our marriage, Iggy bought me beautiful bracelets or delicate porcelain music boxes, took me to dinner and dancing with friends in Sacramento or on a holiday to Monterey or San Francisco. But in the last few years, his gifts had been less than thoughtful.

"I can't help it that your family has scattered to the winds in Texas and New Mexico." He handed me a birthday card that read, "Happy birthday to someone special," with a certificate for a free manicure at Daisy's Salon. It was just signed, "Iggy." Not "Love, Iggy."

He was right that I didn't need him, at least not for much. I was going to make an unforgettable name for myself when I became the first woman in the Gold Seal Club. This town was going to get used to the face of Odilia Delgado, whether Iggy liked it or not.

"Let's see what he thinks about this," I said as I marched into County Commissioner Holson's office that afternoon and gave him a check for $200 for his next election.

"Just be certain the next time you have an opening on the museum board, you put my name in, understand?" I said with a wink.

Then I dropped a check for $500 written to the Buttonbush Southside Boys Charities into the mailbox. It was sure to get me recognition at their annual banquet and I'd made sure they credited the donation only to me, not that no-good Iggy who, I knew, was not actually going to Sacramento for a power plant bill. The powerful smell of his cologne as he dashed out of the house was always the signal that Iggy had more than business to attend to in Sacramento.

HISTORY AS TOLD BY GIN

Irene

Jimmy wiggled something out of his teeth with his fingernail, a sure sign he was thinking hard. The Chrysler lurched around a tight corner as we headed to the museum for the gala, my first big event since getting on the board. I chattered more than usual, fussing with the ends of my hair. He stared at the road, never turning his head to me.

"Give them a bunch of money and set that clock right over my coffin," I said to him.

"What clock?"

"You know. The French Limoges clock I told you about yesterday. The one owned by Lorna Jean Starwood Walker, wife of the founder of Buttonbush. I've only seen a picture of it."

"Oh, that clock."

"That thing has been sitting in the museum basement for decades. I want to finally get to see it … So you make a big donation, subject to getting that clock out at my funeral." I jiggled the fake pearl bracelet on my wrist.

"Little early for planning that, don't you think? You gonna die soon, or something?" he said.

"Not that I know of. But Carlotta has kept that thing locked up and never put on display. Ever."

Jimmy sat silent for a few seconds and waved his arm out the window to turn left into the museum parking lot.

"You know, even if I do get that clock out at your funeral, you still ain't gonna see the dang thing because you'll be dead," he said.

I hated when he pointed out truths to me.

"You'll get to meet Carlotta tonight. Try not to be overly impressed by her cheerfulness." I slapped him on the knee.

Lots of swanky people were in the room when Jimmy and I entered the great hall of the museum. My efforts at helping the museum office girl, Felicia, get the word out about the gala paid off because the who's who of Buttonbush was in the room. I had high hopes for the evening.

I'd never been an official board member at a fancy event, and I wanted to do it right. I'd helped publicize the event, looked over the donor list, memorized who was coming and who was married to whom. Or not married. I knew there would be stuffed mushrooms, canapés, Swedish meatballs, skewered shrimp, and champagne punch. And lots of cocktails, a detail Gwen emphasized.

Jimmy nudged me.

"Are they going to blow a trumpet and announce, 'Mister and Missus James Pickett?'" he asked as we walked in, blowing out a "ta da daaaaa" from his hands.

"For heaven's sake, no," I said. "They just roll out a red carpet and bow."

He laughed and held my hand.

The great hall glowed, decked with round tables covered in white tablecloths, tall ivory candles, and glass vases filled with carnations, the enormous chandeliers polished and lit. Everyone was dressed in fancy clothing and a band played "Some Enchanted Evening." My purple cotton dress, with a square neck, a little bow at the waist, and sleeves that puffed out like balloons, was a little less fancy than the rest and Jimmy was in his best suit and even a tie, rumpled as usual. But we were suitable enough. The men on the board introduced themselves to Jimmy, and I chatted with their wives. Looked to me like we would rake in a good amount of money that night.

Jimmy and I had just wandered to the punch table when a hush fell over the room.

Senator and Odilia Delgado walked into the crowded hall as every head turned to look at them. She wore a dark green sheath dress with a deep-V at the neck, trimmed in gold satin. The sleeves were accented in the same gold and her high-heeled black shoes had little gold tassels on them. Her dark eyes surveyed the room and her chin tilted imperiously upward.

"That's Senator Delgado's wife, Odilia," I whispered in Jimmy's ear.

"Yeah, I know."

"How do you know?"

"I went to high school with her."

"You did? Why didn't you ever tell me?"

"Didn't seem all that important," he said and gulped his punch.

The Senator strolled in behind her and it was like the Red Sea parted. Everyone knew Senator Delgado.

"She's beautiful," I said. Jimmy grunted.

Odilia's long, red fingernails flashed in the candlelight. She stood in the center of the hall next to her husband, eyeballing the crowd and waving hello to people. I was mesmerized by all the mesmerization going on.

"What was she like in high school? Were you friends?" I asked. Jimmy was seven years older than me and went to school in Rye, a town exactly twenty-three miles west of Buttonbush. I wasn't familiar with all his classmates.

"I don't remember. Ain't thought about it."

"Was she in your class?"

"Sure was."

"Do you want to go say hello?"

"Sure don't." Jimmy shook his head and swallowed another stuffed mushroom.

"Good evening, everyone. Hello to all of you wonderful people," Senator Delgado said, bellowing across the room, puffing out his substantial chest and belly. A crowd of around a hundred people gathered as he made commentary on the happenings in Sacramento: the new dam, road construction, the university expanding, the booming economy, and the general progress being made in Buttonbush, all due to his stupendous efforts. I noticed Odilia sneer then make a beeline for the bar.

Money was getting donated right and left. But halfway through the evening, Felicia came whirling towards me.

"Oh my God, Gwen has had a lot of gin. She's going to give her speech soon," Felicia said. "She hates all these rich people. Her ma was a maid for the Rutherfords, and she thinks people with money are awful. Watch out."

I spotted Gwen in a corner, wobbling side to side, talking wildly with her hands moving in all directions, her eyes popping and rolling. The gala was going to go downhill fast if the museum manager was schnockered.

I ran over and grabbed Gwen's hand. She was talking to four ladies, and I don't know what she said, but they looked horrified. I pulled her away.

"Gwen, let's have a little cup of coffee before you do your speech, okay?" I said.

"I'm fine. Right as rain ... right as rain ... I've got a very historic speech planned! I mean a speech about history. It will resonate with this group, these fancy rich people with their enormous diamonds and expensive clothes ... yes, it will ... Why I promise they'll be glued to their seats," she said. You could tell she was revving up, like an engine, but not a nice, purring little engine to run a farm pump, but more like an engine to run a

Boeing B-29. I got her to drink just a bit of coffee, but then the head of the county commission introduced her.

"Good evening," Gwen said, staggering on her heels. She steadied herself and launched into a long talk about why preserving history was so important. Then she veered off course.

"Of course, lots of you have history that's not even in this museum ... fascinating stories that have never been told ... things that don't get printed in books but are nevertheless interesting ... For example, the second mayor of Buttonbush, was rather, shall we say, different ... Story goes that Mayor Fronco liked to put on his wife's nightgown and drink sherry on the backyard terrace ... sometimes pruned his gardenias in a white lace number."

Two men in the back slugged back their drinks and laughed.

"And there was a young man from Germany who became incarcerated in 1899 and was thought to be a model trustee by the Buttonbush County Jail guards. But come to find out, he'd made a sham copy of his cell key and had been escaping every night to burgle homes all up and down Magnolia Avenue," she slurred, and old Emil Johanssen, owner of the Johanssen Cash Register Company, squirmed in his seat. "He was only sixteen, so the judge gave him a light sentence. He returned to society and eventually became a salesman for a cash register company ... Who would have thought that a reckless young man could become a part of civilized society?"

"Oh Lord," I said to Jimmy and grabbed his hand. Mayor Fronco's great-grandson had recently given us a check for $150.

"And who can forget Gertrude Ward? Gerdie McGill before she got married ... Gerdie the Gams ... a dancer in the Pickle Lily Saloon over in Rye. She knew her stuff. Gerdie could dance up a storm and the men loved her! She married up and became one of the grand dames of Buttonbush," Gwen smiled right at the wife of a Buttonbush real estate baron and, if I remembered correctly, the granddaughter of Gerdie the Gams.

Several people started whispering and shaking their heads, but I noticed several others smiling and smirking.

"She's running off our donors," I said to Jimmy.

The chair of the museum board stood up.

"Gwen, I think that's quite enough," he said.

Gwen shook her head.

"Gosh … there's so much more history to go. Isn't it fascinating? I'll bet you all have never heard this … Why, one of our past county commissioners was a founder of a nudist colony in New Jersey before moving to Buttonbush earlier this century," she said and rumbles began around the room as people tried to figure out who that county commissioner was.

"Hope that wasn't Vern Duffy," someone shouted from the back of the room and the audience broke into laughter. Vern Duffy, a retired county commissioner, was as wide as he was tall. And he was tall.

"And finally, there was that inventive hotel owner who, in about 1911, had moonshine and women of the night concealed in a downtown hotel room, making money hand over fist. The police raided the room but couldn't find any liquor until they noticed an unusual chandelier. They pressed a button, and a stream of moonshine came out of the fixture. Pressed another button and wine came out the other side. Imagine that." Gwen chuckled. "Of course, he was arrested … The Brigadier, I believe, was the name of the place."

The audience drew in a sharp breath, and an entire table of people scooted their chairs out and left the room. That hotel owner was the father of Pastor Owens of the Presbyterian church.

"Gwen, let's get on with the party, shall we?" Joanna Mosher, a kindhearted, wealthy donor, stood up and tried to draw Gwen away. I, along with everyone else in the room, was sitting in shock, so all the credit went to Joanna.

"Oh, you ... Joanna ... I don't have anything to say about your family history. Except that you're a spoiled little rich girl. Haaaaaa!" Gwen laughed into the microphone as the audience gasped. One of the other board members jumped out of his chair and yanked Gwen out of the room.

The entire audience started wiggling and buzzing and several ran out the door.

"This is outrageous," Senator Delgado shouted from the back.

"I want my money back. I won't donate to this place ever again," a balding man in a pinstripe suit said.

This was a disaster, and I didn't know what to do. I kept my head down and wandered into the lobby as the audience bolted for the doors. I came upon the rest of the board grouped in a circle, grey and bald heads bobbing up and down, deep voices rising.

"Unforgivable ... Beyond the pale," one board member said.

"So, we're settled. We'll meet tomorrow at eleven for an emergency meeting with Gwen to send her on her way. Such a disgrace. Irene, you are most welcome to join us," another said.

"Gee, that's nice of you," I said, giving them a smirk, but they didn't even notice. I guess they'd forgotten that I was a board member, too.

Six prominent donors called the museum the next morning to say they would never give money to the museum again. Those old men on the board were buzzing like a hornet's nest when I sat down at the board table to discuss Gwen's fate.

"Tom Dogan snatched his three-hundred dollar check back last night," one board member said. "So much for all the repairs we were going to do around here."

Gwen came in looking like she had a lemon peel in her mouth.

"I really don't recall saying anything wrong. I think you perhaps took my commentary out of context," she said. Gwen sat glaring at the board with her half-closed eyes and cemented frown.

Those men were a sight to behold. Gwen's speech had put some kerosene on them and lit a match. They were unmerciful. Gwen got it from all sides. I didn't say anything, because I couldn't get a word in with those men rattling off like machine guns and I didn't want to say anything, anyway. I was too new. But I guessed Gwen didn't realize that you can't insult rich people just because you don't like rich people, especially when those rich people are giving you money to run your enterprise.

Gwen looked like a wilted onion when they finished. She cleaned out her desk and disappeared.

Of course, the *Buttonbush Daily* got wind of Gwen's departure and her juicy stories and ran an entire article the following day, repeating all of Gwen's historical scandals. This had the unfortunate effect of making almost the entire town mad at us over the next month.

It didn't take long for a huge chunk of our steadfast supporters to abandon us, and our budget shrunk in an instant. Fortunately, we had the reserve account set aside for rainy days and it couldn't have gotten any rainier. Attendance declined by fifty percent over the next month and donations tumbled by seventy-five percent. It seemed at every church meeting or women's club or even my bunko group, people were talking about the gossip Gwen had blurted out for all to hear.

"You need to get this museum running efficiently. We can find other uses for this property," said the county budget officer who came to our next board meeting. "We're monitoring you."

I didn't know what that meant. But the men on the board just grumbled and rambled, forming no plan or method to get us out of the financial mess. I supposed they had better things to do at their important jobs.

"Running a museum is a lot harder than it seems," I said to Ma one day as we shelled a box of walnuts.

"Why would people go there when you could go see Humphrey Bogart at the picture show?" she said.

"It might just be up to me to save the place," I said to Ma.

"Lord help us," she said and clamped her hand down to crack a walnut.

★ ★ ★

Felicia called me in late February for a favor.

"Can you give a tour to a couple of ladies? It's one of our last remaining big donors. Bettina Davenport, the new wife of Alvin Davenport."

"I know Alvin," I said. Alvin was friends with my little brother. Smart as a whip, Alvin had gone to college back east. He wasn't much in the handsome department. Alvin had a front tooth so cockeyed that it looked like a blade on a windmill that you could just push round and round if you wanted to.

"Her mother is visiting from Vermont, and she apparently is on the board of some ritzy museum there. I get the feeling she's a bit of a snob," Felicia said. "She'll be impressed with having a board member give her a tour."

When Bettina and her mother arrived, I realized nothing was easy with Mrs. Celeste Shellman neé Bickford, as Mrs. Shellman informed me, her white hair pulled in a severe bun on the back of her head, her jowled neck rolling with every sentence. Bettina, a sweet-faced young woman with a mane of sandy hair, had bloodshot eyes.

"We've been to lunch at the Iron Oak Room, a tea at Parker Hills Country Club, a drive over to the central coast to look at the fabulous views on Moonstone Beach, and a Mozart concert by a small quartet from the Buttonbush Symphony," Bettina said. "I'm hoping Mother enjoys the museum."

"California has such an odd way of displaying things," Mrs. Shellman said as we entered the grounds, the tiny houses and buildings were dappled in the sunshine creeping over the tall oak and mulberry trees. "So very rustic and unsophisticated."

"It is the Wild West, Mother. It wasn't easy pioneering here. So much land and harsh climate." Bettina rolled her eyes.

"We're rough and ready," I said, but Mrs. Shellman pinched her nose.

"It does take some getting used to here. Buttonbush isn't like I expected California to be, with lush lawns and oleanders and beaches. Or movie stars and glittering restaurants and swimming pools," Bettina said.

"It definitely is different here in Buttonbush. It's like someone took a chunk of Oklahoma and set it right in the middle of California, just for fun," I said. "That's what makes it so special."

"My dear, there was nothing at all easy about being the early settlers in Vermont and the rest of New England, but at least they made strong efforts to stay respectable and cultured. Look at this." Her mother pointed to a dilapidated house sitting at the entrance to the museum. It was from an old Buttonbush family but needed attention.

"I'm sure funding is scarce here," Bettina said.

"Perhaps they are too busy spending on plows or pigs or something like that. Or gambling." Her mother cast her nose down.

"I've only been on the board a short time and I'm still learning about this place. Isn't it wonderful? So many interesting historical things here," I said, sweeping my arm out toward the back of the museum.

"At least it's encouraging to hear that there are women on the board," Mrs. Shellman said.

"Yeah, they let us vote and drive cars too," I said. Mrs. Shellman was starting to feel like a blister on my heel.

"Mother is on the board of a museum in Vermont." Bettina bit her lip.

"You are? Well, isn't it just always something? I can't believe how much there is to do around here." I waved them down the path.

"These need renovation immediately," Mrs. Shellman said, pointing to another house. "You have too many buildings to care for here. Didn't anyone think to do a financial overview of all this?"

"I guess not." I crossed my arms. "There is a lot to be done, that's certain."

"Perhaps you should remove them. What significance could they possibly have?"

"Significance? Oh gosh. A whole lot. This place, run down as it is, holds the history of the California that nobody knows," I said. "People know a lot about the rest of the state: Los Angeles, Hollywood, San Francisco, Spanish missions, Yosemite. That's all glamorous and fancy. But they don't know anything about our part of California. It's hot here in the Central Valley and full of tough opportunities. Agriculture and oil. We feed and power the country."

"You certainly know a lot about this place," Bettina said.

"I've done my research. I used to work for the newspaper during the war but, well, you know. The men came home, so I needed something else to do. So here I am." I wiggled my shoulders and laughed.

"Some weren't so fortunate as to come back," Mrs. Shellman said, turning her head and walking away.

"Very true, Mrs. Shellman."

"That is at least something worth saving." Mrs. Shellman pointed up to the main gallery and the old clock tower.

"That's the Walker clock tower, Mother," Bettina said. "Named for the founder of Buttonbush."

"Correct! General-in-Chief of the U.S. Army, William P. Walker. Nicknamed 'Old Brains.' Ha! A veteran of the Civil War and the Spanish American war, an amateur expert on the California missions. He left his papers to the museum," I said.

"Wasn't this once attached to City Hall?" Bettina asked.

"It was. You must be a history buff. The General married Lorna Jean Starwood, and he loved Buttonbush," I said.

"I can't imagine why anyone would want to preserve all this," Mrs. Shellman said, and I frowned. I guess she thought Vermont had the only history worth saving.

As we ambled on and poked our heads into the shoemaker's shack, Bettina inhaled the air deep into her lungs.

"There are smells in a museum, old smells, smells that you can't get in the current time no matter how hard you try. It's the smell of history, of thinking in another time. Their ideas float in the air and seep into the woodwork, the bricks and roofs, creep into the windows and pierce the foundations. They're in there, buried deep. The only consolation is the stories poorly told by the small pieces of furniture, objects, or relics displayed there," she said.

"Whoo-wee! That's a beautiful observation," I said. She sounded like she'd swallowed a poetry book.

"No one can ever know the full human experience that took place in these buildings or with those objects, Mother. But a person can smell them. They're … dank, sweet, soft, warm. Human. Those stories need to be told," Bettina said. "Not only in the buildings and the things in them, but in words and sounds that earnestly carry forth those histories, keeping them moving in the wind and air so that they will never be forgotten,"

Bettina put her hand over her mouth when she realized how much she'd gushed on about history.

"Gosh, you sure can talk pretty. Wish I could talk that … What's the word? Eloquently," I said. "This museum is a government-owned jewel box of stories. We're hard pressed to get people to care. But I do."

"The only way to raise money for a museum, dear, is to ask for it directly or hold events that entice people to give … parties and soirees and lectures and things like that. You'll need to do more, dear," Mrs. Shellman patted my arm. "Bettina, consider getting on the board. Your brother would have taken my seat on the museum board."

"What? I don't know, Mother," Bettina said, but I jumped on that right away.

"You should!"

"How do you obtain a board seat?" Mrs. Shellman asked.

"You have to be appointed. I think it would be great if Bettina joined us whenever we get an opening. I could use another woman on the board."

Bettina stammered a bit, but smiled in a way that made her eyes glow and her cheeks turn pink.

As her mother strolled down the road to survey the rest of the buildings, Bettina pulled me to the side.

"Call me Betty. But not in front of Mother." She winked.

★ ★ ★

With Gwen gone, I spent more and more time with Felicia, who I quickly realized was the backbone of the museum. Spunky and willing to work as hard as an ox, she knew just about everything that was going on. Some might have called that snoopy since she seemed to stick her nose into everything, but I called it enterprising.

One day she took me down to the dark basement stairs and opened the door with a skeleton key.

"They lock this up and no one ever sees any of it. Carlotta will kill me for letting you in."

The basement was jammed with countless, overflowing shelves, chock full of old clothing, hats, guns, teapots, butter dishes, tools, etched glassware, jewelry boxes, Victrolas, maps, clocks, desks, dolls, china sets, wash boards, guns, and hundreds of other old items. There were seven pianos, six spinning wheels, ten sewing machines, fourteen desks, eight rocking chairs, fifteen anvils, and a box of 348 thimbles. Things were piled almost to the ceiling and much of it looked like it had not been cataloged or inventoried. I peeked inside a small box sitting on a shelf.

"Carlotta keeps all this under lock and key?" I asked.

"Gwen hired Carlotta in 1941. She has two history degrees and knows more about Buttonbush history than anyone," Felicia said. "She also has a bad attitude, as I'm sure you've noticed."

"Why on earth do we have three shoehorns from a St. Louis shoe store? And a medal from the Ohio Pharmaceutical Association?" I said. "Not to mention an entire box of postcards from Florida."

"Carlotta takes anything people give her. She always says this stuff can't be exposed to air or light," Felicia said.

"So it all just sits there … unappreciated?" I said. "That seems like a strange way to run a museum. Some of this stuff needs to go."

Felicia nodded.

"Carlotta is almost vicious about putting things out. She won't let anyone near any of it."

I assumed that in about five hundred years, the Buttonbush Museum basement would be like the lost tomb of King Tut, and somebody would open that basement door and be astounded at the ancient treasures. I sincerely hoped that Carlotta hadn't put some curse on it, but I couldn't be sure about that.

★ ★ ★

Carlotta loved it when she knew something I didn't and phoned me one day in March with a major piece of information.

"We're getting three new board members," she said. "Three of the men on the board are retiring due to health problems."

That, right there, should have clued me in that being on the board might kill me.

"They're all women." Her voice sounded like she questioned my reaction to this piece of news.

"Three women! Well, I'll be a monkey's uncle," I said. I wasn't sorry to see the men go. They didn't do much.

Maye Marie Shadwick, a widowed bookkeeper and granddaughter of a California gold rush pioneer, was one of the women. Bettina Davenport, to my delight, was also nominated. Odilia Delgado was the third, which scared the daylights out of me. The new ladies would start in three weeks, and I hoped I could be friends with all of them.

★ ★ ★

Odilia

That check to Commissioner Holson had done the trick.

I had accomplished the first part of my plans and had been nominated to the Buttonbush Museum board of directors, despite Iggy.

Iggy was none too pleased. He set down his briefcase and poured himself a whiskey and soda, the ice tinkling in the glass as he glared at me.

"I thought you'd calm down and stay home a bit, Odilia. Do you need to get involved in everything under the sun? Ever since you had that job during the war you've decided you're some big businesswoman, some big shot."

"I would think you might be happy for me." I poured myself a glass of wine and took a hefty gulp. Wait until he realized just how involved I was going to be in Buttonbush, if I had my way. Besides, what did he expect me to do? We never had children; my family was gone. I needed to occupy my time while he was in Sacramento doing whatever he damned well pleased.

To be fair, Iggy hadn't gotten what he thought he'd had in me. I was a prettily wrapped package that he opened to find a ticking time bomb.

As a child I'd been a well-behaved, traditional girl; my mother and father saw to that. Girls weren't allowed ambitions in our household and Papa put his thumb on Mama in every way. She cooked enchiladas and made her own tortillas, she cleaned our dusty farmworker houses incessantly, she mended all our clothes so they could be passed from child to child, she planted our little garden with tomatillos, chili peppers and squash. Mama raised all eleven of us pretty much on her own as we moved from house to house, place to place, wherever the harvest took us. Papa worked in the fields during the day and spent his evenings with his friends in the smokey taverns or out in the yard drinking beers. Mama took us, without fail, to church on Sunday where the priests reinforced this kind of family arrangement. Mama never asked for anything for herself, never complained, never uttered one opinion that contradicted Papa.

I thought that was my destiny, too, until one summer when I was about thirteen. Papa was running a harvest crew outside of Buttonbush, in a little town called Rye. He took a permanent job there as a foreman on a big farm, run by a man who was mean as a snake and married to a lady who was endlessly kind. The woman was the actual owner of the farm, having inherited it from her parents. I'd overheard Papa and the other men talk about her, partially in awe of her but partially in disgust at being bossed around by a woman. I had never seen a woman boss and Papa didn't quite know what to do about it because they paid well.

"That woman!" he'd spit out of his mouth when he came home. But she checked fields for bugs, turned irrigation water on, ordered the crews into various fields and even drove the tractors occasionally. I loved seeing a woman in charge of something more important than a pot of beans or a basket of laundry even though I knew those things were important, too, and my Mama deserved respect for what she did. But she never, ever got it. I also loved that the woman got under my father's thin skin.

One day I was wandering down a farm road near our little house and the woman drove up in a beautiful red truck, the big chrome grill on the front gleaming in the sun. She stopped near me, the dust kicking up behind the truck.

"Hello, sweetheart. You're Manuel's daughter, aren't you?"

"Yes," I said, in awe of her shiny short hair, like a fairy, with dark, twinkling eyes.

"Would you like to help me with something?"

"Sure." I was eager to see what she had in mind.

"Hop in. I'll take you up to the packing shed."

I got in and she smiled at me, asking me what grade I was in and what I wanted to be when I grew up.

"I guess I'll be a mother." I said. I'd never thought about it.

"Are your grades good?"

"I always get As."

"That's good. You can do a lot of things. Maybe go to college," she said.

"Me? College?" That thought had never occurred to me.

"I went to college. UCLA. You could too if you study hard enough and work at it." She smiled at me, pushing a puff of hair off her face as the air blew through the open windows of the truck.

"I don't think my papa would let me go to college," I said. Papa would never let loose of a daughter who could help around the house.

"Well, let's see about that."

She took me to the packing shed where there was an enormous pile of labels sitting on a table. They were about eight inches across and four inches tall and they had a picture of three little girls dancing in a circle around a cantaloupe, fancifully done in orange and green. The label read, "Merry Melons from Mireles Farms, Rye, California."

"Those are my sisters and me. My papa had that made when we were little. My sisters both married and moved away, so I stayed to run the farm," she said. How wonderful that must have been, I thought, to have a papa so nice that he had an entire picture made for his little girls.

There were wooden packing boxes piled all around, ready for the melon harvest that was coming up in a week. Two women were piling the boxes in neat stacks around the pack room.

"I'm going to have you put these labels on these boxes. These are for our cantaloupe that will be shipped all over the United States and even to Canada. Do you think you can do this?" She handed me a pile of labels.

"Of course I can," I said, thrusting my chin out.

"Of course you can." She patted me on the shoulder and left.

Over the summer Mrs. Mireles put me to many more tasks around the farm. Sorting boxes, counting crates, cleaning out the field office, filing in a metal cabinet she had in her office. She had a slatted chair on rollers that she sat in behind a massive oak desk covered in papers and files and receipts and a little statue of an angel holding a yellow flower. She showed me where to file all the various account paperwork and keep the payroll records in a certain spot. Then she showed me how to use a machine that had number keys on it with little ribbons of red and black ink and a roller that ticked out a small slice of paper. I'd add up columns in the ledgers for her and tally the work hours for various workers, give her totals on the number of boxes packed in a day per field, and add up expenses for the office and for the farm shop. Mrs. Mireles was never cross with me, patiently showing me how to use the machine, often listening to music on a radio while we worked.

Papa didn't like that I was being so influenced by Mrs. Mireles, but he was always willing to overlook things for money. I had to give him my paycheck each week.

Mr. Mireles rarely came into the office, but one June day when I was fourteen, he walked in, foul language pouring out of him.

"Where are the totals for the potatoes? I've been looking for those all day." His gravelly shout rang across the office.

"Odilia, has them, dear," Mrs. Mireles said.

"Hand those to me girl." He glared at me.

I reached for a file across the little table where I was working and my hand shook, bumping the files. Papers, receipts, invoices, and bills of lading flew across the floor, a few landing on his boots. My lip trembled and I couldn't think straight as his wicked eyes bored into me.

"What the hell are you doing, girl? Look what a mess you made. Where are those damn totals?" He shouted and my eyes searched for Mrs. Mireles who was still smiling.

"Dear, there's no need to shout at Odilia. You've made her feel scared. Stop it now, please." She smiled at him, but I could see the steel in her eyes. He could, too.

"Just get them to me," he said, his voice more subdued.

I grabbed the receipts and handed them to him as quickly as I could, my eyes downcast. He took them from me and stomped out of the room.

"Don't let him frighten you, Odilia. Don't let any man frighten you. You are just as good, just as worthy. Trouble is, as women we have to be tough and tender at the same time. It's all too much for the men if we're just tough," she said. "I've found you can slay a dragon as well with sugar as you can a sword. And it doesn't hurt to own the castle they want to live in."

She laughed to herself and winked at me.

I learned a lot from Mrs. Mireles over four summers. Until she, unbeknownst to me, went to my high school principal and told him I needed to go to college and that he should find me a scholarship. So he did. And Mrs. Mireles sweetened the deal by paying $500 for me every year for college as well, provided I came to work for her during the summers. I did just that. When I graduated from the University of California at Berkeley, she was there with my mama. When I said I wanted to work in Sacramento, she helped me get my first job with Assemblyman Obert.

"I don't know why you aren't supportive of this," I said one night after Iggy complained again about me being on the museum board.

"Your head is always three sizes too big, Odilia," Iggy said. "It's not becoming of a woman to be so ambitious."

When Iggy and I married in 1936 and he rose to prominence in Sacramento, I threw away that shadowy belief, that shroud over me that set limits. I wanted something more, something bigger for myself, by myself. I joined the ladies groups in Sacramento, the church council, the Sacramento Junior League, the Ladies Guild, the League of Women Voters. Forgetting what Mrs. Mireles taught me about using sugar as a weapon, I just used my weapons. So when the war came, my reputation for being tough and rather ruthless got me a job running a segment of the shipyards in Richmond, California, leading a group of "Rosies" in producing cargo ships. I got a taste of a man's world, and I liked it.

But Sacramento was a large city, and it was harder to get ahead there, especially for a woman. Buttonbush was a smaller city, with less competition. I could be a big fish in that pond. And I wanted to be a very big fish.

"Do you want me to be like my mother, totally dependent on you so that you can drink and gamble and do what you want, and I have no recourse?" I snapped. "Or like yours? A miserable, grumbling, wretched ... Well, you know how your mother is. Because your father left her for Antonette."

"That's not what I meant, and you know it. I'm going to do some work in my office now. Don't wait up for me," he said then stopped and turned. "But if you're going to do this,

I'd take a tactic of fixing up the place. Spend the donations on improvements to all those old houses. They're disgraceful."

He vanished into his study, the sturdy mahogany doors closing with a sharp slam. A faint odor followed him, something sweet and unrecognizable, like vanilla or caramel.

THE NEXT THREE QUEENS

Irene

Betty and Maye Marie looked like they were straight out of *Look* magazine at their first board meeting in March 1950. Betty's cinnamon-sugar freckles sparkled on her face, and she wore a dark blue dress with matching shoes and purse, eyes dancing with excitement, her hands in a steeple pose. Maye Marie had her sleek blonde hair in a soft bun with a little bow at the crown. Smiling sweetly, she wore a pale maroon dress with black buttons. I knew I should have taken more time with my clothes instead of waxing my kitchen floor. Plus, I'd accidentally left a clothespin attached to my collar which Carlotta gleefully pointed out to me.

Maye Marie brought a gorgeous cake that she cut in neat little pieces and placed on dainty little flowered plates for everyone. She even brought forks.

"Coconut cake. I hope you like it."

Right there I decided these monthly board meetings were going to be a lot more fun already. None of the three men left on the board took a piece of cake, but Betty and I each took a slice.

The three of us sat at the board table buzzing with ideas for the museum. Maye Marie had all sorts of thoughts on how to improve our financial record keeping while Betty wanted to create educational programs, same as me. She'd been reading gobs of Buttonbush and California history books, and I could tell she was quite smart. I wrote down all their ideas in my notebook.

The three remaining men on the board stared at us like a pack of unicorns had entered the boardroom. Unicorns eating coconut cake.

Everyone stopped talking when Odilia, cigarette in mouth and eyes darting, strode into the room. She was dressed spectacularly in a red suit with a black silk blouse and red heels, a rose-shaped rhinestone broach on the lapel of her jacket, and a whiff of perfume which overpowered the cigarette smoke. I pulled down my cotton dress a little lower on my legs, my Woolworth's bracelet dangling from my wrist. Odilia smiled at Betty, nodded to Maye Marie, and didn't glance at me. She took a fancy pen out of her purse, then lit another cigarette, propping her elbow on the edge of the table, staring at the chairman.

He cleared his throat and began reading the agenda.

I kept an eye on Odilia. She sat sharp toothed and watching intently, writing things down, jumping in to state her opinions on everything, not being one bit shy. She directed a lot of her questions at me, which was scary.

"Do you have an endowment?" she asked me and I shook my head. I didn't even know what that meant.

"These events you have … the gala, the children's carnival … these take a lot of work to organize. Are these raising money for you?" she asked.

"I guess so," I said. "But not enough. The gala could raise money but … you know all the donors are mad at us."

"There are better ways." She gave me a snide look and began talking about the budget with one of the men, flicking her cigarette ashes into a shell-shaped ashtray.

Clearly, the three men remaining on the board were scared to death of Odilia. Partially, I guessed, because she was terrifying. But also because her husband had deep connections and great power in Buttonbush. Odilia was smart enough to know that having a senator for a husband gave her a good deal of leverage. She dropped his name into the conversation frequently. I planned to learn a lot from her.

But our finances were in jeopardy, and we had no manager.

"We need to raise money," the chairman said. A small grumbling rose in the room, but no one had any concrete ideas. "Our donations have dropped precipitously and the healthy reserves we had are dwindling. The county is very unhappy with us."

"It appears to me that we need to raise money to refurbish this place. Make it attractive so people will come," Odilia said. "That is what will raise revenue. My husband agrees with me on that."

All the men nodded in unison.

"Maybe we could find the lost treasure of the outlaw Square Foot Fred," I said, only half joking. Square Foot Fred, a rather famous but inept Buttonbush outlaw of the mid-1800s, was so named because his forehead rivaled the size of a church door.

"That sounds like a great thing to waste your time on. Why don't you just sit out in the street and panhandle for money? You'll get more." Odilia crossed her arms.

"I was just joking and …"

"Oooh. He was supposed to have a fortune stashed away somewhere," said Betty. "Maybe we can research him and find it."

"That is ridiculous. A myth. The outlaw Fred Watlington had no such treasure," Carlotta piped up from the side of the room, also crossing her arms. "He was caught red-handed several times and most of the cash was recovered."

"I've read numerous stories about him robbing stagecoaches and banks," said Betty.

"But his hidden treasure is supposed to be from a museum in San Francisco that he blew the doors off of … Kind of impressive if you ask me," I said.

"What did he steal from a museum?" Maye Marie said.

"They had an exhibition from Damascus with over five hundred coins from the seventh century. Valuable stuff. Square Foot Fred knocked down the museum door with dynamite and carried off the coins. He vamoosed to Buttonbush to hide out," I said. "I read that in a historical journal somewhere, so there might be some truth to it."

"That was never verified," said Carlotta. "He was a bumbling idiot. Robbed a stage then dropped the lock box on his foot and broke it. He fell off his horse during a train robbery. I doubt he was smart enough to rob a San Francisco museum."

"Rumors often have an element of truth in them," Maye Marie said.

"People have been looking for that treasure for decades … They've torn up countless acres of ground and old mine shafts and all kinds of things, but it's never surfaced," said Betty.

"Didn't he escape from jail several times?" said Odilia.

"He did. But I assure you, there's no treasure." Carlotta, as usual, delivered a cure for joy and put an end to my hopes for a gigantic pile of gold coins showing up to rescue the museum. Not to mention my chance at being labeled a bona fide treasure hunter.

★ ★ ★

Ma, naturally, had a lot to say about my new board members. She dropped in on a Friday morning to bring me my sister's latest creation: egg salad à l'Agnes. It smelled like it came out of a sump pump.

"Maye Marie Shadwick … Well, you know the rumors there, don't you?" she said to me.

"What rumors?"

"Not to be un-Christian and convey gossip … but you know all the scandal about Ingrid Bergman and all and …" Ma tilted her head and stared at me.

"Maye Marie knows Ingrid Bergman?"

"Don't be sassy, Irene. No … you know Ingrid Bergman had that affair with that older man. Stromboli or Simboli or … I can't quite remember."

"You mean Roberto Rossellini, Ma? By the way, I hate egg salad."

"That's it! Well, I can't say for sure, but my beauty operator says Maye Marie was cozy with Martin Martin. Senior. She worked for him when he was the county accountant. Of course, it was quite a few years ago, before she was married. But he was married. He and his wife packed up and moved to Kansas the very day after Maye Marie got married … So, well, you just can imagine what that was all about."

"That doesn't mean anything. Stop gossiping, Ma," I said, and she raised her eyebrows. I handed her a plate. "Here, try my cobbler."

Ma was really no different from the rest of Buttonbush. Despite it being a fairly good-sized town of about thirty-six thousand with a few stoplights and many stop signs, two high schools, two hospitals, and one bowling alley, it was a big town until there was a juicy piece of gossip. Then it was a small town.

On the other hand, Ma was thrilled about me working with Odilia Delgado.

"Why, she's an amazing person. She's done so many things. She spoke to our ladies' group at the church a few months ago and talked about all that she's done. You can learn a lot from her," Ma said, waving a spoon of cobbler around.

"I thought you didn't want me doing the museum work," I said.

"I don't. But seems like you're going to do it anyway, so you might as well learn something," she said. "But you sure did make a good batch of peach cobbler. Is that your granny's recipe?"

★ ★ ★

After months of searching, we were still lacking a manager. Odilia sat straight as a rail and hard eyed at our June board meeting, a cigarette hanging from her manicured fingers.

"Why don't you let us do it?" she said and took a long puff of the cigarette. "Me, Maye Marie, and Betty ... if they're agreeable to that. We could manage the museum. Temporarily, of course."

Maye Marie and Betty each widened their eyes.

"I think that would be fine," the chairman said, finally. "In combination, you all probably have the skills to run it. For a while. But you'd better get our revenues up. We are $2,832 in the red for the year."

"What about me?" I squeaked. I wasn't even sure I wanted in on the plan except for the fact that I'd been left out.

"I didn't think you'd want to do it," Odilia said. "You have your little farm and all."

"Why shouldn't I?"

"I wasn't sure of your particular skills." Odilia's haughty eyes bored into my forehead.

"Odilia, if Irene wants to join us, why not? She's been here longer than any of us and her newspaper experience will be a help," Betty said. I smiled at her, stifling the childish urge to stick my tongue out at Odilia.

Odilia sat silently for a few seconds.

"Fine. Let's meet at my house tomorrow. Ten o'clock."

My mouth dropped a little when I saw Odilia's home the next day. Tall ceilings with giant wood beams hung over pale green walls covered with paintings of birds and flowers and outdoor scenery. A puffy, scarlet sofa sat in the middle of the living room surrounded by mahogany bookcases that almost reached the ceiling. Antique vases and urns decorated every corner. Walnut paneling covered the dining room walls where a fine silver tea set sat on an immense, round walnut table, and a giant crystal chandelier with countless dangling prisms hovered overhead. Odilia invited us into her office—she had a proper office, all her own—and I couldn't believe what I saw there: plaques, certificates, and trophies all over the walls and shelves and bookcases, awards from all kinds of Northern California places.

Odilia took charge right away, flipping through a leather binder packed with papers and documents about the museum. She had three pages of lists for us which took me twenty minutes to copy into my notebook.

"Maye Marie, you work with Felicia to go over the books. Let's ensure our financials are as efficient as possible. Betty, you work on inventorying all our collections with Carlotta. Let's find out what we have and what we need," she said. "I'm going to work on donations and construction ... Refurbishing our buildings and bringing in more will generate revenue."

"What about me?" I asked.

"You? What can you do?" She flicked open a matchbook and put another cigarette in her mouth.

"I can do all the publicity. Get people to attend our events and lectures and things," I said. "I used to be a newspaper assistant, you know."

"Is that all you can do? Talk about what we're doing?"

"Well ... there are other things. I'm good with the volunteers and I have a ton of ideas on how to bring people into the museum. I've organized school events and church functions," I said, like a fly trying to talk a spider into eating me.

"Fine. I'm sure you'll find some use," she said.

"Odilia, Irene has been doing a lot of things on this board. Why, she publicized the gala that Gwen ruined and there were quite a lot of guests there," Betty said.

"A lot of good that did. They're all mad now," Odilia said.

"I'm sure we can get them back. I'm good at making people aware of things that are happening," I said.

"We'll see," she said, snapping her notebook shut. "Let's meet again tomorrow. Eight o'clock at the museum.

"I can't get there until eight-thirty. I have to get the kids to school," I said.

"We can't wait around for you and your children all the time." Odilia flicked her cigarette into a yellow ash tray.

"Eight-thirty should be fine," Maye Marie said. "Irene needs to be there for her kids."

Odilia shook her head and said, "Fine."

"Did I do something or say something to offend her?" I said to Betty and Maye Marie when we walked outside to leave. "I don't know why I let her intimidate me."

"I don't think it's personal. She's driven. She told me she wants to be the first woman in the Gold Seal Club," Betty said.

"That's ambitious on her part. You have to show a lot of accomplishments to get into that club. And be a man ... so there's that," I said.

"I can't see how the club will let any woman in," Betty said. "My husband says it would be highly unlikely that she'd win a vote. There are a lot of members who would leave the club over that."

"There's no damn reason she shouldn't get in," I said. "We saw all her awards. Odilia is smart."

So maybe Odilia wanting to get in the men's club explained her cantankerous behavior. I never understood the need to keep women out of things like that, but in those days, that opinion wasn't thought of too fondly.

"She's building her case by doing all these things," Betty said.

★ ★ ★

The four of us settled into a peaceful sort of arrangement over the next several months, spending loads of time together. Our camaraderie was so great that we began labelling ourselves the "Four Queens" that summer, even though Odilia still didn't consider me her equal. I'm not really sure why we started calling ourselves that, but I think it was Maye Marie's idea and it seemed to suit the four of us. But it was a misnomer of the spectacular kind. Despite being duly appointed board members of the Buttonbush Museum, most of the time we were there wearing soiled dungarees and work shirts, our hair tied back in red bandanas so we could scrub the tile in the Indian pottery exhibit or polish the wood around the "Outlaws of the West" display or trim the great green hedges that lined the front of our little museum. Except for Odilia, who was usually running around bossing around the staff, wearing some spectacular outfit, furiously waving a pencil in the air like an orchestra conductor doing a Rachmaninoff piece.

We Four Queens believed it was our hidden little kingdom. No one but our families and a few friends knew we were doing the job on a daily basis, handling every little detail and problem, watching every cost, every nick of paint, every school kid who ran through the grounds. The county commissioners paid no attention except to look at our ledgers and county staff just thought we were checking the place over now and then. That kind of attention and daily embrace of all that was the museum got a piece of my heart and my days were filled with museum business and plans. Finally I was doing something that mattered.

"It's a grand, noble endeavor," Betty told us. I would have never thought to phrase it that way, but it fit. I was always in the mood for a grand, noble endeavor.

Maye Marie, a quiet, tiny woman with a head for figures and the body of Betty Grable, took on the financial tasks. I ignored Ma's gossip about her and took her at face value. There didn't seem to be anything nefarious about her and whatever Martin Martin, Sr. had been to her, he'd taught her well about bookkeeping.

"I like to keep busy," she said. "Makes the time go faster."

Maye Marie's husband died during the war, and she seemed awful lonely. Her two daughters were away at college. She frequently wrote in her little ledgers, and she always had a dreamy, sad look on her face. Betty, Odilia, and I invited her to things, but she almost always declined. But she loved working with arithmetic, darting around the museum with a pencil on her ear and ledgers in her hand. She said the word "budget" about thirty times a day.

Maye Marie was a proper lady. She was a churchgoer and Sunday school teacher, but I'd seen her once in a bathing suit and she could have been a pin-up on any sailor's bunk. Even with her funny little swim cap with lilies of the valley on it, like a funeral spray, Maye Marie was a lollapalooza, but she didn't even know it. That's probably how the rumors got started since I could imagine a lot of men taking a glance at her. She planted a beautiful garden every year and cooked like a real chef. Her cakes were her crowning achievement and there wasn't one meeting that we held where she didn't bring some sort of baked good for us. I put on five pounds in those first months just from her delicious goodies. But her true love was those ledger sheets and counting every penny we took in at the museum.

I knew Odilia spent the wartime being a boss of the "Rosie the Riveters." But I also learned she was a college graduate of Cal Berkeley and married the Senator while working in the state capital. She never talked much about him unless she needed to use his name to get a donation or put pressure on someone, a tactic I had never seen employed by anyone, but heck, I didn't know any other senators' wives so maybe they all did it. I learned that after the war she was out of a job, like me, so she convinced her husband to move back to Buttonbush in 1949 so he could eventually retire.

For Odilia, there was no difference between running a company making battleships for a world war and running a little Podunk museum. It was all do or die.

Odilia became the buildings' manager and rode the maintenance crew like Scorpus driving chariots at Circus Maximus. She took over the manager's office—never asking permission, of course—setting up all her files and paperwork on the wide mahogany desk. Odilia marched through the museum each day, pointing out porches that needed sweeping, scuffed paint on the sides of a building and leaks in the drinking fountains. If she didn't get results in a short time, she was back at the poor groundsman, Kosta, with a shaking finger and a face so bunched up she looked like a catfish. She enjoyed construction projects the most and found any little reason to build onto something. Her plan was to build out the museum so well that people would flock in to see it.

She decided to redo the floor in the shoemaker's shack, put new wallpaper in the Haywood House, add trees in front of the great hall and paint the inside of the Peabody House. Odilia ran around the museum in her high heels with sweaty concrete workers traipsing after her and paint trucks following her down the roads, greasy plumbers carrying tools on their backs while she marched into buildings, pointing and demonstrating. One day I saw her sitting in a lawn chair, directing two men who were unloading bricks in front of the great hall while she had some woman doing her nails, the little dust flying in the air from the emory board while the men grunted around her.

Odilia had a real knack for getting donations and pretty much every little project we were doing was paid for by someone Odilia cornered into giving us money. They either seemed to have forgotten about Gwen's debacle or Odilia convinced them to forget it. And by "convinced," I mean "forced." There wasn't a banker, oilman, merchant, attorney, or accountant in town she didn't hunt down like Buffalo Bill on the front range, and she most always got something out of them. She even cornered SueAnn Thornbury at her own sister's funeral.

"I just wandered over and told her how sorry I was about her sister and all and then I mentioned her sister liked hats and that we were going to remodel the old hat shop at the museum and wouldn't that just be a wonderful way of commemorating her sister in a unique and generous way. She didn't seem to mind me talking, so I just asked if she could give us thirty dollars to pay for wallpaper and she said yes," Odilia beamed at our board meeting. The very next day, she marched to the Thornbury house to collect the money, flowers from the funeral still fresh in their living room.

On July Fourth, she did even better. She got the museum's old Methodist church building painted by feeding pound cake and Hamm's Beer to Tom Coyle, owner of Coyle's Paints, at a backyard barbecue. Right in the middle of the rest of the group singing "America the Beautiful."

"He was just sitting there, and he looked kind of lonely. You know his wife is strange, and she wasn't there, so I thought it was an excellent opportunity to talk to him about the museum. He liked that cake, so I brought him more and a little glass ... well, maybe it was a couple of little glasses of beer. And we talked all about the paint business, and before you know it, I was telling him about the poor children that we educate at the museum and how much they love coming to that little church and learning about our history and he remembered going there when he was a child and pretty soon, I had him write down the date when he could start painting the building and here it is. I think a light grey will be nice. What do you think?" Odilia said at a board meeting. All I could wonder is how she got that done so fast during "America the Beautiful," except that maybe they sang all the verses.

I also noticed that at the location of all these little projects, Odilia placed a small sign in a frame that had the name of the donor on it but also her name. "Odilia Delgado, board member, chair of donations." I didn't think we had a donations chair, but apparently, we did. The museum was abuzz with construction workers, far more than patrons, and all that money she got donated came in and went right out in a giant funnel.

As I suspected, Betty took the museum board position because her mother—a woman who could have scared the medals off General Patton's chest—insisted. Alvin told her it would be a good "diversion" for her. She was a graduate of Bryn Mawr with degrees in history and math, and she was smart. It was hard to keep her mind occupied. She knew a lot about the arts and music and poetry by people like Keats and Pope and Blake and some others I'd never heard of. And while she loved the arts, she herself was not the least bit creative and hired an interior decorator to design her living room because she couldn't think of what to do with it except that it needed to be just like her mother's house.

Betty also liked her gin gimlets, and we roped her in now and then at some of our ladies' gatherings because she liked to sneak in a flask and get a little tipsy.

"I don't quite know what to do here," she'd say, but still she volunteered. She went through the packed-to-the-roof storage sheds and threw out all sorts of old things like broken lampshades, burned down candles, and rusty door hinges, even though Carlotta threw fits over it. Betty followed Odilia around, biting her finger every time Odilia tore into some poor fellow who clipped a rose bush the wrong way.

I took charge of advertising and publicity and organizing events, so Odilia called me the "fluff" person in the group. This made me about the most worthless human being around in her eyes. I made up the advertisement posters and flyers. I wrote articles for the newspaper, came up with names for the winter gala which, before I came along, was creatively titled "Winter Gala." I thought of themes like "Magical Merriment" and "Icicle Dreamland." I wanted to call it "Snowballs in Hell" originally, but the other board members didn't think that was too funny. I organized the parties and thought of fun themes and things to do at them with table decorations and fancy food and flowers. I wasn't particularly crafty, but I knew people who were. Or sometimes they were just things I pulled off the roadside or pilfered from my garden.

"I don't know why you think having flowers in the middle of the tables is a big deal," Odilia said to me when I wanted to decorate for the Ladies Guild Lunch. I tried to string little flowers made of paper doilies for the Ladies Guild Night on the Town in May and she told me it was "romantic phooey."

"Why do you waste time decorating?" she said to me, which I thought was strange since she had decorated her house to the nines.

"Why do you waste time rebuilding these houses?" I said, which made her mad as a wet hen. I knew it was a stupid question but dang, those decorations made our parties a lot nicer, and I needed something to do. Odilia just wanted all the money we had to go to her projects, nothing else. I know if not for me, the Ladies Guild lunches would be on old card tables with Melmac plates and nothing but cheese with mayonnaise sandwiches and iced tea. There wouldn't be a pink tablecloth, garland, or vase of flowers for miles if I let those three plan a party and they know it because none of them have any sense of artistry or pizzazz. None at all.

Maye Marie, especially, kindly browbeat me over my spending.

"We don't need that thing to have a nice luncheon, Irene. It's not in the budget," she said when I wanted to buy a three-foot plastic centerpiece replica of the Venus de Milo I'd seen for sale at Dempsey's Department Store. I argued with her for a bit about the need to make the ladies feel "transported to another era." She wouldn't go for it, so I ended up putting out cuttings from some camellia bushes into a large milk can striped with blue ribbons.

I didn't mind being the lowest on the totem pole. Maye Marie, Odilia, and Betty were university graduates. I had just taken a few classes at the junior college before I got married and I tried not to dwell on my lack of education. But I was determined, right from the start, to earn their respect for my creative nature, imagination, and persistence.

Pretty quick, Odilia and I started to bicker.

"We have the next gala coming up in February. I think we can make it even better than ever. How about we hire that swing band from Los Angeles: Don DeShazo and his Swingin' Band. Spend a little money on really good music. We'll get a great turnout. Don't you think we ought to do something like that rather than keep building things?" I said at our July board meeting, almost in a whisper because I figured I was going to get blasted.

"Do something? We are doing something. We're fixing this place up because it was so run down it was embarrassing." Odilia scowled at the men board members who all dropped their heads in shame.

"That band is fantastic. Alvin and I heard them in Ventura at the Yacht Club, and it was so much fun. Let's get them. I'll bet we double our attendance." Betty's shoulders wiggled, like she was dancing. It was so nice to have a young woman on the board who could speak for the younger set.

"Bah. No one cares about dancing at these events," Odilia said.

"My wife enjoys it," one of the men said, but Odilia gave him a firm scowl and he sat back in his chair.

"We could also get some items to auction off. Bigger things like television sets and tickets to plays in San Francisco. Jewelry and antiques," I said.

Maye Marie, who had been sitting quietly, also piped up.

"And Carlotta could display some of our collection from the 1850s. Anything that's one hundred years old or more. I know we have things. Wouldn't that be interesting?" Maye Marie said.

"I don't have ..." Carlotta started her usual excuse, but Odilia took over.

"Carlotta doesn't have time for this. She's got all my projects to get done. There's concrete work that is scheduled in front of the general store and a paint project in the Henderson House. Carlotta has to move all the relics. And the children's area has a terrible lighting problem. Carlotta has to be available. She doesn't have time for gala nonsense, right Carlotta?" Odilia glared at Carlotta.

"Right!" Carlotta crossed her arms.

"Odilia, your projects aren't exactly bringing people in the doors. A new paint job isn't something people are inclined to come look at. We need to have events. Fun experiences." I said.

"Oh, for heaven's sake. We don't have time for that. Do you have time for that Carlotta?" Odilia looked at Carlotta, who, like a golden retriever, shook her head in obedience. Of course Carlotta didn't have time. She never had time.

These little arguments continued, and Maye Marie and Betty tried to keep us from going to battle, but sometimes it was just bound to happen. Odilia didn't like to lose, so she always won. I didn't have the time or energy to put into fighting her so hard. Seemed like no matter what the problem was, she'd stay up all night, make phone calls, find information, and come to a meeting as prepared as a Supreme Court lawyer to argue her case. I couldn't spend that kind of time. And honestly, it was more important to her to win.

Odilia hadn't given me much to do, so I took it upon myself to get rid of some of the unimportant relics—or junk—that we had stored in the warehouse. Betty, Carlotta, and I got together and sorted through piles and piles of stuff. Of course, Carlotta had to approve of us getting rid of it and negotiating that with her rivaled negotiating the Yalta Agreement. She argued something fierce over some items but there was just no justification for keeping things that had absolutely no connection to Buttonbush. Betty helped me haul six loads of junk out in Jimmy's truck. Every time we packed a box, Carlotta took two or things out of it. Whenever I took a box out of the storage room to my truck, covered in grime and sweating like a hog, I'd see Odilia prancing through the museum in her tailored navy-blue dress with white trim at the collar and cuffs or wearing her little candy straw hat with red flowers all around it, looking for all the world like a damn picture postcard.

Then Betty and I focused on the things in the museum that might be museum-worthy somewhere, but just not in Buttonbush. No one, not even Carlotta, knew where they came from or why they were at the museum. I figured I could send them off to wherever they belonged. Carlotta seemed more agreeable to this because at least they would be preserved somewhere, hopefully by a curator less cantankerous than Carlotta.

There were old photographs of Mineral City, Virginia, rocks from Juab County, Utah, land records from Grand Island, Nebraska, and an 1804 jewelry box owned by Anna Hughes, Yonkers, New York. I even found a metal box with some old love letters dated almost a hundred years ago and a locket in it from a British colonel addressed to a woman in London, England. I wrote letters to the Chamber of Commerce in each of those areas, offering to send them the relic if, of course, they paid for the shipping. In the end, I sent out sixty-three letters to twenty-four states and to the Royal Historical Society of London regarding the love letters. I didn't know if any of this would do any good, but at least I was doing something.

"Don't know why we call ourselves queens when we get so dang filthy," I said after Betty, Maye Marie, and I finished cleaning out a tool shed at the back of the museum. Odilia sat near us, making a list of supplies. "None of us are royalty, except maybe Betty. Your ma seems like she might be a queen."

Betty laughed.

"My mother is Celeste Eugenia Shellman née Bickford of the Boston Bickfords. They're in banking," Betty said. "Daddy refers to them as Boston, banking, and bluestocking."

Odilia gave an unimpressed grunt.

"Ooooh. I'm Irene Fanny Pickett née Looper of the Terrell, Texas Loopers. Half of which are in prison," I said.

"Your middle name is Fanny!" Odilia laughed. I rolled my eyes.

"I guess I'm Maye Marie Shadwick, née Maytubby of the Auburn, California Maytubbys," said Maye Marie.

"I'm Odilia ..." she started in, but I cut her off.

"You make fun of my middle name, but she used to be Maye Marie MAYTUBBY, and you say diddly?" I shouted. The Four Queens were all laughing, even Odilia.

We were invincible at that point. So we thought.

HOW TO STEAL AN OLD HOUSE

Odilia

I nuzzled my toes into the thick wool carpet of my office, the one in the perfect shade of sage green, so perfect it was peaceful. I'd spent six weeks scouring Los Angeles showrooms for just the right one two years ago when Iggy and I built the house. It tickled my toes deliciously. I looked out the window, draped in the light blue chintz fabric that matched the wing chair I was sitting in. The nearby mantle, covered in Italian marble, held two pewter candlesticks from an antique store in Pasadena, and the chandelier above cast a light green haze over the room. It was my favorite room in the house but, honestly, I loved them all. I'd designed every piece of the house, every nook and cranny, every little detail, all based on the interior of Mrs. Mireles's house, which she had occasionally let me into for one reason or another. The walnut paneling in the bedroom. The cheery white tile in the kitchen and the high hutch filled with blue and white china. The glossy green bathroom with delicate lilies on the wallpaper. I'd done the same with our Sacramento home. I would not have known how to decorate other than to draw on those memories of Mrs. Mireles. I had to credit Iggy for giving me the means to do it. Iggy and the inheritance from his Uncle Sal.

It was a marked difference from my mama's life, and mine as a child, living in grubby house after house, none of them ours.

Up and down the San Joaquin Valley as Papa abruptly moved us with each harvest. Little farm towns with nothing to offer us but tiny schools and even tinier houses. Mama did her best but she could never do much to make them feel like homes. Once she'd tried to hang some old lace for a curtain and the farmer's wife told her to take it down. The places were all the same. Sad, cold, smelling of babies and the sweat of work, full of furniture that other people used, beds others had slept on, houses where lots of people stayed but no one really lived in. Not until we got to the Mireles' farm did we have a proper home with our own furniture, sparse as it was, and our own little beds, always shared by two or three of us. Now, I had almost everything I wanted.

★ ★ ★

I practically pranced into the August 1950 museum board meeting.

"We've just hit on a stroke of good luck," I said, my curled hair bouncing on my head. "My husband informed me that the old Iversen ranch is going into probate. Belinda Iversen died last year ... one hundred and five years old. Can you imagine? They didn't have any children and they've not found any heirs. The bank is happy to let us have the place if we can move it. Lock, stock, and barrel. They want to sell the land to some big farmer out of Orange County."

"That's an early California ranch house and would fit perfectly in the front east corner of the museum," Carlotta said.

"We don't need another building," Irene said. "We can't take care of what we've got."

"How can we refuse?" Irene was going to go against me again. I wasn't having it. "The bank tells me that everything in it is perfect. Think of how much attention and praise I'll … er … we'll get from the community."

"Irene is right," Betty said. "This is the last thing we need."

"We have quite a bit of new building going on here," said one of the men board members. "They aren't bringing in the revenue."

"We can't pass up this kind of opportunity, can we? That's a ranch house from a historic Buttonbush family. They go back to the … what, Carlotta?" I said, scooting my chair next to Carlotta. The house was so much like the houses of the wealthy farmers my papa had worked for, the ones I'd craved to have as a child, wishing I could go inside.

"Eighteen hundreds," said Carlotta. "Lars Iversen came a few years after the Civil War ended. From Nebraska, I believe."

Once, on Christmas Eve, while Papa was harvesting citrus in Reedley and Mama was making tamales, I'd peeked into a farmer's house to see the whole family sitting around the dining table in their velvet and satin Christmas clothes in deep green and crimson red. They had two candles burning in some type of silver candleholders while the family ate dinner off sparkly china and crystal glasses. I thought that was the most magnificent thing I'd ever seen. The Iversen house likely held scenes like that, too.

"You three need to stop fighting things like this." I glared at Betty, Maye Marie, and Irene.

"We do need to pay more attention to our finances. The county accountant tells me that the new budgets are going to be cut even more and we are always over budget. The commissioners aren't too happy with us right now and may give us a firm goal of raising a specific amount of money," the chairman said.

"That's perfect. This house will bring in lots of people," I said. "It's so beautiful. Everyone will want to come see it."

Irene grunted, and Betty and Maye Marie both sighed and sat back in their chairs, which told me I'd won this battle already.

"Ladies let's just table this for now. Think on it some," said the chairman.

* * *

The state government was in session, so Iggy was in Sacramento. I went home and fixed myself a giant burrito filled with tender beef and beans I'd cooked that morning. I never made Mexican food for Iggy. He didn't like it anymore and seemed to want to shed himself of all his Mexican heritage. He was playing with the big boys in Sacramento and they ate steak and potatoes, baked chicken, and rice pilaf.

I mapped out my plan for the Iverson House while I ate. I called Iggy at nine and told him about the meeting.

"You most certainly need to get that house, Odilia. Don't let them stop you. That will be a showstopper," he said. "That historic house on the property will add a great deal of value to the museum."

"I thought so, too. Glad you agree with me on something," I said, more sarcastically than I'd intended.

"Don't be disagreeable, Odilia."

"When are you coming home?" I knew the answer already but asked the question anyway.

"I can't say for certain. We'll see how things go. There are a lot of new bills up for approval and I have at least three committee meetings later this week. I'll let you know. Don't count on me for anything," he said.

I rarely did.

* * *

Irene

Tabling the decision on the Iversen house was like giving Jesse Owens a fifteen-minute head start. Nothing more was said of the house when suddenly it appeared on the September 1950 board agenda.

"What's this?" I asked, and Odilia grinned.

"We've got the paperwork to get this moving. All we have to do is give the okay to get started," Odilia said.

"Hold your horses. We haven't said we want this, and we don't know what it will cost." My face flushed hot and my hands clenched.

"Odilia, we can't just move forward on this," Maye Marie said. "The budget."

"I've got a rough estimate of $1,600 to move it. Then about $2,500 to place it and renovate it. And I think the bank might make a generous donation since we're taking this out of their hands," Odilia said. "I'm fairly certain we can get the rest donated."

"Fairly certain isn't certain!" I said. "Have you forgotten the county is watching us?"

"We'll make money on this, most definitely. Do you realize how stupendous this house is? They won't dare cut us back," Odilia said. She passed pictures of the house around the room, the men nodding and smiling at the gorgeous woodwork and high-beamed ceilings. She displayed all the bank documents and all the legal items needed.

I argued for about ten more minutes, but all three men seemed entranced by the prospect of the Iversen house, too.

So the three men and Odilia voted to take the house, with Betty, Maye Marie, and I casting "no" votes. Odilia gave us dagger-looks throughout the rest of the meeting.

"We're just building a museum, not being a museum. A broke museum," I said, but Odilia strutted out of the room.

Odilia made a grand deal of getting the Iversen house, letting all the newspaper and radio people know we were in talks with the bank. The entire story of the Lars and Belinda Iversen family was told in the paper with pictures of the family and the ranch. Even some Los Angeles papers picked up on it. *Futile search for missing heir leads to big gift for Buttonbush Museum*, was the headline in the *Los Angeles Beacon*.

Odilia was in near Shangri-La over it all and she and Carlotta spent hours planning and plotting the move of the house. The paperwork and documents to complete the whole deal came about in record time, but costs for the project kept rising. It didn't faze Odilia one little bit.

* * *

Nothing can humble a person more than cleaning out a stinky animal pen, and I nodded in tribute to the sheep who stared at me blandly, possibly in gratitude for my work or possibly in arrogant satisfaction. The pungent smell of dung hung in the air as I raked. I didn't mind. Doing something physical perked me up, and it was nice to be appreciated, even if it was only by a sheep.

The county fair was in full swing and both Pauline and Willy showed animals, which took up enormous amounts of my time. I spent almost two weeks at the fairgrounds helping the kids, hauling supplies, grooming the animals, feeding the animals and the kids. The scorching September sun peeped over the top of the barn when Pauline crept up beside me.

"Mom, this is Deborah's mom, Mrs. Dolley. She wanted to meet you," Pauline said. I turned around, sweat dampening my forehead, dirt covering my work boots. Deborah was a new girl at school and Pauline had become fast friends with her.

I tugged at my soiled gingham shirt and raised my head. There stood this glossy, deep auburn-haired woman, curls dangling around her neck, a baby-blue dress with lace work at the top, carrying a matching baby-blue purse. Her smile was so dazzling I almost had to shade my eyes. I wished I'd worn my Platex girdle under my dungarees. I sucked in my stomach.

"So nice to meet you Mrs. Pickett," she said. Pauline and Deborah were grinning ear to ear.

"Mrs. Dolley used to be a fashion model in Los Angeles. For magazines," Pauline said. "She came all the way down here to the fair just to see my sheep."

Pauline couldn't tear her eyes off the lovely Mrs. Dolley. I pushed my hair off my neck.

"How wonderful," I said. "How on earth did you end up in Buttonbush?"

Her laugh was melodic.

"I met my husband at a car race down in Pasadena. He's in the oil business and we moved here recently. I've been so impressed with Pauline. What a beautiful girl ... Deborah just loves her," she said. "And call me Joyce."

"I'm Irene," I said. "We'll have to get together when this is over and visit."

"We shall," she said.

"Mom, the newspaper called, and they want me to be interviewed for a story on raising my sheep. Deborah and Mrs. Dolley want to see me do the interview. Isn't that great?" Pauline said.

"The newspaper? You didn't tell me that? When?"

"In an hour."

"Oh no. I can't watch it. I've got to finish up here. Then get to a committee meeting at the museum," I said.

"Oh, for heaven's sake, Mother. Can't you just miss once?" Pauline said.

"Honey, I can't."

That Joan of Arc martyr look glazed Pauline's face. Guilt crept over my forehead and into my brain.

"I'm sorry honey but I can't miss. I'm sure you'll do fine without me. I'm glad Mrs. Dolley and Deborah are here with you," I said. But my stomach lurched as I said it. What a terrible thing to do to my daughter.

Pauline rolled her eyes at me.

"Thanks, Mom." She gave me a quick kiss, and the three wandered off, chatting and giggling. I finished cleaning the pen and headed to the meeting at the museum with a hollow feeling in my belly.

* * *

The move of the Iversen house was just a day away when Felicia came to Betty, Maye Marie, and me in a dither, shaking all down her body.

"I don't know how to tell you this. It's just frightful," she said.

"Spit it out, Felicia," I said.

"A few weeks ago, a man came in to see Mrs. Delgado. His name was Mr. Aden ... Paul Aden ... I don't know why I remembered that except that he was very nice and ... Anyway, I took him to her office and after he left, she was upset. Didn't come back for the rest of the day," Felicia said. "I didn't think much of it. The next day, she was in her office ... er, the main office ... with the door closed all day long."

Felicia thought no more of it. But yesterday, while Odilia was out, Felicia went into the office to drop off some papers. She accidentally knocked a file off Odilia's desk and papers scattered on the floor.

"I know I shouldn't have looked but I couldn't help it. It looked so official and important," she said.

There was a long letter that said there was an heir to the Iversen ranch estate. Mr. Aden, an attorney, had been contacted by a woman named Mary Iversen, who said that her husband was a nephew of the late Lars Iversen. A genuine heir.

"You mean that house belongs to somebody?" Maye Marie said.

"According to the letter, it does," Felicia said.

"Why didn't Odilia tell us?" Maye Marie said.

Felicia and I looked at her, and she grunted.

"Never mind. What shall we do?" Maye Marie said.

"You can't tell her I told you!" Felicia said. "I don't want to lose my job."

"Let's go call this Mr. Aden," Maye Marie said.

"Do you have the letter, Felicia?" I said.

"No, I was too scared to take it."

Maye Marie and I went home and spent an hour on the phone trying to find an attorney named "Paul Aden." We finally tracked him down in Long Beach, but he didn't return my phone call until the next day, which was moving day. Maye Marie was at my house when he called. Mr. Aden took a huge breath when we told him what was happening to the house.

"They can't move that house. It belongs to the Iversens," he said. "I told that Mrs. Delgado to have the museum's attorneys get in touch with me."

"How the heck did this happen?" I said. I was becoming sick to my stomach. This was pure treachery on the part of the museum.

Mr. Aden began the long story.

The Iversen family came from Denmark and settled in Chicago around 1835 where they became quite wealthy. There were two children, Lars and Valentin, who grew up and set off for Nebraska together. The parents passed away, leaving them their fortune. Lars and Valentin used the money to acquire a timber limit in Nebraska, which proved to be a valuable document, according to Mr. Aden. After a while, Lars and Valentin headed to California. Valentin went to Long Beach, Lars to Buttonbush County. The brothers lost track of each other and never saw each other again.

"The funny part of this is that it all came out in a joke," Mr. Aden said.

John Iversen, Valentin Iversen's only child, was a typesetter at the *Long Beach Independent Press Telegram*. His buddies in the newspaper office saw the news story about the Iversen house and the valuable estate and typeset a fake news story that said John was the heir to the Iversen fortune in Buttonbush County. John got a good laugh about it and stuck it in his pocket. That's when his wife found the story and thought it was true.

"She started searching through John's family photos and memorabilia … never telling her husband what she was up to, mind you … and came across photos of the Iversen family. Lars, the parents. All of it. And she found the timber limit document, a true legal document," Mr. Aden said. Maye Marie and I had our ears pressed up to the phone.

"John turned dead pale when I told him all this," Mr. Aden said. "He didn't know any of his family history … his father never spoke of it … and John forgot about the old photos he inherited from his parents. He was speechless when I told him what the estate was worth."

That sounded about right to me. My Jimmy could sit on top of the crown jewels of England but wouldn't even notice if there was a plate of pancakes in front of him. I said a silent prayer of thanks for curious and persistent wives everywhere.

"That house is about to be moved across the county today," Maye Marie said.

"I'll be right up," Mr. Aden said.

Maye Marie and I hopped in my car, and we picked up Betty. We found the house already moving on County Road 14, scooting along slowly past a pig farm, right before the railroad tracks. The house was in pieces, with the kitchen, living and dining room sections at the front on a low-riding trailer that was at least twenty feet long, and the smaller bedroom section sitting on a truck with tires the size of elephants. The poor old thing looked like someone had taken a cleaver and ingloriously chopped right into it. You could see the bare insides of the house from the side, like a dollhouse. The bedrooms, the bathroom, the kitchen, the parlor. The windows open as the scenery inched by.

A railroad truck was at the tracks with flashing lights, ready to help the old house over to the other side. Odilia rode in her convertible along with Carlotta, escorting the house, cheering it on like she was queen of the Macy's Thanksgiving Day parade. A few farm workers came out and were watching the slow progress of the building as it squeaked and groaned on its journey.

"What should we do?" I said.

"We need to wait. We can't jump in front of the truck. And we can't let Odilia know we know what she's covering up. We don't have any proof. At least not yet," Maye Marie said. We followed as it made its way down the country roads, poking along behind the house, keeping careful so as not to let Odilia notice we were there. When the house got to Cotton Corners, a car pulled up to the front of the procession and a short, yellow-haired man with an orange bowtie jumped out. We pulled up, out of sight of Odilia, to listen.

★ ★ ★

Odilia

"Stop, stop. You can't do this!"

Paul Aden, the attorney who'd visited me about the Iversen house hopped up and down like a kangaroo right next to the Iversen house as it paused in the road. How did he know where we were? Then I saw Irene's car with Maye Marie and Betty inside, parked at the side of the Cotton Corners auto shop. Sneaky little women.

"What do you want?" I said, getting out of my car.

He waved his arms at the truck driver as the house ground to a creaky stop.

"This house does not belong to you. It belongs to the rightful heir of the Iversen Ranch," he said. "See here, I have the papers from the bank." He waved a file stuffed with papers in front of my face.

This was not going as well as I'd planned.

"You! I talked to you about this weeks ago. You told me your lawyers would call me." Mr. Aden shook the file in my face.

"I didn't think you were really representing an heir. I thought you were a phony," I said, my hand twitching at my waist. "There are people all the time who try to defraud a museum. How do we know you're legitimate?"

"I have all the paperwork. I showed them to you."

"I don't know if that's legitimate. We can sort this out later, Mr. Aden. This house needs to be moved. We're blocking traffic," I said. This man was annoying me. He couldn't possibly have a valid claim. I had plans and this heir nonsense would not deter me.

"Oh no, you will not move this house."

"We must. See here, it's in pieces and already halfway to the museum." I swooped my arm out to show him the chopped-up house.

"And where are the contents of the house? The family items, the valuables from inside? What have you done with them?" Mr. Aden said.

"Don't worry. They're stored safe and sound," I said, not that it was any of his business.

"Put this house back!" Mr. Aden shouted.

I'd had enough of this man. I snatched the papers from Mr. Aden and rifled through them. They did appear to be rather legitimate, now that I really looked at them. I'd been so intent on the project I hadn't paid that much attention to him when he'd talked to me, and I figured he'd just let it go. I went back to my car, grabbed my purse, and walked into the little phone booth that sat outside the general store at Cotton Corners. I dug in my purse, searching for a dime, then called the mayor.

"Look, the house is halfway to the museum. We can't just take it back. I'm going to keep going, okay?" I said. The mayor agreed.

Then I called the museum's attorney and told him what happened.

"You did what?" He was rather loud.

"Calm down now. I can fix this. We're almost to the museum. They're not going to make us take it back now," I said. I was pretty sure they wouldn't.

"Odilia, you just can't haul a house off," he said. "This is going to be a giant legal mess."

"Do you want me to take it back?" I wasn't even sure we could make a U-turn with something so large.

"No. Take it to the museum. It might reinforce our position. Dear Lord, what will you do next?"

I shrugged and walked back over to where Mr. Aden was standing with his arms crossed, glaring at me.

"Mr. Aden, the mayor of Buttonbush is on his way here. We are going to proceed down the road. We can straighten this out later," I said. "If not, I'm going to call my husband, Senator Delgado."

None of that fazed Mr. Aden.

"See here, you cannot move this house any further. It should never have been given to you," he said. "The bank is aware of this issue."

"Until a judge tells me that, I'm moving this house," I said.

Mr. Aden walked over to the driver of the truck and said something. The wheels of the truck turned left, like they were going to head back to the ranch.

"Hey, hey. No! Stop that. Keep going!" I waved my arms.

The driver turned his wheels back.

Then Mr. Aden shouted something again, and the driver turned the wheels left again.

"No! I told you. We're going to the museum. Now get going. I'm paying the bills!" I jumped up on the truck's running board. "Now get this thing moving or else.

The poor driver threw up his hands. He turned back on the original path and moved forward. I smiled and got back in my car. The procession started moving again. Out of the corner of my eye I saw those little sneaks, Maye Marie, Betty and Irene, walk over to Mr. Aden.

★ ★ ★

Irene

Mr. Aden left and went back to Long Beach, vowing to pursue legal matters, and we followed the house until it reached the museum. We approached Odilia, acting like we didn't know anything.

"Some lame brain attorneys from Long Beach claims there is an heir to the Iversen estate, and we shouldn't be taking this house. He says he has papers. I don't quite know what we're going to do," she said. "Someone tipped him off about the move. Do you know anything about that?"

"Not really," I said.

Her top lip curled.

"And you didn't think to bring this up to the rest of us, so that this could be avoided?" Betty said.

"You three were against this from the start. I wasn't going to give you any ammunition to stop this move." Odilia slapped her hands together. "I'll sort this out."

"Odilia, you stole a house. A whole damn house!" I said.

"I wouldn't phrase it that way."

"You stole a house!" I said, louder.

"You better not go forward any more with this until you know for certain that the house can stay," Maye Marie said.

"*You stole a house*!" I couldn't help shouting it.

"Pfffft." Odilia walked away and talked to the moving crew. Soon the movers lifted the house over the foundation but left it on the blocks and platforms and not on the cement slab, a sure sign they were questioning whether it was going to stay there. By the end of the day, the poor old Iversen house embarrassingly perched on cement blocks and wood, still sawed in half and under the hard scrutiny of all of Buttonbush. The newspaper and radio stations got wind of the dustup with Mr. Aden and were hounding Odilia as she walked around the house, pointing things out to the workers.

The headline the next day read, *Buttonbush Museum acquisition of Iversen House under question when long-lost heir appears.*

My Jimmy thought it was a riot.

"You mean Odilia stole a house? Was it at gunpoint or did she sneak in at the dead of night …? 'Gimme yer house or I'll shoot ya in the gut, Shorty. And don't forget the Venetian blinds,'" he said, and I poked him on the shoulder.

"Stop laughing. It's awful," I said. "And stop watching those Cagney movies!"

It got even more awful when word came out that John Iversen, the heir in question, was a poor typesetter, eking out a living in Long Beach, with his wife and four children. To boot, he was a decorated army veteran. The newspaper had a field day, taking pictures of the house sitting on blocks, torn up and forlorn. Mr. Aden filed papers to halt the reconstruction, and everything got tied up in the courts. Odilia was mad as a hornet at Mr. Aden.

"It's very selfish of him," she said, which made me even more upset at the general tenor of our museum board at that point. How low were we going to go?

AMBUSH AT THE BOARD MEETING

Odilia

The Iversen house issue was winding its way through the legal system, and I took that as a cue to assume it was going to go my way. I was going to make it go my way. They would not make us take that house back. Unfortunately, the newspaper skewered the entire board over the Iversen case but fortunately for me, they didn't point to me individually and I wasn't about to single myself out. I had more projects to do.

"What next? A heist at Randall's Jewelry Store? A stick-up at A-1 Grocery?" Irene said.

"It's all going to work out. You'll see." She was such a smarty pants.

We had more to worry about.

"I received a letter from the California Commission on Courts. The state has allocated money to build a new superior court in the valley. They are scouting out locations and Buttonbush is on the list of potential locations. In particular, the county has recommended they look at the museum as a potential site," the chairman told us at a meeting.

"Where would they put the courthouse?" Irene asked.

"I don't know," the chairman said.

"That's a ridiculous idea," I said. The nerve. After all the things I had planned I wasn't about to let a courthouse get in the middle of it all.

"We don't know anything yet and other cities are in the running. So let's not worry about this now. But there's more bad news. The county is asking all departments to take another five percent reduction this year. That means we have to concentrate on raising money for our expenses," he said. "You four ladies have a lot of work to do. I suggested to Carlotta that we do a large-scale Civil War commemoration. It's been ninety years since the war. Unfortunately, we can't pull out our Civil War-era relics and military uniforms because Carlotta said it might damage their integrity. Carlotta is going to take some photographs and we'll have those hanging in the main gallery with captions to tell what's in the photo."

"Sounds boring to me," Irene said, taking a bite of one of Maye Marie's chocolate chip cookies. For once, I agreed with her.

Across the room a little ray of sunshine beamed over the top of Carlotta, her red cardigan practically glowing over her shoulders and her penny loafers shining like bronzed bricks. She gave Irene a dirty look and then smiled.

"What do you mean? We can't actually see the things?" I asked. Carlotta was getting on my nerves, and I needed to put an end to her little reign of terror.

"Yes ... I mean, no." Carlotta jumped into the conversation. "These are incredibly precious items, and they need to stay protected. I can't possibly put these military uniforms out on display for the sunshine to bleach them or the air to cause damage to the fibers."

Betty turned her head to the side, like she was trying to shake something out of her brain.

"You're indicating that you're simply going to take pictures of the things we have in our collection instead of putting the actual collections out ... the uniforms and all?" Betty said, taking a bite of a cookie.

"Exactly. I'll write up something about it for people to read so they'll get a good deal of information that way," Carlotta said.

"I visited the Vatican in Italy once and I distinctly remember a hall filled with artworks and relics and the windows were open. I remember because it was such a pleasant breeze," Betty said.

"We are not the Vatican." Carlotta crossed her arms.

"Yeah, they don't know how to manage museums as well as we do," Irene said, rolling her eyes.

"This will be highly informational. I've already started writing the story of the relics and the public will learn so much from reading about the pieces that we have in our collection," Carlotta said.

After the meeting, Irene cornered the three of us.

"Has Carlotta ever once agreed to display anything from the storage collection?" she asked.

We were quiet for a moment.

"Well, no," I said.

"Have you asked her to put anything new out, and has she ever agreed? Even once?"

"Ummm ... now that you mention it, no," said Maye Marie.

"And every time we ask her to do something new, change a display case or have some new program to educate about something different, does she tell you she's too busy?"

We all nodded our heads.

"Why is that?" I asked.

"I've given up on the why of what Carlotta does. It aches my brain. I only know that every damn time we want to do something, pull something out of the collections, she finds a way out of it.

Irene asked us to meet at the museum on Thursday. She had an idea, so I was naturally skeptical. The Four Queens met in the great hall, Irene pacing the floor like a giddy colt.

"You know, Percy LeRude, that rancher from over in Posse Creek? Jimmy and I were at his house last Sunday afternoon for a barbecue. He has a downright spectacular collection of old guns and Western memorabilia like belt buckles, spurs, and saddles. He's been collecting for years and I hear it's a museum-worthy collection. Not very many people in Buttonbush have seen his relics, and I think it would be a hit," she said. "Percy has often told me he'd love to have an exhibit of all his things at the museum."

"Is he willing to give them to us?" I asked.

"Hell, I wouldn't even want him to. They would never be seen again. He could just lend it to us for an exhibit. It would make money, I think. And it doesn't involve stealing anything."

"Move on, Irene," I said, lighting a cigarette. Honestly, she never stopped jabbing at me. Just like Iggy.

"But Carlotta will have to agree to do this display. She'll have to be the one to organize it and set it out," Betty said. "And you know she'll have every excuse in the world not to do that."

"I have an idea," Irene said, a phrase that always made me shudder.

★ ★ ★

The room was packed at the next board meeting. I invited all the county commissioners to attend, enticed by the promise of double chocolate brownies made by Maye Marie. It was amazing how easily baked goods could increase attendance at just about anything. I, of course, ate nothing, mainly because I'd made myself an enormous plate of huevos rancheros that morning.

Midway through the meeting, Irene made an announcement. "I have some wonderful news. Percy LeRude has agreed to loan us his western collection of guns, belt buckles, saddles, and other cowboy antiquities for a display to begin in January. This will be a very exciting portrayal of our ranching history. We can have a cowboy day for the kids, with roping and calf wrestling. Western arts and crafts and a cowboy cookout. It's going to be something everyone in Buttonbush will love," she said.

Carlotta's face puffed like a balloon and the lilt in Irene's voice made me wonder if she was more excited about the exhibit or about ambushing Carlotta.

The men, all whiskers, gruffness, and grumbles, began whispering to each other.

"Percy rarely lets anyone see his precious items. The four of us Queens looked last week, and we were flabbergasted. It's going to be a feather in our cap to show these pieces, along with having some fine educational programs for the kids," Irene said. "Ranching history, the Vaqueros, cowboy poetry and other Western lore ... We should haul in a good bit of money on this."

"What a momentous idea. Bravo!" said Betty, and Maye Marie and I clapped. I couldn't argue with this idea, even if it came from Irene.

"And, we got a big sponsor. Clemmie St. Onge, who is a ... ummm, friend of Percy's, will give us $400 for the exhibition. Isn't that wonderful?" Irene said.

Irene had enticed Clemmie, a doll-faced, wealthy temptress who was apparently a very, very good friend of the bachelor Percy LeRude, to help.

Carlotta squirmed in her chair.

"But I don't have ..." Carlotta sputtered, but Maye Marie cut her off.

"I think this is a marvelous plan," Maye Marie said.

"We need to think about ..." Carlotta tried to interrupt.

"How wonderful to provide an educational opportunity for our young people. I cannot imagine anyone who would oppose this. I assume this will hardly cost us anything but Carlotta's time to set it up and, well, we're already paying her to work here, aren't we? And we don't even need to dig into our own collection for this, do we? What a great blessing this is," Betty said, and when she sat down, she winked at Irene.

Carlotta jumped to her feet.

"You can't do this. I don't know what these things are. I don't even know if they are museum worthy. They could just be some old junk ... and ... I have things to archive," she said, but no one listened to her as the buzzing sound around the room grew and I sat back in my chair to enjoy the delicious uncomfortableness washing over Carlotta.

"This is a great idea. Everyone loves cowboys!" said one of the county commissioners. He waved his fist in the air and all the board members and other commissioners began smiling and talking. I realized that one surefire way to get grown men to do just about anything is to dangle cowboy lore in front of them. It was like magic. The entire room buzzed with excitement and Carlotta sat crouched in her chair like an angry bear.

Irene whispered to the other Queens.

"I can practically smell the horse manure." We all burst out laughing, even me.

★ ★ ★

Three days before the opening, I padded down the fern-patterned carpet on the staircase of my home, my steps muffled by the deep pile. I rubbed my head from lack of sleep. It was not even five o'clock. Milk. I needed a glass of warm milk to go back to bed.

Soft sounds coming from Iggy's den made my head jerk around. What was he doing? I pushed open the solid mahogany door and saw him standing at his desk, a yellow paper in his hand. He quickly folded the paper. Dressed in his blue pinstriped suit, his dark hair combed back and slick, he looked like a Mexican Walter Pidgeon.

"What are you doing at this hour?"

"Just state business, dear. You know there is always some disaster happening in California." His phony smile didn't fool me.

"That's hard to believe. And why are you dressed in your suit?"

"I'm heading out today. I'll be in Sacramento for the next week. Much to do. Meetings with the governor and the Department of Agriculture."

"But you said you'd go to the Western exhibit opening on Saturday with me. You promised me, Iggy."

"Odilia, darling, I can't just tell the governor to wait, can I? You know I've got obligations still. My term is not over yet." Iggy gathered up his papers and brushed past me, taking care not to touch me. He smelled heavily of some kind of cologne.

"Well, that's just wonderful. Thanks a lot. Good Lord, you're going to have to be fumigated. How much cologne are you wearing?" I put my hands on my hips and stared at his back as he walked out the front door. He stopped, turned, and sneered at me.

"Good luck with your exhibit, dear. I see you're getting quite a bit of publicity. Is that your doing?"

I stuck my chin out and glared at him.

"No."

"Who then?"

"Irene."

"Well, see now. Not such a mistake, was she?" Iggy turned around again and shut the door. I let out a howl and slammed my hand on the hall table.

Iggy was a handsome devil, the kind who swept a woman off her feet just by looking at her with his deep stare that made a girl feel like he was touching her, even though he wasn't. He entranced me from the start. I fell truly in love, and our courtship had been too fast. We met and married within six months, both of us recognizing that the other offered something important. For me, he offered stability and upward mobility in the social and political chain. For him, I was a smart, steady partner with a head for business and a traditional Mexican upbringing that promised a provincial wife dedicated to his ambitions and whims.

At first, I was just that. I kept my job but dialed back my working hours so I could be home to care for the house, make dinner, cater to Iggy. I attended political functions with him and could hold my own in conversations with other political wives and, more importantly, with their husbands. We'd assumed children would come but they never did and I grew more restless, taking on more work as a staff aide to the California Secretary of Agriculture, then as a liaison between the Water Department and the Governor's office. When the war came and I was asked to run the factory, I jumped at the chance to be a boss in a private business. It was the undoing of our marriage. By the time Iggy returned from his service, I was suckered into the power of being the head honcho–the jefa. There was no going back.

Iggy, in turn, threw himself into the state business and soon came home later and later, sometimes not at all. He began making excuses not to take me to things and when, three days before Christmas 1948, I found a note in his coat pocket written to "Darling Iggy" from someone named Suzette, I knew where I stood with him. We'd been in a standoff ever since. Our move back to Buttonbush was a last attempt at resurrecting our marriage but it withered within weeks when Iggy kept getting phone calls late at night. I pretended not to know what was happening but a thing like that sticks in your brain like a deep splinter; painful and annoying, unable to be removed.

★ ★ ★

Irene

Sparkling silver belt buckles, polished brown leather saddles, shiny rifles and pistols, colorful horse blankets, turquoise neck ties and bracelets, tall cowboy hats and fringed leather jackets adorned the great hall as the opening day of the Western exhibit dawned. Carlotta, when she put her mind to it, could actually do something creative and artistic. Too bad we practically had to put a gun to her head to get her to do it, which would have been ironic since there were so many guns on display.

But two hours before the great hall opened, a freakish rainstorm the size of Alaska fell over Buttonbush. Buttonbush only got about seven inches of rain in an entire year and over an inch showed up that day. Rain in torrents pelted the entire county, raising the river and filling creeks to the brim. Slick rivers of mud ran down every road while downtown Buttonbush flooded. Water poured in front of City Hall, the hospital, and the Buttonbush Museum. A farmer's wife rarely curses rain, but I did that day.

Odilia, Maye Marie, Betty, and I came dressed in our fancy Western gear, looking spectacular but feeling horrible. Just three people came through the gate that morning, sopping wet, tracking mud into the exhibit area. We shelved our cowboy barbecue and pony rides for the kids since the outside of the museum grounds turned into a lake. None of the news people showed up because they were out taking pictures and reporting on all the flash flooding going on all over the county.

"Looks like this exhibition is a bust," said Carlotta, a smirk painted across her lips. "I knew January was a bad month for this."

"They can come see it for another four weeks," I said. "It's not just here one day."

"But you've got all this other frivolity going on here. What a waste," she said.

Our sponsor, Clemmie, pouted.

"This is unfortunate that so few people are here," said Clemmie. "I was so looking forward to this."

"I know, Clemmie, but you are just so wonderful for sponsoring this. You're a real beacon for the history of Buttonbush," I said. "We are eternally grateful to you."

Clemmie grinned and fluttered her eyelashes.

"Oh well. You girls are just the tops. Aren't you so clever for putting Percy's things out like this," Clemmie said. "I just love this museum. You know, my granddad was the first one to strike oil down over in Rye in 1902. Did you know that?"

I knew Clemmie from school. She'd once laughed at me when I'd worn Ma's old dress to a dance. But I had her figured out since I researched a news story on her once and learned that just like in high school, if you flattered her, she'd do anything. Clemmie, never married, showed up at all the best parties in town, partly due to the hefty inheritance she'd received—not to mention her famously ample cleavage—but also due to her ability to charm most any man she met, married or bachelor. My Jimmy one time ran straight into the men's room and stayed for thirty minutes when she said, "Hey good lookin,' whatcha got cookin'?" to him at a party.

Clemmie, who had a loose relationship with the concept of loyalty, abandoned her last conquest, the handsome but poor manager of the Bijou Theatre, and took up with Percy. For anyone else, a woman of her appetites would have been looked down on in Buttonbush—or most places, I guessed. But people tend to look the other way when it's someone with a generous bank account. I admired her vigor. And she dearly loved the museum.

Clemmie flitted off on the arm of Percy. Adorned in a flowered skirt with blue fringe, a white Western shirt, tied together by an ornate belt with a large buckle, cowboy boots that showed her long, shapely legs, and her blonde curly head beneath a gorgeous red cowgirl hat, Clemmie paraded around the gallery like Dale Evans. Percy's puppy dog eyes followed her every movement. I felt a little sorry for him.

I could not have been any bluer. We'd gone to so much work and I had a deep resentment for old Mother Nature that day.

"I was hoping we'd raise at least five hundred dollars today. That would put us ten percent of the way there in our budget deficit," said Maye Marie.

"We couldn't know it would rain like this," Odilia said and patted my arm in a rare display of sympathy. "We tried. But maybe we'd better find other ways to raise money."

I heaved a ragged breath and smiled, tears welling up in my eyes.

"Too bad no one came. The county commissioners are cutting budgets right and left. Our money is running out. What are you Four Queens going to do next?" Carlotta said, and the Four Queens looked at each other. None of us had an inkling of an idea.

★ ★ ★

In February, the county accountant went over our books with Maye Marie. He was none too pleased and said the commissioners were going to be making some announcements soon. He wouldn't tell her what that meant but said two of the commissioners were heading to Sacramento that week to visit with court officials about the new courthouse. Maye Marie was frantic that we were dipping into our reserves all the time and they were just about gone. We'd already cut the lights in three buildings and stopped watering some of the grass in the back.

Figuring I needed to make up for our failure at the Western exhibit and the mess of the still undone Iversen house plopped into the museum, despite that one not being my doing, I decided to try another route. I wasn't about to let Carlotta's disagreeable temperament stop me, if nothing else, just to make a point. So I went over to the library to do a little digging on Square Foot Fred and his treasure. Turns out, he often visited the Dewberrys, a ranching family that lived some thirty miles outside of Buttonbush. The Buttonbush sheriff made a lot of visits to the Dewberry Ranch back then, hoping to find old Fred. I knew just who to call.

"Oh, that crazy story. I remember my grandpa talking about Fred, the old sawhorse. They were good friends, but I don't know anything about treasure. Far as I recall, Fred had about as much sense as a pigeon. Grandpa said Fred just always wanted a hot meal and a place to hide out. Grandpa didn't have any fondness for the local sheriff back then," said Glenda Dewberry, a woman I'd met at the Grange, her voice booming through the line. "My Great-Aunt Viola hated Fred. For years, every time his name came up, she'd say something awful about him."

"Did anyone search for his supposed treasure on your ranch?" I said.

"Two of my uncles did, and my cousin Dean. But they just ended up digging a lot of holes, messing up a well and killing a damn nice cottonwood tree. They didn't find anything, although

I think Dean got into a wasp nest and got bit something fierce," she said with a chuckle.

If Square Foot Fred had buried his gold coins somewhere on the Dewberry Ranch, it might be impossible to find. If I remembered correctly, the ranch sat on about 4,600 acres. Someone would find those coins one day, but it wouldn't be me and it would belong to the Dewberrys, anyway.

I also wrote a letter to the San Francisco Museum of Antiquities where Fred supposedly did his dastardly deed and asked if they knew anything about the missing coins. But the letter came back in the mail. Apparently, the museum didn't exist anymore which gave me pause. Apparently, museums could go out of business.

So I kept researching at the library and at the county hall of records, and Felicia snuck me in one day to read some books in our collection in the basement when Carlotta had a dentist appointment.

"A fine thing when you have to wait for her to have a cavity in order to read about some of our history," I said to Felicia.

I came across a small article that talked about Square Foot Fred's taste for expensive clothing. The article said Fred robbed banks by sauntering in looking like a true gentleman in his fine coat, starchy white shirt and fancy neck ties and hat. Then he'd pull out his pistol and rob the place.

"Do we have any clothing in our collection from anyone famous?" I said a few days later, when I wandered into Carlotta's office.

"We have the suit coat worn by Colonel Walker at his inauguration as first mayor of Buttonbush. And we have the dress worn by the first school mistress out in Rye. Plus a few other things. Why?" Carlotta pinched her lips after she answered me. "You know we can't put those out to be exposed …"

"I know. To sunlight, God forbid. The evil sun. That's not what I want to do. I was just wondering, do we have anything from any nefarious characters?"

"Nefarious? You mean like … Oh no, you're not still thinking about Fred Watlington?"

"Do you have anything of his?"

"This is a ridiculous endeavor. Fred Watlington never robbed any museum and there is no stash of gold coins anywhere in Buttonbush. Really, Irene, focus on something else," Carlotta said and slammed down her book.

"Answer my question. Do we have anything from Square Foot Fred?"

Carlotta drummed her fingers on the table.

"We have his suit and a top hat. They took it from him when he went to prison for the third time … and then escaped."

"Can I see them?"

Carlotta rose from her seat and made a huffing sound.

"What a waste of my time," she said, and I followed her down the hallway to the basement doors.

Carlotta didn't know I'd already seen the enormous basement stuffed with relics, memorabilia, and junk. The low ceilings made it seem crowded and stifling. In the far corner hung a long iron rod with coat hangers suspended on it, the clothing underneath covered with old sheets. Above the clothing, were shelves of hats, also covered up with sheets, little feathers and tassels hanging out on the sides.

"Here it is. Fred Watlington's suit. I don't know what you think you can find here," she said, shrugging her shoulders. I believe I could have had more cooperation from a crocodile.

"We won't know until we try," I said, not really believing I could find anything but too stubborn to let go of the quest in front of Carlotta.

"I want to see if there's anything in the clothing. I need to touch it," I said, and predictable as church on Sunday, Carlotta shook her head.

"That is not possible. I can't just let you examine these things and touch them. You'll expose it to … to your … human breath and oils and all of that." Carlotta let out an exasperated grunt.

"There is no reason I can't put on a pair of your spiffy white gloves and examine this clothing, Carlotta. This does not belong to you. It belongs to the people of Buttonbush County, and I'd hate to go to Senator Delgado and tell him you refused a board member access to a relic," I said, crossing my arms.

She gave me a deep scowl and stomped to the front of the room, where she grabbed a pair of white gloves for me and put a pair on herself. She pulled the suit off of the hanger and carefully laid it on a nearby table, fussing over it like it was the dang coronation robe of Henry VIII.

"Don't damage it," she said, tapping her toes while she watched me.

I carefully touched the lapel of the jacket, excited to be looking at Square Foot Fred's very own suit even though I had no idea what I was looking for. A map, a gold coin, a diamond ring? The jacket was quite fancy with a pale-yellow waistcoat and blue and yellow tie. The brown and beige plaid pants seemed small. I pictured Square Foot Fred as a large man, but from the size of his clothing, he was quite short and lean. His gun must have been a big one for him to commit all those robberies. And, of course, there was his forehead.

I took a whiff to see if I could smell anything like gunpowder or explosives, but all I could smell was Carlotta's Helene Curtis shampoo.

I ran my hands over the clothing, feeling for anything in the pockets or sewn into the hems. I tapped my hands and fingers over the entire outfit until Carlotta gave a grunt.

"Oh, for heaven's sake, you will not find anything," she said.

I reluctantly stopped my inspection because it seemed I couldn't find anything. Then I remembered the hats.

"Is that hat up there his?" I said.

"The brown one," Carlotta said, edging her way to the door, rattling her keys impatiently. "Can we please speed this up?"

"Well, let's just see while we're here," I said and stood on my tiptoes to get the hat. "I can't see how he could fit this thing on his big fat head and ... Ooooops!"

"You're going to ... Aaaaaack," Carlotta shrieked.

The hat toppled to the floor and rolled across the concrete into the next aisle of relics.

"Look what you've done! I told you to be careful!" Carlotta shrieked.

I bent over to pick up the hat, but she brushed me aside and grabbed it.

"I'll get it. You can't be trusted and ..."

"Carlotta, look there," I said, pointing to a shiny object on the floor.

On the cold floor lay a very old silver key that must have been stuck somewhere in the hat.

"What does that go to?" I said.

"I don't know. Not what you think. Don't get your hopes all up. It's probably nothing," she said, and grabbed the key.

"You should look around to see if that fits anything. Did Fred have anything else here? A safe, a music box, a trunk? Think, Carlotta, think!"

"There is nothing. Nothing at all. It's just an old key, good for nothing."

"What are you going to do with it?" I said.

"I'll put it in my file on Fred Watlington. We have nothing of his that this could go to, I assure you."

"It must have been important for him to hide it there," I said, and she shook her head. She had about as much of a sense of adventure as a turnip. "You need to see if that key fits anything around here. Show some initiative!"

"I'll do no such thing. This is all idiocy." Carlotta turned and headed for the stairs.

She escorted me out of the basement, slamming the door just a little too hard behind her. I was a bit blue that I didn't find anything noteworthy, but it did warm my insides to have discombobulated Carlotta so much by finding a key she didn't know existed.

"Don't lose that key, Carlotta. You never know when it might come in handy."

* * *

For the life of me, I did not know why Odilia was so hateful to me. Figuring I would use the old catch-a-fly-with-honey-instead-of-vinegar method, I decided to try to win Odilia over. So I invited her and the other two Queens to lunch at my house the week after Valentine's Day. Jimmy said he didn't know why I was trying so hard to win over someone who had been voted the "girl most likely to scare Frankenstein's monster" in high school, as well as "most likely to succeed." I ran Jimmy off the farm to get him out of the way because I was cleaning the living and dining rooms like a madwoman. Then I spent all morning making cream of potato soup, shrimp salad, Waldorf salad, homemade rolls, and an apple pie. There weren't any flowers in my garden that time of year, so I just cut some greenery off some of my trees and put them in two blue vases to add a little touch of style to my dining table.

I used my best lace tablecloth and my granny's yellow china set. I even got out the crystal glasses that I'd only used once before on Thanksgiving.

"This looks lovely," Maye Marie said when she arrived, and Betty gave me a hug, the cool air blowing in the door along with the three Queens.

"How nice of you to fix us lunch. Mmmm, I smell bread or something," Betty said.

"Fresh made rolls," I said, and showed them into the living room.

Odilia marched in and crossed her arms, her eyes sweeping over the house.

"I've got a list a mile long of repairs that need to be done. We need to talk about that," she said.

"Gosh, Odilia, let's eat lunch first. Come sit down," I said, and ushered her into the dining room. She sat down, glaring at the table.

"Odilia don't be so cross. We'll have a pleasant lunch and then talk about the museum," Betty said, patting Odilia's hand. Odilia grabbed her water glass and took a swig.

"I'm not that hungry," she said.

Odilia picked a small black thread from the bottom of her impeccably pressed beige skirt and dropped it on the floor, her rust-colored blouse tucked neatly into the top of the skirt, a chunky sweater on her shoulders. I took a bite of my roll and she gave me a contemptuous look. Odilia never ate.

"Odilia, I know you and Jimmy went to high school together in Rye. What was he like? I didn't know him then," I said.

"He was a buffoon," she said, pushing her salad around on the plate.

"Odilia! Really!" Maye Marie's shook her head.

"He probably was. I know he and his baseball teammates got into some hijinks," I said, a slight laugh in my voice. "But he was smart. He told me his grades were good."

"I wouldn't know," Odilia said. "I was busy as class president and head of the scholastic honor society."

I sat back in my chair and fiddled with my spoon.

"You went off to the University of California after that, right?" I said.

"Cal Berkeley. On scholarship. I graduated magna cum laude," she said.

"What does that …" I started but Betty interrupted me.

"That's impressive. That means with great distinction." Betty smiled at me.

"Jimmy went to junior college and took some agricultural courses. Then he came back to the farm. His dad died when he was just twenty," I said.

"That must have been difficult. Good for Jimmy for becoming a successful farmer," Maye Marie said.

"If that's what you call it," Odilia said, her eyes scanning my living room. I noticed I'd left a little pile of Jimmy's farm magazines under a chair and her eyes rested on the unruly array.

"Odilia, that's a beautiful sweater you have on. It's very elegant," I said.

"I got it in Dublin."

"Dublin, that's up near San Francisco, right?" I said.

"Dublin, Ireland. Known for its fine wool … Sheesh," she said and scrunched her mouth to the side as she sipped her iced tea.

"I'll get the dessert." I stood up and beelined for the kitchen. Maye Marie followed and gave me a little hug.

"Why does she hate me so much?" I whispered.

"I don't think she hates you … she's just cranky, that's all," Maye Marie said.

"She's nice to you and Betty. She respects you but has no respect for me. I know I'm not a college graduate and haven't done that much, but still …" I grabbed the pie and Maye Marie followed me to the dining room. Odilia had lit a cigarette, the smoke creeping over my small dining room chandelier as she leaned on her elbows.

"First, we need to re-roof the shoemaker's shack and put new plumbing in the main gallery," she said. "The county financial officer called us last week. They're coming to our next board meeting to see how we're doing. They can shut us down in the blink of an eye."

"We're not doing very well," said Maye Marie. "We get money for your projects, but it all goes to the project. In and out. We're going to have to let one of the maintenance crew go soon if we don't do something."

"If we fix things up, people will come," Odilia said. "The Senator agrees with me."

"We need to do something entertaining and educational … How about a historic reading of some piece of literature where we act it out? Raise money by getting people there instead of just repairing things all the time," I said. I wasn't going to let her take over my lunch conversation.

Odilia grunted.

"That won't work."

"Why not? People will pay money to come to fun things … or educational things," I said.

"Like the Western exhibit?" she said.

"That wasn't my fault." I took a gulp of water but wished it was whiskey.

"My mother did an entire month of Longfellow readings at her museum. It was quite successful," Betty said. Betty always referred to the museum in Vermont as her "Mother's museum." I knew there was a proper name for the place, but I took to thinking of a large sign that must stand outside the building in Vermont reading "Betty's Mother's Museum." Way too many possessives.

"I was thinking something more exciting. Like the *Scarlet Pimpernel* or *Moby-Dick*."

"You want to act out trying to kill a whale?" Odilia said. "That should be just terrific."

"I think Longfellow is superb," Betty said.

Betty loved to think of historical topics, and I was always game to find some fun way to show kids whatever she wanted to promote, whether or not it pertained to Buttonbush County. She had been reading lots of Longfellow lately, who clearly had nothing to do with Buttonbush history.

"If you think Longfellow is a good idea, I guess …" I said.

"You know his wife lit herself on fire and he, himself, was burned trying to save her. It was quite tragic," Betty said, and decided that we should do a rendition of "Paul Revere's Ride" for the children's Saturday story time in March, even though we weren't remotely attached to the American Revolution in Buttonbush. Still, it was history.

"Hey, I've got that George Washington costume Jimmy wore for Halloween one year. I could be Paul Revere," I said.

"You'll look ridiculous," said Odilia.

"You know he … Paul Revere, I mean … not Jimmy… didn't just ride a horse. He rowed across the Charles River to Charlestown as well," Betty said.

"I could borrow a horse from my brother," I said. "And I've got an old boat we could use, too."

"Revere didn't actually ride his own horse. He borrowed it from John Larkin. And he never gave it back," Betty said in that tone that told me I was behind in my American history tidbits.

"The kids won't care," I said, although I didn't know about either the boat ride or the fact that Paul Revere didn't ride his own horse. "Did he just not have a horse or was it that he didn't want to take his horse because it was too slow? And why on earth wouldn't he return the horse? If you're going to be a hero, you need to follow through on those kinds of things."

Betty had no answer for that.

"Nice lunch," Odilia said as she walked out. "But I think your Paul Revere idea is a bomb."

After the three of them left, I cleaned up the kitchen, noting that Odilia had eaten almost nothing on her plate and I wasn't any closer to making her respect or like me.

PAUL REVERE TAKES A DIVE

Irene

I didn't care what Odilia said and tried on the costume that night. The shirt was a little roomy on me and I rolled up the sleeves. It was less Yankee-looking than I would have liked, but it would do.

As usual, I couldn't leave well enough alone so the following week I decided I wanted to stage the rowing scene so that the boat would look like it was rocking in the waves of the Charles River. I got some old sheets from the storage shed and painted them dark blue and white, like waves, so that Maye Marie and Odilia could hold the sheets, end to end, and wave them up and down to simulate water. Odilia refused, so I got Felicia to do it.

"But you are coming, Odilia. You need to be there," said Betty.

"This is the last thing I want to do," said Odilia. "It's a nutty idea."

"Come now, we're doing it for the museum," Maye Marie said. She had a way of calming Odilia down.

Betty and I propped the boat up on two sawhorses so that I could sit high above the sheet waves, looking out to the crowd of children. Then we cut down some pine trees at the back of the museum property. There were plenty of them and they were scraggly, anyway. We put them in big metal buckets of water and set them behind the boat so it would look like a nighttime scene. It was better than the blank, pea-green wall behind our stage area.

I'd practiced my best Paul Revere gestures all week, holding a whip in my hand, waving dramatically when I heard "one if by land, two if by sea." We hung a yellow papier mâché moon ball up, too, although you could see the wires holding it up. Still, it was a good enough moon. The pine trees were dying, but they gave a forest effect.

Betty was very excited about the whole thing and gushed on about how Alvin was helping her practice the readings.

"He's so sweet. You know my mother didn't approve of our marriage," Betty said as we sat in the museum's foyer, waiting for Maye Marie.

"But Alvin is a wonderful guy. Didn't he graduate from Yale?" I said.

"He did. And by age thirty he had already been named vice president of the Central California Bank and Trust. But for Mother, that's not good enough," Betty sighed and plopped her purse in her lap.

Apparently, Alvin's hometown of Buttonbush was the problem. A place her mother referred to as a "cow town."

"He treats me like a princess," said Betty. "He reads me Keats and Shelley at night and brings me coffee and toast in bed on Sundays. But he wasn't East Coast approved and mother looks down her nose at anyone who's ever ventured west of Philadelphia or Albany."

"Gosh, the only thing Jimmy ever reads me is the weather report," I said, but I knew, in his own way, he treated me like a princess, too. A princess with dirt on her shoes.

"Mother grossly underestimates Buttonbush. I like its rustic charm and the way people always say hello in a most sincere way," she said. "Neighbors wave when you drive past them and salesclerks in the stores smile instead of having haughty smirks."

"You're right. People in Buttonbush are genuine. There's not much vanity going on here. We're ... authentic, I guess," I said. Betty's expansive vocabulary had been rubbing off on me.

"I had everything any girl could want: the best schools, cotillion, a debutante ball, and all the social gatherings of the cream of society in Vermont. Sometimes Mother took me to Boston for parties and soirees. And of course, I was fortunate to attend Bryn Mawr," Betty said.

"I can't even imagine that kind of life, Betty. It must be so strange for you here," I said.

"When my brother, Jamison, died in the war, all those people that we knew at those parties and soirees sent small cards and letters. But no one visited, no one came by to offer a shoulder to cry on or a warm hug. In Buttonbush, three neighbors visited us when Alvin came down with a cold," Betty said.

Poor Betty. A mother who smothered her like a wet blanket all the time with grief and sorrow without any recognition for the fine daughter she had. I was glad Alvin treated her well, and that she had fallen in love with Buttonbush. Like Alvin, we weren't much to look at but there was a lot to love.

"I'm glad to hear you like it here," I said. I don't think anyone ever described Buttonbush so affectionately.

"Certainly, Buttonbush lacks some cultural stimulation, but there is a symphony and two art galleries and a theater group. They all try very hard to be of quality," she said.

"And just think of the cultural stimulation we'll be giving the children tomorrow when we do this poetry reading," I said. I was impressed with myself for my participation in such a cultural adventure, even though I hadn't ever thought about it that way. For once, I was on the brink of being refined.

* * *

Odilia

What a stupid idea. I stormed into the Buttonbush Museum on the day of the reenactment, the fires of hell blazing behind me. I didn't want to be there. It was going to be a bust. But the hall was almost completely filled with children and parents, chattering and laughing in lively fun. Even the *Buttonbush Daily* had a pasty-faced reporter and scruffy photographer there. Irene had done her part to get people there.

"See, Odilia. When you do things, the newspaper does a story on it," Irene said to me. "I told you I could get people to notice this museum."

"We'll see how this turns out," I said. "Don't count your chickens just yet."

We needed to do more than count chickens since the county accountant had visited us again just last week and informed us that the commissioners wanted us to have at least $5,000 in our reserves by September of 1952. The reserves we'd just about depleted. That meant we had to climb out of the hole we were in plus save up five thousand dollars. That included making sure my beloved building projects were completely paid for.

I turned around and there was Jimmy Pickett walking towards me. I had not seen him in years and just like when I was sixteen, my heart fluttered a bit. He looked the same as he did when he sauntered down the halls of Rye High School, sandy hair, dreamy eyes, crooked smile. His eyes widened when he saw me, as if he wasn't sure what I would say, and a wall the size of a skyscraper rose up in front of me. I crossed my arms and glared at him.

"Hello, Odilia," Jimmy said, his head cocked over to one side to look at Irene who was standing behind me, dressed in her ridiculous Paul Revere costume.

"Jimmy," I said.

"How are you?" Jimmy said, shoving his hands in his jeans pocket and shuffling awkwardly from foot to foot.

"I'm fine. I see you're doing well on the farm," I said.

"I guess."

"Odilia is trying to get into the Gold Seal Club, Jimmy. Isn't that amazing for a woman to try to do that," Irene said, her words spilling out quickly.

"I'll bet she is. Well, good luck with that," Jimmy said, scratching his head and flinging it to the side. "The kids are over here so I'm going to ..."

"Okay, enough chatter here you two. We need a picture," Betty said, brushing past Irene and grabbing Jimmy's arm. "Go sit down, Jimmy."

A lump welled in my throat. Jimmy Pickett. I'd risen far above where he was in life so what did I care what he was doing now and how his life had turned out. My life was wonderful. Mostly. Jimmy shuffled off.

"Come on, Odilia, over here," Betty waved her hand at me while the horse stood behind her, swishing its tail side to side.

"I want to send Mother a picture. She'll be so happy to see we did a Longfellow reading," Betty said, patting her hair and straightening her dress. "Maye Marie don't hide behind the horse. Come up here."

I forced a smile for a quick three seconds when Felicia snapped the picture with her Brownie camera, then tucked myself to the side of the stage while the others took their places.

No one cares about Longfellow or Paul Revere. I peeked out to see the audience where Jimmy was laughing with his kids, he and his freckle-faced son playing rock, paper, scissors while they waited for the reading to begin. An emptiness filled my chest and I turned to see Irene, looking like a complete fool, crawl into the canoe.

* * *

Irene

Right before our opening act, Betty took a hefty swig of claret. I thought about it myself but figured I shouldn't be a liquored-up Paul Revere. Although, who's to say old P.R. didn't have a nip or two before he went on his famous ride?

First up was the boat scene, so I climbed into the little canoe. The horse stood behind me, which kind of looked like the horse was in the water, but it was the best we could do. Betty started her reading as I sat rowing in the boat, looking as Revolutionary as I could with furrowed brow and clenched jaw. The horse stared at me like I was nuts. Kosta crouched behind me, holding on to the boat because it was a little wobbly.

Listen, my children, and you shall hear
of the midnight ride of Paul Revere,
On the eighteenth of April, in Seventy-five;
Hardly a man is now alive
Who remembers that famous day and year ...

Betty's voice was full of drama, like she was an actress or famous orator, waving her arms and pointing her finger in the air. She droned on for a few lines and then a hissing sound came from the back end of the horse, followed by a strong odor. I looked down and that old horse had done its business right there on stage. Gales of laughter broke out among the kids, and you could smell that horse all over the room, a development we had not considered. One of the Tucker kids pulled a rubber band out of his pocket, and I knew there was going to be trouble starting right quick.

"Wave the water, wave the water," I whispered to Maye Marie and Felicia, and they started shaking those sheets up and down as hard as they could. I stood up, waving my fist in the air, making what I thought were Revolutionary sounds—whatever those are—to get the kids to pay attention. Kosta, crouching to the side, tried to steady the canoe as I stood.

Odilia stood off to the side with her arms crossed, glaring at me. The *Buttonbush Daily* photographer was snapping lots of pictures of me so I sucked in my stomach and tried to put steel in my eyes to look like Paul Revere, not that I knew he had steel in his eyes, but it seemed like that could be true.

"Yeah, faster, faster," I said, throaty and deep, rowing as fast as I could, while standing up. Which made no sense. But heck, it was a bunch of kids.

He said to his friend, "If the British march
By land or sea from the town to-night,
Hang a lantern aloft in the belfry arch
Of the North Church tower as a signal light,
One, if by land, and two, if by sea;
And I on the opposite shore will be,
Ready to ride and spread the alarm
Through every Middlesex village and farm,
For the country folk to be up and to arm.

Betty was reaching a high pitch now, more like she was singing or calling her cats than reading a fine American hero poem.

Just then Maye Marie let go of her side of the sheet and it snapped over to Felicia's side. Maye Marie lunged over to pick up her end of the sheet, but she pushed on the boat to keep her balance as she bent down. Kosta tried to steady the darn thing as it wonked over to the backside of the room and my head pitched forward. My legs wobbled and I furiously waved my arms to the sides to balance myself, but I was no tightrope walker. Poor Kosta just couldn't hold it and my head went sideways and down right into one of the trees that grabbed at my wig, tugging at my hair underneath, and scratching my face. Spooked, the horse trotted forward and my whole body went in another direction as I tumbled straight into the manure pile. One tree fell over, spilling water all over the floor and running the fresh manure all over me. My yarn wig was stuck in a tree and I sat up and yanked it off my head, my eyes rolling to the back of their sockets in a dizzy tumble.

"Yeowwww," I yelled, and the kids all screamed because it looked like Paul Revere got pummeled by some invisible British shot to the head.

I looked up, and the horse was staring at me and I swear on a stack of Bibles that old nag snickered at me. Camera flash bulbs went off like fireworks. Both my wig and my real hair were covered with pine needles and water which drizzled down my face. I was drenched head to toe in slimy manure which smelled something awful. Felicia and four of the mothers in the audience raced up to help me because Maye Marie and Odilia were on the sides, laughing like a couple of drunks. I sat in the puddle and plucked the pine needles out of my hair, then limped off stage in pure humiliation as the ladies held me by the arms. Betty, as if nothing happened, continued her reading. The kids laughed hysterically while Pauline and Willy were red with embarrassment. None of the kids ever did listen to the rest of "Paul Revere's Ride" or see me ride the horse.

"That went well," Odilia said, smirking at my disastrous appearance. I didn't have a word to say as I dripped across the floor.

★ ★ ★

Odilia

Irene, deliciously covered in muck, hobbled over to her husband.

"You forgot to mention that your wife is a pure vision of beauty," Irene said to Jimmy, and he chuckled, putting his arm around her.

I hoped he enjoyed his wife's little performance. What a naïve, silly woman that Irene was. There was nothing sophisticated or serious about her although I could see she had some sort of basic charm to her. Her rosy cheeks and exuberant laughter could be appealing to some, but I found her annoying and loud. But even after such an embarrassing display, Irene and Jimmy laughed it off together as he brushed the hair back from her face and took out his blue bandana handkerchief to wipe her down.

"Hmmph." I snorted at them. After this little debacle, I wanted Irene to give up on this cockamamie idea of holding events and programs. The museum just needed refurbishment to bring in crowds, not a bunch of circus acts and silly shows to get people there. Irene knew nothing about making money. Her inexperience was showing, and I was unashamedly half-pleased that the Paul Revere reading had gone so very wrong. I fully intended to push my ideas through with even more force now that I'd shown Irene to lack credibility.

"Come in for a drink, Odilia. I need one," Betty said when I dropped her at home after the poetry reading. I was grateful to have someone to have a drink with since Iggy was gone.

Betty poured me a glass of red wine and we sat down in Betty's gold-velvet-covered, high-back chairs when the phone rang.

"Hello, Mother. We did the reading. It went … nicely." Betty's face scrunched up in the lie. "I'm very pleased about it … The crowd appreciated Longfellow even though they are from Buttonbush … I'm sorry you're tired … Oh no … that's unfortunate. Do you need a rest? I'll talk to you soon."

Betty hung up the phone, tears in her eyes.

"What's wrong? Is your mother sick?" I asked.

"She's sick over losing my brother. He died in the war, you know, and she can't seem to get over it. Father pressed her to put Jamison's things in order and she's refusing to throw them out. She's going to send some of them to me, so Father doesn't get angry. It's been eight years since he died so …" Betty gulped down tears.

"I'm sorry, Betty. That must be very hard."

"I miss him, too. Father stays at work much longer these days. Mother cries in her room all the time. Nothing I say or do seems to help."

"I know that feeling of helplessness too well," I said, and patted Betty on the arm. It occurred to me that I often forgot that even young, happy Betty had her sad moments, just as I did.

"I sometimes hate that we live so far away but Alvin and I are so happy here." Betty took a sip of wine and sighed.

"My mother passed away when I was just twenty-two. I'd just graduated from college, and she was so worn out and tired from doing everything for my father that I think she just gave up on life. I miss her all the time," I said, surprised that I'd disclosed so much. "Grief is a terrible thing."

"It is terrible. But enough of that. Tell me how you came to marry the Senator," Betty said. I don't think anyone had ever asked me that.

"Iggy literally swept me off my feet years ago, picking me up off the ground after I'd slipped on a wet marble floor in the Sacramento state capitol. I was there working as an office assistant to a state representative, and he was an aide to a senator," I said, remembering my blue dress drenched at the hem, Iggy gallantly teasing me about needing a wind tunnel to dry out. His devilish eyes should have warned me that the man could charm the hair off a bear, but I was madly in love with him and determined not to repeat my mother's life. Whatever happened, I'd make sure I was accomplished and self-sufficient.

"It must be a wonderful life being a senator's wife. All that political drama and the challenges of government. I'm sure he's very proud of you," Betty said. It always shocked me how easily Iggy and I could portray a happy couple to the rest of the world but be so different at home.

"It's got its challenges," I said. "I'm sure you have your own challenges."

"I do. But Alvin is a darling. Goodness Odilia, it's nice to talk with a friend about all these things," Betty said.

Friend? Is that what this was?

"I rarely make friends," I said.

"Why is that?"

"I guess I'm a bit headstrong for most people. Women seem to resent me, and men can't stand a strong woman. I've always been a loner," I said, remembering in high school when I couldn't find anyone to be my partner in chemistry lab.

"You're not so bad, Odilia. Just a little gruff sometimes. I know you have a kind heart," Betty said.

I hoped I had a kind heart but made a note in my head to think about that more. I'm not sure where kindness ranked on my list of things to do. Betty and I sat and chatted for another hour, the conversation stalling my usual evening sitting in my big, gorgeous house all alone.

I had to go home eventually, so when I got there, I poured myself a glass of red wine and settled down in a green leather chair with a cigarette and a notebook to write out plans. Damn, I loved smoking. After twenty minutes and ten pages of notes, I realized I hadn't spoken to Iggy since yesterday morning.

I dialed his office number in Sacramento, and when he didn't answer, I dialed the Sacramento house. He wasn't there either. He didn't answer when I called him at ten o'clock, or at midnight. I tossed and turned into the night, waking up with a raging headache. I rubbed my head and made a breakfast of chili verde eggs.

Twenty some years into my marriage and I didn't know where my husband was, or what he was doing, or whom he was with. Why was I in the same boat as my mother? I had tried so hard to be more, to be important and wise and noticed. Why wasn't it better that I had elevated myself? Iggy didn't think a woman moving in man's world was an elevation but was more of a competition and he didn't like it. He wanted me back to where I was before. What did it take to get a husband to stick around? Irene seemed to have accomplished it just by being a nitwit. This wasn't what I wanted at all.

I finished breakfast then sat on the back porch, smoking cigarette after cigarette, the neighbor's black cat staring at me from atop the brick fence, the cold sun stinging my skin. I threw a rock at the cat, missed, and went inside.

★ ★ ★

Irene

A photo of "Irene Revere" flying off the canoe and into the muck landed on page two of the *Buttonbush Daily* the next day.

"Is this how the museum board plans to put five-thousand dollars in reserve?" the article asked. Ugh.

Agnes called to simultaneously see if I was okay and then to laugh her head off.

"Don't you need to go crochet a brassiere or something?" I said and hung up on her.

Ma called, too, adding to my embarrassment.

"I see you fell off a horse. Do you need some potato slices for your head?"

Ma thought potato slices could cure anything.

"No, Ma, I didn't fall off a horse. It was a canoe, but it wasn't in water and, well ... never mind. I'm fine."

"You sure did accomplish what you set out to accomplish: getting the museum noticed. Is this what you had in mind?"

I put my arms down on the kitchen table and laid my head in them, groaning.

"Lordy, when are you just going to stay home?" she said, and I listened to her go on and on about how my sister was sewing new curtains for her kitchen, all done in red gingham and bric-à-brac.

When she finished, she said, "Just let Odilia Delgado run it."

I groaned again.

A HANDSOME CUSS

Irene

The worst part about my fall from the canoe was that Jimmy didn't even tease me about it, a sign that it was genuinely embarrassing. He acted overly nice which just told me he felt sorry for me. I knew Jimmy would always love me, which was magnanimous in many ways, him being stuck with an idiot for a wife and all.

When a couple of the other mothers at Willy's school snickered at me the next week, I knew my exploits at the museum were becoming a problem. Willy ducked his head down when I dropped him off. I needed some time to think harder about what should be done, what would work at the museum, and what I was capable of because I hadn't been successful at anything yet.

My performance as a mother wasn't much better.

The teenage years were in full swing with Pauline who had just turned sixteen. Our household was always in a tizzy about her classes, tests, term papers, dances, and everything else a teenage girl wanted.

I spent much of my time running down hosiery, pinning up her hair, finding the right colored purses, turning down the record player, checking English themes, and wrestling the phone from her hands as she lay on the floor, legs and feet propped up on my living room couch.

Willy got the short end of the stick, and I frequently caught him rolling his eyes as his sister's dramatic shrieks swept over our house. I confess, her giggles and unvarnished excitement about life made me chuckle, as she put on a daily, joyous spectacle, despite the bad moments when a boy didn't talk to her, or a girl would say something mean to her.

But I didn't want her to think all this teenage behavior was acceptable, at least not for her lifetime. I spent many days trying to impress upon her the value of being a decent, responsible human being, although, if I thought about it, she was absolutely top-notch with everyone else: teachers, coaches, friends, neighbors. It was just me whom she liked to zing with accusations, pleadings, directives, and admonishments, like Yogi Berra firing balls back to the pitcher.

I was cleaning up the kitchen on a Sunday afternoon when Pauline flounced into the room, her long ponytail snapping back from her head.

"Mom, I don't want to go to Grandma's house this afternoon. I have homework for biology. Biology, Mom. Do you hear that? Serious stuff." Pauline pinned herself to the kitchen pantry door, back flat against the wood, writhing like Joan of Arc at the stake, her arms slung back and her head bobbing forward in agony.

"You should have done that yesterday afternoon," I said, avoiding her sizzling glare by vigorously scrubbing the sink.

"I would have. But you had to go to the museum for something and I had to finish cleaning my room. As you so rigidly ordered me to do." She growled when she said "museum."

Lordy. It is purely astounding to me how a person whom you've borne in your belly for nine months, fed cereal by the spoonful, bandaged every hurt, held over a toilet while they were sick, sleeked back countless hairdos, and carted to endless dance lessons, can shoot so much poison at you. Between

Pauline and Odilia, I sometimes wanted to run off with the circus. Maybe be a lion tamer. It seemed easier.

"Better get to it, young lady!"

"Mother! You realize I met with the Key Club yesterday and that meeting didn't get out until one o'clock and we missed lunch. So I was absolutely starving. We all went over to the Tastee-Fry to eat, and we did some more club business there. We really did, Mom, so I didn't have time to do my biology yesterday, did I?" Her head bobbed side to side like she was trying to catch me. I weaved to the left and grabbed a broom.

"You need to go with us to Grandma's. Sunday dinner. You can do your biology tonight."

"Tonight! But I need to see Deborah!"

"Oh, for Pete's sake, Pauline."

"Deborah just broke up with Kenny and she needs me to come over and console her, on top of doing my biology. I shouldn't have to go if I don't want to. And you can't make me."

"Listen here, young lady, you better snap out of this attitude. Do you understand? You sound like your Uncle Lenny. Is that how you want to be?" Uncle Lenny was my ace in the hole, the trump card I played when I really wanted to get her.

"Uncle Lenny! That's such an insult, Mother! Fine, I'll go but I'm going to be very unhappy the whole time."

I smiled and kept sweeping while she stomped off, muttering. Uncle Lenny was Jimmy's wayward brother that we threw out at our children during key moments when we wanted to threaten them with the possibility of arriving at adulthood as certified lunkheads. Uncle Lenny could only be described as a ne'er-do-well and was famous for ruining family holidays, starting at the age of eight, when he brought a live rattlesnake in a jar to Easter dinner. He came to Thanksgiving one year with a half-eaten apple pie. During the meal, we all went around the table to say what we were thankful for, and Lenny told us he was thankful that the boil on his left leg had popped. The next year, after we'd finished eating Christmas dinner, Lenny excused himself from the table. No one knew where he'd gone, but when I went into the kitchen to clean up, I realized that Lenny, the leftover turkey carcass, and pecan pie were gone, carried off on his motorcycle. Lenny sure did like pie.

Learning to manage a teenage girl gave me powerful experience in arguing, something that would benefit me far more than I could have known for my work at the museum.

★ ★ ★

By April 1951, the Four Queens had been running the show for almost a year, much longer than I'd originally figured. We all had other things to spend time on and were getting tired. Except for Odilia, who had thirty-four hours in a day instead of twenty-four, like the rest of us.

I didn't agree with her plans at all but did a poor job of conveying my thoughts to the rest of the board because every month, we voted to do another project for Odilia, even though our memberships and attendance were down, and she blew through budgets like a Santa Ana wind. But I voted right along with the rest, because she made so damn many good arguments, and I thought it better to go along. And what did I know about building projects?

"Why do you keep voting for it if you don't like it?" Willy asked me one night when I rambled on about the museum. Again.

"How many times have you asked me 'If Janie Winns wanted to jump off a cliff, would you jump off the cliff?'" Pauline said. "I thought you told us to think for ourselves."

Jimmy, relaxing in his easy chair, looked up from his copy of *California Farming News*, peering over his glasses.

"If Odilia wants to jump off a cliff, you ought to just let her," he said, and went back to reading. He sure didn't like Odilia much. She must have done something in high school to make him mad. She'd probably honed her skills back then. Jimmy wasn't one to gossip or say anything bad about anyone and it was like dragging dried paint out of a can to get him to talk sometimes.

★ ★ ★

Maye Marie's little hand erased a figure from the far-left column on the ledger sheet while I looked on one cool April morning. Felicia spouted out numbers to her but Maye Marie was irritated already. She'd gone to A-1 Grocery for vanilla extract and they were all out.

"How am I going to bake a batch of blonde brownies for my Bible study group without vanilla?" I had no answer for her.

"Three seventy-four, eight fifty-two, six sixty-seven. Column B." Felicia counted out.

"We are way over budget on this," Maye Marie said, slumping back in her chair. "We're going to have to transfer money out of the reserves. Again."

I sat at the desk next to her, slathering a jalapeño with strawberry jam.

"What on earth are you doing, Irene?"

"I read that eating spicy food will calm down your temper, but I don't much like spicy food so I'm thinking the jam might help. I'm going to see if this makes me less mad at Odilia." I shoved the whole jalapeño in my mouth.

"Where did you read that?" Maye Marie asked.

I scrunched up my nose and swallowed. The sweet, thick jam soon yielded to a burning down my throat. My eyes bulged and I went into a coughing fit, barely able to speak.

"I read it ... in a magazine at the beauty shop so ... yuck ... you know it's the God's truth. Ack!"

Maye Marie smiled. A tall man stood nearby, cowboy hat in hand, a slight grin creeping around his mouth.

"You want a check for how much?" Maye Marie's little glasses perched on the end of her nose as she looked up at him.

"That would be seventy-six dollars and forty-two cents, ma'am. Made out to Buttonbush Lumber Yard."

"That's not in the budget. We've already paid for the barn."

"You sure have. But I told Miss Odilia that those old beams aren't going to hold up. I recommended she figure them into her numbers but sounds like she may not have informed you all. I guess she wanted to keep your expenditures down," he said. His face was rugged and warm, with twinkly, wrinkly eyes and hair slightly greying at the temples. He would have registered with my ma as a "handsome cuss."

The museum was in the middle of reconstructing an 1844 barn that Odilia got donated from the Contreras family and moved to the museum, much to my objection. No one even knew she'd secured it until she paraded in with the signed documents from Nick Contreras and a donation check for $300. Meanwhile, the Iversen house still sat there while the legal system moved like molasses to sort it out.

"Irene, do you hear this? We don't have money to pay for beams, too," Maye Marie said. "Once again, Odilia's gone over budget."

"Beams! Where's Odilia? This is her doing," I said, closing the jar of jalapeños.

"She's out at the barn, ma'am," he said. "I apologize. I haven't properly introduced myself. I'm Judson Riggs. Riggs Construction. Everyone calls me Jiggs."

I shook his hand, but Maye Marie careened out the door, carrying her pencil and ledger papers with her. Jiggs and I followed.

"You mean Odilia knew those barn beams weren't good?" I said.

"We all talked about it, but I think Ms. Odilia had some high hopes that they'd work out," he said.

Maye Marie, walking much faster than us, found Odilia outside the barn.

"Odilia! See here. Look what you've done." May Marie's face got redder by the second. She pointed to the ledger paper while Odilia crossed her arms and smirked.

"Odilia, there is nowhere in our budget for beams. You said that $800 would cover all the costs. You got $300 from the Contreras family and $500 from the United Ag Bank. That's what you told the board," Maye Marie said, tapping her pencil on the ledger book. "Where is this money coming from?"

"We can't put up the barn without new beams, so we're just going to do it. I'll find the money somewhere. Don't we have something left from another project?"

"We did. But you pulled that into the children's area. You can't keep moving this money around like a game of checkers," Maye Marie's voice was agitated and sharp. Several of the workers stopped working to watch.

"Well, the barn's here. What are you going to do about that?" Odilia said, shrugging her shoulders. Jiggs moved around behind Maye Marie who gave a long sigh. I stepped in front of Odilia.

"Odilia, you can't just spend money like that," I said. "Once again you've …"

"Oh, don't you two start fighting again. I'm mad enough for the both of us, Irene. I'll figure something out. But never again, Odilia. Never again!" Maye Marie swiveled to face Jiggs. I closed my mouth and stepped backwards, hoping Maye Marie had better luck than I. None of my ultimatums ever worked with Odilia.

"Mr. Riggs, we'll get those beams. I'll deal with this problem, never you mind," she said, and stomped off back to the office. He tipped his hat at her and smiled, watching her walk down the path.

"Do you want some jalapeños?" I called out to her.

★ ★ ★

I went home to find Willy on the living room couch, with a large chunk of ice on his head and a sling on his arm. Ma and Jimmy sat nearby.

"What happened?" I said and rushed to Willy's side. "Are you okay?"

"It wasn't nothin.' Me and Ronnie were racing to climb a tree at school and I fell," Willy said. "It's just a bump on the head and my arm's broke. I'm fine."

"Why didn't anyone call me?"

Ma shot me her down-the-nose glare.

"The school tried to call you. They couldn't find you, so they called me. Jimmy and I took him to the doctor. You were nowhere to be found," Ma said.

"I was at the museum and ..."

"I reckoned you were. We called, but no one answered the phone there. Fine thing when a mother can't be found," Ma said.

I looked at Jimmy.

"I'm sorry. I did not know. Sometimes they don't have enough people to answer the phones and ..." Tears wet my cheeks and Jimmy came over and hugged me.

"It wasn't anything big. Don't worry, honey," Jimmy said.

"Yeah, I'm fine Ma," Willy said, moving the ice on his head to the left.

Ma grabbed her purse and headed to the door.

"You need to stop all this volunteering nonsense and concentrate on your family. I thought you'd come to your senses by now," she said.

Hot tears ran down my throat.

"I'm sorry, Willy."

"Better not let this happen again or I'm going to move in with you. Me and Pa," Ma said, and slammed the door when she left. I sat by Willy and rubbed his neck. What kind of mother was I? My stomach hurt for days over the whole thing, and I babied Willy quite a bit until he told me to stop when I tried to comb his hair.

"Maybe I should quit the board," I told Jimmy.

"Don't do that, Irene. Willy is fine."

"I know, but what kind of mother am I when I can't be found to take my son to the doctor? I'm so ashamed of myself."

"There ain't nothing to be ashamed of. You're a wonderful mother and … you got to have a couple purposes in life, Irene. I do. I got you and the kids, but I also got a purpose growing crops out in those dry fields out there. Everyone needs a couple of purposes, not just one. You got me and the kids and you got the museum," Jimmy said, and I hugged him. "You're a good ma, Irene. Don't let this set you back."

"I guess."

"Now, I got me a purpose to go down to the river and catch some fish this afternoon after I check water," he said and pinched me on the cheeks. "Smile, now."

Willy healed up just fine, but I stuck around home more for the next two weeks and babied him. I vowed to make my whereabouts more known to everyone, except for Ma, whom I didn't want to listen to at all. What did she know about being a woman in a man's world and trying to do something bigger?

* * *

Every time I went to the museum to see the progress on the Contreras barn over the next few weeks, Maye Marie was out there, too. I noticed her and Jiggs talking quite friendly one day. His eyes focused on her as she tossed her head back and laughed. I also noticed that she started wearing rouge on a regular basis. One day I took Willy in to get his cast off, dropped him at school, then headed to the museum where I found Maye Marie putting on lipstick. That was my signal that it was a good time to poke her with some questions.

"That Jiggs is a handsome man, isn't he?" I said. "Is he married?"

"I have no idea," Maye Marie said, just a little too fast. She snapped the lipstick top shut.

"But you think he's handsome, don't you?"

"Oh my goodness, Irene, stop being such a nosey Nellie. I haven't even noticed if he's handsome."

"You might ought to notice. Because he is," I said.

A few days later, Betty called me. I was sitting at my desk writing more letters to help get rid of more artifacts. So far, I'd mailed out twenty-three pieces to as far away as Wales and Mexico City.

"I was over at the museum today and I saw Maye Marie sitting on a bench in the garden, having lunch with that building contractor. What's his name?" she said.

"Holy Toledo! Wait, that's not his name. It's Jiggs," I said.

"Maye Marie looked quite happy. Are they an item?"

"Not that I know of, but she sure perks up when he's around."

Betty and I noodled this around a bit. Maye Marie hadn't sought any male companionship since she lost her husband. This was the first time I'd seen her look twice at anyone. Her kids were almost grown and gone, so it was a perfect time for her to look for someone, at least in my opinion, which she was not asking for at all, but that never stopped me.

CLEVE BOSWORTH PICKS A BAD TIME TO DIE

Odilia

Cleve Bosworth couldn't have picked a worse time to die.

"Says right here, you need to bring this property to the museum and preserve it in honor of Cleve," said Ruby Dillsaver, who along with her spinster friend, Iris Stoot, were the president and vice president of the Buttonbush Cleve Bosworth Fan Club. Ruby waved a stack of legal papers at the museum board meeting, dressed in black, clutching a lace hankie.

The property in question was the shuttered Blue Bonnet Saloon, an establishment owned by Cleve Bosworth, the most famous person to come out of Buttonbush. The saloon, once owned by his daddy, had been bequeathed to the museum long ago for preservation. It stood at the north end of town and hadn't been open in decades. No one on the board knew anything about it.

"And now he is dead. *Dead!* Met his maker on May the twelfth, nineteen hundred and fifty-one," Ruby screeched like a wet cat. The entire board stifled laughter, which would have been extremely rude considering that Cleve recently had a heart attack right in the middle of pulling on his britches while on the set of his new movie. I put my hand over my mouth and pretended to cough.

"Cleve is an actor of great acclaim. A Western movie hero. An Oscar winner. A star among stars. A Buttonbush legend. His wishes must be honored," Iris said, dramatically swooping her hand. What a windbag. As I recalled, Cleve Bosworth spent most of his acting time on horseback, riding over hills like any regular ranch hand and not saying too much. But he was quite handsome and so had many movie roles. And wives.

"Why on earth would he want to preserve this saloon? Didn't he have a home in Buttonbush?" Betty asked.

"He did. But this saloon had a special place in his heart. For unknown reasons," Iris said.

According to Iris and Ruby, right after Cleve won his Oscar in 1933, he decided that the saloon, where he'd apparently spent much of his time as a boy, should be moved to the museum upon his death. Rundown, ramshackle, and filthy, the building sat on the edge of Buttonbush and needed lots of work, but no one considered that part. Humbleness not being his strong suit, Cleve dictated that the two-story saloon be put on a vacant piece of land near the front of the museum. And the museum board signed a document at the time agreeing to all this, thinking he'd live at least forty more years and none of them would have to worry about it.

"We know nothing about this. I don't see why we have to take this," I said. This saloon was not in my plans. I had far too many other projects to take on this eyesore.

"At least we wouldn't be stealing this house," Irene said, and I snarled at her.

"You must. We have the documentation." Ruby slapped the papers on the table in front of the board chair.

"We'll take a look at these, ladies, and make a decision at a later time," the board chair said while I steamed. These two were going to be a royal pain in the neck.

"We need this like a hole in the head," I said, shoving a cigarette in my mouth. "I want nothing to do with this."

But the commotion over Cleve's death was unlike anything ever seen in Buttonbush. Hollywood reporters ran all over town, radio and television shows about Cleve and his marvelous life were on constantly. Stories of his brush with the law when he was a teenager. And his notorious love of beer. And his movies with some of the most famous actors in Hollywood. And his three homes and two fishing cabins. And his four wives and thirteen children, not all by the wives. I wasn't interested in keeping up with the antics of Cleve Bosworth during his short but adventurous life but everyone else in Buttonbush was interested.

Over the next few weeks, the Four Queens just ignored the whole thing, hoping Ruby and Iris would fade away. But one evening as I sat down to eat a lovely plate of sopas, it was clear they weren't going away. Felicia phoned.

"Turn on your television. Channel 25," she said.

Sure enough, there was Ruby and Iris, sitting on the broken steps of the Blue Bonnet Saloon. Crying with lacy hankies in their faces, while they ate a plate of chicken-fried steak and mashed potatoes with gravy.

"It was Cleve's favorite dish from Mortie's Diner ... 349 Walker Street ... open six to nine every day except Sunday, free biscuits on Thursdays," Ruby said through sobs. "We can feel him here in this place. He's here ... right here with us."

"His presence is here among us. We know you're here, Cleve," Iris said, shoving a spoonful of potatoes in her mouth.

"Madre Mia!" I said and scooted closer to the television.

The camera swept over to a window of the saloon all boarded up and rickety looking. I expected a ghostly Cleve Bosworth to be standing in the shadows, laughing at those two women chowing down chicken-fried steak.

The newscaster said that the Buttonbush Museum Board was not living up to its agreement to move the saloon to the museum and preserve it.

"Cleve is so beloved in Buttonbush. We know he is with us in spirit and wants the museum to do the right thing by this place," said Iris, tears streaming down her cheeks as she gobbled down a spoonful of potatoes.

"That's the most ridiculous thing I've ever seen," I said to Iggy who was behind me, nursing a gin and tonic in his leather wingback chair.

"It appears you must take that saloon, Odilia. It's likely to bring in customers. It's not as if you've turned down any other building project. You've been completely focused on construction so I think you're going to have to embrace this project as well," he said. I stomped out of the room and went outside for a smoke.

★ ★ ★

Irene

Ma came marching over after hearing Ruby and Iris on television.

"You're taking in that saloon, that den in iniquity? Why on earth would you put that in the museum?" She threw her eighty-pound purse on the couch.

"Why are you so against it? Did you get stiffed when you used to dance on the tables there back in the twenties," I said, and she gave me a dirty look.

"You are not funny, Irene. That place should not be honored."

"Ma, I understand you don't like drinking but what is the problem with it? Other than we can't afford to fix it up."

"You don't know the history of it, do you?" Ma said, plopping herself down on the couch with vigor. "It was a house of ill repute."

"You mean there were prostitutes in there? Ladies of the night?" This was news to me.

"Loads of them. And thank goodness a traveling preacher put a stop to it. I remember it. Back in 1924 or so. Can't exactly recall the date," Ma said. "That saloon was busy all the time with men from the oil fields and farms. Just like Sodom and Gomorrah, it was."

The traveling preacher gave such a fiery sermon about the vice and corruption in Buttonbush at the time that Cleve's daddy closed the saloon right then.

"He took all those girls to the revival meeting and made them confess their sins right there," Ma said. "It was in the newspaper and everything."

"Well, that doesn't seem very sincere to me, but, okay," I said. Dang, were we putting up a house of ill repute at the museum? "I've been against all the other building projects but this one actually has the potential to attract visitors. Don't you think people might come to look at Cleve Bosworth's family saloon?"

"Sinful." Ma snapped her purse open and jingled her car keys. "You should not be a party to this." She stomped out the door.

I wanted the real story because I knew Ma could embellish a thing or two. I went to the county library and searched the newspapers for 1924. Sure enough, there was an article on the fiery preacher.

While more than two thousand men stamped and cheered in the tabernacle yesterday afternoon, Dr. Fernwell paid his respects to the evil businesses of the town. He went after booze and its users, turned loose a volley of shot toward the Blue

Bonnet Saloon and Bandit's Bar, and he hammered away at the liquor traffic in Buttonbush County. Some of his ammunition was spent in attacking the Moose, Elks, and other lodges of the city, and in his conclusion, he asked the men if they would stick with him.

That was when he took off his collar and with outer shirt unhooked at the waist and perspiration streaming down his face, he opened fire with his Gatling gun of oratory.

"What right have these places got to peddle booze day and night and on Sunday?"

He then broke into song: I Didn't Raise my Boy to be a Drunkard.

That might be the best title for a hymn that I've ever heard.

Blue Bonnet Saloon owner, Ellis Bosworth, stood up and declared his sins, bringing with him four ladies who worked at his saloon. The women, wearing gaudy makeup and bright dresses, dropped to their knees.

"I'll be, Ma was right," I said under my breath. I hoped I could find out the words to that song, just so I could embarrass Willy at some key moment. A mom's got to have things like that in her arsenal.

★ ★ ★

I had to make a stop at Willy's school to drop off donations for the clothing drive the next day, and it was recess time when I arrived. Willy and his friends were out on the baseball field playing pop-up. His arm was all healed.

"Hey Ma. Look at the gloves and baseball stuff we got today. The principal said we could use them at P.E. and at recess," Willy shouted at me as he eyed a high fly. He caught it in the new mitt, the ball smacking into his hand.

"Wow. That's pretty nice," I said. "Good catch."

I glanced over and the girls from Willy's class were sitting on the ground.

"What are you girls playing?" I said as I walked towards them.

Mary Margaret Ellis looked up at me and stuck her tongue out.

"They gave us jacks to play with. The boys got the baseball stuff."

"You mean there's no baseball gloves for you girls?" I said.

"No." All the girls answered in unison.

"Only for the boys," Mary Margaret said.

A little fire welled up in me and I took a breath. That wasn't right and I, for once, could do something about it. I was getting kind of tired of women doing lots of things and not being rewarded, myself included in that premise. I marched back to my car and drove to Piedmont Sporting Goods where I bought nine baseball gloves, a bat, and six baseballs. Then I drove back to the school where I cornered Principal Jenkins in his office.

"Mrs. Pickett. How nice to see you ... er." Principal Jenkins saw the look on my face.

"You didn't think the girls should play baseball, too? Girls are good at sports. They don't want to sit and play jacks all recess," I said.

"But we only had enough money for the boys."

"You could have split them. Or taken turns. Or done something so that the girls got some good exercise and team spirit, too," I said. I tossed the bag full of baseball equipment on the desk.

"These are for the girls. See that they get them." I turned on my heel and stomped out of his office.

"Whew! That's something as nervy as Odilia might have done." I said right out loud when I got into my car. It felt pretty dang good. She was rubbing off on me.

★ ★ ★

Odilia

Like a couple of Panzers, Ruby and Iris were undeterred.

"Nothing wrong with the saloon. Mr. Bosworth reformed himself and went to work at the foundry after that revival. Two of those girls became salesclerks at Manny's Five and Dime and one became a secretary at the police station," Ruby said. "Cleve said his formative years were in that saloon."

"I'll bet they were, considering his reputation in Hollywood for chasing women into every corner," I said.

"It's a testimony to Cleve's integrity that he left the saloon to the museum," Ruby said, ignoring me.

Integrity is not what I'd call it and I contemplated what lurid memories Cleve had of being a young boy in that place. He must be laughing in his grave.

But the wheels were turning. Ruby and Iris were imposing women, with robust physiques and ambitious ways. Ruby ran a dairy with her brother and she marched through life like Napoleon in a skirt. Iris was a strict, never smiling schoolteacher. A wiry thing with persistent eyes that followed a person, so you knew she would never forget what she was thinking about you. They had the paperwork and the public sentiment in their favor.

After ten minutes of back and forth at our June board meeting, the board chairman made a decree.

"We have to take this building," he said. "Our lawyers say it's legitimate."

"No! I've got Carlotta and Kosta working on all kinds of other building projects now. And how are we going to pay for it?" I said, my face heating.

"You didn't worry about that when you were moving the stolen Iversen house or the Contreras barn. Or doing all your other projects that went over budget," Irene said. "Are you just against it because it wasn't your idea?"

Irene contradicted me all the time, and I'd about had it with her. What did a piddly farmer's wife know? I had my plans to build the museum out and put my name on all of it so the Gold Seal Club would take notice. After that, who knows? I wasn't about to let two star-struck women, Irene, and a handsome movie star derail it.

"We don't have any money for the Bosworth project. We're draining our reserve account since all our building projects have gone over budget," Maye Marie said, turning the page of her ledger book.

"Over budget. Imagine that," Irene said.

"Don't you have some old junk to mail off or something?" I took a puff on my cigarette.

"At least I'm helping somebody's museum by doing that. I can't seem to help this one. I don't know why your projects always get top priority."

"They do because I said so." I tapped my pen on the table. "Besides, you've been putting up a fight over all these other projects. I think you're just in favor of this because I'm not. That's what I think."

Irene tossed her head to the side.

"Excuse me, Mrs. Stalin. The Blue Bonnet could attract visitors, couldn't it? Won't people from outside Buttonbush come to see it? I mean, it being a cat house and all," she said, crossing her arms as she sat back in her chair. "Your projects never have near the broad appeal this saloon does. That's right. A broad appeal."

"Broad appeal my fanny," I said.

"Honestly, Irene. Do you have to bring up the cathouse all the time?" Maye Marie said.

We argued for about an hour more but settled nothing.

The next day, it got settled for us.

"Clemmie St. Onge is donating $1,500 for the moving of the saloon. We'll have to pay the rest," said Maye Marie. "The county lawyers say that agreement is binding."

"Oh, terrific," I said. "I'm not taking charge of this one. Leave me out of it."

★ ★ ★

Irene

A famous Hollywood reporter, Ralston Huey, planned to come to Buttonbush for the moving of the saloon. Ralston Huey wrote stories about all kinds of movie stars, even interviewing Clark Gable, Tyrone Power, and Rita Hayworth. I'd worked up the nerve and called him myself, offering to walk him through the steps it took to get the saloon, the mechanics of moving it, and how we planned to refurbish it to its former glory. I had Clemmie lined up to talk about why she financed it, and I had to mention Ruby and Iris although I hoped he wouldn't interview those two loons. I also hoped to plead for rich movie stars to donate money for refurbishment.

The Blue Bonnet Saloon, a smelly wreck, moved to the museum on a Buttonbush summer day so hot the house would have to catch on fire to cool off. Creaking and gasping, the poor old thing lumbered down the road to the museum, the windows boarded up and the roof and siding in danger of sliding off. Clemmie, prancing around in a tight skirt and heels, flitted though the crowds of people there to watch the building's journey. I don't think that woman ever broke a sweat. Ruby and Iris stood on the side fanning themselves.

I rounded a corner of the museum just after the building plopped onto the foundation and found Odilia sitting like a slinky cat talking to a man who was obviously a reporter. He was taking notes as she spoke.

"Hello. Are you from the press?" I said. "I'm Irene Pickett. Board member."

"Ralston Huey. You and I spoke. Mrs. Delgado here was telling me all about the Bosworth saloon and how important she thought it was to bring it to the museum. Quite an accomplishment she's made here," he said. "She's been very good at providing me information about the building. Such a tremendous undertaking for her."

"Her undertaking. Really? Do tell." I could not have stared at Odilia harder than if I'd frozen.

"It's been quite an effort to move this saloon, and isn't it terrific that so many people in Hollywood, and all of California, are so excited about this. I'm so pleased to have lent my efforts to this wonderful cause." Odilia kept her eyes on Ralston, but her smile targeted me.

"Do you need any other information? I can take you around and show you the saloon and the rest of the museum?" I said.

"Thanks, but Mrs. Delgado here, Odilia, has already shown me around. I think I have everything I need now," he said, snapping his notebook shut. "Thanks for tipping me off to this, Mrs. Pickett, and thanks Odilia for a great interview."

"How nice. Isn't that just like Odilia to be so … so … Excuse me Mr. Huey, I need to go." I turned on my heel and stomped off.

I found Betty and Maye Marie and told them what happened.

"Do you think if I strangled her with her garter belt I could make it look like she just choked herself trying to get her nylons off? That's plausible, right?

Betty patted me on the back and Maye Marie handed me a chocolate cookie.

"I don't have any jalapeños," she said.

★ ★ ★

Odilia's rotten little face was on page two of the *Hollywood Roundup* the following week, along with Ralston Huey's article, a picture of the saloon, and one of Cleve as a young boy. He credited her as the woman behind moving the Blue Bonnet to the museum. I was ready to spit bullets, but it was nothing compared to what Iris and Ruby wanted to do.

"How dare she take credit for this? She's despicable." Iris called me and talked my ear off for almost an hour about all they'd done to get Cleve's saloon to the museum. "It's an out-and-out lie."

I tried to soothe her over, but the damage was done.

Worse yet, Betty, Maye Marie, and I tried to raise money to refurbish the place. Clemmie had paid to move it but there was no money to fix it up. After I'd pushed to take in the house, partially just to aggravate Odilia, now it needed a lot of help and there was no money for it. Ruby and Iris tried to raise money, too. But Odilia had already gotten to everyone about her own projects and none of us could out-fundraise her.

"Sounds like she's always one step ahead of you," Jimmy said.

I nodded and thought of that damn saloon sitting there, ragged, dingy, and beat-up. I was feeling the same. I could never seem to get anything right at the museum. Odilia, as if the saloon wasn't even there, merrily proceeded along with all her projects.

★ ★ ★

Ground beef smushed through my fingers as I mixed a meatloaf the following day, the eggs oozing through the goo.

"Mom, Mrs. Dolley invited us to a ladies' lunch on Saturday. It's at the Parker Hills Country Club. Say we can go, Mom," Pauline said, bouncing around on her tiptoes, like when she was little. "I can finally wear my blue Easter dress again."

I dreaded the thought of sitting with the fancy Joyce Dolley through an entire lunch, but I knew how much it meant to Pauline.

"Alright, I can go. But what should I wear?"

Pauline appointed herself my fashion consultant, and I said a silent prayer of thanks for Platex girdles and Max Factor. She settled on my purple shirt dress and best nylons and even took out my little silver evening purse.

On the day of the lunch, Pauline smoothed my hair with a comb and straightened my hemline.

"You're wearing a hat, aren't you?" Pauline said.

"Do I have to?" I grabbed my yellow church hat. I never liked to wear hats.

"Oh Mom, you can't wear that with the purple. How about that little black hat you used to have?"

"Good Lord, are we having lunch with Lana Turner? Rita Hayworth?"

"Stop it, Mom. Don't be ridiculous."

"You are making a big deal out of how I look. Are you ashamed of me?"

Pauline's face tightened.

"No. It's just that sometimes you don't make much effort."

"Do you think I have a lot of time for that between you and Willy and your dad and the farm and the museum and everything else?" I stomped out of the room.

"Ack! The museum. Always the museum. Maybe you'd have more time for yourself if you gave up some of that," she hollered from the other room. I rummaged in my closet and reached up to the top shelf. A little black pillbox hat, slightly dusty and worn, toppled down. Pauline came into the room and stood behind me.

"Here, that will work. Let's clean it up a bit," she said.

She wasn't wrong. I looked pretty nice in that hat.

The reason for Pauline's desire to make me more attractive became painfully apparent when we arrived at the club, my first time being there. Women in beautiful dresses—pink brocades with wide skirts, blue and peach satins, embroidered rosebuds, silk waistbands and tulle underskirts—floated around the room. Their hair, obviously styled that very day, was in sleek updos or tightly curled platinum locks. My purple shirtdress and freshly washed hair weren't too impressive.

"Hello, Irene. So thrilled to see you here," said Joyce, who whisked over to us in a rush of pale pink taffeta with a delicate satin bow in the back. Her hair flowed down one side of her face and she had on a perfect shade of magenta lipstick. I bit my lip. I'd forgotten lipstick.

"Thanks so much for inviting us," I said. Giggling, Pauline and Deborah wandered off and Joyce drew me to a table.

"I've so much wanted to talk with you. Pauline is just the most charming girl. So smart and beautiful," she said. "Does she have plans for college?"

"She'll probably just go to Buttonbush Junior College," I said. "Maybe she can go to a university somewhere, but I'm not sure."

"Deborah is still deciding, too. They have an entire year to go but we're pushing her to go to Stanford. But if you push too hard, they push back. So we're being gentle with Deborah," Joyce said. She patted my hand. "Pauline is quite capable of getting into Stanford, too."

"That's a pretty expensive college. I'm not sure," I said. Pauline couldn't decide whether to wear a red blouse or a blue blouse on any given day so deciding on a college wasn't anything she was near capable of doing yet. Joyce stared at me with enormous eyes, like she was petting a lost puppy, and I squirmed in the fancy velvet lined chair.

"Oh, that's unfortunate. Something can be worked out. I'll bet there's some way to get help with that," she said, and I felt my brain kind of cramp, trying to work out what she was referring to, and realized that she viewed Pauline and me as in need of charity.

Typical. People think all farmers are poor and stupid. She didn't know that half the farmers I knew went to college, including my Jimmy, and got degrees in some kind of science. And that they were all smart business people, or they wouldn't survive. They may look sort of hillbilly in their dungarees or overalls but their minds, for the most part, were like fine-tuned machines and it's easy to be fooled by their kind manners and folksy ways. There has been more than one know-it-all city salesman or government bureaucrat who thought he'd come to a Buttonbush farm to sell a product or program and by the time he was done, he was buying a box of oranges from the farmer and donating money to the local 4-H.

I tugged at my dress and took a deep breath. Pauline and Deborah joined us at the table. Three other ladies also joined us, all young, gorgeous, smelling of lilac and gardenia. As if I wasn't feeling enough like a mutt in a roomful of French poodles, Odilia sauntered over, her dark hair shining and large emerald earrings dangling at her neck like a couple of pickles. She threw me a quick glance then turned to Joyce.

"Joyce, as usual, you look adorable. You must have learned your style from your time as a model. It's so wonderful to have women with a sense of style and grace in Buttonbush," she said, turning her snakey eyes to me and running them down to my plain black pumps where my ankles crossed uncomfortably.

"Didn't you say you attended UCLA? Terrific school. I know people around here like little Buttonbush Junior College, which is fine if you can't do anything else, but UCLA! What an education you must have! Where did you attend, Irene? I've forgotten?" Odilia said, and all eyes turned to me.

"Little Buttonbush Junior College, Odilia. As you well know," I said through clenched teeth. Pauline hung her head down.

"Oh well. Joyce, are you going to the Robinson's party next week? It's supposed to be a huge celebration for Cassandra's birthday. Vincent is flying in all her sorority sisters from back East and I hear rumor there are lobsters coming in from Maine. Won't that be great? Were you invited, Irene?" Odilia clutched at the pearls around her neck, and I had a vision of her hanging from the museum clock tower with them.

I ignored her. Joyce gave me a pitying look which was worse than Odilia's taunt.

Odilia, satisfied with humiliating me, wandered away, her swishy ivory dress swaying. I contemplated hurling one of the cocktail shrimps at her but figured my aim wasn't that good. I was pretty sure I could get her skinny little body in a headlock, but I didn't want anyone to see my dress fly up and expose my Platex girdle. Plus, Pauline would disown me. I slumped back in my chair like a clump of cold noodles.

"With your hair like that today, Pauline, why you look just like Donna Reed," Joyce said, and she and Pauline and Deborah burst into laughter.

"What's so funny?" I said.

"We have a long running joke about Pauline looking like Donna Reed and we laugh about it all the time," Deborah said, and I faded into my chair is if someone had punched me as I watched the three of them share something I had no part in.

"I never noticed that," I said, then drew in a breath when Pauline smirked.

"I'm looking forward to the tea next week, Irene," Joyce said, daintily spreading butter on a roll. Pauline bit her lower lip.

"What?" I said.

"The junior girls' tea, the one they put on for the senior girls and their mothers. Next Thursday. What a sweet tradition," Joyce said.

I stared at Pauline. She had not mentioned this tea at all. My eyes started to tear up.

"It's going to be marvelous," I said, and Pauline kept her head down for the rest of the lunch.

I couldn't wait to leave and dragged Pauline out the door as quickly as I could. On the way home, I held back my tears and asked Pauline why she hadn't mentioned the mother daughter tea to me.

"You're too busy all the time. During the week you're always at the museum, so I didn't think you'd want to go to a tea on a Thursday," she said.

"That's not true, Pauline, and you know it. I always make time for you ... You and Willy and your dad come first for me," I said, but she turned her head away from me. Maybe I hadn't noticed how much the museum had taken me off course. It hurt my heart.

"Fine. Come to the tea if you can squeeze it in to your busy schedule," she said. "I was going to ask you eventually, anyway."

Danged if I was going to let Pauline convince me I was a terrible mother. I knew I wasn't, but when my daughter treated me like I'd abandoned her, I knew I'd made some mistakes. I went with her to the tea, but we were still out of sorts and distant. Watching her talk to Joyce Dolley made me so dang mad. Was I that awful of a mother that my daughter wanted to be around another mother more than me? And the answer I heard in my head was "yes."

Figuring I needed to take some course of action, I made a goal to spend more time with my daughter. Bribery being a useful tool, I knew Pauline enjoyed shopping. So I planned an outing with her. I'd buy her some new clothes then have a nice lunch. Maybe she'd start to see me as fashionable and as sophisticated as Joyce Dolley or at least a close second.

On the Saturday before Labor Day, I put on my hat and gloves and even some White Shoulders cologne. The phone rang, and I heard Pauline giggling when she answered it.

She came into the kitchen with a hangdog face.

"Mom, I'm so sorry, but I have to cancel our lunch today. Mr. Foley called a special meeting of the class officers. Something about student council."

"But honey, I had a whole day planned with lunch and everything."

"I know Ma, I'm so sorry. Can I take the car?" Pauline said, and scampered back to her room to change clothes. She scurried out the door before I could talk to her again.

"See you later, Ma."

I put away my nice clothes and vacuumed the house for an overly long time, watching the clock for when Pauline might return.

THE CHICKEN RING

Irene

Come to me my melancholy baby, Jimmy was singing loud enough that I could hear him over the tractor roaring down the road, the smoking September sun heating my back like a cookie sheet in the oven. I chopped at the nasty pigweed on the side of the cotton field that sat to the south of our farm, the stinging smell of the green leaves making me sneeze and itch. The cotton was growing fast, its leafy arms spreading across the fields with the bolls popping out into fluffy little balls. I heard a noise and saw Betty in her fancy car driving down the dirt road, waving out the window at me. I plodded down the deep row to meet her, wiping my neck with a blue bandana.

"Look at this, look at this! I can't believe it. I never win anything." Betty waved her arms as she came bouncing up to me, hair flying mane-like behind her.

"I saw a flyer at A-1 Grocery saying there was a sweepstakes going on with Presley Farms Chicken. I opened a package of chicken today and look what was in it. I won a contest! It's an emerald with genuine diamonds, I'm sure of it," Betty said, and waved her hand in my face, flashing a gigantic ring on her finger. It had multiple circles of diamonds on what looked to be a platinum setting, a big emerald stone in the middle. "I didn't even know they were having a contest, but that must be it. Look, we can auction this off at the museum garden party and raise a lot of money." She was breathless, and I grabbed her arm to steady it so I could get a better look at it.

"It's a genuine J.E. Caldwell ring. Sitting directly under the chicken wing. Do you know what this is worth? Why we could earn oodles of money auctioning this off," Betty put the ring on, her hand moving in and out, around her body, across her chest so she could admire it from various angles. "This has got to be worth at least five hundred dollars."

"Five hundred dollars! I never saw an authentic piece of jewelry worth that much in my life. Are you sure? ... Wait, did you wash this thing?" I stepped backwards.

"Of course I did! I have a Caldwell ring, but mine is smaller, and Alvin paid $350 for mine. Look, see here is the insignia on the inside of the ring."

"J.E. Caldwell" was inscribed right on the band.

"What I know about jewels you could put inside a bottle cap," I said, but Betty knew about jewelry. She owned tons of it, once nearly decapitating me with her ruby bracelet in an over-eager hug.

"But it's yours. Don't you want to keep it?" I said.

"I have plenty of jewelry and precious little opportunity to wear it. No, this is a stroke of luck for the museum," Betty said.

"As my kids would say, that's the bee's knees," I said, abandoning Jimmy to his field work to drive back to my house to call Maye Marie right away.

Pauline ogled it for a bit, too.

"Mrs. Dolley wears rings like that," she said.

"Does she?" My lips pursed in what could only be called a grouchy mom look.

"She wears rings and rhinestone necklaces and beautiful silk scarves," Pauline said, that dreamy look coming to her eyes every time she spoke of Joyce Dolley. "She's so fashionable."

"Maybe she'll want to bid on this ring. I'll invite her to the anniversary dinner." I handed Betty a glass of iced tea.

"Mother, she won't want to come to some boring museum dinner. Please don't embarrass me by asking her to go to one of your silly little events," Pauline said. "She's much too dignified for that."

"Thanks for the compliment, Pauline," I said, a frustrated frown on my face. "I can't wait for the day when you have your own children and they can say terrible things to you."

"That's not so terrible."

"It is. It's uncalled for and hurtful." I slammed the kitchen cabinet. "Stop being so rude in front of Mrs. Davenport."

Pauline glared at me and left the room.

"That girl is going to be the death of me," I said, and sat down next to Betty as a deep sigh escaped my chest.

"She's just a teenager. Don't let her upset you. This, too, shall pass," Betty patted my hand. "I have sometimes wanted to just unleash venom on my mother, but I don't. Don't all daughters quarrel with their mothers until they are grown enough to realize their mothers are right?"

"You sure are wise for such a young woman, Betty. I can endure Odilia and all our arguments, but I am not equipped to deal with my daughter's scorn," I said, and Betty hugged me.

★ ★ ★

Odilia

The Four Queens were in a tizzy for a few days, calculating how much we could get for the ring and how we could light a fire under potential bidders. The ring sat in a little jewelry box in the middle of our lunch table one day, the emerald green catching the sunlight, flashing green all around the room.

"That damn thing is entrancing," I said. It was gorgeous, and if Iggy weren't being so distant, I might ask him to buy it for me. As it was, he barely gave me the time of day, much less an expensive ring.

Twice the other three Queens told me that any money raised was not going to one of my building projects but to our goal of putting $5,000 in reserve.

"Pffffft." I snuffed out my cigarette.

"I'm playing bridge with my ladies' group next week. I'll let it slip that we've got this beautiful ring to auction and wouldn't that look just splendid at Christmas time?" Betty's eyes arched, positively cat-like. "And Dinny Dogan, well, not to gossip or anything ... but her husband, that despicable man, needs a peace offering for her and this would be perfect. From what I've heard, he won't dare say no to any request she makes these days."

Betty's eyebrows rose. I knew exactly what Betty was talking about and Maye Marie said, "Hmmmm."

"What the heck did Tom Dogan do?" Irene practically jumped out of her chair, always excited by a juicy piece of gossip.

Betty shrugged.

"You can imagine. You've met his new secretary, haven't you?" Betty said.

A thought came into my head and I raised my hand, pointing my index finger in the air.

"I hadn't considered this about Tom Dogan. I think we should go right over to his office and see if we can get him to donate to the museum right now," I said. Why hadn't I thought of this before? This was so unlike me to not consider this kind of ingenious money-raising plot.

"Right now? What about the auction?" Betty said.

"He can buy the ring in the auction. But we can get him to sponsor something else, can't we?" I said.

"Odilia, how many times do we have to tell you that ..."

I interrupted Irene. "I know, I know. None of this money goes to my building projects. But it's fair game for anything not at the garden party. Who wants to go with me?" I said.

"I can't. I have to go to a doctor appointment," Betty said.

"I have to meet the plumber at my house. My bathtub drain is clogged," said Maye Marie. "And I need to bake cookies for him."

I looked at Irene, who had a smirky grin on her face.

"Guess you're stuck with me, Odilia," she said. I grunted. She was all I had. We headed to the parking lot and got into my convertible.

"I never rode in a convertible before," Irene said, sitting down in the passenger's seat, running her hands over the white upholstery. I put on my new fancy Ray-Ban sunglasses and tore out of the parking lot.

As we approached Tom Dogan's downtown office, we spotted Tom and a lithe, milky-blonde woman with a long ponytail and very high heels on, talking and laughing in the parking lot. I drove past then turned around.

"Would you look at that?" I said. We watched as Tom led her to his car, a black Mercury coupe.

Tom backed the car out of the parking lot and headed down Eighteenth Street.

"Let's follow them," Irene said.

"We can't just follow them." I shook my head. Irene had so many cockamamie ideas.

"Come on, Odilia. Just go. They're probably going to the courthouse or something."

I gunned the engine, following the Mercury down the street but keeping a suitable distance behind. Then they turned down Porter Avenue. Four blocks later, Tom went right on Harrison Road where we followed him for six miles.

"What the hell is he doing all the way out here? I can't imagine he has business this far out of town," I said.

"Odilia, you know these are traffic signs, not just suggestions," Irene said, so I sped up even more.

"I'm a fast driver. Does that surprise you?"

Irene put her hands on her head in a futile effort to keep her hair in place, but the air whipped all around her, making her springy curls stick out on every side like a porcupine.

"Nice hairdo," I said. "I can't believe you're making me drive all the way out here."

"Just a few more miles. I'm curious now," Irene said. "This is strange."

We followed Tom for seven more miles, all the way to Meeker, a tiny farm town, where he turned down a short gravel road lined with trees. At the end stood the Blackstone Inn, a quaint, two-story brick building tucked in a grove of eucalyptus trees, rose bushes and oleanders. I inched the car behind a patch of the bushes and parked.

"Now what?" I said.

"Let's see what they're doing," Irene said, and she opened the car door, hunched over like a thief, and tip-toed behind a bush.

"For crying out loud you look ridiculous," I said, but then I did the same thing.

"Holy cow!" Irene hissed, her eyes wide. Tom and the woman, now holding hands, entered the hotel. "Let's go. That's more than I want to see."

We got back in the car.

"Horrible man. What a lowlife, no good." I started the engine then rubbed my chin. "But hmmm. Might be to our advantage. Let's wait a bit. We can go to the cafe off the road and watch."

"Wait for what?" Irene said, but I was already pulling into the cafe parking lot, the wheels in my head turning.

At a small table near a window, we ordered Coca-Colas and split an order of French fries while we kept an eye on the Blackstone.

"I feel like a regular Sherlock Holmes," Irene said.

"I'm not your Watson." I popped a fry into my mouth. "Perhaps I'm more like Ingrid Bergman in *Notorious*."

"Didn't she die at the end of that?"

"She did not."

"Good, because I'd have a heck of a time explaining how you died from watching Tom Dogan and his sweetie go to a hotel in the middle of the afternoon," Irene said.

"Why are you always so smart-alecky?" I stared out the window but saw no sign of Tom.

"I don't know. It's just me," Irene said. "Besides, life is too short to be so serious all the time."

"Sometimes you need to be serious, Irene. Sometimes there are serious things happening and you can't just joke about them all the time. He's cheating on his wife."

"Sorry, I didn't know I was offending you so much." Irene took a drink of soda and sat back in her chair.

"Dinny doesn't know this is happening. He's breaking his marriage vows. It's so dishonorable. We shouldn't joke about it," I said. Irene was always making stupid jokes about everything.

"I'm sorry. I didn't know it would upset you so much," Irene said.

"Maybe it's because I know how Dinny feels," I said.

"You mean?" Irene stared at me, her mouth hung open.

"Never mind. I said too much. It's just that people have hard things that happen to them sometimes and jokes don't help. You make fun of me all the time. Did you know kids used to make fun of me at school because we were so poor I had to wear my older sister's shoes that were falling apart? And her old dresses.

I never had a new piece of clothing until I got my first job in Sacramento."

"I understand. I never had any new dresses growing up, either," Irene said.

"Then you shouldn't make so much fun of things all the time."

"I'm sorry, Odilia. I never meant to offend you. It's most always in good fun but I'll try to stop," Irene said. "In my defense, you are kind of funny sometimes."

Reluctantly, I smiled.

"I am a bit much sometimes."

She laughed.

"And you're right, we all have things that are hard and I should be more aware of that." Irene rattled the ice in her glass and took a sip.

"You? What do you have that's hard?" I pulled out my cigarette case.

"Well, my daughter, for one. She's selfish and self-centered and thinks I'm as stupid as a post. She doesn't appreciate or agree with anything I do or say. It's like I'm the enemy." Irene's eyes clouded as she spoke.

"Teenage girls can be difficult. I imagine she'll grow out of it."

"That's what everyone says. Let's hope so." Irene said and dipped another fry into the catsup.

"Finish the fries and let's go. This is making me sad," I said.

For once, she shut up. Tom and his secretary were still in the hotel so we left and rode back to Buttonbush in silence.

When I got home, I remembered I needed to water my poor little lemon tree on the side of the house so I parked the car in the garage and walked through the backyard before going inside. I could hear Iggy in his study, bellowing over the hum of the swamp cooler. He was on the phone, laughing with someone.

"It's a terrific idea if I do say so myself. Perfect. Just perfect and it's going to be easy to pull off. Just you watch. I've already started the process." I walked silently past the open window. "It's a great last project for my legacy. We'll talk more soon." The phone clattered into the cradle and Iggy strutted out of the room. I didn't know what he was talking about since he hadn't mentioned any new legislation or projects to me lately. But we didn't talk all that much.

I watered my lemon tree and two rose bushes, then wandered upstairs and found Iggy in the bedroom closet, putting clothes into his suitcase.

"Where are you going?"

"Business trip, dear. A little fact-finding mission that I need to go on."

"Where?"

"Carmel by the Sea."

I adored Carmel.

"How long are you staying? I can go with you." I opened my closet doors and began pulling out clothes.

"Not so fast, Odilia. I have to be in meetings all day and there won't be any other wives there for you to spend time with. It won't be fun at all for you," Iggy said, closing his suitcase with a crisp snap of the latches.

"I don't care. I can read books or take walks or …"

"No, Odilia, it just isn't a good time for you to go with me. I'm leaving right now. Don't you need to do something for the museum?" He pulled his jacket on.

"But Iggy … I can pack quickly."

"No point. I'll be way too busy."

"It certainly seems like you don't want me around you. What's going on that you don't want me there?"

"It's not that I don't want you there, dear. I just have so many meetings and private negotiations that I'm doing that it won't be any fun for you at all. And don't you have plenty of things to do here?"

"We never spend any time together anymore, Iggy. When's the last time we even had a nice dinner together?" I sat down on the bed, my whole body suddenly feeling heavy.

"Come now, we eat dinner together all the time. Now I've got to get going." Iggy buttoned his jacket and brushed his sleeves with his hands. He certainly was taking time with his appearance.

"Can you just stay and have lunch with me?"

"No time. I need to get on the road, darling. Get to those building projects at the museum. That's how you'll save your museum. You are so good at that. Enjoy your weekend." Iggy whisked out the door. As he drove away, a hard pit formed in my stomach. My life was a series of catching Iggy at home for a few minutes then watching him drive off to live a life without me. We hadn't had dinner together in weeks. I went into the kitchen and made myself a ham sandwich piled with tomatoes, lettuce, and peppers, then ate an apple, a pear, and two pieces of applesauce cake that Maye Marie had given me. I washed it all down with almost a full bottle of wine.

★ ★ ★

The next day, I pranced into the museum waving a check for four hundred dollars.

"I got $400 from Tom Dogan for a new roof on the general store building this morning," I said. "And he promises to bid on the emerald ring at the garden party, too."

"You what? How?" Betty said. "That was supposed to go to our garden party. What did you do?"

"Don't worry. You can get him to buy tickets to the party on top of bid for the ring. In fact, we can get just about anything from him right now. I went over to his office this morning. Told him I happened to be in Meeker yesterday and saw him at the Blackstone Hotel and wouldn't he like to give us some money to re-roof the general store? He had the secretary write the check that very moment," I said. "By the way, her name is Trilby. Have you ever heard of such a name?"

"Odilia, that's genuinely devious," Irene said. "That's blackmail."

"I wouldn't quite use that word. Besides, he deserves it, the big cheater." I was quite proud of myself for delivering a little reckoning to Tom Dogan.

"Dear Lord, what won't you do to get money for this place?" Maye Marie asked.

I shrugged. I couldn't think of anything.

★ ★ ★

Irene

A few days later, Betty stopped by my house again looking as sad as a puppy in the rain.

"I went back to A-1 Grocery today and told them how excited I was to win the ring in the Presley Farms contest. The butcher gave me the funniest look. He showed me the flyer, and it said the sweepstakes was for you to buy five packages of chicken and put your name in to win a set of frying pans. I guess I didn't read it too well," she said.

"So, what about the ring?"

"He told me to wait a minute. So I did, and soon he came back and asked me to go with him to the back office and handed me the phone," she said.

Betty plopped down in a living room chair.

"It was Mrs. Juliet Presley of Presley Farms herself on the phone, calling all the way from Kearney Falls, up north. It's right near Mt. Cree, but in the flatlands, kind of east of Pernot. That's where they have their chicken farm. It's a pretty big farm and they sell all over the Western U.S. and even as far as Missouri," Betty said. "I buy their chicken all the time, more than Farmer Wade's Chicken even though they're from Buttonbush, because that Presley chicken is just so much better and tastier."

I tapped my foot.

"Betty. The story."

"Right. Mrs. Presley told me that a few weeks back, they were short workers at the chicken packing plant, so she helped her husband out. It was hot, and she was sweating. She actually told me that ... and she was working fast because they were getting backed up. She had on her favorite emerald ring and later on she realized she'd lost it. They sent out a call to all the customers, telling them to keep a lookout for it. So now we have to give it back to her." Betty rested her chin on her hands and frowned.

"Awww, no," I said. "We had such high hopes of raising money with that ring."

"There goes our auction. I'm so disappointed. Not to mention I told my mother about it and she, for once, seemed pleased with me. Now I have to tell her it was all a mistake."

"I'm sorry, Betty. That is unfortunate," I said. "But don't worry, we have other auction items, like the satchel from Kirby's Kustom Leather. And my Jimmy is donating twenty hay bales. Who needs an emerald ring when you can get hay bales?"

When Betty told me about the true owner of the emerald ring, all I could think about was Juliet Presley, standing in her rubber boots and butcher's apron, wrapping up slimy chicken legs while her giant emerald ring dangled on the end of her finger. And how much money was there in chicken farming if you could own that kind of ring and wear it around all day like it was nothing more than a hair ribbon?

Betty needed to get that ring back to Juliet, so the Four Queens decided to drive up to Kearney Falls to return it.

We packed some goodies and a jar of water and Betty drove her blue Buick, a whale of a vehicle with a good radio. Maye Marie made a batch of donut holes, and we were stuffing them in our mouths as we talked.

"Isn't there some way to get rid of Carlotta?" Maye Marie said, an out-of-the-blue question, but none of us blinked an eye.

"Did you see *The Wizard of Oz*? I'm thinking a bucket of water aimed right at her head and ..." I said.

"Oh, for heaven's sake. We can't get rid of her. She's the only person in town who knows Buttonbush's history so well. I asked her to find me a teakettle from the 1890s for the Edwards House the other day, and she knew right where to find it in all that stuff in the basement. We'll never find anyone with her knowledge. We're stuck with her," Odilia said.

"Can't we force her to put more of the relics out? It's rather ridiculous," said Betty as she rounded a curve in the road.

"She won't ever. She keeps her house the same way she keeps the basement of the museum," Maye Marie said.

"What? How do you know that?" I said.

"Felicia told me. She gave Carlotta a ride home one night when Carlotta sprained her ankle. Do you remember that? Felicia helped Carlotta into the house which was packed with all kinds of things. Old books piled to the ceiling, all kinds of doodads and dishes and pots and pans and furniture. Felicia said she walked through a path that was surrounded by a wall of old newspapers to take Carlotta into the bedroom. It was frightful," Maye Marie said.

"You mean she piles stuff up in her house, too?" I said. That explained a lot about Carlotta's need to stuff things away from the light of day.

"Felicia said even her bedroom was filled with picture albums and picture frames and pillows piled up, clothes, and so many blankets she couldn't see out the windows."

"Well, I'll be," Odilia said, and we were quiet for a moment as the explanation for Carlotta's crazy curating methods sank in.

"Sounds like she has some sort of mental problem about keeping things. I should try to help her. Get her to organize more. At the museum and at home," Betty said.

"Are you a psychiatrist now?" Odilia said.

"No. But maybe she just needs some gentle advice," Betty said. "It can't hurt."

"Hey, do you think we can get Juliet Presley to contribute to the party?" I said, tossing another donut hole in my mouth.

"She should. I'm returning this precious ring. I would think she owes us something," said Betty. "Of course she'll want to help us out. Alvin says the Presleys are very well off. Very. She was tickled pink that I'd found her ring."

"We might get enough to launch our history in pictures program for the kids," Maye Marie said.

We hatched a plan to get Juliet to donate something, although Odilia was noticeably quiet as we plotted.

The Presley place was a house of the spectacular kind, a white columned brick monstrosity with little hedges all around it trimmed flat and an entire row of petunias underneath that were all white. Rows of red rose bushes lined the circular driveway, and heavy drapery hung inside the wide windows. When Juliet came out of the house, I half expected her to be dressed like Scarlett O'Hara but she emerged wearing a pair of pedal pushers with a polka dot shirt. I sure would have loved to have seen her in a sweeping gown, all satin and lace, swooning in the heat.

But she was a jolly, smiley woman with curly grey hair and blue eyes, and with the look of someone who knows how to work hard. She took us around the side to a wide brick terrace with two sets of little white metal tables, both with small vases of yellow daisies in the middle, and plates of macaroon cookies. She offered for us to use her bathroom facilities and I jumped at the chance to see her house, taking my time to take it all in. I made a mental note to try to duplicate her dining room wallpaper, a delicate, pale green leaf pattern with little ferns etched in cream.

Pink and black tile circled the bathroom and black and white mosaic tile covered the floor where fluffy pink rugs lay in front of an enormous bathtub. Little pink hand towels with lace on the bottom hung on black hooks. It was a delightful bathroom, if a bathroom could ever be delightful.

Betty handed Juliet the ring right away, looking so proud and hopeful about getting a wallop of a donation from her.

"I just can't thank you ladies enough. Why my husband was about to literally choke me for losing that ring. He bought that for me for my… well, you know, a milestone birthday. And I cried and carried on when I realized I'd lost it somewhere. We scoured that pack room for hours, looking for it. I just about wore out my knees crawling around on that concrete floor, thinking it slipped in some crack. We finally determined that it was probably in a pack of chicken. Thank heavens no one cooked it and ate it," she said, laughing as she swallowed her iced tea.

"Betty found it and kept it for you," Maye Marie said, smiling at Betty, who nodded and batted her eyes.

"I can't thank you enough, Betty. Many people would have just kept their mouth shut and hung on to that ring. I am so grateful," Juliet said.

"We were in the middle of planning our garden party for the Buttonbush Museum when I found it," Betty said, edging into our crafty plan. "We're celebrating the seventy-fifth anniversary of the museum and we're hosting a party. You would be so welcome to come. We're holding a dinner and dancing and an auction to raise money for the museum. It's so difficult keeping our place afloat."

"We are always trying to raise money to pay for the educational classes for children and the lectures and tours that we do for our visitors. It's all very expensive to maintain a twenty-one-acre museum," I said. "We depend on our generous donors to help us keep the lights on, and our education and events going."

"We were wondering ..." Betty started in, but Juliet cut her off.

"I've heard how hard you ladies work. And I've heard about all the wonderful things you're doing. In fact, I just donated $200 for tiling the floor in the museum's education area. Why, Odilia called me yesterday and told me about what's going on there and I must say, I am very impressed," Juliet said. "Consider it a little thank you for finding my ring."

You might as well have dropped a boulder on the Queens at that point. None of us spoke for a few seconds. In unison, the three of us turned and stared at Odilia, who sat innocent as a baby. She smiled at Juliet. I had a cookie in my hand, about to take a bite, and it fell on the plate, making a muffled, plunking sound. Finally, Maye Marie rallied.

"Odilia called you? She didn't mention it, did you, Odilia? Isn't that wonderful? Tile ... How generous of you," she said, but her voice shook a little and a quick vision of me dumping the plate of cookies on Odilia's head flashed in my brain. Poor Betty's face deflated like an old balloon. I composed myself and gave Odilia the stink eye. We murmured our goodbyes to Juliet and got into the car. None of us said a word for about six miles.

"All right, I know you're all mad at me, but I called her because I knew she'd want to donate and we need that tile," Odilia said.

"Do we?" I asked.

"How come you said nothing when we were planning on asking her to donate to the garden party? You didn't make a peep on the ride up," Maye Marie said.

"There was nothing to say. I thought maybe she'd donate to your party, too, but you didn't even ask her. You've got to ask to get things," Odilia said.

"That was truly despicable, Odilia. Sneaking around on the rest of us Queens like that. Taking money behind our backs," Betty said. "I had so hoped to get a donation for the children's programs."

"It's not like I took it for myself."

"That is about the most low-down scoundrel thing you've ever done, Odilia," I said. We barely spoke the entire way home. Odilia had bested us again.

FAKE BADMINTON

Irene

*C*ounty zeroes in on museum as new courthouse location, read the headline in the September 23, 1951 newspaper.

The article stated that one quarter of the museum would be demolished.

The museum has always been a money loser for the county so it would be financially prudent to locate the courthouse there and make that location more productive, if the state awards Buttonbush the courthouse location, one county supervisor said in a quotation.

Each of the Four Queens was about to spit nails over this fresh development.

"I can't believe they would do this," Maye Marie said.

"They want to build the courthouse on property they already own rather than buy something new," the board chairman said.

"That would be a travesty. Simply a travesty," Betty said.

"I can't believe our county officials are approving of this. Demolish part of the museum! What a terrible plan," I said.

"It's all about saving money, ladies," the board chairman said.

"Who's ramrodding this?" Odilia said.

"I'm not sure. Might be the county planning department. They don't think our little village of historic houses is all that important," the chairman said, and I pitied whoever worked at the planning department because they were about to get an Odilia special, served hot.

Odilia called a Four Queens meeting a few days later with bad news.

"Those idiots wouldn't listen to me. I even called three commissioners, but the planning department thinks this will save them money," she said. "They're in a pickle because oil prices are down, which means county revenue is down. So they're looking at lower cost options."

"It is a prime piece of property in a central location," Betty said.

"Give me some time; I'll think on this," Odilia said, and the thought of her focusing her energies on something else for a while comforted me.

★ ★ ★

Odilia

A letter from the county commissioners that month infuriated me.

> *"With the interest of the state in building a new courthouse in Buttonbush, we are commissioning a feasibility study to determine the long-term future of the museum. Your books show a $3,738 deficit to date, the second year in a row that the museum has been in a negative financial position. Your deadline is December 1952 to achieve a $5,000 reserve amount. We'll be analyzing your finances to determine whether you can achieve this goal and what action we may need to take. That action may or may not include closure of the museum."*

"They can't do that," I said at a financial committee meeting. "It's a bluff."

"I don't think so," said Maye Marie. "The county is cracking down on all over-spending. They just cut the library budget by eighteen percent. And that courthouse is looking very promising."

I didn't see any reason to change plans. Once the museum was in tip-top shape, we'd have scores of visitors, and it would be the shining jewel of Buttonbush. I could see the potential. I didn't know why others couldn't see it, too.

The day of the Contreras barn opening dawned, and I was in a cheery mood. One more project under my belt. The other Queens were still mad at me about getting that donation from Juliet Presley, but it didn't matter to me one fig. I put on my black lace slip then pulled a dark magenta skirt over it. I looked at myself in the mirror and tilted my head up.

"I'll show them all. Especially Iggy," I said. I buttoned my flowered blouse and tucked it into the skirt, then slipped on a pair of black pumps. This was certain to be on the news and I hoped, that just maybe, all those Gold Seal members would see me. Getting to the top was why I went away to college, defying my parents, even though it was the best decision I ever made. My scholarship was a first in my family and I'd made the most of it. Why shouldn't I run in the same pack as the men? I'd never met one I couldn't outwit. Except maybe Iggy. I patted my tummy, flat and taught. Not a single pound more since high school. Not that Iggy noticed any more.

I could hear Iggy talking on the phone as I came down the stairs, his deep voice rumbling in his study. I pushed open the door and Iggy's voice got louder when I walked in.

"That's right. So good of you to call. I've got to go now," he said, and hung up the phone, the handset clanging into the holder. "All ready for your opening today, dear?"

"Who were you talking to?"

"That was one of the state engineers, asking me about funding for a canal project. Nothing exciting, dear. Now you'd better get going." Iggy stood up. I noticed he was still in his golf clothes from an early morning round.

"You're going with me, aren't you?"

"I'd planned to, but this canal project has put a crimp in my schedule. I've got a state engineer coming here to discuss it this afternoon. Nora can make us lunch, yes?"

Iggy gave me a dry kiss on the cheek.

"But Iggy. I wanted you to be there with me."

"Sorry, Odilia. Got to work on this project. Great work on that barn, darling." He sat down at his desk and began flipping through papers. I ran up the stairs, and stifled a yell, choking back tears, damned if I'd let them run down my cheeks.

★ ★ ★

Irene

I could recognize a woman on the prowl. Maye Marie showed up at the barn opening in a sassy green dress, pale with darker green flowers, a flowing, wide skirt, and red waistband. Her blonde hair was pinned up neatly and a little black purse swung from her arm. She looked like a movie star and Jiggs noticed it, too. His eyes never left her.

We gathered in a little circle to listen to Odilia drone on and on about the Contreras Barn and how wonderfully historic it was and how much work she did to get it into shape. She forgot to mention that we went $459 over budget and were dipping into our reserves to pay for it. There was, of course, her little sign posted on the front wall noting the barn's donation by the

Contreras family and listing "Odilia Delgado, Board Member, Chair of Donations." She sure was keeping the sign company in business.

Jiggs stood close to Maye Marie, and when Odilia mentioned him as the building contractor, he tipped his hat and winked at Maye Marie. That was a signal to me to commence meddling, even though my Jimmy told me to mind my own business.

"Jiggs, we're all going to lunch at the Center Café, if you care to join us," I said, scrunching my new blue pillbox hat down on my head. After Pauline's scrutiny of me at the ladies' lunch, I'd gone shopping. "Maye Marie is coming."

I heard Jimmy groan.

Jiggs tipped his hat and smiled at me, a little too long, and I arched my eyebrows. My Jimmy was handsome, too, but after nineteen years of marriage, I'd quit looking at him that way. And Jimmy had never had that devilish look in his eyes like Jiggs had. I was going to keep an eye on Jiggs.

The Four Queens, Jimmy, and Alvin went to the Center Café and plopped down at a large table in the back. Odilia was particularly prickly and sat as far away from me as possible. I was tiring of her sour moods and when Jiggs joined us, I used the lunch time to grill him like I was Edward R. Murrow.

"So, Jiggs, where are you from?"

"Raton, New Mexico originally. But I've been living in Oak Flats for about twenty-three years."

"Oak Flats is a beautiful place. We went up there last fall, didn't we, Jimmy? Had a nice picnic there. How does your wife enjoy it?" I said. Jimmy kicked me under the table.

"I have never been married, ma'am."

"Oh goodness, I wonder why?" Jimmy kicked me again, harder.

"I guess I get too busy. No time," he said.

"Do you have family there?"

"I have a brother. He and his wife have three children."

"Do you like children?" Jimmy kicked me again.

"Ouch!" I gave Jimmy a look.

"Oh sure. I like them enough."

"No wife and you like children. Strange. How about that?" I said, looking straight at Maye Marie. Jimmy pinched my leg and I let out a small yelp.

"Excuse my wife. She used to work at the newspaper and sometimes she likes to overly question people," Jimmy said. "Persistence is her middle name." Jimmy gave me that "stop talking" look that I knew so well. I ceased interrogating poor Jiggs but still couldn't help having a funny feeling about him.

Maye Marie was shooting rockets out of her eyes at all of us, so we settled down into a regular conversation.

Odilia glared equally at Jiggs and me from the end of the table, stirring her coffee cup as she frowned.

"Why don't you talk about how we're going to get that Iversen house re-done?" she said.

"Why don't we talk about how you stole it," I said, and Jimmy poked me in the ribs. "Well, she did."

"That's for the courts to decide and I can't see how they're going to give that thing back. So we need to get that done. It's going to be a showpiece. Better to concentrate on that than all your other little projects like the ladies' lunches and galas and foo-foo things you do," Odilia said. "My husband, the Senator, agrees."

"Now Odilia, they aren't foo-foo. Those generate money, too," Betty said.

"Not much." Odilia flagged the waitress over. "My potatoes are cold and there's too much salt in them. Can you please get me some others?"

She was more difficult than normal, like something in particular was bothering her. I went back to listening to Jiggs who was relaying tales of his ranch and training thoroughbred horses. He was as charming a man as any I'd seen, perfectly polite—too polite if there was such a thing, but in a masculine way with a slow method of telling stories that made you sit on edge for the ending. Maye Marie's whole face lit up every time she spoke to him. When our meal was over, he insisted on paying, which bound him to my Jimmy forever.

When we left, Maye Marie and Jiggs walked off together and I started to follow them, but Jimmy dragged me away to our car parked on the street.

"You're being a dang snoop," he said.

"I am not. I'm just looking out for Maye Marie. Oh hello." Joyce Dolley and Deborah paraded toward us down the sidewalk, the two of them dressed like bright red robins.

"Hello Irene. So good to see you. We look forward to seeing Pauline again soon," Joyce said, her soft voice floating over the pavement. "We so enjoyed her last month at our pool party. It was last minute, but we were delighted she came."

"At what?" I said. Jimmy opened the car door for me.

"Our pool party. The Saturday before Labor Day. Pauline is an excellent swimmer. It was so much fun, wasn't it Deborah?" Deborah cast her head down, avoiding my puzzled stare.

"Oh, that's wonderful. So glad it turned out well," I said. "Sorry, we've got to get going."

Joyce waved, and I got into the car and burst into tears.

"What's the matter?" Jimmy said, pulling a bandana handkerchief out of his pocket. I blew my nose in it.

"Pauline lied to me. She was supposed to have a day with me on that Saturday. But she told me something serious came up with student government and she had to go. She went to

Deborah's house instead and spent the day with Joyce Dolley." I cried some more tears and wiped my nose.

"Aw, she shouldn't have done that. We'll have a talk with her," Jimmy said.

"She likes Joyce more than she likes me. She's ashamed of me," I said.

"That ain't true," Jimmy said, but I could see the worry on his face. We'd both noticed Pauline being mesmerized by the Dolley family. But we were at a sore loss for ideas to change that.

"Maybe I should quit the museum board and just stay at home," I said. This thought had been rattling in my brain more and more.

"No. That's not the answer. Our daughter needs to learn to tell the truth," he said.

We got home and Jimmy called Pauline on the carpet. She turned dead pale when we told her about seeing the Dolleys.

"I'm sorry. I just wanted to go to that pool party," she said.

"You didn't want to go shopping with me?" I said.

"It's not that. It's just that everyone was going to the Dolley's house, and I didn't want to miss it."

"You hurt your mother. Pretty bad," Jimmy said. "Your ma does everything for you, Pauline. That was a darn ungrateful and shameful thing you did."

He grounded her for the next two weeks. Pauline cried and hugged me. I forgave her but I admit, there was a sinful little piece of me that couldn't wait until she had her own daughter, and she could feel what it was like to be hurt to the bone.

★ ★ ★

A no-good, scoundrel outlaw seemed more likable than my own daughter right then, so I turned my efforts back to Square

Foot Fred's treasure. I made a list of all his known haunts that were still around: the Posse Creek Saloon, the old cabin on Riverbend Road, and the parlor of the now dilapidated Chantilly Hotel. None of these places were exactly swanky. So I wore my old dungarees and wandered into each place, eyeballing every nook and cranny that might hold some treasure. The bartender at the Posse Creek Saloon gave me a dirty look when I started tapping beneath the old bar to try to find a hidden panel and the hotel manager, a smarmy, greasy sort of man, told me to stop trying to upend the floorboards. I wasn't a very good treasure hunter and came home empty-handed except for finding a Texas Ranger lapel pin at the hotel. I didn't want to know why he'd been there. I went home dirty and defeated.

I told Maye Marie about my treasure hunt the next day and she practically fell off her chair when I told her where I'd been.

"You went into the Chantilly Hotel? That place is dangerous!"

"It wasn't so bad. It smelled something awful, but I wore extra cologne so I could sniff myself and not the place," I said. "Besides, they gave me a free 7 Up when I told them what I was doing."

"Ugh, you drank out of one of their glasses. Irene, what will you do next?" Maye Marie shook her head, grinning.

"Hard to say."

Maye Marie had some new life sprung in her, like a lily that opened. Jiggs was in her office regularly, making one excuse or another to be there. Little vases of flowers and boxes of candy began appearing on her desk, but Maye Marie wouldn't give up where they came from. Of course, we needled her.

"Has that Jiggs asked you out yet on a proper date," Odilia said at one of our Four Queens meetings.

"Oh, stop it. That will not happen," she said, but she blushed a bright pink shade.

"That seems odd to me. Why is he charming the socks off you but not doing anything more?" I said. "I think the three of us need to keep an eye on him."

Odilia and Betty nodded in agreement.

"Please," said Maye Marie. "You're all being ridiculous."

Maye Marie deflected us with more budget discussions, so we left it alone.

★ ★ ★

Odilia

The California Court Commission made an announcement in October: Buttonbush was to be awarded the money to build the new state courthouse, a proclamation that came like an icy wind. Money would be awarded in 1952 after the site selection and extensive planning. The county commissioners were over the moon as they hung the chopping block over the museum.

"These buildings require a great expense. Utilizing the property for a higher purpose will be in the plans of the county if the museum board cannot demonstrate fiscal responsibility and sound fundraising plans and success," the chairman of the county commission told us. "We are looking at several locations, but the museum is at the top of the list."

"They're getting serious. It's not funny anymore. We need to raise money," Irene said. "Mostly, we need to work together."

"We're already in the red by $239 this month," Maye Marie reported. "We need revenue."

I tapped my fingers together, thinking hard. What could I build or bring in to raise money? None of us had any good ideas that day and agreed to think about it and come back the next day.

But the next day, Irene and I stood at the front of the museum, arguing as usual. I wanted to replace a rusty iron gate and Irene was against it.

"We don't need a new gate." Irene stomped her foot.

"You are ridiculously short-sighted. Is this what you call working together? This gate is old and needs to go. I think we should ..." I said I but was interrupted by Walt Rogers, a local businessman, who walked up to us. We swung our heads to glare at him.

Walt was well-known in Buttonbush. He made his money by owning lots of property in the shady areas of town where he could charge low rents to people who couldn't afford much. He had run-down hotels, apartments, and houses, and none of them had a decent coat of paint on them or bathrooms that worked well. It didn't seem like a business that could be profitable, but it must have been because Walt threw money around town like a lawn sprinkler. So, lots of folks felt obliged to him. But I knew many didn't like him much, either. He had the soul of a rotten apple, slippery and mean.

"Ladies, I know you're on some kind of committee here. I'm wondering about renting the museum for a gathering," he said with a crooked smile, revealing yellowing, sharp teeth. His hooked nose and balding head gave him the appearance of a hawk.

"We're board members, Walter," I said.

"How nice. What can you tell me?"

"What kind of gathering?" Irene asked.

"Oh, you know, just a group of men who like to get together and talk about politics and business. Important things like that. No ladies allowed, of course! We had a gathering up in Schubert City three months ago and it was very successful," he said, and adjusted his tie with his left hand. "We'll have a barbecue and some other food. It's an important event. We need to keep America pure and we like to plan for that."

Irene, who had a face you could read like the daily newspaper, scrunched up her mouth. I crossed my arms. I'd heard about his group. Men who thought they knew better than anyone how things should be run and they were cruel to those who didn't fit in.

"Well, I'll have to see. I don't know the schedule off the top of my head," I said. "Do you know what date?"

"We'd like it for the twenty-first of October. How's $300 for the full use of the museum that day?" he said. "We're very keen on preserving Buttonbush history so I'm sure that kind of donation would be helpful."

I gulped. Three hundred dollars was a lot of money. But was it worth letting that nasty group use the museum? I was unsure what to say to him but Irene, for once thinking on her feet, nipped it in the bud.

"We're hosting the international women's badminton tournament here that day. October twenty-one," Irene said, and I swiveled my head to look at her, my eyes wide.

"Badminton? International? In Buttonbush? That's strange. I'll have to pay attention to that," he said.

"It's very exciting. We need to go now. Sorry Walt. I'm sure you'll find somewhere to hold your meeting." Irene grabbed my arm and yanked me back into the museum.

"International badminton? What the hell are you talking about?" I had my arms on my hips.

"It was all I could think of. I don't know why. I barely know how to play badminton."

"And international? He's going to find out you lied," I said. "Aren't we supposed to be making money?"

Irene put her hand under her chin and rubbed it.

"He won't know we lied. We're going to do this."

"You've really lost your senses now, Irene." I said and walked away. But over my shoulder I called to her. "But let's not let him on the grounds."

★ ★ ★

Irene

I dialed up Maye Marie right away.

"Walt Rogers wants to rent the museum and it's for one of his group meetings. What are they called?" I said. "But we don't want them here. Odilia and I—hold on to your knickers—are in agreement."

"They're the Righteous Men's Posse and yes, they're bad news," she said.

"Well, I told them we were hosting the women's international badminton tournament."

"You what?"

"I don't know why I said that. Do you know anything about badminton?"

"Oh my goodness, what were you thinking? We don't have any such thing. Did he believe you?"

"I don't think so. Do you think we can set up an international badminton tournament in three weeks?"

Maye Marie shrieked but my wheels were turning. I got the Four Queens together at the museum the next day.

"Well, by right, we should rent the place to anyone who wants to rent it," Odilia said, and I thought she was going to go haywire on me and insist we call Walt back. But she came through.

"They're nothing but a bunch of idiots when they get together, talking about all kinds of awful things," she said. "They don't like anyone who isn't exactly like they are."

"I've got an idea," I said, and we hatched out a plan.

★ ★ ★

Fall never really arrived in Buttonbush. It stayed summer for about seven million days and then we got three minutes of winter. So it was nice and warm on October 21, 1951 when I plastered a giant paper sign over the entry to the museum that said, "International Women's Badminton Tourney," painted in big red letters. We set up four badminton sets on the great lawn in the middle of our museum with a check-in area, judges' platforms, and picnic tables and chairs. Even Carlotta helped. I found some flags in the museum shed although I did not know what country they represented or if they were even for a country at all. They worked well enough for our purposes.

We did our best to make the tournament look international. Betty asked her maid, Anna, and her friend Irma, both Slovenian immigrants, to come play. They showed up in goofy yellow shorts that puffed out like balloons. But they could slam that little birdie across the net like a fighter plane.

I carted in Maria Boni and Gina Allesandro, my Italian immigrant farmer friends who didn't have a clue how to play badminton and kept trying to catch the birdie with their hands.

Odilia invited her two sisters and the whole Gaeta family, a huge group of Mexican immigrants who had a delicious restaurant called Tampico. They didn't know much about badminton, but they were game to try. Their kids ran all over the museum, so much so that I didn't see how those kids could still stand after they'd run up and down the grounds at least fifty times.

I also recruited six Chinese farmers and their families to come into town for the day by promising them beer at the end of the tournament. I had my friend, Ramona, come and wear her father's Spanish hat.

And the Scottish Society sent a couple of women. Not to be unkind but they were beefy women with thick arms and torsos, and they sort of scared me with how hard they could hit that little birdie. They might well have been able to play in an international tournament. The offer of beer also got my Jimmy to show up. And Maye Marie asked the ladies Bible study from the African Methodist Episcopal Church to join us although beer was not a selling point for them. The lemon cookies, however, were.

Everyone brought spectators with them so that there was a friendly crowd of every color, size, and shape scattered across the lawn, with lots of chatter and laughter. After a while, I determined we ought to have the tournament even when we weren't trying to keep old Walt off the grounds. It occurred to me, also, that I was getting dang good at being deceptive.

Long picnic tables lined the perimeter of the field, loaded with every kind of food: chile relleno, lasagna, boiled sausages, sauerkraut, egg rolls, fried okra, corn bread, cabbage rolls, potato salad, chop suey, and Odilia's enchiladas, which were delicious.

With an excuse for needing to check on something at the barn, even Jiggs showed up to watch. Maye Marie bounced around the badminton court just a little bit more when he was there, flouncing around in her little white skirt and flipping up her feet when she went for a birdie.

As the tournament wound down, Walter came storming on to the grounds. I shuddered when I saw him.

"This is your international tournament?" he said, his beady eyes staring at the sweat that was hanging off my forehead.

"Isn't it wonderful? So many people here," I said.

"This doesn't look very organized or official," he said. "Look at these people. They're amateurs."

"Well now, Walter, it's all in the eye of the beholder," I said.

Just then Betty wandered into the conversation, and I could tell she'd had a few nips.

"Why, Walter. How nice of you to come. I know you've been so busy with your new projects and Alvin tells me he's working with you on the finances. So important to have a good relationship with the bank, isn't it," she said, and I swear she sounded like Hedy Lamarr, all sultry and mysterious. Walt gulped. "Here, come sit down and have some food. It's delicious."

Betty yanked his arm so he couldn't refuse and dragged him to the food table. Odilia walked over and began talking to Walt, then wrote something down on a little notepad.

"I got him to donate one hundred dollars for the repairs in the general store," she said to me. "Cheapskate. But at least something good came out of this."

She gave me an ever so small smile.

"You did well to keep him out." Odilia turned and walked away.

Walter stared down at the food, then put his plate down and stomped away. As he was leaving, Estella Gaeta fired a birdie, and it whapped Walter smack in his bald spot. He yelped and I could see a little red mark glowing on his head all the way to the parking lot.

I gathered the other Queens together at the end of the day.

"Do you see what we can do when we work together? We can save this place if we try but we have to work together. Odilia, you can't just go off on your building spree anymore," I said. "It's not working and we're going to lose this place. Look at the good we did today."

She stared hard at me.

"She's right. Odilia, it's time to stop your plans," Betty said.

Odilia gulped.

"I know what you're saying. I still think I'm right. But we need to do something to bail ourselves out. Let's think about it, okay? I'll stop with the building. For a while," she said.

It was the first time in a long time that I'd accomplished something at the museum, in more ways than one. We didn't make any money that day, but we sure did make a lot of friends.

MR. FINI FROM SIOUX CITY

Irene

I couldn't really describe what I thought when Prentice M. Fini strutted in the door of our dingy office at the Buttonbush Museum for an interview with the Four Queens that late October 1951 day. The only thing that came to my head was the word "dandy," which might have been an incorrect description, since I thought dandies were fancy men from the 1800s. He was more of a 1920s sort of dandy, with baggy, pleated pants, a long beige waistcoat, and green bowtie clipped to his peach-colored shirt with a dark brown vest that had some sort of zig-zag design on it. He wore striped socks you could see as his pant legs flopped, and white and brown saddle Oxfords that I hadn't seen a man wear since my Uncle Boone bought some on a lark in Kansas City. His scraggly blond hair poked out beneath a brown derby hat and his pointy face carried a thin mustache above pinched lips. I winced when he walked into the room because his face resembled a woodchuck.

The men on the board had decided that the Four Queens needed to stop running the place and get an actual manager after more than a year without one. I was more frustrated than ever with our lack of shoring up the finances, so I couldn't wait to turn the reigns over to someone else.

"Good afternoon, ladies," he said, and strode over to take a seat right in front of Odilia as he examined us one by one like

I've seen my Jimmy do at the butcher counter when he wants to find a good pork chop but can't.

"Tell us a little about yourself," Betty said, having recovered much faster than the rest of us.

The Four Queens were charged with interviewing candidates for the museum manager's job. With advertisements in not just the *Buttonbush Daily*, but all the way to newspapers in Colorado, New Mexico, Arizona, Nevada, Kansas, Oklahoma, Iowa and Montana, we thought we'd get a good selection of candidates for the job.

The first four were not at all what we were looking for. One sounded like she only wanted to work three days a week, another hadn't bothered to look up any Buttonbush history, and the other two were each dull, timid, unenergetic, and dim.

"I'm so discouraged," Betty said, flopping her head on the table.

"We can always just keep running it ourselves," Odilia said, and the rest of us groaned because we knew Odilia secretly wanted to run the place on her own.

Mr. Fini was a whole different ball of wax.

"I'm from Sioux City where I've been manager, curator, and resident entertainer for the Butler Mansion Museum, a beautiful museum that was in ruinous financial state when I took it over. It simply had to be saved, so I put my pencil to paper and worked out a plan to bring members and donors to the museum for a variety of purposes," Mr. Fini said, without a breath. He drew his leg up over his knee and leaned forward towards Odilia. "I created a magnificent schedule of bringing the wealthy people of Sioux City into the museum for dinners every Tuesday evening. After dinner, I performed for them. I sing and play the piano and accordion, and, well, these events just became the talk of the town.

"Once you get those wealthy people in, you can entice them by having learning days for the children and they love to give money for those types of things, especially if the children are needy and come from less than prosperous homes," he said.

"We already have children's learning days here and …" I said, but he cut me off.

"There are learning days, and then there are properly focused learning days. My plans always include a specific learning skill, such as phonics or arithmetic, in combination with the history lesson. For example, I once orchestrated a Margaret Crary Day, you know, the famous writer from Sioux City. I not only read her stories to the children but I read them my stories which were based on her topics and then I required them to do vocabulary words based on her works and my works. You must give people more than they are expecting, ladies, and you must appeal to their sense of obligation to uplift their children in an educational context. I enjoy that particular skill," he said, clearly pleased with himself for that very detailed account of his focused learning extravaganza.

Betty grinned. Odilia crossed her legs and drummed her fingers on the table.

Maye Marie asked, "Do you know how to prepare a budget?"

"Of course I do. It's a piece of cake for me. A piece of cake." He shrugged and threw his chin up in the air as if she'd offended him.

"What about raising money for this place? What would you do?" I asked. Despite his strangeness, he had some good ideas. "We are under pressure to raise a good amount of money this year."

"As I said, my dinners are very popular with people. The right people. And I would, of course, make my rounds about town to get to know the community and they could get to know me. I love to have presentations, entertaining presentations. As I mentioned, at the Butler I put on an array of entertaining events and I have quite a repertoire of songs—for the tenor voice, which I possess. So right there you have some grand entertainment that you can charge money for, and people will just love it," he said.

I wondered if someone, somewhere, had a bet with him on how many times he could say the word "entertainment."

"You know I have very strong connections with the Buttonbush Country Club, and the Buttonbush Oil Society, and the Petroleum Wives Club. I can provide an introduction to those groups," Odilia said.

"And Irene here knows everyone in the farming business," said Maye Marie.

Mr. Fini just stared.

"You know the county is bearing down on us because of our expenditures. How would you protect the museum from this?" Betty asked.

"Public opinion can highly influence government. I am quite adept at gaining citizen loyalty and mobilizing action. I would most certainly use the museum's fervent supporters as bulwarks against any kind of county onslaught or hindrance," he said. I wasn't sure what he was talking about.

"Mr. Fini, do you know anything about history?" Odilia asked.

"Ladies, I have a vast knowledge of the history of the U.S., and I read constantly. Historical biographies mostly. I've done research on the great ragtime musicians and on surrealism, which I think could be quite popular around here if presented correctly," he said.

"But we're a history museum, Mr. Fini, not an art museum," Odilia said.

"Of course. But surely you ladies realize that all are intertwined. A culture and its history are deeply wedded to its arts and music which tell the story of the times. They give you the very essence of those eras via an impression on all your senses. At the Butler, I was enormously successful at attracting people from miles and miles around who wanted to blend their history with cultural and artistic enrichment. I'm certain you all have been working on this sort of thing as well," he said and we all nodded, even though it was a big old lie to say we'd ever thought of that.

"Those are wonderful insights, just wonderful. You are well prepared to deal with our ill-informed and overbearing county officials," Betty said.

"Have no fear. I've dealt with city and county governments before. They just need to be shown that we are a force to be reckoned with. I have no problem stridently conveying the importance and worth of a museum to government officials," he said.

After he'd gone, the Four Queens went giddy with the thought of this learned and enthusiastic gent taking over the reins of our beloved place, even though there was a generous dose of strangeness to him. My thoughts and feelings for Mr. Fini were as mixed as a fruit salad with turnips and horseradish. Was this the person who was going to save us?

"He's simply perfect. Just perfect." Betty swooned and put her hands to her cheeks.

"He's odd. But he might be able to do the job," Odilia said.

I thought we were acting like the buck tooth girl at the dance, all desperate and such, but I went along with the other three Queens and really, we didn't have anyone any better. We went to the next board meeting and nominated Mr. Fini as our new museum manager.

It was a relief to me. The museum had taken up way too much of my time and I had high hopes that Mr. Fini could save us.

* * *

Odilia

On November 5, 1951 Mr. Fini swept into the museum office. The first thing he did was hand me all my paperwork and files, running me out of my office which I supposed was appropriate, but it bothered me, nevertheless. Over the next few days, the Four Queens had to adjust our habits somewhat. Maye Marie quit going in daily to assess the till for admissions money. Irene typed a list of all the upcoming activities, parties, exhibition openings, invitation lists, menu plans, and decorations and gave it to Mr. Fini, but he didn't look at it. I could tell he didn't appeal to her because he didn't appeal to me either, but I took a deep breath and decided to give him some time. He quite entranced Betty.

I thought leaving him alone for a few days was quite enough, so I went in on Thursday of his first week of work and told him I planned to take him to the Kiwanis Club meeting on the following Tuesday.

"I've already scheduled myself there. No need," he said.

"Well, then I have you booked at the Parker Hills Country Club Ladies Luncheon on the fourteenth. They want you to say a few words about yourself and about the museum," I said.

"I know. I already spoke to a Miss Reynolds there. I'm all set for that."

"Hmmmph. How about the Elks Club barbecue next month?" I was getting a little agitated at his boldness.

"I did not know about that, but I'll make a call. I'd rather do these things on my own, if you don't mind, Mrs. Delgado." Mr. Fini dismissed me by picking up his phone and dialing, waving to me with a crooked smile as I walked out.

"Well, he thinks rather highly of himself," I muttered under my breath. But over the next few weeks he attended the

Library Guild annual breakfast, the Buttonbush Cattlemen's Hoedown Supper, the pancake breakfasts at the Presbyterian, Catholic, Baptist, and Lutheran churches, two meetings of the Buttonbush Cooperative Extension, the Ladies of Oil Auxiliary, Buttonbush Kiwanis Club, and the 4-H meeting at the Grange. He also got himself invited to supper at the homes of some wealthy Buttonbush folks. He was everywhere except at the museum. And so far, he hadn't walked away with any money from anyone, a situation I was watching closely. Irene and I had daily phone calls about what he was doing as she was as skeptical of him as I was. It was finally something that we could agree on.

★ ★ ★

Irene

Mr. Fini was the sole topic of conversation when I arrived at Betty's house to pay a call on her mother who was visiting again.

"How wonderful that you've hired someone so cultured and dignified," Mrs. Shellman said. Betty had apparently given her every detail of his activities and her mother seemed pleased, which pleased Betty.

"He's kind of different," I said. "Not exactly the kind of person I would have pictured for the job."

"It sounds as if he's bringing new ideas and refined culture to Buttonbush. Surely that's a commendable effort." Mrs. Shellman raised her eyebrows at me as if daring me to disagree.

"We'll see. I haven't quite figured out yet if we've got ourselves a pretty, wrapped package with nothing but a dead gopher inside," I said.

"Really!" Mrs. Shellman gasped.

"There's a veterans salute today, Mother, and Mr. Fini has some wonderful entertainment planned," Betty said, pouring more coffee for her mother.

"Veterans from all over the county should be there," I said. "Are you coming, Mrs. Shellman? My mother and my son will be there."

"No, I don't think so. I'm not feeling all that well. But please do remember your brother in that salute, Bettina. We cannot forget his sacrifice." Mrs. Shellman fanned herself.

"I will. I'll tell you all about it."

Mrs. Shellman got up from the table and quickly left the room. Betty sighed and I patted her hand.

"She'll be okay someday. It takes a long time to get over losing someone. Especially a child," I said.

★ ★ ★

"Where's Mr. Fini?" Betty asked when we arrived at the museum. Felicia said she hadn't seen him all day. "Where are our volunteer ladies?"

"Mr. Fini said we didn't need to use them anymore. We could handle it ourselves. That's how they do it in Sioux City," Felicia said, brushing the sweat from her forehead as she poured tea into glass pitchers. "Iowa, good lord."

Predictable as ants at a picnic, Carlotta had done minimal work on the exhibit, putting only a few photographs, a couple of medals in glass boxes, three framed newspaper articles, one bugle, and two pistols on display. I knew there were at least seventeen military uniforms and loads of weapons in the collection buried in the basement.

Mr. Fini waltzed through the door at four o'clok, just as the bulk of families were arriving. He swayed side to side, meandering down the hallway to the exhibit hall. His arms reached out like Jesus at the Sermon on the Mount, as if he thought all the crowd would rush towards him.

Wearing his usual bow tie, baggy pants, and saddle shoes, he'd chosen to wear a Panama hat, stuck sideways on his head.

"He looks glorious," Betty said.

"Welcome, welcome everyone. Welcome Buttonbush citizens," he bellowed as he entered the room, and old Clyde Perkins startled, like he thought there was an incoming mortar shell.

"We're so happy you are here. Welcome veterans and their families. I'm Prentice M. Fini, most recently from the Butler Museum in Sioux City, Iowa, and I'm so happy to see all of you."

He beckoned Felicia over, and she appeared carrying a ukulele. Odilia, Maye Marie, and I gave Betty a quizzical look.

"I thought since we are celebrating World War I and your great service, I'd do a few little songs for you to remind you of that time. Such a courageous time. A patriotic time," Mr. Fini said then began strumming the ukulele and singing "K-K-K-Katy."

Hank and Howard Speller started laughing in the back and Colonel Prendergast spit a lemon seed out the side of his mouth and coughed. But Betty swayed to the music, transfixed by Mr. Fini and his ukelele.

"Mother thinks he's just what we need," she whispered to Maye Marie.

Mr. Fini's voice was rather off-key, even I with not much of an ear for music could hear that. It wasn't exactly off but just a hair which made it all the more painful and he had a habit of jerking his head quickly from side to side when he finished a stanza.

I'll be waiting at the k-k-k-kitchen door. Whoosh!

I wondered if I could refrain from laughing if his head flew off his skinny neck.

Odilia yanked my arm.

"Did you tell him he could do this?"

"Me? No. I don't tell him anything," I said in a hiss.

"Hush, you two. He's going to sing 'My Buddy' now," Betty said, and both Odilia and I groaned. Willy and Ma scooted next to us.

"It's hard to watch a woodchuck sing," I said, and Maye Marie giggled. Betty hushed her, too. Mr. Fini swayed his shoulders from side to side, his eyes tightly shut as he warbled. He wasn't that bad, but he wasn't that good, either.

"Mom, he's kind of strange," Willy said.

Mr. Fini's face scrunched in determination to convey the heartfelt love in the song but when he sang the word "buddy" it sounded funny.

"Is he saying 'my body'? because that's just weird, Mom," Willy said.

"It's 'buddy,' Willy. Not body. Let's remember to be kind. We can't ..." I said, but Ma interrupted me.

"Willy's right. He's stranger than a chicken in a church," Ma said. "He looks kind of like ..."

"A woodchuck?" I said, and we both stifled a laugh.

"Quiet!" Betty hissed.

"I thought this was a veteran's salute. Do I have to stay here and listen to this?" Willy whispered.

"You have to stay. I didn't know he was going to do this," Irene said.

"I thought you were the boss here," Willy said.

Mr. Fini sang three more songs and by then most of the veterans had shuffled out the back door.

"That was wonderful Mr. Fini, just wonderful," Betty said, and I snuck up close to her, sniffing to see if she'd had a nip of the old gin.

"How much did you drink?" I said to Betty.

"I didn't drink at all, Irene. Honestly."

Betty turned to chat with Mr. Fini.

"Thank you, Mrs. Davenport," he smiled, and Betty beamed. A few other older ladies also gathered around him, praising his singing with giggly voices and melodic murmurs.

"You know you're supposed to just introduce the exhibit and let people look around Mr. Fini," Odilia said, and he turned on her with a sour frown.

"People love entertainment. This is what we did in Sioux City. They enjoy it more when they attend these types of things and there's not only an exhibit but lively music. Plenty of time to see the exhibit. Why look, they're all viewing it now," he said, pointing to the six stragglers left in the room.

When it was over, the Four Queens met in the parking lot for a little discussion.

"What the hell does he think he's doing?" Odilia said.

"Did you see the Spellers? I thought they were going to fall over laughing when he sang," I said.

"Why he's so cultured, and he's showing all the things they did in Sioux City that were so marvelous and successful," Betty said, hands on hips. "You all knew he was an entertainer in Sioux City."

"This isn't Sioux City, Betty," Odilia growled.

"But he's written books on arts and entertainment. Music. He's quite accomplished. I think we're fortunate to have attracted someone so versatile to Buttonbush, " Betty said.

"I don't think we quite knew what he meant by entertainer," Maye Marie said. "I guess it's our fault for not questioning him more about that."

"We keep trying to tell him that Buttonbush is different. Folks expect different things here, Betty. He's acting like he can just come in here and change everything. That's not what we want in Buttonbush, is it?" I asked, but Betty, Mr. Fini's biggest fan, gave me a nasty frown.

★ ★ ★

Mr. Fini was shining his beige Oxfords at his desk the next day, whisking back and forth as his yellow-sock-covered feet gripped the floor, when he informed me he'd scheduled himself to go before the county commissioners on Monday.

"Do they have some sort of vote coming up about the museum?"

"No. But they need to realize what I'm doing here. I want them to have a clear picture of all the good I'm doing for the museum to keep it stable and financially sound," he said.

This development terrified me. After his ukelele performance at the veterans' event, I was nervous about what he might do in front of the county commissioners. I called the other Queens. The following Monday, we crept into the commissioners' chambers, which was full of people, to see what Mr. Fini was going to do. The four of us sat in the back row, hoping no one would notice us. Mr. Fini was not in the room.

We listened to the commissioners drone on about sewer problems, misaligned property lines around the tax assessor's office building and difficulties hiring a dog catcher. Then the county clerk called for Mr. Fini.

"Our next presenter is Prentice M. Fini, manager of the Buttonbush Museum."

Right then, Mr. Fini burst into the room wearing a red, white, and yellow striped cowboy hat with a chin strap on his head, a yellow feather sticking out from the brim. He wore a blue and black plaid jacket and red pants, white and black Oxfords with red pom-poms attached. He was carrying his ukulele. The commissioners were at first stunned, then a few laughed.

"Hello, hello Buttonbush County commissioners," Mr. Fini shouted. The chairman tapped his gavel.

"Mr. Fini, you have, er ... five minutes to present to us," he said.

"Excellent," said Mr. Fini, and he began strumming the ukulele.

Oh, you beautiful doll... Mr. Fini sang, his lips in a semi-smile as he nodded to the commissioners, each of whom looked like they wanted to run out the room.

The Four Queens were trying to crawl under our seats at this point. At least three of us were. Betty tapped her toes and bounced her head. It was downright painful to watch. Finally, he finished the song.

"Ladies and gentlemen of the commission. As you can see, entertainment attracts people. It's what people want. And this is what we're doing at the Buttonbush Museum. Weaving history with entertainment is how we plan to entice many more Buttonbush citizens to visit the museum to enjoy a day or evening of entertainment and education. History and art," he said. "Do you see how easily you were entertained just now with a simple song? Why, I will do things like this all the time at the museum, and I guarantee we will see throngs more coming through the door. People will be lined up to get into the museum. That is why you need to reconsider your courthouse plans, because the museum will be just too vivacious for you to pare down."

None of the commissioners spoke for a few seconds, and finally one cleared his throat.

"Thank you, Mr. Fini, for that very ... um, interesting song and performance. I'm sure we'll see more of you at the museum.

We will consider your points," he said, his face nearly bursting. "Just make sure you're making some money over there."

Mr. Fini took a slow bow and sashayed out the door. The Four Queens waited a few minutes and slipped out of the back.

"Wasn't he just stupendous?" Betty said. The three of us stared at her.

"Stupendous! How about stupid?" Odilia whipped her head in my direction. "You're supposed to be in charge of our public appearances and our entertainment. Why did you let him do this?"

"Me! I didn't know anything about this … I don't know what in the hell he was trying to do there, but that was overly embarrassing," I said.

"You're all being very narrow-minded. He's trying to do something different. Bring people in. Become a cultural center. Haven't you been saying that we need to do more at the museum, Irene? Haven't we talked about needing the money from admissions and events to strengthen our financial position?" Betty argued.

"This wasn't quite what I had in mind," I said. "I don't think this is going to appeal to most Buttonbush folks."

"That's shortsighted and negative. We need to give him a chance," Betty said. "Let's see what he can accomplish before we tar and feather him."

For the next week, Jimmy sang "Oh, You Beautiful Doll" to me at every opportunity until I pelted him in the head with a potato. I, for one, had grave doubts about anyone whose best friend is a ukulele.

WHY NOT THE MOSQUITO ABATEMENT DISTRICT?

Irene

Ma had an unsettling gleam in her eye when she and Pa came over the first Sunday in December.

"I think I can solve all your problems," she said, straightening a doily on my mahogany table. Pa looked away and shuffled his feet. A sure sign of impending doom.

"What problems?" I said. "Do I have a problem?"

"Your problems with the museum and all the time it takes you ... and your burning desire to do something more than just be a wife and mother, although for the life of me I can't figure why you don't ..."

Pa cut her off.

"Now, dear, get to the point."

"You know your father is in charge of the Mosquito Abatement District. And he needs some office help. Not a full-time job, but just a few hours a day, answering phones, taking messages, typing notices ... things like that," Ma said. "So we thought ..."

"You thought I'd like to work at the Mosquito Abatement District?"

I jumped to my feet, pacing the room.

"Was this your idea?" I stared at Pa. He looked as assertive as a deboned chicken.

"Your mother said you might be interested, so I said we had a little need for help."

"I knew it! Ma! You don't need to get me jobs and send me to things you think are better than what I'm doing. I'm doing what I want."

"At least you'd get paid for working at the Mosquito Abatement District. Not like the museum," she said. "Maybe Pauline wouldn't be spending so much time at the Dolleys."

"Ma, you need to stay out of my business!" Her commentary stung deep, and I held back tears.

"You're always running off ... No one knows where you are. At least we could find you at the Mosquito Abatement District," Ma said. "And it wouldn't be so much time."

"I'm doing just fine as I am. I can be a wife and mother and do the museum," I said.

"Do you think that's true, Irene?" Ma said, and my hair lit on fire.

I stomped out of the room. Jimmy came to find me in the kitchen.

"It's okay, honey. She means well. You're doing good things over at that museum and it makes you happy, so I'm right there with you," he said, and I hugged that dear man.

"The Mosquito Abatement District!" I said. "We could use the money, I guess."

"We're doing fine. The potato deal was pretty good this year and prices for alfalfa are up."

I took a deep breath.

"But Pauline and Willy ... maybe I'm neglecting them."

"You ain't doing that at all."

"Maybe I should do something more ... normal. Answer phones for the district," I said.

"Nah, I hear it's a fly-by-night job," Jimmy said, and I laughed as I laid my head on his shoulder.

★ ★ ★

Odilia

Over the next few weeks there were rumors swirling all over town about the county coffers. Someone had embezzled from the library funds and there was ridiculously over-budget spending by the county sheriff. The powers that be were scrutinizing the museum ledgers. The *Buttonbush Daily* ran a front-page article listing all the county department budgets and financial information, and the museum was in it, looking none too good.

Iggy made it worse.

"The citizens of Buttonbush need accountability for these expenditures. I am particularly noting the sheriff's department and the museum for being greatly overspent. This surely needs the attention of our county commissioners," he was quoted as saying. "The museum board can't even seem to balance a budget and the Bosworth and Iversen houses sit in disrepair."

Iggy sat at the breakfast table buttering a piece of toast when I stormed into the kitchen shaking the newspaper at him.

"How could you say this? You've made us look terrible. You've made me look terrible." The curlers in my hair shook along with my head.

"It's just the truth, Odilia dear. You are not managing that museum well." Iggy took a long sip of his coffee then set it down to add more cream. "You need to find the money to finish those two houses."

"You sound just like that ninny Irene."

"Great minds and all, you know, dear." Iggy cracked his hard-boiled egg and began peeling off the shell one tiny piece at a time. "She's right and I'm right."

"Do you even consider that what you do might impact me? You used to pay attention to me, Iggy. You used to care about what I was doing and how I felt." I said more than I wanted to say, sputtered out more emotion than I wanted him to see.

"Odilia, that's because you used to behave like a wife. Like a woman. Now you're just running around trying to be a man. So I'm treating you like one. What I do is based purely on sound thinking and policy choices. Not emotion." He put his knife down and reached for the butter.

"I'm your wife."

"Maybe you should act like a wife," he said, not looking up.

"I might if you were ever here. If you weren't up in Sacramento doing whatever you are doing with whoever you are doing it with."

"I don't know what you're implying, but I go up to Sacramento to get the job of the state done. That requires time and attention. You knew that when you married me." He dabbed at his lips with his napkin.

"I did know that. But I sure as hell didn't know a lot of other things. I thought you'd at least respect me."

"Your tone and attitude are becoming tiresome. I'm finished talking to you." Iggy picked up the newspaper and raised it over his face, cutting off his view of me.

I screamed and ran out of the room. That man had completely forsaken me. He wanted a delicate little flower, a submissive, traditional woman, and I was just not that anymore. I knew that, in actuality, I never was.

* * *

Irene

It may have been the sharp odor of permanent wave solution or maybe it was the tight curlers in my hair that might have been pulling my brain in all directions, but not for the first time an idea came to me at the beauty shop. I was thinking about that damn newspaper article and what we could do to bolster our finances when Glenda Dewberry walked in.

"Irene, I've been thinking about you and Square Foot Fred."

"Did you remember anything more about him? I still haven't found a clue," I said, pulling the dryer off my head and patting the pink rollers.

"No, but I mentioned him to my cousin, Katie. She said Aunt Viola used to say terrible things about him, but when she died, they found love letters from her to him that were never sent. Katie said one letter mentioned that Square Foot Fred had been sweet on Suzanna Edwards and had spent time with her after leading on poor Aunt Viola. She never forgave him," Glenda said. "You know, you never think of your old auntie as having had a romance, or a broken heart or anything like that, do you?"

"No … you sure don't," I said. "Wait, Suzanna Edwards? Of the Oscar Edwards family?"

"I think so."

"Hot dang! Thanks Glenda, I grabbed my pocketbook and started to bolt out the door when Glenda hollered.

"Irene, your hair!"

***

Romance was on my mind when I gathered Maye Marie and Betty and Odilia with me the following day at the Edwards House at the museum and told them about the love affair between Square Foot Fred and Suzanna Edwards.

"And just our luck, we have the Edwards House where Suzanna grew up, right here in the museum. Remind me not to complain so much about all these buildings, will you?" I said.

"Oh, that will surely not happen," said Odilia.

"Maybe ... just maybe those gold coins are here somewhere. I'll bet no one even looked here," I said. "Square Foot Fred might have given them to Suzanna for safekeeping. This might save the museum and Odilia. We need to save it. Together."

"I know we do. Let's see if this crazy idea pays off," she said, unusually compliant. She looked tired.

I opened the front door and crept in.

"Fred must have been quite a ladies' man, although I saw a picture of him and he wasn't much in the looks department, at least in my opinion. Who knows how many hearts he broke around California while he was botching all those robberies," I said.

"Why wouldn't he take the treasure back? Did he ever marry Suzanna?" Maye Marie said.

"No, he got hauled off to the hoosegow in about 1869. For the fourth time," I said.

"But surely they looked this house over when they moved this here ... what, thirty years ago?" Maye Marie said.

"Maybe, maybe not," I said. "Let's try it."

The Edwards House was a simple house but with a sprawling farmhouse kitchen, a cheery oak paneled dining room, three bedrooms, and a cozy parlor. We tapped on walls, prodded closets, looked for loose paneling, even gently poked the ceiling with a broomstick to see if anything gave. We spent four hours scouring the house that day, then came back the next day for more, working quietly so Carlotta would not get wind of our search. Even Odilia got herself dirty looking for that dang treasure.

"Keep looking, ladies," I said, and Betty brushed her hair back from her sweating forehead, despite the December chill.

I was sticking the broom up the fireplace, looking for loose bricks, when Carlotta burst through the door.

"What are you four doing in here?" she shouted. I jumped back from the fireplace and pretended to sweep the floor.

"Never mind us, Carlotta. We're just cleaning," I said.

"You are not. You're looking for that stupid treasure, aren't you? How many times do I have to tell you ... look here, give me that broom. You're doing more harm than good," Carlotta lurched over to grab the broom from me and I scooted back, my arm pulling the broom backwards so she couldn't get it.

"Stop it, Carlotta!" I hollered.

The stick end of the broom hit the old grandfather clock that stood behind me and a loud popping sound emanated from the bottom. Carlotta screeched, and I turned around to see a large wooden panel from the clock on the ground, and a hole appearing in the interior of the clock.

"Look what you've done now." Carlotta stormed over to the clock then stopped dead still.

"What is it?" I said and bent over to look in the hole. There sat a wooden box, about the size of three shoe boxes put together.

"Don't touch anything," Carlotta said. "I need my gloves. I mean it. Touch nothing. I'll be right back."

She ran from the room.

The Four Queens sat on the porch steps of the house in giddy anticipation.

"Do you think that's it? The treasure?" Betty said.

"Don't get your hopes up," Maye Marie said, but I was tapping my fingers together. What a story it would be if Square Foot Fred saved the museum.

Carlotta appeared with her white gloves and we all went inside the house. She pulled on the box.

"It's heavy," she said.

She tugged at it and when it pulled out of the clock, she almost dropped it on the ground.

The initials "FW" were carved on the box.

"Square Foot Fred!" I said.

"Fred Watlington," Carlotta said.

She tried to lift the lid, but the box was locked.

"The key, Carlotta! Go get that key," I said.

She gave me a disgusted look and went out the door, returning in a few minutes with the old key we'd found in the top hat. She put it in the lock and the box popped open.

"Hot dang!" I said.

The Four Queens scooted closer and bent our heads over the box in a huddle. We peered inside the old box and I gasped.

"Are those gold bricks?" I asked, my heart pounding in my chest.

"Looks like. They look heavy," Odilia said. The bricks were nestled in a bed of old cloth, yellowed with age and ragged at the ends. A small piece of paper sat folded on top one of the bricks.

"Look at that!" Maye Marie said.

"You were right," Betty said and patted me on the shoulder. Odilia, for once, was speechless.

"I'll be danged," I said. "But I thought he had coins. Not gold bricks. Maybe there are coins somewhere, too …"

"Don't get carried away," Carlotta said.

"Read the note, Carlotta." I stretched my neck to look over her shoulder to peek at the note.

Carlotta carefully unfolded the fragile paper. I could see scratchy handwriting on the page.

> *My dearest Suzanna: I've left this in your generous keeping. If I should perish in my endeavors, please enjoy the riches and comfort this may bring you. Our love will endure, even if I don't. Yours forever, Fred.*

The four of us broke into a string of chatter and laughter that echoed up to the roof of the house. We were squawking and babbling about how we were going to save the museum from the clutches of the courthouse.

"I need to take this to a gold assayer and find out what it's worth," Carlotta said. "This is not the gold coins you've been talking about."

The Four Queens stood with our arms around each other, even Odilia, as Carlotta lugged the gold bricks out, all of us filled with hope for what it could bring to the museum. We were in a tizzy, trying to estimate the great wealth we'd stumbled upon and what we might do with it.

"Maybe I should call the newspaper. This is a great story. It's a genuine treasure hunter's story," I said. "And we can stop the courthouse."

"Just like *King Solomon's Mines*," Betty said. "Except that was fiction. We're real treasure hunters!"

It was as giddy as we'd ever been.

I should have known better, but I ran into the museum office and called up the newspaper to tell my old editor about our find.

"Women treasure hunters find lost treasure of Square Foot Fred." The newspaper ran an article the next day, waxing on about how the treasure was going to save the museum from destruction. The Four Queens were walking on air thinking we'd found the answer to our financial woes.

Three days later, Carlotta served up the cure for happiness.

"Looks like Fred, once again, bungled it," said Carlotta when she called the Four Queens to come to the museum to give us a report on the gold bricks.

"How?" I said feeling a cloak of disappointment was about to land on me.

"These bricks are made from those seventh-century coins that Fred supposedly stole. They would have been worth hundreds of thousands of dollars but …" Carlotta said.

"I knew it!" I said. For once, I'd out-relic-ified Carlotta. I made up that word in my head.

"Hundreds of thousands!" Maye Marie practically spat it out.

"But they're not. They're almost worthless. Fred melted the coins down, making them lose all their value. The value was in the coins," Carlotta said.

My face fell like Ma's support hose on a hot day.

"That idiot melted his fortune into nothing?" Odilia said, looking at me.

"They're worth about $514," Carlotta said. "It's not nothing but it will not save us."

I hung my head. All that work to find a treasure no one else had ever found, and it was peanuts. It was just another one step forward, two steps back for me at that museum.

"Stupid Fred," I muttered as I drove home. "Stupid me."

The *Buttonbush Daily* ran another story about our disappointing find, poking fun at us and poor old Square Foot Fred.

Treasure hunt at museum a bust. Square Foot Fred melts away fortune.

Once again, I was a laughingstock and Pauline and my sister, in equal measure, reminded me of it for days.

THE JIGGS IS UP

Irene

The best part of the St. Aloysius Parish Jamboree was that Mr. Fini was out of town and wouldn't be there.

The church rented the museum grounds for a family barbecue every March where most everyone in town attended. The Four Queens were no exception and gathered at the front of the museum to peruse the event.

"Mr. Fini is doing nothing but attending parties and dinners around town. He hasn't brought any money in," Odilia said, never stopping a moment to enjoy the festivities. She was still griping when my head shot up.

"Lookie there," I punched Maye Marie in the arm.

There was Jiggs sauntering down the main museum road, in a fancy white cowboy hat, and looking as handsome as any movie cowboy. Maye Marie straightened her shoulders and patted her hair. Jiggs didn't notice us but headed our way, his head high above the noise. As he passed by the general store building, a familiar blonde head popped up. Clemmie St. Onge stepped in front of Jiggs and we could hear her sing-song voice.

"Jiggs, I'm over here. I wasn't sure you'd come after I kept you out so late at the picture show last week." Clemmie's yellow hair floated in the breeze as she talked. "I missed you, sugar. Come on, let's go get some fried chicken."

Clemmie hooked her arm in Jiggs' arm and pushed him forward. He waved to us as they walked past with Clemmie still chattering. Maye Marie's face was still.

"That no good chiseler!" said Odilia, and Betty put her hand on her hip. We circled around Maye Marie as Jiggs brought a plate of chicken over to Clemmie, smiling at her while she continued to talk.

"So much for Percy LeRude. They look pretty damn chummy," I said. I knew there was something up with Jiggs. He was just a little too handsome.

"Who cares what Jiggs does?" Maye Marie said. But her eyes were clouded and her top lip trembled. We grabbed her arms and dragged her for a stroll through the museum, trying to get her to play lawn croquet or throw pennies in a bottle. She was having none of it and stayed quiet. We wandered over to the museum pavilion to get some iced tea where, unfortunately, we spotted Jiggs holding Clemmie's hand as they sat listening to a banjo group.

"Enough of this," Odilia said, and dragged Maye Marie towards the outside parking lot. There were several baseball fields next to the museum, so we headed over there where Jiggs wouldn't see us. We stood at the edge of the outfield, huddled together in solidarity for poor Maye Marie, guzzling our iced teas like they were beer.

"Never mind him. He wasn't any good for you, anyway." Betty said. "What a reprobate. Is there a bar here?"

"It's a church party, Betty!" Maye Marie said.

"Right. I forgot." Betty put her hand to her chin. "Sorry, Maye Marie."

"I don't care. What makes you think I care who he sees?" Maye Marie said, and we all patted her shoulders.

"You can't ever trust an overly handsome man anyway," Odilia said. "They're completely despicable."

We continued our assault on Jiggs's character when something knocked into me from behind and I fell forward, my iced tea splashing all over Maye Marie's white blouse.

"What in the hell ... Oops, sorry," I said, remembering I was at a church get-together. I turned and there was Arky O'Dell, Jimmy's Rye High School classmate—and Odilia's for that matter. A hulking hardware store owner and former college football star, Arky had a baseball glove on his left hand and a startled look on his face. He was sweating top to bottom but grinning as he eyed his glove.

"Hey there Irene, sorry, geez ... I guess I ran into you. I was trying to catch the pop-up fly and look ... well, I got it." He tossed the ball in the air, grabbed it with his right hand and fired it back to the pitcher's mound. "Hi Maye Marie. You sure look pretty."

Arky took his ball cap off and nodded at Maye Marie. He smiled at Betty, then spotted Odilia.

"Oh, hello Odilia." His face turned serious.

"Good Lord, Arky, you're still a bull in a china shop," Odilia said. Arky shrugged and tucked his chin down.

"Oh, for heaven's sake, Arky, look what you've done to me," Maye Marie said, frantically wiping the tea off her blouse and her skirt.

"Cripes, I'm such a lunkhead," he said, and pulled a large handkerchief out of his back pocket.

"What are you doing?" Maye Marie jumped back when Arky started patting her down, pressing the handkerchief on the wet spot on her chest.

"Maye Marie, I'm sorry. I just wanted to help clean up your pretty dress." Arky chewed on the top of his baseball glove like a chastened child. "I owe you, I do."

"Never mind. This day couldn't get any worse," she said, and stomped off.

We walked back into the museum where we spotted Jiggs and Clemmie sitting on a picnic bench. Clemmie was talking, using quick hand gestures and patting his leg now and then. I glared at him, and he must have felt it because he looked up and saw me. I gave him the stink eye and, surprisingly, he smiled. A genuine, friendly smile, as if he had no indication in his mind that his flirtations with Maye Marie might come into question by him parading around with Clemmie on his arm. I marveled at his ability to misunderstand himself so very much.

"I need to go clean up. And I have a headache. I'm going home," Maye Marie said, and she took off down the path to the parking lot.

★ ★ ★

Over the next few weeks, we all noticed that Maye Marie didn't come by the museum much and when I'd call her, she'd get off the phone as quick as possible. Betty and Odilia didn't fare any better with her. It was heartbreaking. She was so nice, so sincere and so obviously lonely. That Jiggs had just tickled her heart and walked away, and I wanted to pinch his nose off. We all hoped she would come out of her blue mood soon. Besides, we all needed her to participate in our disliking Mr. Fini as much as we did, which was pretty much all we talked about then. Except for Betty, of course.

What bothered me the most about Mr. Fini was not his strangeness but his lack of interest in learning about the Four Queens, or about Buttonbush. We'd been holding the place together for a long time, but he never asked what any of the Four Queens did around the museum or what we had done in the past that would indicate we were useful people. He had no idea that Maye Marie was broken in two when her Daniel died in the Pacific or that she was an ace bookkeeper. He never bothered to find out that Odilia churned out cargo ships during the war, plus made sure forty-seven women under her watch didn't get hurt or killed doing it. He never knew Betty went to Bryn Mawr where she won two poetry contests and graduated with honors. And he never learned that I spent my earlier years as a newspaper assistant and knew loads about agriculture, plus every farmer in the county. And he showed no interest in the fact that Buttonbush farmers fed a good portion of the nation and the local oil business powered cars everywhere. He just didn't care unless it happened in Sioux City, Iowa. It all made me both mad and sad.

Frustrated with lack of anything I could do to help the situation, I fortunately received some responses from various museums and galleries about returning relics to them, and most agreed to pay for mailing costs. I spent a good amount of time packaging up old items and mailing them off all over the country. Carlotta was busy with all of Odilia's projects, so she didn't know the half of what I was doing, which worked out well for me. It was all stuff we didn't need. The British group also asked for the locket and love letters but didn't send a payment. I shipped it anyway.

Mr. Fini hadn't done any planning for the gala which was scheduled for April. In fact, he hadn't done much of anything except go to dinner everywhere in town. I took it upon myself to organize a committee. I was tiring of waiting around for everyone else to do something and tired of fighting Odilia and Carlotta. Teenage hellion Pauline was driving me crazy at home, insisting that I let her drive out to Rye Lake with her girlfriends for an overnight camp out and screeching because "Tommy Niksich was so gorgeous" and he'd asked her to the dance. She'd forgotten my birthday, and I was cross and short-tempered with her. A fact which she barely noticed. I asked her to come help me set up for the gala, but she was busy, no surprise to me.

I'd named the gala "Moonlight and Satin," which sounded pretty fancy to me. We needed to raise at least five hundred dollars from it, and we had over one hundred people coming, an attendance rate down from our last gala. Betty and I joined a few volunteers to string the yards of satin material across the ceiling of the great hall. We hauled out the big ladders and she and I spent two hours draping the material across the room, propping it up with fishing line I'd stolen from my Jimmy's tackle box. The workers, as usual, were busy with Odilia's priorities and I fumed inside over that. Maye Marie came in later and I set her on making the sparkly stars and moons to glue to the satin.

We set up the tables and chairs, and Felicia covered the tables with a lacy white fabric that we bought for cheap at Dempsey's last year. We added candles and little white paper flowers that the children made in art camp. Betty, Maye Marie, and I spent the afternoon with heads and backs bent up on ladders, gluing stars and moons to the satin. I was hot and sweaty by the time I needed to get ready for the party. I sped home to change clothes, then came back with Jimmy.

We hadn't seen Mr. Fini all day.

Ten minutes before the first guests showed up, Mr. Fini came through the back door wearing a white tuxedo jacket with black pants, a bright red cummerbund, and a red carnation in his lapel that contrasted sharply with his pasty face. He wasn't wearing a hat, and his slicked back hair had something shiny in it.

"Hello ladies," he bellowed, barely glancing at us.

"What a beautiful night this will be! Are the musicians here? I'd like to go over their set up," he said, twirling around the room. He disappeared into the back, not bothering to wait to hear our answer.

Folks began arriving soon after that and Mr. Fini stood in the foyer with the Four Queens, greeting the guests as if he'd planned the entire evening.

"I had no idea you ladies obtained so many wonderful auction items," Mr. Fini said to the four of us.

"You'd know that if you bothered to pay attention to what we were doing." Odilia flounced off to pester another donor for more money.

"Oh, Odilia." Betty patted Mr. Fini's arm. "Don't mind her."

Near the end of the event, Mr. Fini gave a beautiful speech, long though it was, and Betty swooned like a dying swan.

"Good Lord," I said to Maye Marie when it ended and we started to clean up. "What a windbag. Did we make any money?"

"We did. Not quite the five hundred we needed to make but we're close. Four hundred thirty-seven dollars." Maye Marie crossed her arms and shivered. "I think quite a few people didn't attend because they're not thrilled with Mr. Fini."

As usual, the Four Queens and anyone we could corral jumped in to clean up. Jimmy was dog tired from a full day's work, but I got him to help load the tables and chairs. Alvin was a delicate sort so I wasn't sure he could do much, but he swept the floor. Odilia and I cleared the tables. Maye Marie climbed up a ladder to tear down the satin. I was hauling a load of glassware into the kitchen when I bumped into Mr. Fini. He had his briefcase and umbrella in his hands. I had my dress hitched up and my feet ached. A tray of dirty glassware perched on my middle as I bent to pick up a stray napkin.

"Do you need help?" he asked, putting the umbrella and briefcase down.

"Sure," I said, and let him take the tray from me. He put it on the kitchen countertop. I stooped down to grab the napkin and when I stood up, he was holding his briefcase and umbrella again.

"Good night," he said with a nod of his head.

My mouth may or may not have hung open, I'm not sure. But I know I just stared at him. With that he walked out, past Maye Marie up on a ladder, Alvin out back loading leftover liquor bottles into the car, Odilia crawling on the floor picking up shards from a broken glass, Felicia and Jimmy breaking down the tables and chairs, Kosta heaving several trash cans around the room and loading them with paper and empty liquor bottles, Betty coming out of the men's room carrying a trash can and nine other volunteers helping to clean up.

"I'll see all of you later. Good evening," he said, and was gone into the winter night. You could have heard a pin drop.

The four of us huddled in the back of the kitchen two hours later, after we'd cleaned everything up.

"He left! He just left!" Maye Marie said.

"My Jimmy spent all day out on the farm and has to get up tomorrow at four to do it again, and that man walked out on all of us cleaning up. I've never seen such an arrogant buffoon." I could have spit nails.

"I can't defend him on this," said Betty, her mouth downcast. "I still think he had some fine ideas about entertainment and activities. But a leader doesn't just walk out when there are responsibilities to fulfill."

And that right there, is what prompted the Four Queens, even Betty, on that very next Monday to call a special meeting of the board. Despite the protests from the male board members, who thought we were all crazy, the Four Queens stood their ground and made them vote to show Mr. Fini the door. We let the men call him in and tell him he was being fired because not one of the Four Queens ever wanted to set eyes on Mr. Fini again. Because you could have lots of great ideas and you could make a lot of grand plans and proclaim your ambitions. You could even sing at the top of your lungs. You could do a lot of things in Buttonbush, but the one thing you just couldn't do was walk out when there was work to be done.

* * *

Odilia

Not having a manager had the benefit of saving the museum money. But Maye Marie, Irene, and Betty were tired of filling in. I was not. Not in the least. And the specter of that courthouse was weighing on me. We were running out of time.

Still, the men on the board said we needed to hunt for a new manager. According to Irene, no one wanted the job due to the "overly engaged" board members. I knew whom she meant but didn't care at all. I knew more than any of them about running a business and certainly more than Irene.

I dug around and found someone perfect. By perfect I meant easy to give directions to and by directions I meant, my directions. I thrust him into interviewing for the job, even though he was retired and said he was quite happy working on his stamp collection.

Dick Beeman came sneezing and wheezing with three bandages on his forehead to the interview for museum manager. A respected Buttonbush accountant, Dick didn't have any experience in museums, but he had a head for business and could match Maye Marie number for number in her ledger books.

"Her eyes glow like rubies on a Maharajah's turban when he says words like 'net income,' 'bottom line,' and 'depreciation,'" Irene said when we interviewed him.

With the courthouse looming over us, I thought a money-oriented fellow might do the trick. He might have been the most boring person I'd ever met as well as the person with the most ailments. But that was neither here nor there. Lacking anyone better to hire, we went with Dick.

It didn't take a genius to figure out the bank accounts were dwindling, and Dick pointed out all the over-budget spending at his first board meeting. I was well aware of this but still certain my plans to refurbish the museum would soon pay off. Iggy agreed with me and told me the state would never demolish a refurbished museum for a courthouse. So I paid little attention to Dick's budget commentary.

But Dick's plan to fix the financial situation was to do nothing, much to my surprise. No projects, no new buildings, no parties, no educational days, no lectures. Nothing. He didn't want to spend a dime. He sat in his office all day staring at the bank statements, making little notations on the side. Maye Marie and he became fast friends over the beloved ledger books, Maye Marie smiling as she worked her little pencil over the pages with Dick doing the same, each speaking some strange accounting language that no one else could understand. It was Maye Marie's version of heaven even though Dick was getting all the credit for it.

Dick was an odd little man who loved to tell you about himself and his personal problems, every ache and pain and illness until a person couldn't wait to get away from him for fear of catching something. Irene started bringing him batches of chicken soup or sweet potato casserole to settle his stomach.

"I don't want him distracted from shooting down Odilia," Irene said when she handed Dick a bowl of Jello salad one day. "I mean Odilia's ideas."

I glared at her. Dick wasn't quite working out the way I'd hoped.

"This will be over our budget," is all he'd have to say in a meeting, and the men on the board would nod their heads. It hadn't mattered when Maye Marie said the same thing or when

Irene harped about projects costing too much. Dick apparently could sway the men with his finance voodoo. Plus, he was a man.

★ ★ ★

Irene

The car screeched like a crow when Betty pulled up in front of my house, a cloud of dirt puffing up and snaking through the air. I was dusting the front window blinds and saw her jump out of the car and careen up the porch steps.

"What the heck?" I opened the door, curlers in my hair, bobby pins sticking out at the sides. "What is going on with you?"

Betty burst through the door, threw her handbag on the chair, and paced around the living room.

"You won't believe what I saw today," she said. I sat down, feather duster in my hands like a bouquet.

"Spit it out, Betty."

"I went over to Maye Marie's to take back her pie plates. She made me two apple pies last week for the dinner I hosted for the bank managers from Sacramento. They were amiable people, not at all as stiff and formal as I expected. But one was from New York and a bit more reserved. You know how that can be."

"Betty, the story. What are you going to tell me?"

"Right. So I went up to Maye Marie's front porch. This was just about an hour ago, and I peeked in the living room window to see if she was home. And she was."

"So?"

"She wasn't alone."

"Who was there? Dang, Betty, spit this story out or I'm going to explode!"

"Okay, okay. She was kissing someone. A man, I mean. In the hallway. I could see from the window. I couldn't get a good look, so I don't know who it was." Betty finally sat down, exhausted.

"Hot dang! Was it Jiggs? Could you tell?"

"I could not tell. It was dark in the hallway."

"What about his truck? Was it parked in front of her house?" I stood up, hands on hips, my fingers tingling with this new information.

"I didn't notice. Gosh, maybe there was a blue truck or a blue car or maybe a white car. I don't know. I didn't think to look. I was so embarrassed and excited I just left. I put the pie plates on the front porch chair," Betty said.

"That sneaky little Maye Marie. She and Jiggs have been seeing each other and she never told us," I said. "Well, now the Jiggs is up!"

CHIANTI AND SOFT SPAGHETTI

Irene

A box of chocolates in her hand, Betty surprised me one Monday morning, arriving on my doorstep.

"For you. Because you're so sweet."

"You must not have been talking to my children," I said, and she laughed. "A little early for my birthday. What's the occasion?"

"We have an opportunity. A big one," Betty said, and plopped down on the flowered couch, sighing as she sunk into the cushions. "Your house is so comfortable. Not like mine with all those brocades and velvets and dark furniture. I shouldn't listen to my mother about decorating."

"Your house is stunning," I said.

"I decorated my house in the Celeste Shellman school of stodgy design style. Alvin is a peach to let me decorate it to the nines, but your house is a home," Betty said.

"What's the real reason you're here?" I sat down in a chair, swinging my legs up on the armrests.

"It so happens that a well-known—at least in European circles—choir of Florentine singers is touring California. Do you know Gerald Vickers? He's a local attorney and somehow he has the opportunity to bring this Italian choir to Buttonbush," Betty said. "Gerald wants to host a dinner and a concert in our museum's great hall since the choir will be passing through Buttonbush. And he'll pay for it all, charge admission and donate the proceeds to the museum."

"That's great." I said. "I can plan the menu and decorations and …"

Betty cut me off as she cleared her throat.

"The thing is … he wants me to organize it. Me and his wife, Sabella. Alvin and I know them and … well, I hope you don't mind."

"Not at all. You'll do a fine job. That will leave me more time for other things," I said.

"I won't be as good as you but I'll try. Hopefully, we'll raise some money." Betty gave me a quick hug and left.

I wasn't too upset at being left out. Mr. and Mrs. Gerald Vickers were a highbrow couple that lived in Buttonbush's spiffy Parker Hills Estates where they had a swimming pool, chandeliers the size of Buicks, two turrets at each end of the house, a dining room to seat twenty and an outdoor bar complete with a refrigerator, according to Betty. Gerald and Sabella were what Pauline called "tony." Gerald was a Stanford-graduated attorney, Rotarian, Gold Seal Club member and hunt club owner. Sabella was head of the Parker Hills Country Club Ladies Auxiliary and the chair of the Buttonbush Women's Club. They wielded great influence in Buttonbush social circles, for those who cared. I sure as shooting did not. In my mind, they were the most vainglorious, snobbish, hoity-toity, nose-in-the air prigs in all of Buttonbush, and that may have been an understatement.

The word "prim" was coined for Sabella, a tiny-featured, perfectly coifed, wooden-faced woman. She studied art history in Florence and Paris, often traveled to Singapore and Hong Kong on an Oriental antiquities quest, and played hostess to the most ta-ta of Buttonbush women. Odilia and Betty were included in that bunch. Gerald, a very tall man who never failed to mention his Stanford degree, had thin arms and legs and a knobbish, protruding belly that moved solidly on him like a half-side of the globe. His nose and mouth were cast in an eternal uplift, as if he were sniffing strongly all the time.

I had been introduced to Gerald at least twelve times over the years and had even interviewed him when I was a news assistant, but he never once remembered my name and acted like he'd never set eyes upon me at each new introduction. It was purely offensive. After a while, I started giving him a different name when someone would introduce us.

Once while attending the Buttonbush General Bank's farmer appreciation dinner, I found myself in a group of people that included Gerald. He was moving in the circle, greeting everyone, and came to me and stuck his hand out. I'd met him three times before.

"Gerald Vickers, nice to meet you," he said.

I put my hand out.

"Good evening. I'm Jaqueline. Jaqueline Hyde," I said, then pinched Jimmy beside me, who almost spit out his drink. This happened several more times in the next two years, with me once introducing myself as "Tish Hughes," and once with my personal favorite, "Olive Hoyl." Gerald never noticed.

But the Vickers had money and knew people with money so we were beholden to them at the museum. They had donated in the past. I was getting good at swallowing my pride, a situation that rankled me.

Just to educate myself, I went to the library and researched the choir. They were a first-rate operatic group with a tip-top dramatic soprano named Lilliana Noemi Merlot, who was quite the looker. The article I read said the choir *gave audible proof that they are artists in every sense of the word. The ideal was higher and deeper than making beautiful sequence of harmony. They were worshipping with the voice and showing what a glorious organ it can be made.*

That made me sort of glad I wasn't involved with the choir since I had no idea what all that meant.

Betty planned a lavish chicken and rice pilaf dinner with creamed spinach, something called "arugula" salad, butter crescent dinner rolls, and lemon cheesecake for dessert. I offered to assist with publicity, but Betty said Gerald was having his office girl make up the invitations and write to the newspaper.

I must admit that while I was happy the museum might profit from this event, I was in an oppositional state in my mind. A good part of me was relieved that I didn't have to do much, but the other half felt a bit put to the side.

"Irene, this whole thing would go so much better if you were in charge, but aren't you glad you aren't? It's taking up a lot of my time," Betty said, and I appreciated her noticing that I was a bit in the blue about it.

Five days before the dinner, Betty called me in a panic.

"It's a disaster, Irene. The choir is threatening to cancel on us," she said, raspy voiced. I figured she'd had a little drink. "The Vickers are in an uproar. Sabella was practically screaming at me on the phone."

"Why are they cancelling?"

"You will not believe me when I tell you. They're threatening to go back to Italy and stop all the rest of their U.S. tour. Seven more cities. And you know why?" She was huffing and puffing over the phone line. "Their lead soprano is demanding good Chianti wine and they say the American spaghetti they've been served is cooked too soft. Too soft! They want good, Italian spaghetti."

"Why don't they just order it rare?" I said, but my joke didn't go over too well.

"Stop kidding, Irene! Their star soprano is ready to walk out. What are we going to do?"

"Why don't you ask old Gerald? He knows everything about everything."

"Come on now, help me."

"You could promise them a genuinely Italian spaghetti dinner. And good Chianti."

"Where am I going to get that, Irene? Where?"

I took a deep breath.

"Betty, you know we have Italians in Buttonbush. Lots of them. And who knows them, hmmm?"

"My gosh, you're right. You know all the Italian farmers. Do they have Chianti?"

"I'm no judge of good Chianti, but Bernie De Luca is a genuine wine expert. And I know for a fact that he drinks Chianti because Bernie and Anna come over to play Canasta with me and my Jimmy every other Saturday night, along with their bottle of Chianti. They order it by the case from some Italian liquor store in San Pedro," I said.

"Could he get us some?" Betty sounded a little calmer.

"I think so. I can ask."

"But what about the spaghetti? What are we going to do?"

"You know Joe and Rosa Toloni are from Luca, Italy and they are first-rate Italian cooks. My Jimmy can't get enough of Joe's ravioli. We could get them to cook up some spaghetti and be sure not to boil the noodles too much," I said. Joe was a cotton farmer from south of Buttonbush.

"Who's going to do all this?" she asked.

"Don't worry. I'll get you a bona fide Italian cooking crew and I'll even help. Go see if you can cancel that fancy chicken dinner. Arrivederci!" I said and hung up.

★ ★ ★

I was patting my face, looking into a compact mirror when Maye Marie popped into the museum office the next day.

"No cookies today? What is wrong with you? You haven't baked anything for weeks. Are you dying?" I said. My nosey mind wanted to know if she'd tell me about canoodling with Jiggs and how often. My curiosity was killing me. But Maye Marie was tight-lipped.

"Stop, Irene. I've just had other things to do."

"Other things, huh? Like what? ... Never mind ... Do I look dewy and with a glow?" I said, turning my head from side to side.

"Of course you do," Maye Marie said, a lilt in her voice.

"I bought some new DuBerry lotion that's supposed to make me look supple and smooth. That's what it says." I patted my cheeks. "I'm getting older, you know."

"You're younger than I am and you look wonderful." Maye Marie sat down in front of Felicia's desk.

"I do not. The other day I put my mirror on the table to clean it and when I bent my head over it, I could see what I look like when my head tips down. Lord! It was frightening, all the wrinkles and folds there. Let me tell you, I will be careful from now on not to be in a particular overhead position when Jimmy gets frisky. Nope, it's only on my back for me, if you know what I mean," I said, snapping my fingers.

"Irene!"

"Sorry. Too much information for you?"

"Way too much." Maye Marie shook her head then giggled. "The things that come out of your mouth!"

"You always look great so you don't have to think about it," I said, putting my compact in my purse.

"I do not. I've got plenty of wrinkles coming on."

"Maye Marie, you always look like a dang movie star so stop talking. And why are you so perky today?" I leaned forward, ready to start my barrage of questions. "And your fingernails are painted pink. I've never seen that. What gives?"

"No reason. Now where are the ledgers?" Maye Marie grabbed the papers on Felicia's desk and began flipping through them. I gave up on the inquisition.

★ ★ ★

By the time the choir arrived in Buttonbush a few days later, I had a whole host of Italian farm families coming to the rescue. Joe kept saying something like "al dentay" in Italian. I looked it up, and it meant "to the tooth," but in cooking meant "tender but not soft." So those Italian singers were right on the money in the way they liked their spaghetti, which you would naturally expect from a bunch of Italians. I confess, there was some amount of resentment in me that I was going to bail out that pompous Gerald.

We set up a cook station in the museum's kitchen which was adjacent to the great hall, with the Tolonis making a crowd-size batch of the spaghetti sauce at home the day before. When Joe walked in the door, I couldn't believe what he was carrying. The pot was so large it looked like you could cook a basset hound in it.

Soon the luscious smell of spaghetti sauce was wafting through the building, making everyone's mouth water. The Cabbibis, Civitellos, Tessaros, my Jimmy, and a few other volunteers were busy putting the meal together. They were shouting and scurrying all over the kitchen, chopping lettuce and tomatoes for salad, cutting large crusty loaves of bread and stirring the pots of noodles.

"Americans no eat spaghetti right. They eat like it horse-a-radish," Joe said. "Americans, they smart but ... bah ... they no good with spaghetti dinner." He carefully measured his noodles and set them on the counter as he waited for the water to boil.

Bernie and Anna came in lugging several cases of Chianti, popped a few bottles open right quick, and served the cooks first.

"You can't cook a genuine Italian meal without drinking wine," Bernie said, and he and Joe toasted each other with a clink of glasses.

"Chin, chin," echoed across the entire kitchen.

Joe gave me a glass, and I took a few sips. It wasn't too bad.

The Vickers wanted lacy, white tablecloths, fine china serve ware, and huge vases of flowers for the tables, polished silverware, and crystal drinking glasses, all fancy enough to look like a coronation. It must have cost a fortune, but for once, it wasn't the museum paying for it. I was setting out silverware when Sabella Vickers brushed past me with two of her friends, dressed to the nines, shuffling about like little glittered rabbits, titter-tatting at their hair and gloves.

"Dear, do make sure you get those napkins straight. The silverware must go exactly in the middle," Sabella said to me, straightening the place setting I'd just put down, her icy eyes glaring at me as I moved along the tables. "Now, where are those bartenders?"

"Come on Minnie, she'll get it right," said her friend, and they pitter-pattered over to the cocktail table.

Odilia came into the hall.

"Why did that woman call Sabella Vickers 'Minnie'?" I said. "Is that a nickname?"

Odilia chuckled.

"That's her real name. She changed it to Sabella because it sounds more European. But she's straight out of Tallulah,

Louisiana," she said. "She fools people into believing she was born in Madrid or London or Greece."

"Holy cow. She's got no accent at all," I said.

"She's done her best to shed her roots, but she came from a rather humble household. Rumor is there was a long-lost grandmother who took a shine to her and helped her break away from her hillbilly family. She never talks about her mother or father or any siblings," Odilia said. "It's very sad that she's ashamed of her family."

"Well, I'll be," I said, and I pondered over the unlikelihood of pompous Sabella coming from poor Louisiana kin. I couldn't think of what I might change my name to, if I could, but nothing sounded good with "Pickett." Anyway, all I could hear was Jimmy saying something like "Anastasia Lusitania Joannabellonia, can you please drive the manure spreader out to the north field?"

"Where's Maye Marie?" Odilia said.

"You know, I haven't seen her yet. She bought a ticket to the dinner. I told her she didn't need to help us. We've got plenty of people. Have you noticed her acting kind of different lately. Like sort of giddy or chirpy or like she's got something up her sleeve? Like Jiggs." I fiddled with a napkin, refolding it at a place setting.

"I have. I wondered what she was up to," Odilia put a cigarette in her mouth. "Is she seeing him?"

"We're not sure. Betty saw Maye Marie kissing someone. We think it was Jiggs." I whispered.

"I'm not sure I'd trust him." She lit a match.

"Maybe she's bringing Jiggs tonight or maybe she's bringing us a cake." I fluffed a tablecloth corner. "My money is on the cake. I hope it's a big ole chocolate one."

It wasn't a cake and it wasn't Jiggs that walked in the doors of the museum that night. It was Arky O'Dell with Maye Marie on his arm. She wore a rhinestone bracelet on her wrist, a new yellow dress, and a shiner on her left eye.

"Irene, close your mouth. You'll catch a fly," Maye Marie said.

Arky, looking like a stuffed bratwurst in his nicely pressed suit and tie, smiled a mile wide as they entered the great hall.

"Arky O'Dell?" I pounced on her when Betty and I cornered her in the kitchen.

Maye Marie grinned.

"After he spilled that tea on me at the picnic and ruined my blouse, he showed up at my house one day ... out of the blue," she said. "He had a new blouse for me he found at Dempsey's. It was five sizes too big, but, but I thought it was so nice of him to replace it."

Arky felt terrible, she said, so she invited him on the front porch for a glass of lemonade. He ended up staying all afternoon and even through dinner.

A widower with four strapping sons, Arky rarely got a good home-cooked meal, and Maye Marie said he looked like he'd died and gone to heaven when she fed him at her kitchen table.

"He ate three helpings of pot roast and two helpings of mashed potatoes. I thought I was going to have to make sandwiches, too," she said.

"How did that work out to you showing up here as his date?" Betty asked.

"He went back to Dempsey's and found my size and was so proud of himself. I can't imagine that strapping man wandering through a ladies' department," she said, giggling. "I just thought it was the kindest thing for him to got to all that effort. We've been seeing each other ever since."

"And you didn't tell us, you little secretive minx!" Betty hugged Maye Marie. "Him! It was him you were kissing at your house. Not Jiggs."

"What? Jiggs! No! You saw us? Dear Lord."

"We thought it was Jiggs. You little sneak," I said. "Jimmy always said that Arky was a good egg."

"He is a good egg." Maye Marie couldn't help but smile when she said it.

"But your eye. What happened?" Betty reached over and dabbed Maye Marie's face.

Maye Marie laughed and touched her eye like it was a gold medal.

"Two of Arky's boys were home from college … you know they all play football … and my kids were home so we played a backyard football game. I'm not too good at it, as you can see," she said, and her entire face shone like the lights on a football field.

★ ★ ★

The cocktail hour commenced and soon all sorts of fancy Buttonbush people wandered into the great hall of the museum, dressed in their finest. Tables dressed in fine white linen, tall vases overflowing with lilies, roses, and hydrangeas, crystal wine goblets and linen napkins trimmed in crocheted lace lined the room. Odilia had changed into a black cocktail dress with a chiffon cape on the back that made her look like a little swallow. She was thin enough to pull anything off which perturbed me to no end. But her face was tight, her fists were balled, and her jaw jutted forward like she was angry. The Senator was not with her. He hadn't come to much at the museum with her lately.

Betty changed clothes and put on a cream taffeta dress that complimented her sandy hair. Because I was working, I was in my same old blue cotton dress, which was fine by me. Thirty minutes into cocktails, when about half the room was feeling mighty good about themselves, the choir descended upon them.

Thirty-five robust, sparkling, hearty Italians with quick smiles came into the room. The noise level rose notably, and they swallowed up the bar like ants on sugar. I kept hearing them ask for something called a "negroni" but the bartender didn't have it. Their second choice was martinis. The roar of voices was echoing around the ceilings of the great hall when the leader of the chorus clapped for attention.

"A toast to our host. We are looking forward to a fine Italian meal," he said in a thick accent. Gerald and Sabella stood up, smiling prettily. I went back in the kitchen and Joe and the rest of the crew were sitting at the large kitchen table, table drinking wine and playing a card game called "scopa." I didn't know what it was, but it looked fun. Jimmy was watching from behind them.

"We're just waiting for you to tell us to go," said Anna. "They must be about ready, no?"

"I think they'll be ready to serve soon. They're almost done with the cocktails," I said. I sat down. My legs and back hurt and the smell of the delicious sauce made my stomach growl.

The kitchen door burst open and in strode the soprano lead herself, Lilliana, dressed head to toe in a black velvet gown with little feathers on the sleeves and a red scarf around her head. Her thick black hair framed her face, as exotic as Scheherazade.

"Who cook this meal?" she said in a heavy accent, and Joe stood up.

"This is Mr. Joseph Toloni and his wife, Rosa," I said, and Joe made a little bow but she patted his hand.

"It smells marvelous. I smell all the way out there. Taste please?" she said.

"Si, si," Joe said, and he grabbed a hunk of bread and dipped it in the sauce. The soprano took the full piece of bread in her mouth and moaned.

"Delizioso, how you say in American ... top notch?" she said. Bernie handed her a glass of Chianti, which she enthusiastically sipped, her big brown eyes batting at him as she drank. Then she noticed the card game at the table. She and Joe exchanged some quick Italian talk and Lilliana hiked up her dress and sat down on a wooden kitchen chair. Six more of the chorus members entered the room until all of them had a plate of spaghetti in front of them and were sitting at the table, watching the game, drinking Chianti, shoveling the noodles in their mouths in apparent rapture. More chorus members joined them, so that soon the kitchen and kitchen table were packed with Italians engaging in vigorous fun.

"Food for the gods," said one alto after she dipped her finger into Joe's spaghetti sauce and Joe smiled, his broad lips stretching across his red face. They began talking in Italian, pointing at the pot, back and forth until she hugged him. I had no idea what they were saying, but they were laughing. Two of the male chorus members talked to Bernie, wildly gesturing with their hands so that if you couldn't hear the good nature in their voices, you'd think they were about to get into a row. Joe's wife, Maria Toloni, drank wine with three of the chorus women, toasting over and over, clinking the little glasses, each time they took a sip. It was glorious fun.

Almost the entire choir was in the kitchen, flinging cards down with great enthusiasm, laughing and moaning as they got something they wanted or not. Plates of salad, crumbs of bread and spaghetti droppings were everywhere. My Jimmy joined in, even though he hadn't a thimbleful of knowledge about the game. The giant baritone stood next to him, punching Jimmy in the arm when he did something wrong, both of them belly laughing despite my Jimmy's not knowing one word he said. The high-brow soprano was having the wildest time of all. A little bead of sweat wound down the side of her face and her red lipstick smudged across her lower lip. She looked like a peach. She said something to one of her fellow choir members and they laughed so hard the soprano fell off her chair, causing them to laugh even harder.

"I think you might have given them a little too much of what they wanted," Betty whispered to me as we saw a tenor bend over in convulsive laughter, spilling wine on the floor.

The pots and pans in the kitchen rattled as the card game grew wilder and the noise increased. The soprano and alto were still on the floor, ankles splayed out, dresses crinkled over their knees, drinking. Everyone forgot about the fancy dinner outside the kitchen door.

"Do you think we should start serving the people in the hall?" Betty asked me. I nudged Joe, and he started ordering his crew around, filling plates and running food out to the gathering.

The robust tenor, wide and thick, yelled something in Italian as he pulled a card from a pile while all the men yelled.

"What a shame!" said Bernie, and everyone cheered.

Three bottles of wine were being passed around the group, some spilling down their arms and onto the floor. Some other mysterious bottle of yellow liquor was going around the room, too, something that sounded like "lemon jello." They were drinking straight from the bottle. Betty and I were laughing when Sabella and Gerald burst in the door.

"Whatever ... what is going on here?" Sabella's eyes popped like plums while Gerald's nose pinched upward in a doughy scowl.

The first alto let out a shriek.

"Che culo," she shouted. The crowd roared and kept playing.

Betty jumped up and ran to Sabella's side.

"They're just having a little fun," she said. "No harm done."

"That's the dramatic soprano ... on the floor with her dress pulled up ... and ... and. This is horrible. Outrageous ... Why ... Why ... What in dad gum tarnation hell has gone on here? Git off the floor! Ain't ya got no sense?" Her full Louisiana accent revealed itself in a screech and Sabella startled herself so much that her teeth almost rattled loose from her gums. She fanned her face with her purse.

"What have you started in here? You need to stop this ... this unbecoming behavior ... um ... um ..." Gerald glared at me but realized he couldn't remember my name.

"I'm Gail Force. Pleasure to meet you," I said, and extended my hand.

He stared at me, then turned and stomped out the door while I giggled. Sabella was trying to get the soprano to come back into the party but she was having none of it.

"No, no. We have good time here. A good time," Lilliana said. She was standing up now, a bit unsteady, but there was no moving her since it was her turn to deal. She shooed Sabella away. Sabella ran out of the room moaning.

Realizing we might have a bit of a catastrophe on our hands, I got Joe to serve the remaining people in the great hall. Betty and I made coffee.

"Here you go. Have some of this," I said to Lilliana, who was as liquored up as anyone I've ever seen. But she sat up, draining the coffee cup.

"Another per favore," she said, so I got her another cup. Maye Marie and Betty were foisting coffee on the rest of the choir, too. Within thirty minutes, those Italians put themselves back together looking like they'd done nothing more than lounge on a chair with a glass of lemonade. I admired their sturdy constitutions, since that kind of drinking would have set me back for about three days. They walked back into the great hall as dignified as cloistered nuns.

The concert went off without a hitch and I was in amazement at that soprano who could sit on the floor laughing in a most unladylike way, although charming to me, then half an hour later sing like an angel.

Maye Marie's early calculations showed we made over $700 for the museum. That was enough to keep the lights on for a few more months. She gave me a pat on the back.

"Good job getting those Italian cooks. What a fun time it was," she said. "And good for our budget."

"What would we do without you here?" Betty gave me an enormous hug. "And we made money for a change!"

I was taking my apron off in the kitchen when Carlotta came in.

"I wasn't too sure this was going to go well when the Vickers asked us to do this at that country club dinner but it turned out pretty well," she said.

"Country club dinner?"

"The one where the Vickers approached us about this. Odilia invited Maye Marie, Betty, and me to that dinner," she said, a slight glint in her eye. "Everyone was there."

"I guess I didn't know about that."

"It was a beautiful dinner. Lots of our museum patrons were there," Carlotta said. "I'm surprised you didn't know about it."

I wrapped my apron around my arm and headed for the door. Odilia had not invited me to that but had taken Betty, Maye Marie, and Carlotta, of all the disagreeable people in the world. Why on earth did she hate me so much? And Betty and Maye Marie had concealed it from me, likely to spare my feelings.

I walked into the hall on my way out and saw Gerald talking to Betty.

"That turned out quite well, Bettina. Thank you for your work on this and all the wonderful details you took care of," he said, then turned to me with his hand out.

"And thank you too ... er ..."

"Iona Ford," I said, extending my hand. "Nice to meet you."

★ ★ ★

What did I care about an ole country club dinner? I couldn't make Odilia like me no matter what I did. I stayed away from the museum for a while and concentrated on other things: Mending Jimmy's pants. Cleaning all my light fixtures. Learning to make gnocchi. Watching *The Guiding Light*. My anger would not get me anywhere. Let Odilia run the damn place. So much for working together. I didn't go down there for two weeks.

Betty and Maye Marie came over one night armed with a bottle of whiskey and begged me to keep going. I poured us each a glass and even Maye Marie, who almost never drank liquor, had some. We sat on my front porch, watching the moon move across the sky as the television blared in the living room where Jimmy and the kids were watching Jack Benny.

"We need you," Betty said.

"I'm not sure why."

"You've always got good ideas. You are an expert at getting people to come to things," said Maye Marie.

"We're not getting anywhere. We make a bit of money, like with the choir. Then Odilia just goes and spends it all on one of her buildings. Nobody in Buttonbush is sitting at their house right now thinking they'd like to go see one of our buildings again. They want to come to experience things," I said. "But I can't get any of these things accomplished because Odilia runs the show."

"You're right. You've always been right. But we're only three votes on the board," said Betty.

"Hey, where is Odilia anyway?" I said.

Neither of them answered me.

"Oh, I get it. She didn't want to try to talk me back."

"Well ..." Maye Marie said. Betty shrugged.

"You know, I've had it with her. I'm going to give her a piece of my mind for once," I said, and stood up and wobbled a bit. That whiskey was strong and I stumbled to the front door. "I'm going to tell her what I think of her, that bossy, pig-headed, conniving, old ... witch."

Betty and Maye Marie grabbed my arms.

"Now don't do something you'll regret," Maye Marie said.

I shook them off and grabbed the phone. Jimmy, sitting on the couch, turned and shook his head. I dialed Odilia's number and she answered on the second ring.

"Odilia, this is Irene. I've got something to say to you," I said. "Something important."

"What is it? I'm busy and you're bothering me," she said.

I paused.

"Well, get on with it," she said. "Honestly, you can be so annoying."

"Do you ... You know you ... I was wondering why ... I want you to know that ..." I couldn't force my anger to come out in words and my tongue grew thick in my mouth. It was one thing to throw snarky comments at Odilia but another thing to tell her off completely.

"Spit it out ... what is wrong with you?" she said, growling.

My stomach lurched.

"Odilia, is your refrigerator running?"

Betty shrieked and Odilia hurled curse words at me through the line. Loudly.

"*Better go catch it*!" I screamed and hung up, no better than a nincompoop teenager. Betty, Maye Marie, and I fell on to the living room couch in complete hysterics, tears streaming down our faces. Jimmy and the kids looked at us like we'd gone lunatic.

My head hurt quite a lot the next day.

THE GHOST OF THE DENVER HOUSE

Odilia

That Irene was going to get the chewing out of her life for making that ridiculous phone call.

But then I read the headline of the May 10, 1952 *Buttonbush Daily*, which said, *Ghost spotted at Buttonbush Museum*, and I nearly dropped my coffee cup on the floor.

Early morning risers, Victoria Perko and Davida Munoz, spotted a ghostly apparition in the Denver House at the Buttonbush Museum on three occasions this month during their pre-dawn walk down Hastings Avenue. The two women tell this reporter they saw a "ghost-like figure of a woman" moving through the house. The Denver House, an elegant mansion once owned by the prominent Edward Denver family, can be seen from Hastings Avenue."

"The first time we saw it we thought it was just a figment of our imagination, but then when we saw it twice more, I thought I was going to turn my hair on end," said Mrs. Munoz. The ladies say the "ghost" moves from room to room, turning and twisting, before it disappears.

"It's quite frightening," said Mrs. Perko.

Three other people also confirmed the sightings, over the summer months, one hearing music.

"I was walking down Hastings after getting off work at The Moondrop Pub when I heard some music. It was kind of eerie and all. I could see someone in the house, sitting at the piano. Looked like a woman to me but it 'bout sent me to my grave," said bartender Ivan Roskowski.

"I drive my milk truck down Hastings every day and once or twice in the last month I've seen something moving in there. I thought it might be some sort of kids doing pranks, but it's at four in the morning, so I didn't think kids would be up that early to do mischief," said milkman Sonny Brewer.

Paperboy Michael O'Reilly also said he saw something once, a woman staring out the window as he drove past on his paper route.

Museum curator, Carlotta Eustice, could not be reached for a comment on the ghost sighting.

Before I could get to the phone to call the other Queens, it rang. It was Betty.

"Did you see the paper?" she said. "Heavens, I've never heard anything like this."

"I saw it and I don't know what they're talking about. What a crazy story. But we'd better get over to the museum and look around."

As usual, spring had skipped Buttonbush and summer was in full swing, hot as Hades. The Four Queens assembled in front of the Denver House by nine-fifteen only to find Dick and Carlotta already there. Carlotta, face fierce, was even redder than normal as she paced in front of the house with her hands behind her back, grumbling. An unusually large crowd for a Monday morning stood outside the house. They were pointing up at the windows and whispering. Carlotta shoed them away, telling them there was nothing to see. The Four Queens went in the front door of the house with Carlotta.

"The nerve of the paper printing that nonsense." Carlotta was steaming, her hair frizzing up over her forehead. "We do not have ghosts at this museum. That is a fact."

"What do you think all these people are talking about?" I asked, and Carlotta grunted.

"They're imagining it or trying to get attention," she said. "I've looked around and there's nothing out of order here."

The Four Queens scattered across the rooms, not knowing what we were looking for.

"The first time I saw Bela Lugosi in Dracula, I slept with a scarf around my neck for three weeks," Irene said.

"Oh, please." I looked into a dark corner but saw nothing.

One of the few museum structures that needed little work, the Denver House was the crown jewel of the museum: a stately house built in 1867 and moved to the museum in 1939. The family made their money in mining and real estate, selling pieces of land to the railroads and then to the army for a military base out in the desert. Its wide Victorian porch, painted soft grey, wrapped all the way around the front of the house, and the interior had the original mahogany, cherry, and oak woodwork on the grand staircase and the walls of the foyer. The parlor was a cozy blue color with soft furniture in velvets, lace doilies on the tabletops, and a picture-perfect upright piano. Upstairs, the four bedrooms were each charming, with brass bed rails and headboards and cheery floral quilts, oak armoires, and gilded-framed portraits on the walls. It was one of just five buildings on the property that had a swamp cooler because of its beauty and value, so a visit to it was quite comfortable, even in the summer. It was a gorgeous house, always popular on a tour, although Carlotta kept it locked up most days. She didn't want anyone inside of it who wasn't in a firmly disciplined tour group.

"Is there any history of ghosts in this house?" Irene asked Carlotta, and she shook a disgusted head at her.

"No, there is not."

"Are you sure there's no legend of some dastardly deed here or some terrible event?"

"That's ridiculous, and we shouldn't even talk about it. Just think how the Denver family would feel about their gift of this house being smeared with phony ghost stories," she said, but I sensed something odd in her voice.

"I don't think there are any Denvers around anymore. But what aren't you telling us, Carlotta?" I said.

Carlotta whirled around and stomped her foot.

"Nothing. There's nothing, do you hear? Stop all this nonsense." She barreled out the door.

"She needs to stop saying that there's no ghost to the newspaper reporter. That's directly contradicting eyewitnesses. She needs to say we're looking into this," Irene said to Dick, who was white as a ghost himself.

"I'll mention that to her," he said, but his voice quivered.

"Dick, head back to your office. I brought you a little rice pudding," Irene said, and he gave a faint smile and got out of the Denver House in a hurry.

I chuckled. What a strange, little man.

"There's something fishy here. I'm going to find out what it is," Irene said, and shooed out the door, leaving us standing there.

★ ★ ★

Irene

I headed straight for the offices of the *Buttonbush Daily*. My old friend, Swinky Coe, worked there as a copy editor, a position she'd held for about seven hundred years. She knew everything about everybody.

"Swinky, tell me about the Denver family," I said when Swinky, skinny as a garden hose, beckoned me into her cramped little office, lipstick marked cigarette butts stacked high in a brown ashtray, papers piled to her neck bones, and half a dozen worn down red pencils on her desk. A shaggy, thin swath of grey and white hair framed her wrinkled face. Bright red lipstick plastered her mouth.

"The Denver family, now there are some stories," she said. "Is this about the ghost? Whoooooooo?" She made a whooshing sound and put her hands to the side of her head and twisted them, laughing while she winked at me.

"What do you know?" I said. I knew some of the history of the Denvers. Swinky knew the real stories.

"You're the museum lady. Don't you know?" Swinky's little eyes stared at me, a smile edging her lips.

"Swinky, come on now. I can't know everything," I said, and she laughed, a smoker's cough catching in her chest.

"Old man Denver was a shrewd one. Not much for being community minded, but he sure had the Midas touch. They made a fortune, then their worthless granddaughter wasted it all during the Depression. Dropped all their money on gaudy jewelry, a lousy art collection, and a gambler husband," Swinky said.

"I thought they were pillars of the community," I said.

"Ha!" Swinky grunted. "She never had kids, so her money paid his gambling debts and all the creditors she owed. She was quite beautiful, but not much for brains, no siree."

"How did the museum get the house?"

"I think the estate lawyers gave it to the museum because the damn thing cost too much money for upkeep and no one in

Buttonbush wanted the thing. It was too big and dilapidated. You suckers at the museum took it off their hands," she laughed, and I shook my head. Even Swinky knew how flat stupid we were to take all these old houses.

"Is there any history in that house?"

"Oh, there is … Let's go look in the archives," she said. I followed her to a dry smelling, long, dark room of racks and shelves up to the ceiling, all packed to the gills with folded copies of the newspaper. Swinky toddled over to an oak and brass card file case, searching for the "Ds." She thumbed through it for several minutes, then pulled a card up.

"Ah ha! I just couldn't remember the year … but here it is. There is indeed something about the Denver house. Let's find the February 9, 1889 edition," she said, her thick black eyeglasses gleaming in the dingy light of the room.

We rustled around the stacks until we came to the 1889 pile. Swinky pulled out the February 9 paper.

"Look here, there it is," she said, and showed me a front-page headline.

Lena Denver cruelly stabs her father then poisons herself. I grabbed the paper from Swinky. Sure enough, Lena Denver, an accomplished musician, in a fit of rage over being disowned by her father for *egregious social failings* had taken a hunting knife from his travel gear and stabbed him in the neck. He flung himself down the staircase, landing at the bottom in a bloody heap. Then Lena took a dose of rat poison. I wrote all the pertinent facts down in my notebook with an exclamation point at the last sentence. Whew!

"My stars, that's a terrible story," I said, thinking of that poor man dead as a doornail, right in the foyer that we'd just wallpapered at twenty-three dollars over budget.

"I think her egregious social failings were that she was dating an actor from Spain," Swinky said. "Now it's coming back to me. I really shouldn't drink gin fizz when people are telling me good stories. Anyway, Joan Peters, who worked here way back when ... She had the longest blonde hair I ever saw ... She knew the Denver family. Did you know Joanie? No, you were too young then."

Swinky smacked her hands together.

"Joanie did the society reporting and knew all the juicy gossip. I knew there was something more. Anyway, Joanie said Mr. Denver was in an uproar because this handsome, slimy, flea-bit Spaniard actor was nosing around Lena, trying to worm his way into the family fortune. Lena already bought him a gold watch and an apartment in New York."

"Why didn't the reporter research this for his news story?" I said.

"Oh honey, you know that would require some amount of effort on his part." Swinky chuckled.

"Hell's bells," I said. "A murder and suicide in the Denver House. No wonder Carlotta was acting so cagey about it." I gave Swinky a quick hug and headed to Betty's house, where she, Maye Marie, and Odilia were eating green grapes from a platter on the front porch.

"Here is a news flash," I said, out of breath as I ran up the front walk. "There was a murder and suicide in that house in 1889."

"You have got to be fooling us, Irene," Odilia said

"Lena Denver stabbed her father, then poisoned herself. How in the hell did we never hear of this before?" I said, and read them my notes.

"It was over sixty years ago, so few people would remember that," said Maye Marie. "But why didn't Carlotta mention it?"

"Carlotta is absolutely rigid about not letting anyone think there are ghosts at the museum. She would never have divulged this," Betty said. "She doesn't want us to be known for ghosts."

"And there aren't any Denvers left in town," Odilia said. "I think they're all dead."

The Four Queens pondered over this turn of events over two more pitchers of iced tea.

I went home, and Pauline informed me she and her friends wanted to spend the night in the Denver House.

"We want to see if we can catch the ghost, Mom. Can you let us do that?"

"I absolutely cannot," I said.

"I thought you were some big shot over there. We just want to see if we can prove there's a ghost and have an exclusive story for the school newspaper. I guess you don't have any say-so there," she said.

"I'm on the board, Pauline."

"That doesn't seem to have any purpose at all," she said, and marched out of the room.

My Jimmy spent the rest of the evening popping out of corners at me, scaring me to death because he thought it was fabulous fun.

★ ★ ★

When I went to the museum the next day, there were crowds of people lined up at the door.

"You should see how many we've let in already today," Felicia said. "They're all coming to see the Denver House. Carlotta finally opened it when she found some volunteers to watch over it, but she's standing at the door telling everyone there is no such thing as ghosts.

The guest sign-in book at the front desk showed that sixty-seven people came through the doors that day, more than triple our normal crowd. The next three days were the same. This ghost was turning out to be a cash cow.

On Sunday, another story ran, this time with quotes from a retired Army sergeant who liked to exercise in the early morning hours.

"It was dark out and I was walking by briskly when I heard music. Piano music. I looked towards the museum and I could see a small light in the downstairs of the Denver House and the music was coming from there. It was quite disturbing, I say ... but I don't believe in ghosts or any fiddle faddle like that," he said.

The article ended with a paragraph that told how the museum was facing serious cutbacks by the county and could be partially demolished for a new courthouse.

Perhaps the ghost is angry, the article concluded.

That week, even more folks showed up to look at the house, some driving from Fresno.

"I told you people would come to see these buildings," Odilia said to me at the board meeting that week.

"They aren't coming to see the house. They're coming for the ghost," I said.

Carlotta crossed her arms and sat straight up in her chair.

"I'm going to have Kosta add extra locks to the house. There is absolutely no possibility that there is anything happening there and I think people may be seeing a light reflection from the streetlights or something like that," she said. "This is all getting out of hand."

"Is the museum locked up at night?" someone asked. "Has the perimeter fence been breached?"

"Kosta locks up every night. All the buildings and the front and back gates are locked. Only Dick, Kosta, myself, and Odilia have keys," Carlotta said.

Of course Odilia had a key.

"Has anything in the house been disturbed or moved? Do you notice anything out of the ordinary?" asked Odilia.

Carlotta hesitated.

"Spit it out, Carlotta," said the chairman.

"Now this means nothing and there's a perfectly good explanation. But the piano bench has been moved several times and I've found some cushions on the parlor couch disturbed. I'm sure it's from visitors or volunteers and I've just not noticed this before," she said. "But also ... There's a picture frame on top the piano that keeps getting moved. I've positioned it exactly so that I know where it sits and it's been moved several times."

"Have you been out to the museum at night to observe?" the chairman asked Carlotta.

"No," she said.

"We're getting lots of good attendance out of it. We're up forty-three percent as of today," Maye Marie said and Carlotta grimaced.

The ghostly sightings continued on and off through June, with some folks setting up camp on Hastings Avenue to observe the spirit. It appeared in fits and starts and talk was all over town about the "winsome ghost" that played the piano and drifted around the house.

WE'VE ALL LOST OUR MINDS

Odilia

The ridiculous plan, of course dreamed up by Irene, was to spend the night in the Denver House and find out what was going on with this ghost nonsense. All this, plus Iggy on the phone every night at midnight, using his bedroom voice but pretending he was talking about power plant legislation, put me in a foul mood when I joined the other three Queens at the museum just after dark. I don't think any of us thought to tell Dick. I was getting sick of this working together nonsense.

"Complete idiots," I said, slamming my car door.

I had all the keys, which was the only reason I was taking part in such a crazy caper. The Four Queens crept inside the back gate, a hot, full moon overhead no less, which only added to the spookiness of the night. The summer heat held at over one hundred degrees, a temperature so fierce that I feared my shoes might dissolve into the ground like a drop of sugar on a griddle. The air sweltered around us as we approached the mansion. Dry trees around the front lawn baked in summer intensity while the pavement glowed. The steps up to the house groaned as we tiptoed up to the front porch, me in the lead. Maye Marie brought a jug of water and it swished back and forth in her hand like a pendulum. My hand shook as I shoved the key into the lock. The wooden door swung open with a loud creak.

"We've all lost our minds," I said, and we crept into the house, four normally fearless women acting like bunnies.

"Long as we don't lose our heads, too," Irene whispered. We paused in the foyer where, to the right, the parlor, adorned with lush blue wallpaper with tiny flowers embroidered in it and two massive sofas, was still and peaceful and didn't look the least bit threatening, which made me feel more at ease. Then I examined the piano, a sturdy, steadfast upright and the picture frame Carlotta mentioned. I made a mental note of where that frame sat on the utterly off chance that something moved it.

"This is where Malcolm Denver landed when he tumbled down the stairs," Irene said, and Maye Marie jumped away from the carpet that covered the foyer.

"Stop scaring us, Irene," she said, and clutched at her hair.

We'd brought blankets to place over the chairs and sofas so as not to disturb Carlotta's precious relics and Betty carried four taper candles but we didn't need them. The light of the moon and the streetlights from Hastings Avenue were enough.

The Four Queens settled down on the furniture, Betty and I on one sofa, Maye Marie and Irene on another.

"If that piano plays on its own, my teeth will fall out of my mouth," Irene said and I snorted.

"Well then, you won't eat so many ham sandwiches," I said, and Irene snickered at me and sucked in her stomach.

"I brought this to protect us." Maye Marie pulled out a meat mallet.

"What are you going to do, tenderize the ghost?" Irene said.

"Don't worry. I brought my pocketknife," said Betty, proudly displaying a red knife the size of toenail clippers.

"That thing couldn't harm a grasshopper," I said. "For someone so smart, you can sure be dim."

"You're awfully cross tonight, Odilia. What's wrong?" Maye Marie said.

"It's nothing."

"Tell us. We've got nothing better to do," Maye Marie said.

"Except wait to get murdered," Irene said.

I shook my head and looked out the window.

"You know I've been trying to get into Walker Gold Seal Club for the past year or two. I've done all the things you're supposed to do to get in. I manage all our property around California. I do all these projects at the museum, I'm chair of the Library Foundation's education committee, the Chamber of Commerce Ladies Committee, and the Ladies Committee of the St. Boniface Orphanage. Not to mention I'm a member of the finance committee at the Parker Hills Country Club and a member of the Duplicate Bridge Club. I give money, er, Iggy and I give money, to at least fifteen Buttonbush charities including this museum. I have way more on my list of accomplishments than half the men in there. But I got a letter yesterday denying me. Again," I said.

"That's ridiculous," said Betty. "They should let you in that club. What are they thinking?"

"You know I call them the Buttonbush Woman Haters Club?" I said.

"Then why do you want to get in?" Irene sat back on the couch.

"Because anyone who's anyone—and a man—can get in. I do more by Tuesday mornings than most of them do in an entire month. It's a matter of principal," I said. "They do a lot of business deals at that lunch. It's an opportunity for connections that women can't get. And I'm aiming to get into it."

"You're right," Irene said. "I've heard Jimmy buy new farm equipment after going to one of those lunches."

"That's not the worst of it," I said, and sat back in my chair. "I did some nosing around and found out it was my husband, the Senator, and big bazoo who kept me out. Told them I had plenty of other things to do besides joining that club. I'm so angry at him."

"Why did he do that?" Maye Marie asked.

"He doesn't like me getting involved in things. He's furious that I got nominated to this board. Thinks I should be home, knitting doilies for him, I guess. Ever since the war ended, he decided I needed to be more traditional. Bah!" I said.

Sitting there in the shadowed room, all my childhood sorrows bubbled up. It was like when I was a little girl watching my father brow-beat my mother into staying home from visiting with the ladies in the camp who sat drinking hot coffee and eating pastries in the mornings or chattering and laughing late on Saturday afternoons with cold glasses of beer, their cheerful sounds echoing up and down the neighborhood. Instead, Mama stayed home to wait on him, bringing him food to eat while he sat on his wooden rocking chair and listened to the radio, giving up everything for him to do whatever he wanted and him never giving her anything in return. All the light left Mama's eyes by the time she was forty. I think death was the only time she got any peace.

★ ★ ★

Irene

I felt sorry for Odilia. As much as she made me mad, you couldn't argue with her ambitions and perseverance. What a small-minded husband. Then it occurred to me that part of Odilia's dislike of me may have been because the Senator nominated me to the board first instead of her.

"You wanted to be the first woman on this board, didn't you, Odilia?" I said.

"You took that spot," she said.

"Sorry. If I'd have known."

"Doesn't matter. He was going to do his best to keep me off this, and everything else for that matter, but I find ways to go around him. He's up in Sacramento all the time so he doesn't know what I'm doing here," she said.

Poor Odilia.

I could hear the chug-chug of the cooler out behind the house. Thank goodness our ghost picked one of the cooled buildings to haunt. I put my legs up on the sofa, crosswise, and shivered.

"My cousin Shirley swears she saw a sure-fire, genuine ghost over at the abandoned church in Bruno. The one right off Wexler Road," Maye Marie said. "She was taking a walk, and she says a skeleton appeared next to her and tried to snatch her, right in broad daylight in the church graveyard, over near the tombstone of Thomas Shelton Jobson. His own brother gunned him down in cold blood. They were fighting over a woman, of course. Shirley said its hands grazed the top of her wrist and she can't pass by that place anymore without having every hair on her body rise like porcupine quills."

"Doesn't Shirley enjoy a nip of the old gin often?" I asked, and Maye Marie nodded.

"As do I," said Betty, and she pulled a little flask out of her purse and took a gulp.

"Anyone want any? She waved it around the room. Odilia grabbed it from her and took a swill, too.

"Many people have documented ghost sightings in all areas of the world. There is a well-researched phenomenon at the Belle House in St. Louis and at the St. Nicholas Croatian Catholic Church in western Pennsylvania. Knocking sounds and a robed figure, I believe. It even blew out the eternal flame in the church," said Betty, and Maye Marie tugged at her blouse like she had something crawling on her.

"My Jimmy knocks around in his robe sometimes, and if he's had lima beans for dinner, he blows things out, too," I said, and Maye Marie let out a hoot.

"For Pete's sake, stop all this nonsense. I think the scariest thing we're going to see is a squirrel that comes in here and runs across the piano keys," Odilia said, and it comforted me to have at least one of us who wasn't getting goosebumps.

"I brought some peanut butter cookies," Maye Marie jumped up, holding a paper bag with small splotches of grease on it.

"We can't eat those in here. Carlotta will skin us alive," Odilia said, but Betty and I were already reaching for them.

"You'd better clean up every damn crumb," Odilia said. She never ate anything that wasn't in a cocktail glass.

We chatted some more, and the night wore on, the temperature outside still hot, so the cooler kept rumbling. We grew sleepy, but my mind couldn't help thinking that if Dracula or some ghoul appeared, I was going to hop over the sofa table like a track hurdler and make a beeline for the door.

At midnight, the clock tower chimed and the Four Queens all stared at each other, our eyes wide as saucers. Nothing happened.

Twenty minutes later, Odilia had had enough.

"There's nothing going to happen tonight. Let's go. This sofa is uncomfortable," she said.

As she stood up to fold her blanket, a soft rattling noise came from the back of the house. A door clicked shut and I heard rustling, like something was coming. Odilia sat down quickly, and we all straightened up in our seats. No one said a word. Maye Marie grasped my arm, and I leaned into her. Footsteps padded down the back hallway, slowly coming towards us in tiny, quiet steps like the shuffling of bare feet. I braced myself, terrified.

Betty gulped, and we stared straight at the parlor entrance as a womanly figure in a flowing gown appeared, pushing her long hair behind her and tossing her head.

"Light a candle, light a candle," Maye Marie whispered, but Betty dropped the candle on her lap and was fumbling for it. The figure stopped still.

"This is nuts," Odilia shouted, and flipped on a flashlight. She beamed it straight at the figure which then shrieked a loud, high-pitched cry that sent a freezing river up my spine. We all screamed and Maye Marie dropped the cookie bag, crumbs scattering across the parlor floor.

"Alma!" the Four Queens shouted in unison when we saw Alma, Kosta's wife, standing there in a white cotton nightgown, her long brown hair in damp tendrils down her back and in her hands, sheet music.

"Oh no, oh no. I'm so sorry! I'm so sorry. Please don't fire Kosta. He ain't got nothing to do with this," she said as she dropped the sheet music on the ground and brought her hands to her face.

"What the hell is going on here?" Odilia said, and Alma sat down on the piano bench, tears streaming down her red, puffy face.

"I just came in here to cool off. Kosta ain't fixed our cooler, and it's blisterin' hot in our house and, well … I'm goin' through the change and feel like I could pert near light on fire every night. I knew this place was cooled, so I pinched Kosta's keys and came over here one night and well … it was just so peaceful and quiet here and I could get some sleep without sweatin' all night and Kosta snorin' … I kept comin' back," she said. "Please don't fire Kosta for my poor behavior."

Kosta's house was next to the museum grounds, so I could see how she accomplished her deception.

"Did you know people thought there was a ghost in here?" Betty said.

"Yep, I heard that. I figured it wouldn't do no harm if people thought there was a ghost here and I kept an eye out for when there was people watchin'. I could see them from my house so's I kept away when they was out there," she said.

"But the piano? What are you doing playing the piano?" Betty said.

"Oh, that ... Well, I been learnin' piano in my spare time, which there ain't much of. My daughter and grandkids seem to come by all the time and I never get time to practice with them runnin' all over my house. And this piano is so much better than mine, so I sometimes play a little bit before I sleep or when I get up. I know it ain't right what I done," Alma said, clenching her nightgown in her hand and wiping sweat from her forehead, biting her bottom lip.

"Alma, I remember when my mother went through the change and she felt like an ice cream cone on a July sidewalk all the time," I said, and all the other Queens nodded.

"You just can't do this any ..." Odilia started to chastise Alma, but I cut her short. Maye Marie crawled on the floor, picking up cookie crumbs.

"Alma, you just keep coming over here. Don't you worry," I said, and I grabbed Odilia by the arm and dragged her to the door. She tugged her arm and tried to pull away but I was a lot stronger than skinny Odilia. Maye Marie and Betty scurried after us.

"Enjoy yourself, you hear?" I called over my shoulder as I shoved Odilia down the front steps of the house. We formed a circle on the front lawn and I whispered.

"Be quiet, Odilia. I got an idea. Maye Marie, how much has our daily attendance improved since this ghost sighting happened?" I said.

"We're above seventy-three percent for the month of July. In June it was sixty-seven percent," she said. "We're going to be in the black for the summer if this keeps up."

"And summer is our worst time for attendance, correct?" I said.

"Always the worst, but …" Odilia said.

"Then let's just let this be. Alma won't be going through the change forever and the summer won't last forever, either. Why not just keep this to us and see how many people we can get in the door?" I said and Betty smiled.

"We can't just let her sleep there when she wants to," Odilia said.

"Think of it as her guarding the house," Betty said. "And adding a little spice to the museum as well."

"Odilia, we need money. We get money when people come through the door. Look at all the people coming in. Why would we put a stop to this?" I said. "We're not telling people there's a ghost. They're getting these stories on their own. So what's the harm?"

"They should be coming just to see the house. For its aesthetic value," she said. "Still …"

"Should we tell Dick?" asked Maye Marie.

"No, he's got to get some plantar warts removed. Don't bother him. He'll be happy to see the income rising," I said.

"Alma better not do this again next summer," Odilia said. "But I'll keep quiet about it for now."

I was tired the next day.

"Well, Mother, did you catch a ghost?" Pauline asked, spreading strawberry jam on her toast like it was a work of art.

"No. We did not."

"Seems like you spend a lot of time doing nothing over there. I don't know why you bother with that place. Oh … I need to go get my hair cut today. Can you drive me?" she said, and just like that, my life and contributions to society disappeared into Pauline's always pressing desires.

Jimmy showed up at breakfast with a white sheet over his head, chasing me around the kitchen yelling, "boo." I wacked him with the spatula, told him the story and swore him to secrecy. Then I called Swinky.

"Swinky, why the hell hasn't that reporter dug up the information on the Denver House?" I said, and Swinky grunted.

"Because that kid is lazy. Don't know what he did in the Navy, but I have it on good authority he was a paper pusher then went to college after. He's nice enough but he needs a fire lit under him," she said. "He's been grumbling about covering the damn ghost story."

"Can you just give him a little tip about Lena Denver and the murder and suicide?" I said. "Don't tell him how you found it."

"Sure, I can do that. The kid needs a little kick in the pants if he wants to be a good reporter. Too bad you aren't here anymore. You were a crackerjack," she said.

I hung up and traipsed back over to the museum to see if anyone got a whiff of our mischief. Maye Marie was with Felicia, looking at some billings. Right when I got there, Carlotta walked in.

"Any more ghost sightings?" I asked.

"No, well … no, not exactly. There aren't any ghosts, I keep telling you! But this morning when I went in the house to check on it, it smelled like peanut butter. There must be some kind of rodent in there," she said, and stomped off.

Maye Marie and I almost exploded in laughter. The next day, the paper had a front-page headline.

Denver House has history of murder and mayhem, it read, and there was a picture of Lena Denver, dressed in a fancy ball gown with her handsome Spaniard.

The Buttonbush Daily has uncovered more to the mystery of the Denver House, upon finding that a murder and suicide took place there in 1895. Lena Denver fatally stabbed her father, Malcolm Denver, in a fit of rage, then ingested rat poison to kill herself. No member of the Denver family currently lives in Buttonbush and the curator of the museum could not be reached for a commentary.

The story told about the love affair between Lena and her Spanish boyfriend.

"That reporter finally dug up the goods, didn't he?" Odilia said, and gave me a hard look, but I just shrugged.

Over the next month, visitors flooded the museum, even a caravan of members of the Los Angeles Séance Society which troubled us Christian women but they paid full price admission for all thirty-two of them on a Saturday, so we turned a blind eye. On one occasion, a Hollywood film crew came up to see the house for a potential movie location. They were a greasy, slimy lot, and I hoped they wouldn't come back. Carlotta was near losing her mind over it all.

"I just don't understand all the commotion over this. I don't have time to answer all these ridiculous ghost questions and I refuse to talk about Lena. One lady fell to the floor twitching and mumbling because she felt some presence in the house. This is getting out of hand," she said, but the more people poured in the doors, the more the Four Queens pushed her to give tours of the house.

It was more attention than we could ever hope for and, embarrassingly, brought in more people overall than any educational lecture or exhibit ever did. But it was hard to keep a straight face. Jimmy and I went to lunch over at the Rigger Café, and the lady in the booth behind us told her husband she was sure the ghost was Lena Denver, who came to tell Buttonbush citizens to repent of the evils of whiskey and gambling.

And the church ladies around town were in a dither about it, making up all kinds of stories. My ma was the worst.

"I heard that Lena Denver operated an opium den in the parlor and that Malcolm Denver scuttled away millions in gold bricks down one of his mines but an earthquake caused them to fall so far that he couldn't find them," she said one day when we were sorting through the seeds we'd saved from last year's garden. "And that the Spaniard Lena was in love with was a bullfighter who lost an arm in a bullfight."

"None of that is true, Ma."

"I wish you weren't involved with all this mumbo jumbo voodoo seance baloney," she said. "You know it's right there in the Bible ... in Micah ... *And I will cut off sorceries from your hand, and you shall have no more tellers of fortunes.*"

"Ma, there's no fortune telling or sorcery going on. Except for maybe Carlotta." I laughed.

She ranted on. *Do not turn to mediums or necromancers; do not seek them out, and so make yourselves unclean by them*, and *Do not believe every spirit, but test the spirits to see whether they are from God, for many false prophets have gone out into the world*, and a whole bunch of Leviticus, which I already knew. I did not ask her about what the Bible thought of deception since I already knew that, too.

Opinions were divided among Christian faiths around town but all of them, at one time or another, came to see for themselves, including Ma, whom I caught snooping around the Denver House one afternoon with her friends.

"Ma! What are you doing here?" I said as she strolled down the steps of the house. She made a nasty face at me, pulled her purse close to her body and hurried away, nose to the sky. She never said a word, even when I laughed.

I should have been ashamed for perpetrating such a genteel hoax, but I comforted myself with the fact that we never said there was a ghost and we never told anyone to come by to search out the ghost at the Denver House. We just never mentioned anything about Alma and her dreadful womanly afflictions and our admissions were up over seventy-six percent for the year. We were on our way to making $5,000 but we had a long, long way to go.

"Odilia," I said. "People coming through the doors bring in money. And they weren't coming in to see a house. They were coming in for an experience ... with a ghost."

★ ★ ★

Carlotta burst through the door like a rabid dog one week later as the Four Queens were sitting with Felicia to go over the budgets. She pointed her finger at us, her other hand on her hip.

"I'm resigning. Quitting! I spoke to Kosta yesterday and he confessed his wife had been going into the Denver House to get cool. She was the ghost and you four knew it." Carlotta's face turned bright red, and I feared her head might explode on the spot.

"Uh-oh," I said. "We did. But we kept quiet for good reasons."

Carlotta bared her teeth.

"You had me running in circles, trying to figure out what was going on. Answering ridiculous questions all over town, in the newspaper. Even on television. Everyone thinking it was a ghost and it was just Alma. You four are despicable," Carlotta said. "I'm quitting and I'm letting everyone know what you did."

"Now, Carlotta, think here. We're sorry, aren't we ladies?" Betty said. "Please don't give away this secret."

"We brought in seventy-six percent more revenue than we normally do," Maye Marie said.

"I don't care. What a terrible hoax. You four have no business running a museum." Carlotta's fists balled up and a little bead of sweat dripped down her temple.

Odilia cleared her throat.

"Carlotta. We're sorry we kept you in the dark. But we had our reasons. Now if you want to resign, I think we understand. But do you really want to reveal this little indiscretion? I mean, you're going to want a reference for another job, and, well, you were in charge of Kosta, so, actually, you should have known about this. How can we give you a good reference if you were so unaware of what your staff was doing? Hmmm?"

She arched her eyebrows while I shuffled my feet and looked down, trying to conceal a smile.

"You can't … I won't let you … You four are awful people. You are running this place into the ground. I'm packing up my things and leaving today." Carlotta stomped her foot and when she did, a little clump of dirt went flying across the room.

"Don't leave on bad terms, Carlotta," I said.

Carlotta's neck stiffened and she stuck her chin out. She clenched her fists in front of her body like a boxer.

"Argh!" She stormed out of the room.

★ ★ ★

Between Dick's budget cuts and the deceitful ghost money, we were at almost break-even for the year. But then we went right back into the red again when Odilia put in new flooring in the shoemaker's shack and went over budget. Dick had had enough, turned in notice, and was gone. The Four Queens were again in charge of saving the museum and I was getting damn sick of trying.

The county hired a private assessor to determine how much the place was worth, a bad sign for the museum. The newspaper ran an editorial, listing all the board members' names, saying, "The museum board members seem unable to operate profitably. Just what are they doing over there and who is running the show? One quarter of it may be gone soon."

"Now we don't have a manager or a curator. This museum is in a deep hole," Betty said, and all Four Queens sunk into chairs and sighed.

"Something must be done," Odilia said.

THE MOMENTOUS IDEA

Odilia

The December 31 deadline to have $5,000 in reserve hung like a guillotine over us as the summer stretched on. We had to do something, that much was clear, and I was at a loss on what to do. With the public stain of the Iversen and Bosworth houses still sitting at the museum all undone, no manager, no curator, and the county breathing down our necks, I was getting nervous. We only had twenty-seven dollars in the reserve fund. We'd been ahead a bit more until a pipe broke in the great hall and we had to pay a plumber to fix it, plus redo some flooring. Maybe I'd been wrong about just building things. But Iggy had agreed with my ideas and Iggy was, if nothing else, a smart man.

"We need something big," I said as I stared at the front page of the *Buttonbush Daily*. "Something momentous."

The Four Queens sat in Betty's dining room eating muffins and drinking coffee out of little blue-flowered cups and saucers, stirring cream and sugar with fine silver demitasse spoons. Irene was uncharacteristically quiet, thank heavens.

I threw the newspaper down on the table. A picture of the county commissioners with a drawing of the new courthouse was on the front page. They were going to decide about where to locate the new courthouse soon. The state architects were coming down to discuss locations and they planned to visit the museum next week.

Failing museum deemed perfect location for new courthouse, the headline read.

The article quoted several local officials who were overjoyed at receiving money for the courthouse from the state. I'd badgered Iggy to find out how Buttonbush was selected to receive this money but he blamed it on some lobbying by local officials and real estate developers who wanted Buttonbush to grow. The only other location the county was considering was a plot of land on the edge of downtown Buttonbush that housed an abandoned hotel, but it wasn't as picturesque as the museum grounds.

"The museum has just nine months to show profitability or face partial demolition," the story read.

"We have a little time while they study it. Thank goodness the state moves in slow motion," Maye Marie said. "They have a construction company with detailed plans to demolish part of the museum. All our hard work will be for nothing."

"I can't believe the county would do this," Betty said.

"All they see is a museum that loses money every year," said Maye Marie. "Why wouldn't they consider this?"

"We need to do something. More than we've ever done," I said.

"What? Bake sales, historic walks, auctions, flea markets? None of those are big enough," Betty said.

Irene cleared her throat like something was welling up in her. Her eyes darted to me but then looked down, fluttering like a bird.

"What about some kind of festival?" she said. "Let's do something grand that will bring people in from all over the county. All over the state. A really, huge festival."

"Like what?" Betty said.

"Like that Lodi Grape Festival or that huge festival in Los Banos. Thousands of people come and they get businesses to sponsor them."

"Could we do something like that? And would it raise enough money?" Maye Marie said.

"We could, and it could raise enough. If we do it right. Much bigger than the Halloween carnival or the gala. We'd have to advertise all over the place. Advertising, that's the key." Irene stood up from her chair and began pacing the room. "This would be an endeavor like we've never done. But think of it: Carnival booths, food, music and dancing, a bit of demon rum being served if you know what I mean. Contests, auctions, who knows what else we could do?"

"That's a great idea," I said. Irene spun around on her heel and stared at me.

"What's in that coffee? Are you tipsy?" she said.

"Stop it. I realize we need money. It's not that the building projects won't bring in money, but we need some cash in a sizable chunk. Quickly. That's all," I snorted at her. I wasn't stupid, after all. I still believed my long-range plan was right, but we needed cash right now. It was a bit of a bitter pill to swallow. I hoped Irene wouldn't rub it in my face, but she continued to chatter about the possibility of a festival. Sometimes you could literally feel the creativity seeping out of her.

"This could be something everyone will want to come to. Get every club or group in town to have a booth or display. That will get them and their families to come," Irene said. I could almost see the ideas bouncing around in her head. "We take a percentage of whatever money an exhibitor makes. I can see just about everyone in Buttonbush coming to a festival like that."

"And the sponsors to cover our costs," Maye Marie said. "Cash up-front."

"Who's going to organize this?" said Betty.

"I can do it. We can do it," Irene said. "The Four Queens."

"The Four Queens? Are we capable of putting on a big festival?" Maye Marie said.

"Of course we can. We've done every other damn thing around there," I said. "We're rather unstoppable."

"I've had plenty of experience putting on events ... nothing this big ... But I've done lots of things at the fair and at the school and church ... although not too much at the museum since until now, we haven't had cooperation from all parties," Irene said, staring straight at me.

"Oh, stop bellyaching. I'm on board now. Let's get something going," I said. Not only was Irene's idea a good one, I reluctantly admitted to myself, but it could put me on the map for the Gold Seal Club.

We wrestled round and round about what kind of festival to have. Maye Marie wanted a crafts festival where ladies could bring in their sewing, knitting, and crocheting creations. Quilts, blankets, doilies, caps, clothing.

"That sounds about as fun as watching my Jimmy pick corn out of his teeth after dinner," Irene said.

It annoyed me to no end how she always referred to him as "my Jimmy." I would never refer to Iggy as "my Iggy," but that was because I didn't feel like he was mine. Not any more. Irene never doubted Jimmy's affections.

Betty didn't care what kind of festival we had, as long as there was somewhere for a saloon or bar and she could get a drink. She also correctly pointed out that liquor could raise a lot of money, so we agreed no matter what we did, we'd have some lively drinks available for sale. This was bound to ruffle the feathers of the Baptists in town, but they'd come anyway, if we had enough fried food at the festival. And there was profit to be made in the booze from all the Catholics.

Irene pushed for a farm festival.

"Buttonbush is known for farming. We could feature our local farmers, all their crops and food made from their crops, but also offer an opportunity for all our charitable groups, schools, and other businesses a chance to get involved," Irene said. For once, she was making sense, and, although I would never say it, I was starting to have a slight amount of respect for her opinions.

After a healthy debate, we embarked on the creation of the Buttonbush Farm Heritage Festival. People from around the state would want to come and I could not wait to get started. Finally, a way to change our fate, and a way for me to get noticed. This was going to be big, and I was going to be big right along with it.

★ ★ ★

Irene

There wasn't one second of doubt in my head that I could tackle this festival. Maybe there should have been, given my dubious history, but I was tickled pink to put on a festival, scheduled for October.

The Four Queens decided that Odilia and I should be co-chairwomen for the event but Betty and Maye Marie would handle quite a few tasks as well. That meant diddly to Odilia. She decided she was the head of it all. It was just Odilia taking charge, whether or not the rest of us wanted her to. She was good at self-appointing, noting that her husband could help advertise the festival all over the state.

I got myself organized with little notebooks and files with all the categories for the festival: food, entertainment, sponsors, volunteers, displays, activities. Every morning I got up and sorted through all my paperwork, making sure I had my plans in place for every little detail, making phone calls, ordering supplies. For the first time, I knew I was doing something huge for the museum.

Overall, Odilia and I were working well together. At least at first. She'd warmed up to me in some small measure and that made me happy. We talked once a day, went over plans and schedules, and our working relationship was smooth. I created all the entry forms and contest rules, guides for the exhibitors, and the layout for the booths. I found the musical entertainers, the bands and singers, magic acts, artists, and jugglers. And I got little tidbits of the festival into the paper and on the radio regularly, to keep it in people's minds and build up expectations. My name even got in the paper once or twice.

"Gee, Ma, you look different," Pauline said one day when I put on a new red dress with white lace at the collar. I took that as a winning ticket just to have her notice me in a good way for once.

As usual, Odilia was a wizard at raising money. No one in Buttonbush was safe from her and the sponsor money came pouring in. I had to hand it to Odilia: She was a bare-knuckle fighter when she wanted to do something.

"Can they do it?" the *Buttonbush Daily* asked in a headline with all four of us in a picture, holding our heads high, shoulders back, standing tall. They even labeled us "The Four Queens of the Buttonbush Museum."

If only things had gone as well as we looked in that picture.

I'm not certain when I realized things were going south but it might have been when Odilia chewed out a sign maker for being two hours late with a delivery. Odilia was taking the festival a little too seriously. When she found out the Ladies Guild of the Buttonbush Episcopal Church was having a crafts bazaar on the same day as the festival, she marched over to the church and brow-beat the poor women into moving their bazaar to the following weekend. When the Buttonbush Department of Health said we couldn't have over five food-selling booths at the festival, she paid the head of the department a visit as he got out of his dentist's office. The rule changed. She was amazing and terrifying at the same time. Odilia was sorely driven, a good deal more than most people would be with any given project, like Dr. Frankenstein, who was hell-bent on creating that monster. And we all know how that ended.

It was apparent to me and the other Queens that Odilia was making this festival her own personal Holy Grail. But I was deeply involved in it, too, and I'm ashamed to say that I started acting like Odilia. I quarreled with Jimmy more often, and was short-tempered to my hairdresser, which never happened before. My brain was behaving like Odilia's, and when I wanted something done, I wanted it done immediately and exactly as I wanted it done. That was new for me, especially when one night Jimmy asked me if it would be okay if he could turn on the hallway light.

"What do you mean by asking me that?" I said.

"You got mad at me the other night when I turned it on. You said it was a waste of electricity to turn it on when I could see down the hallway just fine," he said.

"Well, can you?"

"No, I can't. You know my eyes ain't as good as they used to be and I need the light on when I'm going back and forth from the bedroom to the kitchen. Is that okay with you?" He gave me his puppy dog look, but I wasn't in the mood.

"Oh for Pete's sake, that's a dumb question. Just turn on the damn light," I said. "It's your house."

"Don't feel like it," he said, and stomped away to go check water.

★ ★ ★

On the top of my list to help with the festival was the Buttonbush Ladies of the Grange led by Vida Lee Rupnik. Vida

Lee was a tall woman with a wide nose and full lips who ran a farm with her two sons. She always walked slowly, as if she were surveying everything she saw, and when she talked to you, she looked right at you with the kindest blue eyes. There wasn't anyone in town who didn't like Vida Lee because she was sweet as pie. She fed every bum who came around and taught the Bible to the kids at the Lutheran church. When someone robbed the A-1 Grocery and hit the owner over the head, Vida Lee said, "He just needs our prayers," and never once said, "I hope he gets what's coming to him."

It was rumored that once when a California Highway Patrol officer pulled her over for going ten miles over the speed limit, the officer thought she was so nice he bought a ticket from her for the school raffle, showed her a picture of his new baby, and never did give her a traffic ticket. But she was also tough as nails with rough hands to prove it. The interior door handle of her truck was a seven-and-a-half-inch wrench, and she told me herself that one of her favorite pastimes was to sit outside on her back porch and shoot at snakes.

Vida Lee was a key person for the festival, and she was quite keen to be part of it. She agreed her ladies would take over the agricultural displays and create tables full of Buttonbush crops and things that are made from the crops like breads, pies, rolls, butter, jams, jerky, ice cream, bacon, and such. She would organize the cotton gin to bring in bales and loose cotton, the potato farmers to set out boxes of newly picked spuds, boxes of garlic, and onions, and the grape farmers to bring in loads of beautiful fruit. Vida Lee and I were working together splendidly, planning out how to design the displays, making sure we put out nice informational signs to tell people all about our Buttonbush farmers.

I was feeling pretty good about things, like I might just do something successful at the museum for once. But like always, Odilia put a monkey wrench in my happiness.

Vide Lee wanted to lay out her farm tables in front of the old general store at the museum, using the front to hang a sign about the Grange, and the inside for displays. I told Odilia this when I ran into her at the beauty shop. She was getting a permanent wave and went into attack mode as I sat under the dryer.

"Tell Vida Lee no. I already promised the general store to Fred Bagby," Odilia said, her little head bobbing, the small pink rollers bouncing around. The scent of ammonia stung my nose.

"From Bagby Auto? Ouch!" I pitched forward and my curler'd head hit the inside of the dryer.

"They want to be an exhibitor."

"What does he need it for?"

"That store belonged to his great-uncle. Also, he promised to give me $400 to bring in and refurbish the Fortuno House."

"You mean it's not even money for the festival?"

"Well, no. That Fortuno House is historic. Romeo Fortuno was the town's first eye doctor, and that house was beautiful." Odilia put her hand on her hip and tapped her toe.

"That two-story fire hazard that's all dilapidated and falling apart? The board hasn't voted to take in the Fortuno House, Odilia." I slammed my hand on the side of the chair, a familiar hot rash crawling up my neck. "And I'm in charge of displays. Bagby Auto has not filled out one of my exhibitor forms. Vida Lee needs that spot."

Two ladies poked their heads from under the dryers to listen to us, eyes wide.

"He's very excited about it and when you get a donor who wants to give you money, you can't turn him down, now can you, Irene?" Odilia pursed her lips, a sure sign that she already assumed this would go her way.

"So what does he want to do at the festival?" I said. I should have stomped off. But I was snarled in the fight with Odilia, like two bobcats in a laundry sack. Plus my hair needed to dry.

"He wants to put his cars out on display. He's got some nice ones. New Fords that are just beautiful."

"What the hell has that got to do with the festival?" I said, my voice was rising. The two ladies sitting next to me rustled their movie star magazines and looked away.

"Farmers drive cars, Irene. Automobiles are important in Buttonbush," Odilia said with the smug tone I knew so well.

"Too bad for him. I promised that spot to Vida Lee, and she's got actual farming exhibits. Crops and products and hay bales and all sorts of harvest things from the Grange," I said. "That's what we're focusing on. Not Bagby's donation."

"Vida Lee can find somewhere else to put her displays. Put them in front of the Denver House."

"That's not as good a location, and the store suits a farm exhibit. It's supposed to be a farm heritage festival, Odilia. Not a festival to make money for things you want to do but that nobody else has agreed to do," I said.

"It's too late. I can't give the check back."

"You took the money?" I almost yelled it.

"Of course I did. Deposited it in the museum account today," she said. She looked down at me, pointing her finger at my face. "This is my festival, and I didn't ask you to tell me what to do."

"Your festival! Your festival! I'm the co-chairwoman of this thing. It's not just you in charge." I was now shouting over the hum of the dryer. More ladies came out of the shampoo room to watch us.

"I don't share power," she said, and stomped off to sit back in a chair. One of the ladies gasped, and I turned around. In the doorway of the shampoo room stood Joyce Dolley, a towel wrapped around her head, her enormous eyes wide with surprise. The other ladies ducked their heads away from me but their ears tilted towards me.

Fuming, I sat back and let my hair dry, my eyes burning into Odilia's little head as she finished her permanent. Later, I careened out the door of the shop without a word to her and poor Jimmy got an earful over dinner. He was none too happy to hear it.

"What's wrong with you?" I snapped my napkin in my lap.

"Can we just have a decent talk here without talking about Odilia again? Just for a change?" he said.

"Am I boring you?"

"No. Well, yeah, kind of. I'm sick of hearing about her and all the trouble. Can you just talk about something else?"

"I can't help it if that woman causes so much trouble. I guess I'll just not speak any more," I said, sitting back in my chair with my arms crossed.

"It's not that. It's just that, geez, I'd like to hear about something besides her. The weather. Your new shoes. Pauline's math class. Willy's Cub Scouts. Even your mother. Anything but Odilia." Jimmy's voice rose and my anger went right along with it.

"Fine!"

I got up and stormed out of the room.

★ ★ ★

I called Vida Lee that night and it was the first time I've ever heard her mad.

"Who does Odilia think she is? Doesn't she know I'm making the festival authentic? I thought it was supposed to be about farming," she said. "Don't you have the authority to override her?"

"I'm so sorry, Vida Lee, but she's not budging. I've tried everything I can think of," I said, embarrassed by my lack of clout. "Is there somewhere else that would work for you? I'll help you set up."

We tossed around a few other ideas and settled on putting her displays in front of the Contreras Barn, even though it was in the back and not very grand.

★ ★ ★

Ma came over two days later and read me the riot act for giving in to Odilia. Ma loved Vida Lee, just like everyone else did.

"Why couldn't you do what Vida Lee wanted? Seems like she's doing you a favor," Ma said.

"She is. But Odilia already secured the general store for something else and she's not budging," I said.

"Can't you muster up some gumption to tell off Odilia?" Ma said.

I cleared my throat.

"Ma don't lecture me on this. You don't know anything about putting this kind of thing together. You never wanted to do anything like this, so don't tell me how to do things." I was getting tired of everyone telling me how to handle Odilia. It was like telling me how not to get run over by a train when I was tied to the tracks.

"You don't know anything about what I ever wanted to do," Ma said, pouting.

"When have you ever wanted to do something like this?" I said. "Seems like you just want to tell me what to do all day."

She stuck her chin up and scowled.

"For your information, I wanted to be a manager down at Connors Department Store in Texas. I worked there, you know, as a salesgirl before I married your daddy. They were so impressed with me they wanted to make me a department manager. Said I was an astute businesswoman. That's exactly what they said." Ma stood with her arms on her hips. "Astute."

"Why didn't you do it?"

"Because my Ma and Pa said I needed to get married and not have foolish notions like that. They didn't have career girls back then. When I met your Pa, they told me not to talk about my ambitions because it wasn't right for a woman to have those kinds of thoughts. So I gave it up," she said.

"I never knew that," I said and put my hand on her shoulder. "They told you not to have ambitions?"

"My Pa said it was fighting against my female nature to want a job like that. That my husband should be my career. And I knew I could do that job better than anyone."

"I'm sorry I never asked you about this before," I said. "Guess I've been selfish."

"Kids know nothin' about their parents, especially their mothers," she said, and I realized how often I must have treated her as badly as Pauline was treating me.

"Sorry, Ma. I wish you could have done what you wanted," I said.

"I'm fine," she said, and put my dishes away in the sink.

★ ★ ★

Later that week, I saw Vida Lee at the market. She was still mad, and that was unusual for Vida Lee, as she usually forgave everyone for anything.

"What goes around, comes around. I've been praying for Odilia," she said ominously, which made me think good-hearted Vida Lee might have a special pipeline to the Almighty and might have asked for heavenly retribution on Odilia. Surely that was sinful thinking, but then the idea of just a small swarm of locusts descending upon Odilia didn't seem too terrible. Anyway, I was pretty sure Odilia could order the locusts around, too.

★ ★ ★

Odilia

I was not wicked. Or mean. Or evil. I just wanted to get things done. I don't know why Irene always got so upset at me. Her sarcasm was hurtful, although I'd do everything I could not to show it. Every meeting we had turned into an argument because she didn't like the way I was handling things. It was annoying to say the least and very unfair since I wanted so badly to make the museum prosper, even if at the same time I was getting myself noticed around town.

Our beauty shop brawl was just the tip of the iceberg and I suspected a lot of people were coming to our meetings just to see us fight. Like a sport.

But I was used to it so maybe Irene had some valid reason for her attitude towards me. My sisters used to get mad at me, too, mostly because I always won at whatever game we were playing, even if it was who could throw the heaviest rock the farthest. We played hide and seek and I never got caught. When the school teacher at one school we were at held a contest to see who could sell the most Christmas wreaths, I won because I stood at the corner near the market all day on a Saturday and sold to all the ladies before they went in. My sisters went door to door, which took time. I won the contest and got a set of paper dolls.

I had a very specific plan for the festival and Irene was too herky-jerky about it. She changed schedules, allowed for excuses when people didn't show up to meetings, made wild estimates on budgets instead of methodically calculating them, and, most of all, she was always so concerned about making everyone happy. I found no plausible reason for that. When plans went well and people did as they were supposed to, they would be happy. There was no need to kowtow and Irene was a giant kowtower.

MEAT PICKLES

Irene

If you were going to have a festival, food had to be at the top of the list, so I assembled a group of very talented Buttonbush cooks to do cooking instructions, the kind where they talked as they made something delicious and spoons and knives would fly as they gave a first-hand look at how to make their particular dish. It took a good measure of talent to do that, I thought, since I could ruin a cake in no time by Jimmy interrupting me with some question, and soon I'd have put in two cups of salt instead of sugar.

The cooks would use Buttonbush crops in their recipes, so they fit right in with the theme. I'd secured a small refrigerator, a portable barbecue, a little range and oven combo, and a table for the cooking demonstration from Spinny's Spectacular Appliance. The cooks were all very excited to show off their special recipes using garlic, tomatoes, grapes, onions, melons, milk and cream, apples, potatoes, beef, peppers, and plums—whatever they could find that we grew in Buttonbush. Scalloped potatoes with bacon and onions, gelatin mold with grapes and oranges, buttermilk chocolate cakes, squash bread, stuffed peppers, and cheese mostaccioli. I hoped I'd get time to watch farmer Joe Toloni make his famous risotto.

One day I had to take Ma to the doctor and couldn't go to the cook's meeting. So Odilia handled the meeting for me, a job

I gave her with a bit of hesitation. With good reason. Later that afternoon, I found Joe at my doorstep. I could smell his agitation before I even said hello. He was pacing on my porch like the dog did when there was a rabbit nearby.

"That woman ... that *woman*," he said in his thick Italian accent that I could barely understand. He gripped his straw hat in meaty, strong hands, twisting like bread dough. "She ... she told me I shouldn't do my risotto because it takes too long and she ... she had a, what you call, a ske ... ske ... she make a time plan and she tell me to stick to it. Stick a to it!"

"I'm so sorry, Joe. Would you like to come in?" I said, debating on whether wine or whiskey would do the trick. He was so hopping mad he couldn't find words.

"No, no ... I just come here to tell you because I respect you and your husband and I know you got something to do with this festival but that woman is rid- rid- ridi ... she *crazy*! A time plan for cooking! You got to be careful, and you got to do it right to make things. She don't care. She got her plan."

"I'm sure we can work something out."

"What she know about cooking? Nothing! She skinny. Skinny, skinny woman who eat like a little bird ... looks like a chicken. She don't know nothing about food."

"Look, I'll talk to Odilia. I'll make sure we get you the time you need."

"No talk to her!" he said, his voice was deep and loud, the anger in his face red and shiny. His eyes bulged, as if they might shoot out of the sockets, right across my front porch and land in the zinnia planter. "She tell me to make something different ... something like ... like ... you know ... salad ... no not a salad ... the ... salad that's wet, you know ... I can't even think straight she got me so mad!"

He was struggling, the Italian language in him wanting to explode as he fumbled for the English words.

"Wet salad? You mean soup?"

"Ya, ya that's what she said. Zuppa. Soup. I no make soup! I do risotto or I don't do nothing. She no want to have good food at this festival … Food takes time to make … You got to love food and enjoy it when you cook. She no enjoy nothing but her time plan. She ought to just have people make those … those meat pickles!"

"Meat pickles?" I said.

"Yeah, you know … those meat things you boil for ten minutes and put ketchup and mustard on. Like at the base-a-ball games. Easy. Takes no talent."

Hot dogs. He was talking about hot dogs.

"Look, don't worry, Joe. I'll fix this. You make your risotto. I hear it's the cat's meow."

"The what? Cat?"

"I hear it's just delicious, Joe," I said, patting him on the shoulder. He got in his truck and drove off, much more calmly than when he arrived. I called up the other cooks, and they were also mad as all get out from the meeting. A couple threatened to pull out, but I talked them back in, words dripping like chocolate syrup from my mouth but a now always nagging anger clump in my throat for Odilia.

I never discussed Joe's visit with Odilia because, by this point, it was apparent she was on her own damn path with the festival and wasn't inclined to listen to anyone about anything. So I took the cook's committee back over and reworked the schedule a bit to accommodate Mr. Toloni. The rest of the cooks were glad I would not subject them to any more of Odilia's time planning. I told Odilia not to worry about the cooking show. All the other committees were just as angry with Odilia.

"They better be on time and ready at the festival or they'll answer to me," she said, and it never registered with her that there was something wrong in her approach, that people who are volunteering for things don't want to be bossed around. I couldn't figure how someone as sharp as Odilia couldn't see that her methods were more destructive than helpful but she was convinced she was a danged expert in managing people.

★ ★ ★

The new General Electric ovens had nothing on Buttonbush summers in the heat department. I wandered into the museum one day in August, beads of sweat forming on my neck. It was so hot that the paint appeared to bleed off the buildings and the stucco looked like it might char and turn to ashes. The little dirt roads winding around the back of the museum were bare. Not even a dandelion could make a living out there. The little rocks and pebbles in the road were hot and stinging on the feet. Not that anyone would be brave enough to go barefoot.

I hoped the swamp coolers in the main building were working enough so that I could sit in front of them. Felicia's office had a powerful set of coolers and I wanted to stop sweating a bit and dry the drenched strands of hair hanging all over my face. Felicia's office got the coldest, and it was why she didn't get much work done in the summer. Too many visitors.

I sat down with a thud.

"Betty called. She's not feeling that well today," Felicia said. "She wants you to call her."

"What are you doing on the floor?"

Felicia was crouched on the ground, wearing a coral and white skirt and top that matched perfectly, looking as sunny as if she'd just come out the pages of *Red Book*. This led me to have a momentary pause to dislike her because I was sweaty and sticky and she looked like a million bucks while she writhed around on the ground. She was on the hunt for a lizard that she said crawled across her foot and given her near a heart attack. A ruler in her hand, Felicia was on her knees, trying to pry the poor thing out from behind the wastebasket that stood under her desk.

"Here lizard, little lizard," she cooed as if it could hear her and obey like a puppy.

She got to her feet and sighed. The pile of papers on her desk was easily twelve inches tall. It was all Odilia's endless paperwork.

"See here, I have a paper cut from this giant pile she gave me today. These are all her required forms for the sponsors. I think she asked them for their tax returns, last will and testament, and their high school report cards. It's a bit much, don't you think?" she said, and I nodded. Odilia viewed piles of paper as valuables akin to piles of gold.

"Mrs. Holiday called. She resigned from running the children's area for the festival. Said it was because Mrs. Delgado told her she was disorganized and flighty," Felicia said. "And the guy who was supposed to supply ice to the festival told me we could sweat to death for all he cared. Miss Delgado insisted he supply an ice truck for free."

"Hand me the phone, please," I said. Felicia stood up and handed me the phone. I called Betty and filled her in on Odilia's latest fiascos.

"You're doing such a good job, Irene. Odilia is causing you so many problems and you deserve some acknowledgment for all this," Betty said. "All these people are so mad at her!"

"It's like trying to stop a charging elephant with a butterfly net," I said.

"I feel guilty for even asking but I do have a favor to ask," Betty said. "Could I be in charge of the nighttime event at the festival? The supper club we talked about. I think I could organize that nicely, very chic."

"That would be terrific, Betty. You'll do a fabulous job and it would take so much off of me if you would handle that. I have so much to do," I said. "But I'm always here to help you. Unlike some other people, you are good at fixing problems, not causing them."

Felicia, who failed to find the lizard under her desk propped her legs up on an extra chair.

"I'm not letting that thing crawl on me again," she said.

I spent the rest of the afternoon athletically weeding my flower bed. I had to call three more people to apologize for the things Odilia had done, all of them saying they wouldn't bother coming to the festival. The festival couldn't get here fast enough because I was tired as could be, both in body and mind. I was weary of Pauline and her teenage antics ... and between me and the rest of the committee—and possibly all of Buttonbush—we'd all had enough of Odilia.

★ ★ ★

Odilia

Everything was going smoothly. I had all the festival details nailed down tight. Like a military general, I'd put all the pieces together in precision order. It didn't matter to me if the festival was Irene's idea. I was in charge of it and everybody knew it. I made sure they knew it.

"I am thrilled to announce that we'll be doing cooking demonstrations using Buttonbush crops as ingredients all day long at the festival. You won't want to miss that," I said. I was at the Ladies Auxiliary luncheon at the Buttonbush Methodist Church to promote the festival and encourage ticket sales.

They'd called to invite Irene and I to speak but I never mentioned it to Irene and did it myself. I didn't need her to come along. This festival was going to be my crowning achievement and I'd made it my mission to make sure my name was associated with it at every turn. It didn't matter to Irene. She wasn't interested in glory or attention. She had no ambition to get into the Gold Seal Club or any other club for that matter. But for me, this was my apex.

Besides, neither Irene nor Betty nor Maye Marie had the skills to organize the festival. I'd taken it on just like I'd run the factory during the war, with sharpness and discipline. Food, vendors, entertainment, finance, clean-up, and children's committees were all organized and properly prepared. This would not be some thrown-together event with unorganized pieces and parts. I had it all firmly plotted out, exacted, and pinned down. No detail escaped my notice and I let everyone know that I, Odilia Soliz Delgado, was going to single-handedly save the museum from demolition. Sure, Irene, Maye Marie, and Betty had helped, but I was the mastermind behind it all and the architect who designed and built it. No one was going to want to put a courthouse into that museum after I showed what I could do. No one.

THE FESTIVAL

Irene

I ate three jalapeños dripping with maple syrup and honey the morning of October 28, 1952, the day of the festival. It just about made me sick to my stomach, but I figured I was dealing with Odilia all day long and I needed all the help I could get. I got to the museum grounds just as the sun was coming up.

"Look at us all dolled up," said Maye Marie, who, along with Betty, also arrived early. "And we match!"

The festival colors were green and tan so we wore the same. Betty, Maye Marie, and I had on khaki pants and matching green gingham shirts. Maye Marie put a little green bow in the back of her hair and Betty wore matching green shoes. I was lucky to get my hair combed that morning but it was clean, shining, and cut more stylishly than it'd been three months before, and I had new Kedettes on. I was gaining in the fashion department.

"Betty, I can't wait for all your delicious cocktails tonight," I said. "Jimmy wants to try your whiskey sours."

"It's going to be so fun," she said. "But no cocktails for me."

"Why?" Maye Marie and I said in unison.

Betty smiled and made a rounding gesture over her belly.

"You're expecting!" I said.

"Due in April."

"That's marvelous, Betty, so marvelous," Maye Marie said, and we both hugged her.

"Where's Odilia?" I said.

The three of us set down the main museum walking path as hundreds of people drove in to set up their booths or stations. We would open the gates in two hours. At a corner, we spotted Odilia and stopped dead in our tracks.

"What in the holy hell?" I said. Maye Marie and Betty stared wide-eyed.

Odilia, head imperiously swiveling, sat in a horse-drawn wagon driven by Kosta. She wore a long, gold, Grecian-type gown that bared her thin shoulders and draped around her in folds. The gown had little felt farm animals sewn on it: pigs, cows, chickens, sheep. A fake grapevine wrapped around her shoulders, and her skin was tinted golden, too. On her head perched a gold turban to which she'd glued plastic fruit, like Carmen Miranda, little apples and grapes and oranges sticking out of it. She carried a cornucopia filled with a bunch of potatoes, corn, wheat, and cotton stalks, and she wore gold beads on her neck and lots of gold bracelets. She was a mobile farm show.

"Odilia, what are you supposed to be?" Maye Marie said.

"I'm queen of the harvest: Demeter," Odilia said.

"As in the goddess?" Betty said.

"That's right," Odilia smiled, and hopped down from the wagon. She paraded in front of us, swooping the cornucopia to the side. I couldn't rightly form any words.

"Did you make that costume?" said Betty.

"I did. My housekeeper helped. Took us all last weekend," Odilia said, beaming.

"Do you have gold on your arms?" Betty said, and she grabbed Odilia's arm and held it close to her eyes.

"I just took a little kid's paint and mixed it with some gold paint I kept from Christmas. It should come right off with a good scrub," she said.

"Good Lord," said Betty, and she let go of Odilia's arm like it was a hot iron.

"We already have a queen for the festival. You know that, don't you?" Maye Marie said.

"She's queen of the festival. I'm queen of the harvest," Odilia said.

"Oh, that's the distinction. Clever," Betty said, and she couldn't stop staring at Odilia, whose golden tones were sort of blinding all of us.

"Don't get near the pen with the billy goats 'cause they'll likely eat your costume off and then you'll be the goddess of naked," I said, and she lifted that giant cornucopia like she was going to clobber me with it.

"Maye Marie, where are we in our accounts? I know we are about $133 to the good this month, but where are the reserves? I want to know exactly what we need to make today," Odilia said. I wanted to know that, too.

"I did a last-minute balance, and we need to raise exactly $4,432 today. We'd have needed less, but we had to spend money on that broken toilet in the kids area last week," Maye Marie said.

"Okay, Queens. Four, four, three, two. Let's do this. Let's get that money today," I said, fist in the air.

"We can do this," Odilia said. "Nothing can stop the Four Queens. Or Demeter." She swooshed her cornucopia in the air.

"Awww geez, Odilia. You look like the Statue of Liberty went grocery shopping," I said.

"Never mind that," Betty said, stepping in front of me. "I told the other Queens my news and I'll tell you. There's going to be a little baby coming in April."

Odilia's face fell, then lit up with a smile.

"That's great news. Congratulations," she said in a short tone, and climbed back on the wagon. "I need to go check on the ticket booths. See you all later. Onward, Kosta. Four, four, three, two. Four, four, three, two. Say that over and over ladies." Kosta snapped the reins and drove off.

The three of us burst out laughing.

A literal excitement crackled through the air that day. I was nervous as a lark, but proud of what we'd accomplished. Betty twisted her fingers in her hands. Her mother had come to visit, specifically to see how the festival went. Already counting off ticket sales in her head, Maye Marie just fretted about our profits. And Odilia, well, she was never nervous about anything.

The Four Queens had taken on this mammoth task, and there were scads of exhibitors, hanging lights, tables and chairs, food and libation booths, decorations and posters all over the grounds, along the walking paths and on the open green areas under the trees. I was so proud.

Colorful booths of arts and crafts, games for kids, balloons, and trinkets for sale, and lots of tractors, balers, cotton pickers, and other farm machinery filled the museum. The aroma of popcorn, hot dogs, barbecue, and cotton candy permeated the air, and there were several music stages featuring banjo players, barbershop quartets, and dancers. We'd decorated the museum grounds with beautiful banners and signs with the festival emblem, life size papier mâché figures of some of Buttonbush's founders, plus some fun ones for the kids like Rapunzel and Robin Hood. We hung a huge welcome banner at the entrance, perfectly lettered and cheery.

Odilia marched around like General Patton in her gold dress, barking orders, chewing out vendors, pointing her finger every which way. It was classic Odilia doing what she does best: bossing people around. I couldn't help but laugh.

Vida Lee, true to her word, put up festive agricultural displays of everything grown in Buttonbush: oranges, cotton, garlic, apples, onions, tomatoes, potatoes, grapes, hay, and melons. There were dairy and beef cows housed in little pens for the kids to see. She'd even got farmer Choddy Obermeyer, our biggest donor, to bring in a huge truckload of garlic and they were handing out little brown bags of free garlic to folks from the tailgate. Vida Lee made a colorful poster showing Buttonbush's top crops and how much our area grew each year. In the food area, the smell of cinnamon rolls wafted through the air. It was going to be a great day for the museum.

★ ★ ★

Odilia

It was my shining moment. My splendid success. My "I told you so" to Iggy, whom I grew more angry with by the hour. But I would not let him ruin this for me. He'd see. I was a somebody. He promised me he'd be there later in the afternoon and I was looking forward to showing him all the things I'd done. I waltzed down the paths at the museum, each one lined with people enjoying themselves.

By noon, there were throngs of people in the museum. I strolled over to the game booths where I saw a ruckus going on at the Calvary Bible Church booth, which was manned by Irene's mother, Mrs. Looper, and Gertrude Schmid. Their loud voices carried across the path and I saw Mrs. Looper point at the booth next to them, which was the Buttonbush Junior College band booth. A long line of patrons encircled the band booth. Mrs. Looper wagged her finger at two of the band students and they argued back at her.

"What's the matter here, ladies?" I said.

"These students are having a kissing booth. Right here. Next to our booth where we're promoting our Bible study classes and giving away little pamphlets from the gospel of Mark," Mrs. Looper said. I noted that Irene had the same hazel eyes.

"For a nickel you can stick your hand in our Jacob's Wishing Well and get a prize, too," said Mrs. Schmid.

"What's wrong with the kissing booth?" I said, and I eyeballed the young people who squirmed under the two ladies' gaze.

"This is highly immoral," Mrs. Looper said, and she put her hand to her face and stared sadly at the two attractive young women who were at the college booth. Three young men were with them as well, and all were rolling their eyes and dropping their heads back in disbelief at the two church ladies. "I'm ashamed that you've allowed this at the festival. Where is Irene? I'm going to tell her a thing or two."

Irene must have seen the commotion, too, and wandered up, puzzled.

"What's going on, Ma?"

"They have a kissing booth. Kissing!" Mrs. Looper put her hands on her hips as Irene stood in front of her.

"We're raising money for the band," one student said, peeking out from behind Mrs. Looper. "There's no harm in this. What's the big deal?"

"You filled out an application for the booth, correct?" I said to the students. "Did you mention it would be a kissing booth?"

"I don't know. Our band teacher filled out the application," one boy said.

"You are out of compliance with festival regulations," Mrs. Schmid said.

"You need to crack down on this, Irene. These children are forging a path towards indecency and moral decay," Mrs. Looper said, and Irene grunted.

I wandered across the path to the Scottish Heritage Society booth that was directly across from the two dueling booths.

"What happened here?" I said to Duncan Gilday, a stout, friendly faced man with a wiry beard and fingers like sausages.

"It was something. The ladies had their booth all set up, and they were getting a nice trickle of customers there ... handing out their pamphlets and so on ... and then those kids showed up late, like kids do, and put up the kissing booth. They were charging a dollar for a kiss ... boys and girls ... Just a small buss on the cheek, nothing passionate, but they were getting a line all the way down the path here and those ladies got mad. No one was coming to their booth," he said.

"Wonderful," I said, and watched as Irene tried to negotiate between the two sides.

"And then Gertrud spied her husband in the line and she nearly beheaded him when she pulled him out. Bible class or kiss a comely lass, eh? Who do you think is going to win?" Duncan laughed.

I walked back to the church booth and whispered in Irene's ear.

"These kids were charging a dollar for a kiss and were getting a mile-long line. Do you know what that does for our profits?" I said, and Irene nodded. "You distract your mom and I'll move the kids. Look at the money they're piling up."

Irene looked over at the pile of dollar bills in the kids' booth and nodded.

"Okay, Ma, Mrs. Schmid, let's go back to your booth and Odilia is going to take these kids away now," Irene said.

"Praise the Lord. I never," Mrs. Looper said, and shuffled back over to her booth.

"Kids, gather your things," I whispered. "The Rugby Club never showed up to their booth spot. Why don't we move you over there?"

The students smirked at the church ladies who returned to their booth, scowling all the while. I helped the students gather their signs and band information. A kissing booth wasn't so bad. I remembered my first kiss at that age and inwardly smiled, then rousted myself and shook the thought out of my head.

"They shouldn't be offering kisses up for money ... It's shameful," Mrs. Looper called from her booth.

"We'll make sure they don't slip into the den of iniquity at the festival, Ma," Irene said. She winked at me and I winked back.

Ten minutes later, Irene found me at the kissing booth.

"Our descent into depravation is complete," Irene said, and I laughed. The line was getting longer and longer for the kissing booth. If nothing else, Irene and I could unite in our determination to make money. Sometimes she wasn't so bad.

It was just about two o'clock when I wandered to the main office where I found Maye Marie with Felicia, counting out receipts and cash.

"Just as soon as you get some sort of estimate of our take for the day, let me know," I said.

"It's going to be big. We're already way over our estimated attendance. We might just pull this off," Maye Marie said, and yanked a pencil off her ear to write something in her ledger book.

I giggled, sure of our success, and walked out the door. I made my way behind the Henderson House, checking to see if the electrical was still plugged in for the microphone for the watermelon toss when I spotted Iggy on the front porch talking to three of the county commissioners. Their heads were bent over in deep conversation so I pressed my back to the side of the house and scooted closer so I could hear them.

"I don't know, Senator. Looks to me like they might just pull this off," one commissioner said.

"Don't worry about it. They'll never do it. And even if they do, I'll get Odilia to spend it all. It doesn't take much to get her to want to spend money around here. I've got a lead on another house that someone wants to bring in here and it will cost them a fortune. She won't be able to turn it down," Iggy said.

"This courthouse project needs to start soon. We've got contractors breathing down our neck," another commissioner said.

"Fortunately, gentleman, as chairman of that courts commission, I can control those contractors. We'll have that project going here in no time. It's going to be stupendous," Iggy said, chuckling, and my head started to spin.

"I'm all for it, but, personally, I don't know how you're going to pull this off at home. What's your wife going to say when she finds out the entire museum is going to get demolished, not just part of it?" Commissioner Holson said.

My stomach lurched. I held my breath and listened.

"This fire hazard of a museum needs to go and that new courthouse needs to be put right here. Don't worry about Odilia. I've got her under control," Iggy said. The men patted each other on the back and walked down the sidewalk.

I could barely breathe. My own husband was chair of the courts commission that was trying to take over our museum. And they were going to demolish all of it, not just part of it. Iggy had betrayed me, lied to me repeatedly. I was a fool. All those projects of mine that he told me were a good idea were just a way to bankrupt the museum and set me up for failure. I wanted to cry and the tears crept into my eyes, but I took a strong breath and stopped them. There was no time to be stupid and weak. I knew my marriage was in trouble but I didn't know it was in shambles. I'd have to think about that later. But I needed to stop Iggy. I probably couldn't save my marriage, but I needed to save this museum. I needed the other three Queens to do it.

★ ★ ★

Irene

It warmed my heart to see so many Buttonbush people at the museum, the little buildings and houses surrounded by young and old, laughing and having fun at the various booths. Everyone from the Elks Club to the Junior League to the Jefferson School P.T.A. had a booth up and down the paths that wound through the museum. I couldn't have been more pleased with the festival. Thirty-five children got flat on their bellies and tried to roll cherry tomatoes across the great lawn with their noses. It was a sight. Twenty-seven babies crawled on the lawn in a race while their parents screamed and cheered. It might have been the cutest darn thing I ever saw. The pie-throwing booth was a huge success, since the Kiwanis Club picked some of the top targets in town: the police chief, Judge Herrera, two high school principals, a County Commissioner, and Gabby Bozanik, who lost the championship bowling tournament for the Kiwanis last year. I knew, but of course never mentioned, that those Kiwanis could have doubled their income on that booth if they'd put Odilia in there, and some of that money would have come from me, although she was acting like an actual human being that day.

There were a couple of men who threw out their shoulders in the watermelon toss and at least three kids ended up with stitches after crawling on some tractors on display. All the kids had a ball, with baseball games and races at the end of the afternoon that Arky managed on the fields next to the museum.

We kept our word, and the festival had plenty of libations with a genuine, European-type beer garden that was busy all day. Jimmy especially enjoyed this area, and he and Betty's husband, Alvin, contributed to the profits steadily. We'd put out flowers and checkered tablecloths, and even the serving ladies and men wore little German-looking aprons with bric-à-brac trim. You could hear the laughter and joking across the museum. It was sure to make money, and those cash boxes filled up, my sense of pride in the festival going right up with them.

"You did it, honey," Jimmy said. He'd walked up behind me with Pauline. She was dead silent and had only come to the festival begrudgingly. "You got this whole thing going."

Jimmy put his arm around my neck and hugged me. I fell into him, happy to have a quick break from all the commotion.

"I did, didn't I? Kind of proud of myself."

"Yeah, Mom. Good festival." Willy tapped me on the arm. Pauline still pouted, but I didn't care. Even her teenage sullenness couldn't dampen my day.

At seven o'clock, the dance music started in the main courtyard and Betty had gone all out for this. She made a cocktail lounge-type area with a stage for the band, little tables covered in green fabric, and garlands of paper flowers hanging overhead. She strung twinkly lights and surrounded the area with new-fangled tiki torches, something hardly anyone in Buttonbush had ever seen, like something out of a Hollywood movie. There was an elegant bar and a little food section where people could buy hot sandwiches or a plate of spaghetti. Pauline and Willy, wearing green checked aprons, were working in the food line, scooping spaghetti on the plates.

I knew Betty was on pins and needles since her mother was coming.

"It looks spectacular, Betty, just spectacular," I said, and she beamed.

Her mother swept through the plaza right as the band started, with Alvin on her arm.

"This certainly looks cheerful, Bettina. It looks like you've done a good job setting this up," Mrs. Shellman said.

"Come get a drink, Mother. It's going to get very crowded soon," Betty said, and pulled her mother over to the bar. Alvin and I sat down and were soon joined by Jimmy, Maye Marie, and Arky. Soon, throngs of people flowed in, twirling around the dance floor.

Betty plopped her mother next to me while she ran to the ladies' room. Her mother, wearing an overly draped woolen dress, frowned as usual. I scooted closer to her.

"You know, Betty … er, Bettina has done a wonderful job on this festival. Why, if it weren't for her, we wouldn't be organized at all. She's the tops at making lists and keeping track of schedules," I said. "And she put this entire area together. Planned it all herself."

"Really? Bettina?" Mrs. Shellman said.

"Your daughter is a great benefit to this museum," I said. "She is so good at thinking of educational ideas, especially for the children. And she's the best at organizing. I never met anyone smarter than Bettina."

"I had no idea."

Mrs. Shellman watched Betty dance with Alvin, who was a terrible dancer, but it didn't seem to faze Betty. She was smiling ear to ear.

I was sipping my beer when a clawing hand gripped the back of my neck. .

"Get over here. We need to meet." It was Odilia. She grabbed Betty from the dance floor then Maye Marie from Arky's arm.

"What is so important, Odilia?" Betty asked, fluffing her hair. We huddled behind the stage. Odilia quickly filled us in on the Senator's treacherous plans and the jeopardy the museum was in from the courthouse.

"You mean we put this festival on for nothing?" My chest tightened.

"It's been a ruse, a complete setup. I cannot believe it," Maye Marie said fanning herself, and Odilia dropped her head into her hands.

"I'm sorry. My own husband has betrayed all of us. Me included. I'm so embarrassed," she said.

Betty put her arm around Odilia and hugged her.

"It's not your fault. You ... We all have been trying our best to save this place," she said, and Odilia's eyes welled up in tears.

"What are we going to do?" Marye Marie said.

"Do we have any kind of estimate on our earnings yet?" Odilia said.

"I can go run some numbers. They won't be final but I can get something," Maye Marie said. We all traipsed after her to the office and sat down in a dejected heap while she worked her ledger magic.

"I can't believe my own husband did this to me," Odilia said. Her bottom lip quivered.

"I'm sorry, Odilia. Truly I am," I said. And I was. What a shameful thing for a husband to do to his wife.

"They're going to demolish this whole museum. All of it. All our hard work will be gone," Odilia said.

Betty patted her arm and hung her head. Maye Marie yanked the adding machine tape and waved it in the air.

"We did it! We are way over our goal!" Maye Marie jumped up and down with the tape flying in her hand.

"We've raised $7,834, and that's after our expenses. I've looked at our budget and unless there's something I'm missing, there shouldn't be any other big expenses coming. We've saved this place." Maye Marie did a little dance across the floor.

"Yee haw," I said, hugging Betty.

"Okay, but that's not going to stop those devious men. I've got something else in mind," Odilia said, and in hushed tones, she told us what she had up her sleeve.

YOU OLD HEARTBREAKER

Irene

When we got back to the dance floor, Maye Marie went to powder her nose, and Jimmy went to get more drinks from the bar. I scooted next to Arky, who was sweating from dancing.

"You sure put on a good festival. Glad you and Odilia could work together," he said. "She's not easy."

"I guess you could say we worked together. She tolerates me." I laughed. "Amazingly, we haven't argued all day today."

"Well considering her history with Jimmy, I'm surprised she even talks to you."

"What? Her history with Jimmy?" My forehead pinched together.

"Yeah, you know. In high school. Didn't Jimmy tell you?" Arky turned pale. He stood up to leave, but I grabbed his arm.

"What happened in high school?"

Arky sighed and sat down.

"Nuthin'." He cleared his throat.

"Spit it out, Arky." Butterflies fluttered in my head and Arky cowered like a cornered cat. He cleared his throat again.

"Odilia and Jimmy dated in high school. Nothing important." Arky nervously tapped his meaty fingers on the table. "But Jimmy broke it off. I'm surprised you didn't know."

"What?" I felt like someone punched me. I might punch Jimmy.

"Aw, I shouldn't have said anything. I thought you knew." Arky's face was ashen, like he might get sick.

"First I'm hearing of it. What happened?"

"Jimmy broke her heart. You're the only girl Jimmy ever looked at, but you didn't come along until later," Arky said. He patted my hand which just made it worse. I'm certain my face went every shade of pale.

"Odilia! And Jimmy? I can hardly believe it. Why didn't he ever say anything?"

"Jimmy probably just didn't want to upset you, and here I've gone and done just that."

I sat for a few seconds, taking it in. This was the last thing I would ever imagine.

"That might be the first time Odilia couldn't get what she wanted," I said. Holy hell, did she still love my Jimmy?

It's a terrible thing when someone you trusted without fail has hidden a secret from you and I couldn't believe Jimmy could do this to me. I couldn't ever remember a time when he hid anything from me, even the time he spent eighty-five dollars on a new table saw. My stomach was nauseated and my temples throbbed. I still couldn't quite picture the two of them together, but maybe Odilia was a little nicer back then, a little more shy. I couldn't see Jimmy being attracted to her now but maybe I didn't know him as well as I thought I did.

Jimmy came back to the table, and I looked hard at him. I didn't know him in high school, and as a wife, I'd forgotten how handsome and sweet he was. Of course Odilia had a crush on him back then.

"We need to have a little talk later," I said to Jimmy.

"Uh-oh. What did I do now?" He laughed and slapped Arky on the back.

"Arky was just filling me in on your high school days. The part about Odilia and you dating," I said. "The part you forgot to mention to me, dear."

"Oh, it wasn't like that," he said, his eyes peering over the top of his glass as he took a long sip of beer.

Arky looked like he wanted to crawl under the table.

"Don't worry, Irene. The day Jimmy met you he was so lovesick. It was pathetic." Arky smiled at me, but I wasn't buying it.

"Might have been nice if I'd known this. You didn't think it was important to mention this to me. No wonder Odilia hates me," I said. Did all husbands keep secrets?

"I wouldn't call it hate, honey. Odilia's moved on in life," Jimmy said, a nervous laugh in his voice.

"Has she?" I asked.

"Jimmy, you heartbreaker, you," Arky said.

"Yes, Jimmy, you old heartbreaker, you," I said, my tongue poking into my cheek.

"Thanks for filling her in on everything, buddy," Jimmy said, slapping Arky on the back.

Jimmy patted my hand while I stewed, but the music and noise was too distracting and I couldn't concentrate on my thoughts. Jimmy! My Jimmy, the object of Odilia's affections. I didn't know she even had affections. I sucked in my stomach and fished in my purse for my lipstick.

The band was churning out a version of "Walkin' My Baby Back Home" when Odilia interrupted the festivities and took over the microphone.

"There's your old girlfriend up there, dear," I said.

"Aw now, come on, Irene." Jimmy slouched in his chair.

Still in her gold gown, which was now rumpled a bit at day's end, Odilia swayed back and forth as she went on and on about the museum. She, of course, mentioned herself as chair of the festival but neglected to mention Betty or Maye Marie or me. Some things never changed.

The Senator appeared at the side of the dance floor and Odilia stared at him for a long moment.

"I want to thank everyone for coming to the first Buttonbush Farm Heritage Festival and making it so successful," Odilia said. "In fact, we have been so successful that I believe our county commissioners are in for a surprise. According to our financial wizards, the festival, so far, has earned over seven thousand dollars. That doesn't even count what we might raise here tonight. That far exceeds the amount of money the county told us we had to raise by December 31 in order to save the museum from demolition. Isn't that tremendous?"

Odilia smiled and held up her thumb.

"We will continue to preserve Buttonbush history," she said. "Including building even more incredible features here."

Maye Marie and Betty walked up to the stage arm in arm with Tom Dogan, who seemed to have turned a pale shade of grey.

"In fact, just tonight, we've secured a tremendous donation from Tom Dogan for a new portrait gallery, to be built next year on the museum grounds. The gallery will feature portraits of our local leaders and famous residents," Odilia said. Tom's forehead was in in a knot, his eyes darting from his wife to Odilia. She was so good at putting the finger on someone. "What a generous gift from Mr. Dogan."

I stood up, my knees shaking. I wasn't sure if it was from the news I just heard about Jimmy or what I was about to do. I walked over to Senator Delgado.

"Senator, will you join me on stage?" I said, my voice ragged and soft.

The Senator squinted and his top lip curled on one side, but he rose and walked with me.

Odilia handed me the microphone, giving Iggy a sly smile. I took a deep breath.

"The very first portrait that will be placed in the gallery will be that of our own Senator Ignatius Delgado, our dear legislator and current chairman of the California Courts Commission. That's the commission in charge of building a new courthouse in Buttonbush. Although, it won't be at the museum anymore since we've raised the money the county commissioners required of us, having given us a specific goal of five thousand dollars. Which we have far exceeded. I actually took notes at that meeting and have all the details written down if anyone is ever interested in the fascinating history of our county and its inner workings," I said.

"The state will decide, so you really have little say in the courthouse," the Senator said.

Odilia grabbed the microphone.

"Since we've reached our goal, the county commissioners surely will rethink this, especially since we have their promises in writing. I can't imagine our dear and honest commissioners going back on their word," Odilia said. The crowd buzzed and the Senator tried to say something but stammered, his Adam's apple going up and down as he gulped repeatedly, glaring at Odilia and then at me.

The county commissioners sitting at table in the front looked like a pack of rats on the Titanic.

"Isn't that a terrific honor that you'll be the first portrait in the gallery your wife has raised money to build?" I said. Senator Delgado clenched his fists and tightened his jaw. Odilia's gold arms were sticking out from behind her husband, and I waited to see if she might reach up and choke him from behind.

The crowd rose to their feet in applause, and the country commissioners, lacking any other thing to do, did the same. Senator Delgado gave Odilia a nasty stare, and I knew there was going to be a barn-burner of an argument at their house later. Tom Dogan, looking relieved, sat back down next to his wife. I went back to our table. Mrs. Shellman was actually smiling at Betty, which I didn't think her mouth was capable of doing.

The museum was in the clear, and despite my anxiety at what I'd learned about Jimmy and Odilia, I enjoyed the rest of the night and even danced a little. I did step on Jimmy's toes quite a bit, on purpose. I had a touch of burning in my stomach. I'd spent all this time thinking Odilia hated me for my work on the museum board. But now I knew it was personal.

★ ★ ★

When Jimmy fell asleep that night, I rifled through our bookshelves to find his high school yearbook. Sure enough, there he was with Odilia. But they called her "Dilly," and her last name was "Solis." I'd heard that name before but never put it together. I always knew he'd dated someone named "Dilly" in high school, in fact the only other girl he'd dated besides me. I thumbed through the yearbook and there it was: Jimmy and Dilly, at a dance, smiling for the camera, his arm around her waist and Odilia looking up at him all goo-goo-eyed. I might have to kill him.

I couldn't think of two people more different than my Jimmy and Odilia. I tossed and turned all night, looking over at Jimmy every once in a while to wonder how the hell he could sleep when I was so keyed up. After a time, I realized I'd probably gotten to take him for granted, forgetting what a handsome, kind, loving man he was, and how it shouldn't be surprising that he'd had girls falling for him back in high school. But I couldn't for the life of me reconcile in my head that one of those girls had been Odilia, and after knowing her and her do or die ways, it was shocking to me that Jimmy hadn't ended up marrying her.

YOO-HOO

Odilia

Iggy was fast asleep when I got home, snoring like an old bear. I poked him in the side to wake him. He sat up in bed, pulling the sheets up over his chest.

"What is it? It's very late."

"How dare you lie to me! You were the chairman of that courts commission. Plotting to close the museum. You are despicable." The words spat out of my mouth.

Iggy shrugged.

"Odilia, don't get all in a dither. You should have never been on that board. You were supposed to be a wife to me, a homemaker. I didn't marry you so you could run around doing all these things. And that museum is a disgrace," he said, and scratched the top of his head.

"It is not a disgrace. I've done a lot to fix that place up. I've put in countless hours to raise money to refurbish it and you've been sabotaging me all this time. How could you?" I was near tears but didn't want him to see me cry.

"You may have won this battle, dear, but you lost the war. I hope it was all worth it to you," he said, pulling the covers around himself with a smirk.

"Worth it? You bet it was worth it. It was worth it to defeat your plans. The plans you've been sneaking behind my back along with all the other things you've been sneaking. Don't think I don't know what you've been up to, Iggy. But I pulled it off, didn't I? Me and the other Queens. We all think you are a terrible, awful human being!"

"You're over doing this as usual. I just didn't want you to know about the commission because you'd think I was too involved and I knew you'd over-react. And you are doing just that," he said, and laid back down. "Now go to sleep."

"Sleep! You expect me to sleep here, with you? You haven't even apologized." I stormed out of the room, grabbing my robe and slamming the door. I knew my marriage was over and I wasn't sure how I felt about it just yet. There was a wide sense of relief sandwiched between fear and anxiety. What would I do? Could I be on my own without the security of a husband? I made fun of Irene and her itty-bitty life with Jimmy, but maybe she had it right. I'd overshot by getting a husband with power and way too much pride. I spent the night in tears in the guest bedroom. Iggy was gone when I woke in the morning.

My coffee went cold in my cup as I sat to think about what I was going to do. Money wouldn't be a problem. Iggy and I had plenty to split. But what would I be without a husband to anchor me? On my own, no real role in the world. I smoked even more than usual, then got dressed. No use feeling sorry for myself. I had things to do.

★ ★ ★

Irene

I got up with Jimmy at five the next day and cornered him at the coffeepot.

"I still don't understand why you didn't tell me you and Odilia had a romance in high school?" I said, handing him a steaming cup. He had a sheepish look on his face, like he was scared of what I might do.

"That's a stretch to call it a romance, honey. And, well you kind of knew I dated Dilly. I just didn't mention that it was Odilia. That's all," Jimmy said, shrugging his shoulder like I should just let it go. Of course, I could not.

"Don't you think it might have been important to let me know she might hate me so much because she's been carrying a torch for you all these years?"

"That ain't true … Geez, Irene. I'm sorry. I don't know anything about women, and I sure didn't know about teenage girls back then. Or now, for that matter. Don't you see how I can't hardly understand anything Pauline is doing? They're a mystery to me."

"That was all of it, right? You didn't see her after high school, did you?"

"She moved out of town."

"But did you?"

"Well, no … not really. Kind of," Jimmy stammered, and I gave him a fierce look.

"Spit it out."

"She called me the week before we got married."

"She what?"

"She called. To congratulate me and then she asked me if I was sure about you. I hadn't seen her in about six years. I told her I was sure about you. 'Cause I was. Still am," he said, grabbing my hand but I pulled it away.

"I can't believe I had to find out all this from Arky and not you." I slammed my coffee cup down.

"It was nothing. She was never going to be anything to me, and you know I ain't never looked at another woman since I met you." His eyes were soft, warm, and just a little bit teary. "I shoulda told you."

I heaved a deep sigh and looked at him. I could tell he wasn't sure if I was going to throw a coffee cup at him. A raging flare of anger welled up in me, but then it burst like a bubble and dissipated. I knew my Jimmy. I knew he was true blue. There wasn't anything untruthful about my Jimmy. Except of course for this little recent exclusion of details.

"I sure wish I'd known this. It would have explained so much," I said, and grabbed the frying pan to cook him bacon.

"You gonna hit me with that thing?" Jimmy had that boyish glint in his eye, and I turned my back to him.

"Maybe."

"Do it after church. I got some prayin' to do," he said.

"You sure do," I said.

Who'd have guessed that my Jimmy was such a playboy?

★ ★ ★

Buttonbush, as usual, forgot there was such a season as autumn and by Tuesday, temperatures soared to over ninety-five degrees. There was still a lot to clean up. Choddy Obermeyer's giant truck, overflowing with garlic, was still at the museum. It was smelling something fierce, the beautiful garlic cloves turning mushy and rank. I called Vida Lee.

"Choddy's man is on his way. He's been so busy he couldn't get there any sooner. Thanks, Irene." She was always upbeat, but I sensed something unusually cheery about her. I hung up and went about putting away tables and chairs, taking down posters and banners and tossing out all the paper decor. Maye Marie and Betty were also out on the grounds picking up while Odilia was in the office, phoning people and thanking them for their participation and donations. She was all business today, never mentioning what happened with the Senator.

We were all exceedingly tired.

That afternoon Betty, Maye Marie, and I were sitting in Felicia's office draining a pitcher of ice water when Odilia burst into the room, bellowing to the rooftops.

"That garlic truck dumped a huge load of smelly garlic all down the side of my car. All on the driver's side. I can't get in. It's disgusting! Felicia, get someone to shovel that out of there. It's seeping into my upholstery," she said, her temples pulsing.

I ran outside and sure enough, there was stinking, slimy garlic piled up and over the side of that beautiful Cadillac convertible and large clumps spilled into the driver's seat, smattering Odilia's white upholstery. Spoiling garlic has a powerful odor, and it was seeping all into her car. I swear there was a little puff of steam coming out of Odilia's ears.

Odilia almost pulled the phone out of the wall when she called Vida Lee. She held the phone so I could hear.

"Vida Lee! Your truck driver dumped garlic all over the side of my car," Odilia spewed into the phone. "My upholstery is going to smell like garlic for weeks. Weeks!"

"He did? That was Choddy Obermeyer who went and picked it up himself. I'll call him and see what happened," Vida Lee said with just a touch of a giggle in her voice. "I'll call you back, right soon."

I smiled.

"Choddy is our biggest donor to the festival, the one you're trying to get to donate to your building projects," I said. I could almost hear the wheels in her head grinding together. The "raise money" wheel turning right against the "I'm angry enough to spit nails" wheel. Ten minutes later, Vida Lee called back.

"Choddy said he's very sorry and didn't realize that happened. He said while he was backing the truck up, trying to avoid hitting your car, a cat ran out and he slammed on the brakes real fast. That must have been when a bit of garlic flew off the truck. He said he hopes it's nothing too bad, but he sure did like the festival and was glad he gave you all that money. He was proud to be your biggest donor."

"Well, okay, but ..." Odilia's tongue was in a knot.

I could almost see Vida Lee smiling over the phone line.

"I heard you, at the festival dance. What a shame you didn't mention Irene since she did so much of the work for the festival and it was only because we got to work with her that we ladies at the Grange kept going with it. Too bad you didn't give her any credit, Odilia. The Lord rewards those with a generous spirit, you know."

I smiled and made a note in my head never to cross Vida Lee Rupnik because she had some way to tap into the wrath of God. At least a small dose of garlic wrath.

Odilia made the maintenance crew clean out the garlic and she drove away in a spirited huff. I'm ashamed to say the rest of the Queens and Felicia couldn't stifle our laughter. But something about the garlic incident didn't ring true to me, something that defied the laws of physics. I went home and made Jimmy load up the back of his truck with a big pile of loose straw.

"Now drive forward and slam on your brakes. Hard!" I said and Jimmy gunned the truck forward, then slammed on the brakes. The straw stayed on the truck.

"Do it again," I said, and Jimmy launched forward, then stopped with the same results.

After ten minutes of trying, Jimmy told me I was going to wear out his brakes and we quit. That right there convinced me that Choddy shoveled that garlic onto Odilia's car to avenge Vida Lee, who was much beloved by most everyone, but especially all the farmers and who, apparently, possessed a hidden knack for sneaky revenge.

For the next three days Odilia smelled of garlic and we took to calling her "Mrs. Ravioli," which she did not appreciate at all.

★ ★ ★

After all the news of the festival, the newspaper got on our side and called out the county for wanting to destroy Buttonbush's history. The commissioners decided to put the courthouse in a downtown park. We'd done something remarkable by working together. And I was so tired.

"The county wants us to do the festival every year," Odilia told us at a meeting the next week.

The thought of doing the festival every year made me nearly faint. But if it would save the museum, then I'd do it again. Others were not so inclined. Vida Lee, Choddy, and Joe Toloni all said "never again," as did several other volunteers.

"Odilia is too hard to work with," one told me.

"We all need to get back to normal," Maye Marie said, and she and Arky took up golf together. She was terrible at it, but true to form, Arky was a standout.

It took six weeks, but I got back to normal. I prayed I wouldn't ever get so worked up about anything again, which, if I'd thought about it, was a funny one. It didn't take long.

We were just in the early stages of planning the next festival when Betty called me.

"I don't know how to tell you this. So I'm just going to say it," she said, and I sat back in my chair.

"You know The Buttonbush County Commissioner's Dinner … the one we're all going to tomorrow night? Oh gosh, I can barely speak," she said.

"Spit it out, Betty," I said. We always attended the annual dinner. Even Pauline and Willy were going. Willy's Scouts were presenting the flag and Pauline's choir was singing.

"The commissioners give an annual award for a community leader who does something spectacular. They're giving it to Odilia for the festival. She's accepting the award at the dinner. I just found out. I wanted you to know before it was in the newspaper," she said.

"You mean she's accepting an award for putting on the festival without letting them know I was her co-chair and did every bit as much work as she did?"

"I can't believe she's doing this," she said. "I tried to call her, but she's not answering."

I sat dumbfounded and I think my heart actually hurt a little. I knew one hundred percent that I'd done just as much, worked just as hard, contributed as many ideas and hours as Odilia. She had not changed. But I had. I was hopping mad, and this time, I wasn't going down without a fight.

The next night, I put on my best cocktail dress and headed over to the county dinner with Jimmy and the kids, where about two hundred people were sitting down to eat.

Betty and Maye Marie were waiting at our table in the back. I told them I was going to cause a commotion when Odilia got up to take the award.

"All of us, The Four Queens. We put that festival together just as much as Odilia did. I don't want to sound braggadocios, but it's not right that she gets all the credit," I said.

"But you, most of all. You were officially her co-chair," Betty said. Maye Marie nodded in agreement.

"I'm going to stand right up and let the commissioners know they've made a mistake. Right in front of this entire crowd. I hope I don't chicken out."

"Are you sure you want to do that?" Maye Marie said, and patted me on the arm.

"I'm sure. Does Odilia know we're here?" I said.

Betty shrugged.

"You know Odilia. She's never too interested in what we're doing. So, no."

* * *

Odilia

There was an art to sashaying around a room and I had it mastered. I moved seamlessly from front table to front table at the county awards dinner, talking up the museum while at the same time talking up myself. There was no way the Gold Seal Club could refuse me after this, and who knows what might come after that? Who needed Iggy? I was doing just fine on my own.

As I visited a table at the far right of the room, a young woman with a familiar face stood up and wrapped me in an enormous hug.

"Mrs. Delgado. It is so nice to see you again." The woman appeared to be in her thirties, with a dimpled smile and wavy hair tied up in a bun. I couldn't quite place her.

"I'm sure you don't remember me. Francie Simms. Sheetmetal worker. Oakland Shipyard."

"Francie. Good to see you." I was impatient to move on. I'd spotted City Councilman Baines at the next table.

Francie grabbed my hand.

"I have to tell you thank you. You were a great boss during the war and helped get us that childcare center so us women could work. You always made us feel like we were part of a team. Working hard but also feeling like a family. All us gals. I'm forever grateful to you for that," Francie said.

A lump came into my throat. I didn't know the crew thought of me that way.

"I see you're still helping people. Leading by example. So good to see you. My husband and I just moved here," Francie said. "I know you're busy here but so terrific to see you. You were a shining example to me during a tough time."

I walked away, a funny feeling in my head, and went back to my seat, ignoring Councilman Baines. I spotted Maye Marie, Betty, and Irene in the back and felt a pang in my chest. Irene was going to see me get an award. An award she rightly deserved. A burning feeling washed across my face, and it felt like sadness, if sadness could be physical. Had I once been a team player, a good leader, a nice person? Was I still? Nothing affirming came to mind. As the awards ceremony began, the announcer talked about what a fabulous festival I'd created, the sound ringing in my ears. I'd waited so long for recognition and here it was.

"Odilia Delgado, please come up and receive your award."

I walked up to the stage, my brain still in a fog, but I managed to smile and shake hands all around.

"Thank you all so much," I said. "This is just so ... so ..."

I stood at the microphone for a long five seconds. My head rang with questions. Questions for myself. Something wasn't right about this.

★ ★ ★

Irene

So there she was, in all her dang glory.

"Odilia, aren't you forgetting something? Or someone?" I shouted across the crowded hall.

Odilia's head turned left and right. Her sunken face wildly searched the room. I waved my arms.

"Yoo-hoo! Yoo-hoo! It's me. Your festival co-chair. Also, the person who created the festival, who put it together, and who did as much as you did, on equal footing. Your co-chairwoman. You all might want to research your award winners a little more thoroughly because you only got it half right this time," I said. The room was dead silent, and Odilia froze. I was on a roll, and it felt pretty good, for once, taking control over Odilia, whose mouth was hanging open.

Betty stood up.

"That's correct. Irene was co-chair of the festival and did every bit as much as Odilia." Maye Marie stood up, too.

I stepped forward from the back of the room and crossed my arms. The room buzzed with whispers.

"Well now ... why you ..." Odilia's voice was shaking.

"Never mind, Odilia. Get your award. But every time you look at that, I want you to remember just how devious and selfish you were to accept this without Betty or Maye Marie or me. Never forget that taking all the credit for the festival was more important to you than being an honest and a true friend. Or just a decent person," I said. I turned my back and went back to my seat. The crowd burst into applause and murmurs.

"Oh my lord, you were magnificent," Betty said, hugging me. I was exhausted, like I'd run a mile. Jimmy grabbed my hand.

"I think I must have lost my mind there," I said. I'd never done anything so contrary to my nature.

"Odilia should hang her head in shame for this," Maye Marie said.

"She won't," I said. "But I got my licks in."

Odilia was still standing at the microphone, the silence weighing down the room. Her mouth moved in slow motion, like she wanted to say something, but she didn't. One of the county commissioners stepped up to the microphone, scooting her over, carrying a piece of paper.

"Ladies and gentlemen, we'll sort this out. But the timing of this could not be more perfect. Earlier today I was handed two letters by the county clerk. We have some stupendous news.

"First, the Iversen estate has agreed to let the Buttonbush Museum keep the Iversen House and they are donating $1,000 for its refurbishment."

There was a smattering of applause and Odilia smirked.

"That's wonderful news. You know I ..." she said.

The commissioner interrupted her.

"But even better, let me read you the second letter. It's quite something."

> To whom it may concern: My name is Viscountess Anna Philpott, a resident of Kent, England. I received a correspondence six months ago from the Royal British Heritage Society regarding a letter written by Irene Pickett of the Buttonbush Museum in California.
>
> Mrs. Pickett's letter detailed the discovery of an old love letter and locket sent from John Penn, a colonel in the British army who perished in the United States just after writing the letter. My beloved great-aunt, Mary Ophelia Philpott, was the intended recipient of that letter, but it never arrived. My aunt spent her life mourning the loss of Col. Penn., never marrying, and always carrying his picture with her. I am overjoyed to receive this letter which proves the love of the colonel for my dear aunt, even though she has been deceased for decades. Aunt Mary has blessed me with a sizable inheritance and so I would like to thank the museum and Mrs. Pickett for her efforts to return this cherished letter. Irene Pickett diligently searched for our family, and in her honor, we'd like to make a donation to the Buttonbush Museum. I am wiring five hundred thousand dollars to the museum and hope that you will continue to preserve history and educate your citizens. My deepest thanks to Mrs. Pickett for making

the effort to find this letter's rightful home. Yours truly, Viscountess Anna M. Philpott.

"Mrs. Pickett, please come to the front," he said.

"You found a treasure, after all," Maye Marie said to me, grinning ear to ear.

My face felt flushed, and I thought I might faint as the entire audience stood on its feet. Maye Marie jumped up and down and Betty fanned herself. I grabbed the two of them and dragged them to the stage with me. Odilia's eyes were popping out like apricots.

"That's my mother," Pauline shouted.

Willy pumped his arms above his head.

"Hip hip hooray!" he yelled.

For all my failures and misdirected intentions, I'd actually secured half a million dollars for the museum in a turn of events no one could have predicted.

Jimmy grinned from ear to ear and waved to me.

"I think I've finally become relevant," I said to Betty and Maye Marie. "But what the hell is a viscountess?"

★ ★ ★

Buttonbush Museum gets half-million in donation from Brit, the headline in the *Buttonbush Daily* read the next day. With a sub-head of, *Festival co-chairs get in heated argument at county dinner*. It was the first time I'd been acknowledged as the co-chair publicly.

"Wow! Wow!" was all I could say.

Jimmy stuffed a pancake in his mouth.

"Now what?"

"Now what? I'll tell you what. I, me, Irene, finally did something important for the museum," I said. "And all it took was a little research and effort."

"Good for you, honey," he said, smiling. "Feel better?"

"I do," I said, and spent the rest of the day answering phone calls about my illustrious deeds, even from newspapers in Los Angeles and San Francisco.

Even Ma, who'd learned all the nasty details from the church lady grapevine, called to give me praise.

"About time you stuck up for yourself with that woman," she said. "I wondered when you were going to get tired of her bossin' you around and takin' all the credit for the good things you do for that museum."

You could have knocked me over with a feather with that phone call.

Later, I was in the living room dusting the furniture when Pauline came running into the house to grab me by the waist.

"Mother, you're legendary," she said, bouncing up and down like a ball.

"Who? Me? Whatever for?"

"All my friends heard about you. And well, I saw you in action. You really were something, Mom. The ginchiest!" Pauline hugged me.

"I wasn't that good," I said.

"You were like Dorothy up against the Wicked Witch."

"Oh, come on now, it wasn't quite like that," I said, blushing. My daughter giving me such praise was not something I expected.

"Mother! Take the compliment, will you? I think it's wonderful ... Now, I've got chemistry homework."

I sat down on the sofa and smiled. Ma was proud of me, and Pauline was proud of me. Wonders never cease.

A whole ray of sunshine had filled my head and seeped down into my heart. I guess that's what success felt like.

★ ★ ★

The next day I heard a slight tap at my front door. I opened it to see Odilia, flowers in hand. And a cigarette.

"These are for you," she said, and burst into the living room.

"Why?" I said.

"That money you brought in is going to let us do an enormous amount. I've got a list of twenty-seven major projects that we can do right away," she said, and I groaned.

"Not this, Odilia. We can't use all that money for projects. Good lord." I flung myself down on the couch.

"Of course we can do them. Why this museum will turn such a corner now. All thanks to you." She plopped down on the couch next to me.

"But no more building … We have money now for more staff. We can do more educational programs and events, things people want to come to." As I said it, I realized it was the same thing I'd said one million times before.

"That's not all and I'm not really here for that. I'm here to apologize. You were the co- chairwoman and I should have told the county about that before the awards ceremony. I've been selfish."

Her face was softer than I'd ever seen and she seemed sincere. Even so, I was skeptical. I handed her an ashtray and she squashed her cigarette into it.

"I just don't understand why you're so dad gum hostile to me."

"I don't know why. I just am."

"That's not my fault." I said.

"I know." She bit her lower lip and frowned.

"I know about you and Jimmy in high school. I don't know why no one told me about this earlier. Are you still pining for Jimmy?" I had to know, even if the answer was yes.

"No."

"I don't know why you're so resentful of me. I'm just a nothing ... You have so much ... a successful career, travel all over the world, a beautiful house, awards for a million things, a senator husband ... People respect you. They admire your drive and ambition. I'm just a nobody in Buttonbush," I said.

Odilia took a long look around my living room, the pillows mussed from Pauline laying on them, Willy's shoes under the end table, the dog—none too clean—laying on the rug. She sighed.

"You have everything. Everything," she said, and a few tears welled in her eyes.

"What do you mean?"

"You have the important things. The things everyone wants. A husband who loves you. That's plain to see. Two wonderful children. Newspaper experience that's going to get you something big in the future. A life that's filled with family and friends. I have none of that. No one comes to my house because they're a friend. They come because I'm doing something for their cause or because I can influence something in a way they want. They don't really like me. My life is all behind me. I can't even get into the Gold Seal Club. All I've really got are awards on my wall, a husband who doesn't care for me, and I've never had a man love me like Jimmy loves you."

"I'm sure your husband loves you," I said.

"Ha! He's had a sweetheart up in Sacramento for four years. I hear him phone her late at night when he tells me he's working. My marriage is falling apart." Odilia wiped her eyes.

"Oh no, Odilia, I'm so sorry."

"He filed divorce papers last week. He's not going to run again for office. He's got some cushy government job lined up in

Sacramento so he doesn't care about Buttonbush anymore. Or me," she said, a slight cry in her voice.

"That's awful. You must be so hurt."

"I just wanted to make a name for myself somewhere. I ran that whole manufacturing plant during the war and then he came back and he tells me to stay home and be a good little wife. I guess I just can't be that," she said. I realized Odilia was just trying to get what I was trying to get: a mark in the world. Only I had the good fortune to be married to a man who was behind me in that. I had probably been too harsh on her.

"Is there anything I can do?"

"Not really. Just be my friend," she said, and I sat next to her and put my arm around her shoulders. She bristled, at first, then settled in with a sigh.

We sat quietly for a few minutes, then Odilia handed me the flowers and walked out the door.

★ ★ ★

Betty, Maye Marie, and I were sitting on Betty's back porch the following Tuesday, watching a pair of bluejays bicker. Odilia's apology went a long way to soothe my agitation, but I was still keyed up. The three of us were unusually quiet in our thoughts.

"Poor Odilia. She's losing her marriage. I feel badly for her," I said. Odilia had given me permission to tell Betty and Maye Marie. They were as shocked as I was.

"Awww. That's terrible news. Can we help her in any way?" said Maye Marie.

"Not really. But I think she's going to throw herself into the museum even more. That money windfall is going to give her lots of ideas. She already has a list of new building projects," I said.

"Oh no. We should have known," said Betty.

"It means more fighting, more squabbling over projects versus activities. We never win and she'll have all the money she needs. I'm tired just thinking about it," said Maye Marie. "But I do feel sorry for her. For all her ambitions, she really has done a lot of good for the museum."

"She has. I feel kind of bad for fighting with her so much. Although, I confess, sometimes it was kind of fun," I said.

"I feel bad, too. But we have to do what's right for the museum. With no husband to hold her down, she's going to be even more dogmatic about things. I don't know how we're going to control her spending," Betty said.

Their faces were heavy with weariness and frustration. Our generous English donation had made us all feel so excited, but knowing how Odilia would commandeer it didn't give any of us a sunny outlook for the future. Odilia may have softened a bit, but she was still do-or-die Odilia.

"I have an idea," I said.

"Uh-oh, here we go again." Maye Marie laughed.

I looked at the two of them They were such good women with integrity and drive. I couldn't think of two friends I ever could count on so well. I'd won the real award.

★ ★ ★

Betty, Maye Marie and I made a proposal at the next board meeting. We nominated Odilia to be the museum manager, a move we should have made long ago.

"You're the only Queen now, Odilia," I said. "But we have the voting power so things will be a little more balanced."

Her eyes bugged out for a moment but then a slight smile crept onto her face. I knew it was what she'd wanted all along. And she was going to enjoy the battles the four of us would still have, but they'd be a little more challenging for her with our voting power. The vote was unanimous, and Odilia took the manager's seat. Everything was as it should be.

The money from the viscountess came and Odilia had grand plans for it. We mostly let her run with it. She was the last Queen standing and she had her treasure in hand.

It was only fitting. After all, who has more than one queen? Not England, not Denmark, not bees.

Me, I spent time with my friends, who were the real treasure.

1988 ANOTHER QUEEN

Pauline

"Next on our agenda is Pauline Pickett Fonseca, chief financial officer for the County of Buttonbush," the clerk of the board said at the July 1988 meeting of the Buttonbush County Board of Commissioners.

"Thank you, ladies and gentlemen. I'd like to go over the proposal to close the Buttonbush Museum. But before we get into the financial details, I'd like to relay an incredible story to you. It's the story of the Four Queens of the Buttonbush Museum," Pauline said, smiling straight ahead at the commissioners.

Photo by Manuel Heartbreaker

ABOUT THE AUTHOR

BETH BROOKHART has been a storyteller since childhood in Colorado, beginning with a book of poems written for her mother. A journalism graduate of Colorado State University, Beth spent two decades reporting on agricultural news, often found tromping through farm fields in pursuit of a story. Later, her career shifted to communications roles with several agricultural organizations in Bakersfield, CA. In 2010, she embarked on her fiction-writing journey, leading to the completion of *The Book Project*, a prestigious two-year program at the Lighthouse Writers Workshop in Denver. An avid volunteer, Beth was inspired by her seventeen years of service on the board of her local museum to pen *The Four Queens of the Buttonbush Museum*.

ACKNOWLEDGMENTS

This book exists because of the incredible people who stood by me on this winding, unpredictable writing journey. Your unwavering encouragement, even through years of waiting and uncertainty, has meant the world to me. I could never thank you all enough, but please know that every kind word and gesture kept me moving forward.

First, my heartfelt gratitude to Sibylline Press—Vicki and the entire team—for believing in me and my story. Hearing the words "we love your book" will forever be one of the most joyous moments of my life. Thank you for taking a chance on me and for cheering me on every step of the way.

To the Lighthouse Writers Workshop in Denver, especially William Haywood Henderson and Ben Whitmer, thank you for teaching me how to let go of journalism and embrace the art of fiction. You helped me find my voice and transform my ideas into meaningful words. Lighthouse is a gift, and I'll always be grateful for the guidance I found there.

To my dear friends (too many to name) who read my manuscript or heard about it: your thoughtful advice and encouragement were invaluable. I want to especially thank those who helped edit the book: Eleanor Brown, Shana Kelly, Jonna Kottler, and Jackie Cangro. Thank you for your edits, insights, and belief in me. You made every draft better and every step brighter.

My deepest thanks go to my incredible children, Shay and Curtis, and their wonderful spouses, Andrew and Gianna. Your unwavering support and "just get in there and do it" pep talks gave me the courage to keep going. You four (and your children) are my greatest treasures.

To my parents, Irene and Jack Brookhart, your love and confidence in me have always been my foundation. Mom, though you're watching from heaven now, I know you're still cheering me on. Thank you, Dad, for telling me to keep going. And to my siblings, especially my sister Ann who always tells me I'm doing well, even when I'm not, I'm so thankful for your love and support.

A special thank you goes to my loyal writing companions—my dogs (some long gone), Macy, Woody, Hal, Nitschke, Lola, Vinny, and Gus. You were there with me through every slog at the computer, always listening patiently (mostly snoozing) as I read my words aloud. I know you'd happily chew this book to pieces if given the chance, but your quiet presence was a comfort beyond measure.

To the queens who inspired this book—Sheryl, Jackie, Tracy, Barbara, Cathy and Kaye—thank you for the unforgettable journey we shared. The laughter, frustrations, stories, and characters we experienced together gave me countless ideas and endless inspiration. We kept saying "you can't make this stuff up." Well, I did!

I need to give a shout-out to anyone who has ever volunteered for anything. Those non-profit leaders, volunteers and staff, who endlessly raise money, try new projects, beg, borrow and almost steal to keep their organizations going—you are warriors. Working for and with non-profit organizations for decades provided tremendous inspiration for this book and I hope my readers recognize the dynamics of volunteers in the novel, which are sometimes wacky, uncontrollable and unbelievable.

Finally, to my wonderful husband, Andrew—you are my rock, my partner, and my biggest champion. Your steady encouragement, patience, and unwavering belief in me made all the difference. Thank you for standing by me and for loving me through every twist and turn of this journey. I am endlessly grateful for you.

To everyone who's been part of this adventure, from the bottom of my heart: thank you.

BOOK CLUB QUESTIONS

1. Irene desperately wants to fit in somewhere and make a small mark in the world. What is holding her back?

2. Odilia also wants to make a mark in the world. How does Odilia differ from Irene in how she sees herself and how she goes about getting what she wants?

3. Why do Odilia and Irene argue and disagree so much? Are Odilia's plans for the museum beneficial or harmful and why can't Irene get her ideas across?

4. Maye Marie and Betty have their own reasons for being on the board of the museum. What are they?

5. There are many characters who come and go at the museum. Which characters have been helpful and which have been harmful to the museum's cause?

6. Discuss the relationship between Irene and her mother and Irene and Pauline. Are there any similarities? Do you relate to any of the mother/daughter dynamics?

7. Discuss the differences between Irene and Jimmy's marriage and Odilia and Iggy's marriage.

8. What finally unites the Four Queens?

9. Why does Odilia feel justified in accepting an award without including the other Queens? Does Odilia truly change at the end or do you think it's a temporary period in her life?

10. One of the main themes of the novel is the role of volunteers in organizations and the sometimes beneficial and sometimes detrimental impact they can have. Discuss your experience in volunteering. Have you ever had a "Queens" situation where volunteers go way beyond their responsibilities, either for good or bad?

Sibylline Press is proud to publish the brilliant work of women authors over 50. We are a woman-owned publishing company and, like our authors, represent women of a certain age.

Made in the USA
Las Vegas, NV
24 April 2025